Healing Hearts

Riverbend Valley Book #6

Tara Baisden

Sterling Ridge Press LLC

Copyright

Cover designed by Sterling Ridge Press LLC

Published by: Sterling Ridge Press, LLC www.sterlingridgepress.com

ISBN: 978-1-966093-27-5 Printed in the United States of America

First Edition: June 2025

For permissions, contact: tara@tarabaisden.com or visit www.tarabaisden.com

Dedication

To those brave souls who run toward danger while the rest of us run away—the firefighters who battle nature's fury with courage and conviction.

To everyone who has ever taken a leap of faith, bought the ranch, changed careers, or started over.

And to you, dear reader, understand that sometimes the greatest act of bravery isn't fighting flames or breaking horses—it's trusting your heart to someone else's keeping after it's been broken.

May you always find the courage to choose love, even when it's risky.

And may God bless all the Luke Hardings and Sophie Lawsons of the world who remind us that healing happens in the most unexpected places, often in the company of those who have known their own kind of brokenness.

With gratitude and love,
Tara

About Riverbend Valley

Welcome to the fictional town of Riverbend Valley, Montana!

Nestled in the shadow of the breathtaking Sapphire Mountains, Riverbend Valley is a place where life flows as peacefully as the rivers winding through it. Surrounded by rolling ranch lands, dense forests, and the rugged peaks of Montana's wilderness, this picturesque valley is the perfect setting for tales of faith, love, and second chances.

A Rugged Heritage

Founded in the late 1800s by homesteaders drawn to the fertile land and expansive views, Riverbend Valley began as a ranching settlement. Riverbend Valley's roots run deep, forged by generations of ranchers and cowboys who've worked the land with grit and determination. This is a place where faith has always been a cornerstone, guiding its people through hardships and celebrating their triumphs. From the well-worn pews of Riverbend Valley Community Church to the lively gatherings at the rodeo grounds, Riverbend Valley's traditions reflect a steadfast commitment to God, family, and the land.

A Community of Faith

Riverbend Valley offers a refuge for weary souls and a chance to redis-cover the beauty of life's simple pleasures. Whether it's through a quiet moment of prayer along the river, a moonlit ride under Montana skies, or the laughter of a community united in celebration, this is a place where hearts are mended, faith is renewed, and love abounds.

The Essence of Small-Town Life

With a population of just over three thousand, Riverbend Valley re-tains its small-town charm. Main Street is lined with family-owned businesses, from the Bluebird Café, famous for its huckleberry pies, to the General Mercantile, where locals gather to swap stories and stock up on supplies. Seasonal festivals bring the community together, from the Spring Rodeo to the Fall Harvest Festival, celebrating the rhythms of life in this ranching town.

A Haven for Visitors

Visitors to Riverbend Valley are captivated by its rustic charm and natural beauty. Whether it's horseback riding through the foothills, fishing in the Deer Run River, or stargazing from Silver Bluff's iconic overlook, there's something for everyone to enjoy.

<u>Experience the Heart of Riverbend Valley</u>

Here, under the endless skies and among the resilient people of Montana, you'll find stories of redemption, second chances, and unwavering faith. Riverbend Valley isn't just a setting—it's a celebration of the rugged heritage and timeless grace that make this place unforgettable.

Welcome to Riverbend Valley, where faith is strong, family is everything, and love always finds a way.

I hope you fall in love with its enduring spirit.

Contents

Chapter 1

Sophie Lawson eased her foot off the brake, every muscle in her body protesting from the two-day drive as the U-Haul groaned along the winding Montana highway. Her knuckles had gone white against the steering wheel an hour ago, the oversized truck shuddering beneath her while the BMW trailing behind added another layer of complexity to an already challenging journey.

"Nearly there," she murmured, the words a prayer as much as reassurance. The habit of talking to herself had developed somewhere around mile two hundred, her voice the only companion through long stretches of highway that seemed to stretch toward eternity.

The landscape beyond her windshield—a vastness that made her chest expand with something she'd almost forgotten how to feel. Hope, maybe. The rugged mountains rose like cathedral spires against a sky so blue it seemed painted by an artist who'd never learned subtlety. Late June sun poured honey-colored light across rolling grasslands, where prairie grass danced in waves that reminded her of worship.

This was God's country.

Seattle felt like another lifetime now. The city's concrete embrace and Dr. Marcus Brennan had slowly strangled something vital in her spirit, though she hadn't realized it until she'd watched the skyline shrink in her rearview mirror.

You'll never succeed without me, Sophie. You're throwing away everything we've built to play cowgirl.

We. As if her innovations, her surgical techniques, her exhaustive research had been anything but her own. As if Marcus hadn't systematically claimed credit for each breakthrough while chipping away at her confidence with the patience of water wearing stone.

Sophie drew a deep breath, filling her lungs with air that tasted of freedom. "That chapter is closed," she said aloud. "You chose faith over fear. You chose something better."

Better meant buying a horse ranch sight unseen in a town she'd never visited. It was either the bravest decision she'd ever made or evidence that heartbreak had finally driven her to complete madness. The jury was still out.

The GPS directed her to turn onto Elk Run Road, where smooth asphalt gave way to gravel that sang beneath her tires. For the first time since leaving Seattle, doubt crept in like an unwelcome visitor.

"What have I done?" The whisper escaped before she could stop it. She'd put down a deposit on a property she'd only seen in photographs, fleeing to a town full of strangers. Her entire life sat boxed in this truck—her Seattle apartment sublet, her job gone, every bridge thoroughly burned.

Rounding a curve, Sophie caught sight of a weathered wooden sign suspended from a black metal archway. Hand-carved letters proclaimed: "Ironwood Creek Ranch - Est. 1985."

Her heart performed an unexpected flutter. This was it. This was home.

Sophie pulled the U-Haul to the roadside just before the entrance, checking her watch. One o'clock—two hours early for her appointment with the realtor. She studied the long driveway through her windshield, bordered by split-rail fencing weathered to the color of old silver.

What harm could there be in arriving early? Perhaps the owner would be willing to show her around before the realtor arrived with contracts and sales pitches.

"Lord, if You brought me this far, You must have a plan," she murmured, guiding the truck through the entrance.

The driveway stretched ahead like a promise, leading her toward a sprawling ranch house with a wraparound porch and steep metal roof that gleamed in the afternoon sun. Her pulse quickened. The photographs hadn't done it justice.

Sophie parked in the circular drive and turned off the engine. Sudden silence wrapped around her, broken only by her own heartbeat drumming in her ears. Through the windshield, she drank in the view—the house, the outbuildings, pastures rolling toward pine-covered mountains that looked close enough to touch.

"Well, here goes nothing."

She'd barely stepped down from the cab when a shout from the direction of the barn shattered the peaceful moment.

"Need help over here!"

The voice was male, urgent but controlled. Sophie turned toward the sound, spotting a cluster of buildings beyond the main house. Years of veterinary training overrode everything else as she hurried toward the voice, her legs grateful for movement after hours of driving.

As she approached the largest building—a traditional gambler-roofed barn painted white with red trim—the voice came again, issuing calm instructions to someone inside. Sophie quickened her pace, rounding the barn's corner and entered.

"Easy with her head. We can't afford to stress her any more than she already is."

The authority in his voice suggested someone accustomed to being obeyed, but there was something else there too—genuine concern that spoke to her veterinarian's heart.

"Excuse me," Sophie called, approaching with purposeful strides.

The man turned, surprise registering on a face that made her breath catch unexpectedly. Handsome was too simple a word—he was striking, with dark hair and serious brown eyes that widened at the sight of her. Tall and lean, he carried himself with the easy strength of someone whose work demanded both muscle and endurance.

"This isn't a good time," he said, as he walked toward her. "If you're looking for directions—"

"I'm Dr. Sophie Lawson," she interrupted. "I'm a veterinarian. What's the problem?"

The surprise in his expression deepened, transforming into something like cautious hope. "Luke Harding," he replied quickly. "Mare in foal. Our vet's an hour away and tied up with another emergency."

Sophie nodded crisply. "I can help."

Luke's hesitation lasted perhaps half a heartbeat before he nodded. "This way."

The barn's interior enveloped them in dimness scented with hay, leather, and the sharp tang of fear—both equine and human. At the far end of the central aisle, Sophie spotted the source of the emergency: a chestnut mare lying on her side in a stall, flanks heaving with labored breathing. Two men knelt beside her, their weathered faces creased with worry.

"Ray, Gus—step back," Luke ordered as they approached. "This is Dr. Lawson. She's a veterinarian."

The older man—Ray, apparently—gave her a skeptical once-over. "Thought Patterson was coming."

"He is," Luke replied, "but we might not have that long." He turned to Sophie, his brown eyes intense with concern. "This is Moonbeam. Four years old, first foal. Labor started about three hours ago, progressing normally until twenty minutes back when she went down and started showing real distress."

Sophie was already moving, kneeling beside the mare and running expert hands along her distended belly. The familiar rhythm of diagnosis calmed her racing pulse. "What have you tried so far?"

"Kept her as calm as possible, checked for presentation," Luke answered, kneeling across from her. "Called Doc Patterson, but he's dealing with a downed bull at the Morrison place."

Sophie nodded, continuing her examination. Moonbeam's breathing was rapid and shallow, her coat slick with sweat that spoke of prolonged distress. "I need gloves"

"Medical kit," Luke said, turning to the younger ranch hand. "Gus, tack room. Move."

As Gus hurried away, Sophie leaned close to the mare's head, stroking her neck and murmuring in the low, soothing tones that had calmed countless frightened animals. "Easy, sweetheart. We're going to help you and your baby." The mare's eyes rolled toward her, dark with pain and fear, but something in Sophie's voice seemed to reach her.

"She's valuable?" Sophie asked, not taking her attention from the animal.

"Very," Luke confirmed. "Championship bloodlines."

Gus returned with a large plastic container. Luke opened it with practiced efficiency, revealing a well-stocked and organized medical kit that earned Sophie's professional approval.

"I'll need warm water with antiseptic," she said, pulling on the gloves. "And clean towels. As many as you can find."

Luke nodded to Ray, who moved to fulfill the request. While they waited, Sophie continued her assessment, checking vital signs with the methodical precision that came from years of emergency work.

"What brings you to Ironwood Creek, Dr. Lawson?" Luke asked, his tone conversational despite the tension crackling through the barn.

"I'm your three o'clock appointment," she replied, offering a brief smile that seemed to surprise him. "I decided to arrive early and have a look around. I didn't expect to jump straight into work."

Luke's eyebrows climbed toward his hairline. "You're the buyer? From Seattle?"

"Guilty as charged," Sophie confirmed as Ray returned with steaming water and an armful of towels. "Let's save your mare and foal first, then we can discuss real estate."

Something shifted in Luke's expression—surprise giving way to what might have been admiration. "What do you need from me?"

"Hold her head, keep her as calm as you can," Sophie instructed. "Ray, I may need help to reposition the foal. Gus, stand ready with those towels."

Sophie performed her examination with careful precision, her expression revealing nothing as she assessed the situation internally. Please, Lord, she prayed silently. Guide my hands.

"Dystocia," she confirmed aloud. "Posterior presentation with one leg retained. I need to reposition before delivery can proceed."

Luke met her gaze across the mare's body, his brown eyes steady despite the gravity of the situation. "Can you do it?"

Sophie didn't hesitate. "Yes."

What followed was thirty minutes of intense, focused work that reminded Sophie why she'd become a veterinarian in the first place. This was her calling—not the politics and manipulation of Marcus's world, but this pure intersection of skill, compassion, and faith.

"Almost there. Luke, when I give the word, encourage her to push—gentle pressure on her side, keep talking to her. Ray, be ready with those towels."

Luke's hand was steady on the mare's neck, his voice joining Sophie's in a low murmur of encouragement. There was something deeply right about working alongside him, their efforts synchronized with shared purpose.

"Now," Sophie said, and everything came together in perfect coordination.

Minutes later, a wet, dark foal slid into the world. Sophie worked quickly to clear airways and check vital signs as Luke continued monitoring the mare, their partnership seamless despite having met less than an hour ago.

"Filly," Sophie announced, unable to suppress the smile that transformed her face. "And she's perfect."

The barn's atmosphere shifted instantly from desperate tension to joyous relief. Gus let out a whoop that made the mare startle, earning him a sharp look from Luke.

"Sorry, boss," Gus said, though his grin remained undimmed.

Sophie turned her attention back to the mare, checking for complications with the same thorough care she'd shown throughout the crisis. Satisfied that both mother and daughter were stable, she stripped off her gloves and rinsed her hands in the fresh water Gus provided.

"She'll need monitoring for the next twenty-four hours," Sophie said, drying her hands on a clean towel. "The foal should nurse within the hour—make sure she does."

Luke nodded, his gaze moving between the mare and foal before settling on Sophie with an expression that made her pulse flutter unexpectedly. "You just saved both their lives," he said quietly. "Doc Patterson wouldn't have made it in time."

Sophie shrugged, though warmth bloomed in her chest at the recognition. "Right place, right time."

"Right person with the right gifts," Luke corrected, rising to his feet and extending his hand. When she took it, his palm felt warm and work-roughened against hers, callused from honest labor. "Thank you, Dr. Lawson. I mean that."

"Sophie," she corrected, suddenly aware of how close they were standing and the way his brown eyes seemed to see more than she was comfortable in revealing. "If I'm buying your ranch, we should probably be on a first-name basis."

Something flickered across Luke's features—surprise, perhaps, or something more complicated. He released her hand, taking a careful step back. "About that," he began, then glanced toward the mare and her foal. "Why don't we let these two bond while I show you around? Since you're early, anyway."

Sophie nodded, following Luke out of the stall toward a sink near the barn entrance. The soap and cool water felt refreshing against her skin as she washed away the evidence of the emergency, though the satisfaction of a life saved lingered warm in her chest.

"You mentioned Seattle," Luke said as they stepped into afternoon sunlight that seemed somehow brighter now. "That's a long drive."

"Two days," Sophie confirmed, squinting slightly as her eyes adjusted. "Worth every mile to get here, though."

Luke studied her with an intensity that made her suddenly self-conscious. "Most people want to see a place before they buy it."

"Most people aren't running from something... or maybe I should say running toward something ..." Sophie replied, then immediately wished she could recall the words.

But Luke merely nodded, no judgment in his expression. "Fair enough. We all have our reasons for the choices we make." He gestured toward a path leading away from the barn. "The main pastures are this way. You'll want to see where the best grazing is."

As they walked, Sophie absorbed the full scope of the property spread before them. Rolling pastureland stretched toward forests that climbed mountainsides, while Ironwood Creek—she presumed—cut through the landscape like a silver ribbon, its water catching and scattering sunlight. The beauty of it made her chest tight with an emotion she couldn't quite name.

"It's magnificent," she breathed, meaning every word. The land possessed a wild grace, untamed yet somehow welcoming.

"It is," Luke agreed, quiet pride warming his voice. "My uncle built this from nothing. Loved every acre."

"And now you're selling it," Sophie observed, studying his profile. "Why?"

Luke's expression tightened almost imperceptibly, a shadow passing across his features. "Same as you, I suppose. Everyone has their reasons for moving on."

They continued walking, Luke pointing out features with the knowledge of someone who'd spent years learning every inch of the property. He showed her the swimming hole where the creek deepened, the meadow where hay grew thickest, the spring that had never run dry even in drought years. Sophie listened intently, asking informed questions about water rights, grazing rotation, and fence maintenance.

"You seem to know quite a bit about ranching," Luke remarked as they crested a small rise that offered a panoramic view of the entire ranch.

Sophie smiled, tucking a wayward strand of hair behind her ear. "I grew up on a ranch in Colorado. My grandparents—Grandpa was the local large animal vet, and Grandma ran the books and a therapy program. They taught me everything they knew before I went to veterinary school."

"So this isn't just an escape," Luke said, his assessment shrewd. "It's a homecoming."

The word hit her with unexpected force. Homecoming. Yes, that was exactly what this felt like—not running away, but returning to something she'd lost without realizing it.

"Yes," she admitted, her voice softer now. "I suppose it is."

Chapter 2

"Twelve hundred and forty acres," Luke said, gesturing toward the distant tree line as they approached the house. "The property extends to that ridge of pines to the east and follows the creek line to the north."

Sophie shaded her eyes against the afternoon sun, drinking in the vastness of what might soon be hers. Her chest tightened with equal measures of excitement and trepidation. The land stretched before her like a divine canvas—wild, breathtaking, and humbling in its scope.

"It's much larger than I imagined from the listing photos," she admitted, mentally calculating how many horses the pastures could support. The mathematics of her new life were beginning to take shape.

Luke checked his watch, a silver piece that looked well worn and practical. "Janet should be here any minute. Would you like to wait on the porch? I can get you something to drink."

"That sounds wonderful." Sophie climbed the three wooden steps, each board singing a soft creak beneath her boots—the kind of welcoming sound that promised home. She settled into one of the Adirondack chairs, its weathered surfaces worn smooth by years of use, and felt her travel-weary muscles finally begin to relax.

"Water, coffee, or sweet tea?" Luke paused at the screen door, his hand resting on the frame.

"Sweet tea would be perfect, thank you."

As Luke disappeared inside, Sophie settled into the Montana silence—a profound quiet broken only by the whisper of wind through grass and the distant whinny of horses. She closed her eyes briefly, letting the peace of it settle into her bones. This was what she'd been searching for: space to breathe, and room for her soul to expand.

From inside came the homey sounds of domesticity—ice clinking against glass, cabinet doors opening and closing, the gentle thud of the refrigerator door. The intimate glimpse into daily life stirred something unexpectedly tender in her chest. This would be her kitchen, her routine, and her peaceful evening ritual soon.

The screen door squeaked open, and Luke emerged carrying two tall glasses beaded with condensation. He handed one to Sophie before settling into the chair beside her, close enough that she caught the scent of sunshine and honest work on his clothes.

"Thank you," she said, taking a grateful sip. The tea was perfectly balanced—sweet but not cloying, with a hint of fresh mint that brightened the flavor. "This is delicious."

"My Uncle Carter's recipe. He swore the secret was brewing it under the morning sun." Luke's voice carried a note of affection that spoke of cherished memories.

Sophie smiled, warmth spreading through her chest. "My grandmother had her own sweet tea ritual. She'd add a sprig of lavender from her garden."

Luke's eyebrows lifted with genuine interest. "Lavender tea? That's a new one for me."

"It's subtle, but lovely. It always reminded me of summer, even in the depths of winter." The memory surfaced without warning, bringing with it the familiar ache of loss. She rarely spoke of her grandparents anymore; their absence still felt too raw, even years later.

"You mentioned Colorado earlier," Luke said, his tone carefully casual. "What part?"

"Near Durango. My grandparents had a ranch there—smaller than this, but similar terrain. High country, with mountains all around."

"Horse ranch?"

Sophie nodded, settling deeper into her chair. "Grandpa was a large animal vet who specialized in equine medicine. The ranch was his sanctuary from the clinical work—a place where he could see his horses thrive rather than just treating their ailments. Grandma ran a therapeutic riding program for kids who needed healing."

Understanding dawned in Luke's expression. "So that's where your interest in therapeutic riding comes from."

"You saw that mentioned in my offer letter?"

"Janet brought it up. Sounds like a perfect use for this property—giving it a new purpose while honoring what came before."

The distant hum of an engine grew steadily louder. Luke rose, setting his half-finished tea on the small table between their chairs with deliberate care.

"That'll be Janet," he said, moving to the porch railing.

A silver SUV emblazoned with "Myers Realty" pulled into the circular drive, parking beside Sophie's conspicuous U-Haul. A woman in her mid-forties emerged, professionally dressed despite the afternoon heat. Her auburn hair was perfectly styled, and she carried herself with the confidence of someone who'd closed countless deals.

"Luke!" she called, her face lighting up as she approached. "And this must be Dr. Lawson."

"Janet, good to see you. Sophie arrived early and helped deliver Moonbeam's foal, and then I gave her a quick tour of the ranch," Luke said, his tone carrying a note of admiration that made Sophie's pulse quicken unexpectedly.

Janet's eyebrows shot up as she looked between them. "Well, that's certainly diving in to ranch work headfirst!" She extended her hand to Sophie, who had risen to join them. "Janet Myers. It's wonderful to meet you in person, Dr. Lawson."

"Sophie, please," she replied, shaking the realtor's firm hand.

"Well, welcome to Riverbend Valley, Sophie." Janet's smile was genuinely warm. "Would you like to tour the house first, before we tackle the paperwork?"

"I'd love that," Sophie replied, turning expectantly toward Luke.

He gestured toward the door with easy grace. "After you."

Sophie paused just inside the threshold, her eyes adjusting to the gentler light. The living room welcomed her with comfortable leather furniture arranged around a magnificent river-rock fireplace that commanded one entire wall. Large windows framed the mountain views like living artwork, bringing the wild beauty indoors.

"The main living area," Luke said, his voice carrying the quiet pride of someone who'd spent countless evenings in this space. "Kitchen's through there, dining room beyond. An office and three bedrooms down that hallway, with the master suite at the end."

Sophie moved deeper into the living room, trailing her fingers along the buttery-soft leather of a sofa arm. The house had the lived-in warmth of a true home rather than a showpiece—exactly what her heart had been yearning for.

"The fireplace is original to the 1985 construction," Janet explained, slipping smoothly into professional mode. "Luke's uncle hand picked the river rock."

Sophie nodded, drawn toward the kitchen like a magnet. The space exceeded her expectations—butcher-block countertops worn smooth by years of use, a commercial-grade gas range that made her inner cook sing with anticipation. A deep farmhouse sink nestled beneath a window overlooking the creek, while a kitchen island with four stools promised casual conversations with friends over coffee.

"I imagine you've spent many hours in this kitchen," Sophie said to Luke, who leaned against the island with his arms crossed, watching her exploration with unreadable eyes.

"Many," he replied.

They continued through the dining area, where a solid oak table sat beneath a wrought-iron chandelier that cast intricate shadows on the walls. Down the hallway, each bedroom offered its own character—simple but comfortable furnishings, windows showcasing different views of the property. The master bedroom, with its adjoining bathroom featuring a claw-foot tub and generous walk-in closet, felt like a sanctuary.

"The west wing expansion was completed in '98," Luke explained as they returned to the main living area. "My uncle wanted more space for guests—visiting pilots, mostly. He was a crop duster and rancher."

"That explains the aviation collection," Sophie said, nodding toward a display of model planes arranged on built-in shelves. Each piece looked carefully maintained, lovingly preserved.

Luke's expression softened visibly. "He loved flying almost as much as he loved this land."

Janet cleared her throat diplomatically. "Well, shall we settle at the dining table and review the particulars?"

They gathered around the oak table, Janet spreading papers with practiced efficiency. But Sophie's attention kept drifting to the view beyond the windows—rolling grasslands painted gold by afternoon light, distant mountains standing sentinel, horses grazing in perfect contentment. This was the dream she'd carried in her heart since childhood, finally within reach.

"As we discussed over the phone, Sophie," Janet was saying, "the property includes the main house, all outbuildings, twelve hundred and forty acres, and all the existing equipment detailed in Appendix C."

Sophie forced herself to focus. "And the current staff?"

"All ranch hands have been informed of the potential sale," Luke said. "They're all willing to stay on if you'd like to keep them."

"Absolutely," Sophie replied without hesitation. "I'll need their expertise."

Janet smiled approvingly, making a note. "Excellent. Now, regarding the livestock—"

"All livestock remains... non-negotiable," Sophie interrupted, her voice firm with conviction.

Luke studied her with new interest, something like respect flickering in his brown eyes.

"Moonbeam carries Conquistador genetics, doesn't she? Her shoulder marking is distinctive."

Luke nodded slowly, clearly impressed. "Fourth generation. The stallion I mentioned earlier, Thunder, is even more remarkable. You'll want to meet him properly."

"I'm looking forward to it." Sophie turned back to Janet, her business instincts engaged. "The agreed price covers all livestock, correct?"

"Yes, everything except Luke's personal belongings, and—" Janet paused, glancing at Luke.

"I've retained thirty acres on the western boundary," he explained. "It was legally separated from the main property months ago. I'm building a cabin there."

Sophie blinked in surprise, her carefully constructed plans suddenly shifting. "You're staying in the area?"

"Yes. I'll be taking a position with the Forest Service."

"Luke is one of our region's most experienced aerial firefighters," Janet added, pride evident in her voice. "The whole valley is grateful he's returning to active duty."

Sophie's mind raced with this unexpected development. Luke wasn't disappearing entirely—he was simply trading ranching for firefighting. And he would be living just beyond her property line, close enough to... what? Watch her fail? Offer unwanted advice? The thought made her stomach clench with familiar anxiety.

"That's... good to know," she managed.

Janet efficiently guided them through the remaining paperwork, explaining terms and conditions, property boundaries, and water rights with professional thoroughness. Sophie listened attentively, asking informed questions, but her thoughts kept circling back to the enormity of her undertaking.

Twelve hundred and forty acres. An established breeding program. Ranch hands to manage. And she would be doing it alone, with only theoretical knowledge, veterinary training, and childhood memories to guide her.

As Janet outlined the closing timeline, doubt crept in like an unwelcome visitor. She knew horses, understood veterinary medicine inside and out. But running a ranch of this magnitude was different from treating animals or helping her grandfather with daily chores. There were business aspects, management decisions, seasonal considerations she'd only read about in books.

She glanced at Luke, who was listening to Janet with the relaxed posture of someone who knew every fence post and water source on the property. He had grown up here, learned from his uncle, understood the rhythm of the land in ways that would take her years to develop.

And he was leaving. Just as she was arriving.

The realization crystallized something in Sophie's mind. She had fled Seattle to escape Marcus's controlling influence, determined to prove her independence and follow her dream. But true strength didn't mean refusing all help—it meant choosing whom to trust and on what terms.

"I'd like to confirm my full cash offer stands," Sophie said when Janet paused between sections. "But with one additional condition."

Luke's eyebrows lifted slightly. Janet looked between them, her pen hovering over the contract.

"What condition?" the realtor asked cautiously.

Sophie turned to face Luke directly, marshaling her courage. "I want you to stay on for sixty days after closing. To teach me everything I need to know about running this ranch."

Luke stared at her, surprise evident in every line of his face. "Sixty days?"

"Two months," Sophie clarified, her voice steady despite her racing pulse. "Paid, of course. Consider it a consulting fee. But I need someone who knows this property, these animals, and the local conditions to show me the ropes."

Janet looked as though she might speak, then thought better of it, watching Luke for his reaction with obvious fascination.

He leaned back in his chair, studying Sophie with an unreadable expression. "I start with the Forest Service soon."

"Then I'll work around your schedule," Sophie countered, leaning forward slightly. "But I need those sixty days of your expertise, Luke. This ranch is too important to risk failure through ignorance."

Silence settled over the table as Luke considered her proposal. Sophie held his gaze steadily, refusing to show the vulnerability churning beneath her confident exterior.

"I can't commit to being here full time," Luke finally said. "Not with fire season starting."

"I understand completely. We can figure out a schedule... arrange specific days, even partial days. But I want sixty days total of your time to ensure I understand every aspect of this operation."

Luke's mouth quirked in what might have been the ghost of a smile. "You're remarkably determined."

"I am. This is non-negotiable."

Janet cleared her throat delicately. "This is... highly unusual. I've never facilitated this type of arrangement."

"Then we'll be pioneering new territory," Sophie replied, not taking her eyes off Luke. "What do you say? Sixty days total, working around your firefighting schedule."

Luke drummed his fingers once against the table, then nodded with what looked like reluctant admiration. "I'll do it. But with conditions of my own."

Relief flooded through her. "Name them."

"Two days a week are mine completely dedicated to the Forest Service, non-negotiable. I'm all yours the other five, but during active fire season, I might be called away for emergencies."

"Agreed, as long as I get my full sixty days on the ranch."

"My cabin isn't ready for occupancy yet."

Sophie frowned. "Where will you live?"

"The bunkhouse, I suppose."

Janet looked between them with wide eyes. "This is highly irregular. We should probably draft a separate contract for this mentoring arrangement."

"Absolutely," Sophie agreed. "But do we have a verbal agreement, Luke?"

Luke extended his hand across the table, his expression serious but tinged with something that might have been respect. "Sixty days total, teaching you everything about running Ironwood Creek Ranch. Starting the day after closing."

Sophie took his hand, noting the strength in his grip and the calluses that spoke of years of hard work. His palm was warm, steady—the handshake of a man whose word meant something.

"Deal," she said.

Janet cleared her throat again. "Well, this is certainly a first in my twenty-year career. I'll need to consult with my broker about..."

"You're the expert, Janet, do whatever you need to do," Sophie assured her, reluctantly releasing Luke's hand. "The important thing is that we've reached an agreement on the sale."

"Indeed we have," Janet said, still looking slightly bewildered. "I'll draft the official offer with your... unique condition... and bring everything by tomorrow for signatures."

Luke stood, signaling the meeting's end. "I'll walk you both out."

"Actually," Sophie said, rising as well, "I was hoping to see more of the horses before Janet leaves. Especially Thunder, after everything you've told me about him."

Luke checked his watch again. "We have time. Janet?"

"I'd love to join you," the realtor replied, gathering her materials with obvious relief. "I rarely get to see the enjoyable parts of the properties I sell."

They exited through the back door, crossing the porch to a well-worn path leading toward the barns. The afternoon was beginning its graceful slide toward evening, golden light softening the landscape into something that belonged on a postcard.

As they approached the main barn, Sophie could hear the rhythmic sound of hooves on packed earth and the low murmur of voices. Rounding the corner, she saw Gus and another ranch hand exercising a magnificent black stallion in the round pen.

Sophie stopped in her tracks, her breath catching audibly. The horse moved with liquid grace, his coat gleaming like polished obsidian in the sunlight. His conformation was nearly perfect—powerful hindquarters, strong back, proud head carried high as he cantered around the pen's perimeter with controlled energy.

"Thunder," Luke said simply, coming to stand beside her.

"He's absolutely magnificent," Sophie breathed, her professional eye cataloging his exceptional qualities. "Arabian crossed with...?"

"Quarter Horse, third generation. Uncle Carter's masterpiece."

The stallion noticed their presence, ears pricking forward alertly as he changed direction, moving toward them with an arched neck and lifted tail that spoke of both power and intelligence. He stopped at the fence, nostrils flaring as he assessed the newcomers with obvious curiosity.

"May I?" Sophie asked, already extending her hand slowly toward the fence rail.

Luke nodded approvingly. "He's spirited but well-mannered. Gus, bring him closer."

The young ranch hand clicked his tongue softly, and Thunder approached the fence with a regal bearing. His dark eyes were intelligent and assessing as Sophie held out her hand, palm down, allowing him to catch her scent. The stallion's velvet muzzle brushed her fingers, warm breath puffing against her skin in greeting.

"Hello, handsome," she murmured, the connection immediate and electric.

Thunder nudged her hand with gentle insistence, seeking more contact. Sophie obliged, running her fingers along his sleek neck, feeling the powerful muscles beneath his silk-smooth coat. The trust he offered felt like a gift.

"He likes you," Luke observed, genuine surprise coloring his tone.

"Horses usually do," Sophie replied without taking her eyes off the magnificent animal. "My grandfather always said I had the gift."

"It's more than that," Luke said quietly, his voice carrying a note of something that might have been wonder. "Thunder doesn't warm up to strangers this fast. Ever."

Sophie looked away from the horse to meet Luke's gaze, finding something unreadable in his expression—a mixture of respect, curiosity, and perhaps a touch of awareness that suggested she'd just passed some unspoken test.

"Animals sense intention," she said simply. "They know when someone genuinely cares."

Luke's mouth quirked in that almost-smile that was becoming familiar. "Sixty days to teach you everything about this place, Dr. Lawson, but I'm starting to think you already understand the most important part."

The compliment warmed her in ways she hadn't expected. Coming from someone who clearly knew and loved these animals, it carried weight beyond mere politeness.

"Please, just call me Sophie," she reminded him gently. "If we're going to be working together for the next two months, formality seems unnecessary."

"Sophie it is," he agreed, and something about the way her name sounded in his voice made her glance quickly back at Thunder, who was still demanding her attention with aristocratic persistence.

Eventually, they made their way back toward the barn, where Moonbeam and her filly were resting comfortably in a spacious stall bedded deeply with fresh, golden straw. The mare lifted her head as they approached, recognition flickering in her gentle eyes as she spotted Sophie.

"May I go in?" Sophie asked, gesturing toward the stall door.

"Of course," Luke replied, unlatching it for her.

Sophie entered quietly, moving with the slow, deliberate care that had become second nature around new mothers and their babies. The foal was on her feet, wobbling slightly. Her rich bay coloring promised to match her mother's, complemented by a distinctive white blaze down her delicate face.

"She's absolutely perfect," Sophie said, kneeling beside them both. She ran professional hands gently over the foal, checking joints and conformation with practiced expertise. "Strong legs, excellent chest depth. She's going to be a beauty."

"Thanks to you," Luke said from the stall doorway, his voice carrying genuine gratitude. "We would have lost them both if you hadn't arrived when you did."

Sophie glanced up, meeting his steady gaze. "Maybe this ranch and I were meant to find each other. God's timing and all that."

"Maybe so."

As Sophie rose, brushing straw from her jeans, a profound sense of rightness settled over her like a blessing. This place, these animals, this new beginning—it all felt like coming home in ways Seattle never had. Even the prospect of depending on Luke for the next sixty days, which would have sent her running in panic a month ago, now seemed like a reasonable step toward the true independence and the dream she'd always wanted.

The foal stumbled against her legs, then steadied herself with determination, looking up with liquid dark eyes that held all the innocence and promise of new beginnings. Sophie stroked her impossibly soft neck, a smile tugging at her lips.

"Does she have a name yet?" she asked.

Luke shook his head. "Naming rights traditionally go to the owner."

"Then I'll call her Serendipity," Sophie decided without hesitation. "Sera for short. Because some of the most beautiful accidents are divine appointments in disguise."

She looked up to find Luke watching her with an expression she couldn't quite decipher—something between curiosity and challenge, as if he were trying to solve a particularly intriguing puzzle.

"Sixty days," he said quietly, pitching his voice so Janet, who was cooing over the foal from a respectful distance, couldn't overhear. "That's all I'm promising."

"Sixty days is all I'm asking for," Sophie replied, meeting his gaze with steady confidence. "After that, this ranch—and everything on it—becomes my responsibility alone. You'll be free to pursue your new life without looking back."

But even as she said the words, Sophie found herself wondering if sixty days would be enough time to learn everything she needed to know. Not just about running a ranch, but about the man who was going to teach her—and why the thought of him leaving made her chest tighten with something that felt dangerously close to regret.

Chapter 3

Luke stood on the porch, hands braced against the railing, watching Janet's silver SUV disappear down the gravel driveway with Sophie following in her U-Haul. He exhaled slowly, shaking his head as he tried to process what had just happened.

Sixty days.

He'd just agreed to stay on this ranch for sixty more days—two months of his life he'd planned to spend fully committed to aerial firefighting.

"What were you thinking, Harding?" he muttered, rubbing the back of his neck where tension had already taken root.

The position with the Forest Service was supposed to be his clean break from Ironwood Creek Ranch. A chance to return to the sky where he belonged, where the ghosts of loss couldn't follow. Yet somehow, in the space of a single afternoon, a beautiful, determined blonde veterinarian with striking blue eyes had derailed his carefully laid plans.

And he'd let her.

Without hesitation.

Luke pushed away from the railing and paced the length of the porch, the boards creaking beneath his boots. Sophie Lawson had walked onto his property, saved a valuable mare and foal with breathtaking competence, and then somehow convinced him to extend his stay. The woman possessed a quiet strength that reminded him of someone—his uncle, perhaps, in her unwavering determination to see something through properly.

That was the part that unsettled him the most. Not the change to his Forest Service schedule—Chief Roberts would understand, even if he wouldn't be happy—but the immediacy of his response to Sophie's request. As if some part of him had been waiting for a reason to linger here longer, despite his eagerness to return to the sky.

Thunder nickered from the paddock nearby, drawing Luke's attention. The stallion paced along the fence line, his black coat gleaming in the late afternoon sun, head high as he surveyed his domain with the pride of a born king.

"She knows horses," Luke acknowledged aloud, his voice carrying across the empty porch. That much was undeniable. The way she'd handled the emergency with Moonbeam spoke of years of experience and natural talent. And Thunder—suspicious, standoffish Thunder—had taken to her immediately, as if recognizing a kindred spirit.

Lord, what am I getting myself into?

Luke settled into one of the Adirondack chairs, stretching his long legs before him. The mountains rose in the distance, their peaks painted with the first blush of evening light. This view had been the backdrop of his life for twenty-three years. Even during his time away, flying tankers and helicopters over wilderness fires, the memory of this panorama had been his anchor, his true north.

And now he was selling it.

Leaving it behind for a life in the clouds, where the ache of Uncle Carter's absence wouldn't follow him around every corner of the barn, every pasture, every room of the house.

Yet for sixty days, he would remain, teaching Sophie Lawson the rhythms and requirements of the ranch. Showing her the irrigation schedules, the breeding program records, the hidden springs that never ran dry even in drought years. Working alongside her, watching her take ownership of the legacy his uncle had built with calloused hands and stubborn love.

An image of Sophie kneeling beside Moonbeam flashed in his mind—her gentle confidence, the soothing murmur of her voice, the competent way her hands had moved to save two lives. Then, later, the spark of pure joy in her eyes when she'd named the foal Serendipity, as if the moment itself had been a gift.

"Get it together," Luke muttered, pushing to his feet. This was a business arrangement, nothing more. She needed his expertise; he needed the sale to proceed smoothly so he could move into his future. End of story.

Luke pulled his cell phone from his pocket, grimacing at the three missed calls from Chief Roberts. The conversation he needed to have couldn't be delayed any longer, even though he dreaded explaining his change of plans. He dialed the number, steeling himself for the discussion ahead.

Mark Roberts answered on the second ring. "Luke! Been trying to reach you all afternoon."

"Sorry about that, Chief. Had an emergency with one of the mares, then the ranch sale meeting ran longer than expected."

"How'd that go? Are we still on schedule for your start date?"

Luke hesitated, looking out over the pastures where Ray and Gus were moving a group of yearlings to fresh grazing. The familiar sight of well-managed ranch life tugged at something deep in his chest. "That's actually why I'm calling. There's been a... complication."

A pause from the other end. "What kind of complication?"

"The buyer wants me to stay on for sixty days after closing. To teach her the operations."

"Her?" Chief Roberts's voice sharpened with unmistakable interest.

Luke sighed, already regretting the slip. "Dr. Sophie Lawson. She's a veterinarian from Seattle."

"No ranching experience?"

"Some. She grew up on a ranch in Colorado, but this place is bigger than what she's used to, I suspect. She wants to make sure she understands everything."

"And you agreed to this?"

"It was a condition of the sale," Luke said. "Full cash offer, no inspection contingencies. It was too good to pass up."

Chief Roberts was quiet for a moment. When he spoke again, his tone was carefully measured. "We've been holding this position for you, Luke. Fire season's already in full swing. We need experienced pilots in the air."

"I know that." Luke ran his free hand through his hair, tension building in his shoulders. "I told her I'd need to work for the Forest Service two days a week, with potential emergency call-outs. She agreed to work around my schedule."

"Two days a week?" The incredulity in the chief's voice was unmistakable. "Luke, we discussed full-time deployment. The lead pilot position requires complete commitment—"

"I understand," Luke interrupted, familiar guilt tightening his chest. "But this is temporary, after I give her the time I promised... I'm all yours."

Another long pause. Luke could almost see the chief's frown, the way he'd be leaning back in his chair, fingers drumming on his desk as he weighed the options against personnel needs and fire season demands.

"The Sapphire District has three active fires already," Roberts finally said. "Weather predictions point to an above-average season. We need experienced pilots, especially with your skills in the Super Scooper."

"I'm not backing away from the job," Luke assured him. "Just asking for a modified schedule to fulfill this obligation. Then I'm committed one hundred percent."

"Is that what this ranch is to you now? An obligation?" The question held no judgment, only genuine curiosity.

Luke's gaze drifted to the Ironwood Grove stand of trees and the creek that gave the ranch its name. Uncle Carter had begun planting those first saplings beside the creek the year he bought the property, nurturing them through drought and harsh winters until they stood tall and strong—a living legacy of faith and perseverance.

"It's complicated," he admitted, the understatement of the year. "This place was my uncle's dream, not mine. But I owe it to him to make sure it passes into the right hands."

"And you think this veterinarian has the right hands?"

The image of Sophie's capable fingers moving confidently during the foaling flashed through Luke's mind again, followed by the memory of Thunder's immediate acceptance of her touch. "I do."

Chief Roberts sighed heavily. "Two days a week plus emergency call-outs. Then you're mine full time after this sixty-day arrangement you got yourself into, Harding. The district can't function with a part-time lead pilot indefinitely."

Relief eased some of the tension in Luke's shoulders. "Thanks, Chief. I appreciate your understanding."

"Don't thank me yet. Captain Walsh isn't going to be happy about reworking the schedule, and you'll need to stay current with all the training requirements. That means some of your 'ranch days' might get eaten up with Forest Service obligations."

"I understand. I'll make it work somehow."

"You'd better," Roberts said, but the gruffness in his voice had softened with something like paternal concern. "How's the cabin coming along?"

"Getting there. Should be move-in ready in a couple of weeks."

"Good. Are plans still in place for the helipad, right? Might need to pick you up directly during emergencies."

Luke smiled despite himself. "Already covered, Chief. Level area cleared a good distance from the cabin site."

"That's why you're my first choice for lead pilot, Harding. You're always thinking three steps ahead." A pause, then, "So this doctor—she attractive?"

The question caught Luke completely off guard. "That's not relevant."

Roberts chuckled, a sound rich with experience and knowing. "Which means yes. Watch yourself, Luke. Sixty days is a long time to work closely with someone. Things have a way of getting complicated."

"Not going to happen," Luke said firmly, though his pulse quickened at the memory of Sophie's smile when she'd named the foal. "I'm coming back to flying full time. That's where I belong. I have no room in my life for anything else."

"If you say so." The skepticism in the chief's voice was unmistakable. "Keep me posted. I'll work with Walsh on your modified schedule."

"Will do. Thanks again, Chief."

"Don't make me regret this, Harding."

The call ended, leaving Luke with a mixture of relief and mounting uncertainty. He'd secured the modified schedule, but at what cost? Chief Roberts was right—the lead pilot position demanded complete commitment. These next couple of months would test his ability to balance competing obligations while staying focused on his ultimate goal.

And then there was Sophie herself. Roberts's implication hadn't been subtle, and Luke couldn't honestly deny the immediate attraction he'd felt. But getting involved with the new owner of the ranch would be foolish on multiple levels. She was starting a new life; he was returning to a dangerous profession where emotional attachments could prove fatal distractions. Their paths were crossing temporarily, nothing more.

Help me keep my priorities straight, Lord, he prayed silently. Don't let me complicate something that should be simple.

The sound of someone approaching broke into his thoughts. Luke looked up to see Ray and Gus making their way toward the porch, their workday clearly finished.

Ray, the ranch foreman, climbed the steps first, removing his dusty hat as he approached. At fifty-two, he'd been with the ranch longer than anyone, having started working for Uncle Carter fresh out of high school. His weathered face was creased with curiosity and something that might have been concern.

"Saw Janet and that city doc leaving," he said without preamble. "How'd it go? We got ourselves a new owner?"

Luke nodded, gesturing for both men to sit. "Looks that way, assuming the contracts get signed without issues."

Gus, the youngest of the ranch hands at twenty-nine, dropped onto the porch step, his lanky frame folding like a pocket knife. "She sure knew her way around a difficult foaling."

"Dr. Lawson is an equine veterinarian," Luke explained. "She grew up on a ranch in Colorado."

Ray's grizzled eyebrows rose with approval. "Better than some investment banker looking to play weekend cowboy." He studied Luke's face with the shrewd perception of someone who'd known him since childhood. "You look like you've got more to tell us."

Luke leaned back against the porch railing, crossing his arms. "She made a full cash offer, no contingencies."

"That's good news," Ray said cautiously. "Isn't it?"

"With one condition," Luke continued. "I've agreed to stay on for sixty days after closing. To teach her everything about running this place."

Gus let out a low whistle. "Thought you were all set to get back in the air full time."

"I'll still be flying two days a week with the Forest Service. The rest of the time, I'll be here."

Ray frowned, his foreman's mind immediately jumping to practical concerns. "And where exactly will you be staying? Your cabin isn't finished yet."

"That's the other thing," Luke said. "I'll need to move into the bunkhouse until the cabin's ready."

A moment of silence followed this announcement. Luke could almost see the wheels turning in Ray's head as the foreman processed all the implications.

"So let me get this straight," Ray finally said, his tone carefully neutral. "You're selling the ranch to a female veterinarian from Seattle, staying on to teach her how to run the place, moving into the bunkhouse with us, and still planning to fight fires two days a week?" He shook his head slowly. "You sure you thought this through, boss?"

"The sale of the ranch was always part of the bigger plan," Luke pointed out, though he heard the defensiveness in his own voice. "The rest is... an adjustment to circumstances."

Gus grinned, his boyish face lighting up with mischief. "An adjustment, he says. More like a complete overhaul of the exit strategy."

Luke shot him a warning look, but there was no real heat behind it. These men knew him too well to be intimidated by his occasional scowls.

"She seemed nice enough," Gus continued, undeterred. "Pretty too, if you don't mind me saying so."

"I do mind," Luke said flatly. "Dr. Sophie Lawson will be our employer soon. That's all that matters."

Ray and Gus exchanged a knowing look that Luke chose to ignore, though heat crept up his neck.

"What does she plan to do with the place?" Ray asked, mercifully redirecting the conversation to safer ground.

"Continue the breeding program for sure. Eventually start a therapeutic riding program, from what I understand."

Ray nodded thoughtfully. "Like what the Morrison kids have been doing over in Hamilton? That's good work, helping people heal."

The mention of the Morrison family sent a familiar pang of guilt through Luke's chest. Katie Morrison, Jake's widow, had started taking their children to therapeutic riding sessions after Jake's death. Luke had helped fund the program anonymously, his small attempt to support the family of the man who'd died while he survived.

"Similar, I think," Luke confirmed, pushing away the memories. "She mentioned her grandmother ran something like it back in Colorado."

"Well, I'm all for it," Gus declared with enthusiasm. "Beats selling to some corporation that would subdivide the whole place into vacation lots."

Ray scratched his grizzled beard, eyes narrowed in thought. "Sixty days isn't much time to learn everything about a place this size and this complex."

"It's what she asked for," Luke said with a shrug, though privately he'd wondered the same thing.

"And you didn't try to talk her into more time?" Ray pressed, his tone holding a note of challenge. "Seems to me a full year would be more reasonable for a proper transition."

Luke's jaw tightened. "I'll be starting full time with the Forest Service after I've done my sixty days. That's the commitment I made."

Ray held up his hands in surrender. "Just saying, boss. This place was your uncle's pride and joy. Hate to see it struggle under new ownership because the transition was rushed."

The observation struck closer to home than Luke cared to admit. He'd been so focused on his own escape from painful memories that he hadn't fully considered what the ranch needed for a successful transition. Sixty days was indeed a compressed timeline for transferring decades of accumulated knowledge and wisdom.

"Dr. Lawson strikes me as a quick study," he said, more defensively than he'd intended. "And she'll have all of you to help her after I'm gone."

"True enough... we'll be here to help her," Ray conceded. "Though none of us knows the finer details of the breeding program, like you do. Or the water rights agreements. Or the deals with neighboring ranches."

"I'll make sure she understands all of it before I leave," Luke promised, though the weight of that responsibility suddenly felt heavier.

Gus stood, stretching his long arms overhead with a satisfied grunt. "Well, I, for one, am looking forward to having you in the bunkhouse, boss. Maybe now we can finally convince you to join our poker nights."

Luke's mouth quirked in an almost-smile. "Don't get your hopes up. I've seen how you play cards."

"That bad?" Gus asked with mock offense.

"Worse," Luke confirmed. "Your tells are so obvious a blind man could read them from across the room."

Ray chuckled, rising to his feet with the careful movements of a man who'd spent decades in the saddle. "Better watch yourself, boss. Close quarters have a way of revealing all sorts of things a man might prefer to keep private."

There was more meaning in those words than the simple warning about poker tells, and Luke knew it. Living in the bunkhouse meant giving up the solitude he'd cultivated since Uncle Carter's death. No more silent evenings alone with his thoughts and memories. No more private struggles with guilt and grief in the dark hours before dawn.

"I'll manage," he said shortly. "It's only temporary."

Ray studied him for a long moment, then nodded with the wisdom of someone who'd seen many changes come and go. "Everything is, I suppose. Life's just a series of temporary arrangements when you get right down to it."

The philosophical observation was unexpected coming from the practical foreman. Luke met the older man's gaze, recognizing the truth born of hard experience and steady faith.

"Some more temporary than others," he acknowledged quietly.

Ray replaced his hat, adjusting it with practiced hands. "We'll clear space for your things in the bunkhouse. When do you figure on moving in?"

"After closing. Probably tomorrow evening if everything goes smoothly."

"And the new boss? When does she arrive for good?"

"After closing, I imagine. That U-Haul she was driving suggests she's ready to move in immediately."

Gus whistled again, shaking his head in amazement. "Lady doesn't waste time, does she?"

"No," Luke agreed, thinking of the swift, confident way Sophie had handled the foaling emergency, and the decisive manner in which she'd made her offer. "She doesn't."

The men headed off toward the barn to finish the evening chores, leaving Luke alone on the porch with his swirling thoughts. The conversation had forced him to confront the practicalities of the arrangement he'd agreed to—not just the scheduling complications with the Forest Service, but the day-to-day reality of living and working alongside Sophie Lawson.

Sixty days of close proximity.

Sixty days of teaching her everything he knew about this land, these animals, this legacy his uncle had built with such love and determination.

Sixty days of trying to ignore the immediate connection he'd felt with Sophie, the spark of interest that had flared between them.

Luke entered the ranch house, knowing he should start sorting his belongings, deciding what to move to the bunkhouse and what to store until the cabin was ready. Instead, he walked slowly toward the office, the room which had remained largely as his uncle had left it. From the aviation maps pinned to one wall to the breeding records meticulously organized in leather-bound volumes on the shelves. Luke hadn't had the heart to change anything significant, treating the space as both workspace and memorial to the man who had raised him after his parents' tragic death.

Carter Harding had been a man of fascinating contradictions—a skilled pilot who loved the freedom of the sky, yet equally devoted to the earth beneath his feet. He'd built Ironwood Creek Ranch with his own calloused hands, turning a large cash inheritance into a thriving ranch operation through sheer determination and an intuitive understanding of horses, land, and the delicate balance between them.

Luke moved to the massive oak desk, running his fingers along the smooth surface worn by decades of use. This was where he'd have to start with Sophie—teaching her the business side of ranching. The breeding program documentation, the grazing rotation schedules, the water rights agreements that had taken Uncle Carter decades to negotiate and maintain.

A framed photograph on the desk caught his eye—Luke at sixteen, standing proudly beside his uncle in front of a yellow crop duster. His first official flying lesson, though Carter had been letting him handle the controls for years. His uncle's arm was slung around his shoulders, both their faces split with identical grins of pure joy. Flying had been their shared passion, the thing that bonded them across the generation gap.

"What would you think of all this, Uncle Carter?" Luke murmured, picking up the frame and studying the captured moment.

"Selling your life's work to a city vet with big dreams and untested determination?"

He could almost hear his uncle's gruff laugh, see the crinkles around his eyes as he considered the question with the careful thought he'd given every important decision. Carter Harding had been a pragmatist at heart, but also an incurable romantic—a man who believed in following your calling, whatever form it took.

"She loves the horses," Luke continued his one-sided conversation, his voice barely above a whisper. "Knows her way around them like she was born to it. You'd approve of that, at least."

Setting the photograph down carefully, Luke moved to the window overlooking the property. From here, he could see the mountains in the distance and distinctive groves of trees silhouetted against the deepening sky. Beyond those trees, not visible from this angle, lay the thirty acres he'd retained—his compromise with the past and future.

The cabin being built there represented more than just a place to live. It was a bridge between worlds, a way to honor his connection to this land while pursuing his calling in the sky.

Lord, help me honor Uncle Carter's memory while following the path You've set before me, he prayed silently. And help me keep my heart focused on what matters most.

Luke turned from the window, his gaze sweeping the organized chaos of the office. He would need to explain everything in this room to Sophie—every file, every record, every system his uncle had developed over decades of careful ranching. The task seemed suddenly monumental; the time allotted woefully inadequate.

And beneath that practical concern lurked another, more troubling thought: How was he supposed to maintain a distance from a woman who had walked into his life and, in the space of a single afternoon, upended all his careful plans? A woman whose determination matched his own, whose connection with the animals was immediate and profound, whose presence stirred something in him he'd thought permanently buried?

"Sixty days," he repeated aloud, as if saying it might somehow make the challenge less daunting. "Just sixty days, and then everything goes back to the way it's supposed to be."

But even as he spoke the words, Luke couldn't shake the feeling that some things, once changed, could never be returned to their original state. Some encounters left permanent marks on the soul, reshaping the landscape of the heart in ways that couldn't be undone.

The thought should have worried him more than it did.

Chapter 4

Sophie placed her suitcase on the floral quilt covering the bed at the Riverbend Valley Inn & Spa. The room—charming in a stuck-in-the-nineties kind of way—smelled faintly of vanilla pot-pourri and furniture polish, but it was clean and welcoming after her long journey.

By this time tomorrow, or the day after at the latest, she'd be the official owner of Ironwood Creek Ranch.

A thrill shot through her as she smoothed a wrinkle from a blouse she had removed from her suitcase. Owner. Not an employee, not an associate, not "the promising young doctor who works under Dr. Marcus Brennan." Owner.

The sight of the blouse brought an unwelcome memory—the last time she'd worn it, the day she'd walked out of Pacific Northwest Equine Medical Center for good.

Marcus had been in the break room, holding court among the technicians and junior associates as he often did, his voice carrying that authoritative tone he cultivated so carefully.

"The procedure I developed for treating navicular disease has shown remarkable success rates," he was saying, his chest puffed with false pride. "Ninety-two percent improvement in our trial cases."

Sophie had frozen in the doorway, a coffee mug halfway to her lips. The procedure he developed? The one she'd spent eighteen months researching, documenting, and refining while he dismissed her work as "interesting but unproven"?

"Fascinating approach, Dr. Brennan," one of the new veterinary assistants had gushed. "How did you ever think of using that particular combination of therapies?"

Sophie had watched Marcus smile—that practiced, camera-ready smile that had once made her heart race, but now only made her stomach clench with revulsion.

"Sometimes innovation requires looking at old problems through new eyes," he'd replied smoothly, as if he hadn't dismissed that exact insight when Sophie had shared it with him months earlier.

Their eyes had met across the room. No shame flickered in his expression—only a slight narrowing, a silent warning to play along. After all, wasn't his success their success? Wasn't that what being a team meant?

Team. The word had lost all meaning over the past year, as Marcus systematically claimed her innovations while undermining her confidence. His manipulation had been so gradual, she hadn't recognized it until she was thoroughly enmeshed—professionally, financially, and emotionally.

Sophie shook her head firmly, banishing the toxic memory as she tucked her empty suitcase under the bed. That chapter of her life was closed. Marcus belonged to her past; Ironwood Creek Ranch—and whatever God had planned for her there—was her future.

She grabbed her purse and room key, eager for fresh air and something to eat. The drive from the ranch back to town had awakened her appetite, reminding her she'd had nothing but gas station coffee and a granola bar since early morning.

The inn's proprietor had mentioned several dining options in town when she checked in. After two days of driving and an emotionally charged afternoon, Sophie craved something simple and comforting.

Outside, Sophie paused on the inn's front porch, orienting herself to the small-town center visible just down the street. Riverbend Valley's main street stretched before her like an illustration from a Western novel—historic storefronts with wooden sidewalks, vintage lampposts, and hanging flower baskets swaying gently in the evening breeze.

Sophie walked slowly, drinking in the details. The hardware store with fishing gear prominently displayed in the window. The small bookshop with a hand-painted sign reading "The Book Wrangler." A group of men in work boots and Stetsons emerging from a building called the Branding Iron Grill, their easy laughter carrying on the wind.

Everything about the town spoke of permanence and community—so different from the transient, career-focused atmosphere of Seattle, where new restaurants and businesses seemed to open and close with each passing season.

Halfway down the block, a cheerful yellow building with blue trim caught her eye. A wooden sign swinging gently above the door depicted a bluebird perched on a steaming coffee cup. Through large windows, Sophie glimpsed several tables with mismatched chairs and a glass display case that appeared to contain an impressive array of homemade pies.

The Bluebird Café. Perfect.

A bell jingled merrily as Sophie pushed open the door. The café's interior smelled gloriously of coffee, cinnamon, and something buttery baking in the oven. Several tables were occupied with locals engaged in quiet conversation, though a few heads turned curiously at her entrance—not unfriendly, just interested in the newcomer.

"Be right with you, honey!" called a voice from behind the counter, where a woman with silver-streaked hair was filling a coffee carafe with practiced efficiency.

Sophie chose a small table near the window and settled into a chair that creaked pleasantly beneath her weight. A laminated menu tucked behind the napkin holder offered simple fare—sandwiches, soups, salads, and an impressive selection of homemade pies that made her mouth water.

"Well now, you must be Dr. Lawson!"

Sophie looked up to find the woman from behind the counter standing at her table, coffeepot in one hand and a warm smile that reached all the way to her eyes. She wore a blue apron over a floral dress, and her smile crinkled the corners of her eyes in a way that suggested it was her default expression.

"I am," Sophie confirmed, surprised and oddly pleased. "How did you—"

"Honey, news travels faster than wildfire in Riverbend Valley," the woman said with a warm laugh. "I'm Lily Hawthorne, owner of this establishment and unofficial town crier, according to some." She gestured around the room with her coffeepot. "Coffee, while you decide what you'd like to eat?"

"Please," Sophie nodded, turning over the empty mug that sat on the table.

Lily poured the steaming coffee with a steady hand. "Janet Myers called me not twenty minutes ago to say you'd checked into Vickie's place. Said you'd had quite a day out at Ironwood Creek Ranch."

Sophie wrapped her hands around the mug, savoring both the warmth and the easy acceptance in Lily's voice. "Word really does travel fast here."

"A blessing and a curse of small-town living," Lily confirmed cheerfully. "Though mostly a blessing, if you ask me. Means you're never truly alone when you need help." She tucked her order pad into her apron pocket. "Now, what can I get for you? After a long drive and an afternoon saving prize foals, I'd recommend the chicken pot pie."

Sophie blinked in surprise. "You already know about Moonbeam and the foal?"

"Eric Thorne—one of the ranch hands out at Ironwood Creek—stopped by for coffee and pie about an hour ago. Said a city vet with magic hands saved a prize mare and delivered the prettiest filly he'd seen in years." Lily's eyes twinkled with genuine warmth. "He was mighty impressed, and Eric Thorne doesn't impress easily."

A pleased flush warmed Sophie's cheeks. It felt good to be recognized for her skills rather than having them dismissed or claimed by someone else. "It was fortunate timing, that's all. Right place, right time."

"Humble too," Lily observed approvingly. "I like that in a person. So, pot pie? Or would you prefer something lighter after your travels?"

"Pot pie sounds perfect, actually," Sophie decided. "And maybe a slice of whatever smells so amazing baking right now?"

"Peach cobbler with cinnamon streusel," Lily replied with obvious pride. "Good choice. Won't be ready for another thirty minutes, though."

"I'm not going anywhere."

Lily nodded approvingly and headed toward the kitchen, pausing to refill mugs and chat briefly with other patrons along the way. Sophie sipped her coffee—rich and smooth without a hint of bitterness—and let her gaze wander around the café.

The walls were decorated with local photography—mountain vistas, wildlife, and ranch scenes that captured the rugged beauty of Montana. Vintage tin signs advertising coffee and baked goods added a nostalgic touch. The overall effect was homey and inviting, the kind of place where people lingered over conversation rather than hurrying through meals.

"Here we go," Lily announced, returning with a ceramic dish containing a golden-crusted pot pie that looked like something from a cooking magazine. "Careful now. It's a bit warm."

Steam escaped as Sophie broke through the crust with her fork. The aroma of chicken, herbs, and buttery pastry made her stomach growl audibly. She took a careful bite and her eyes widened in appreciation.

"Oh my goodness," she said after swallowing. "This is incredible."

Lily beamed with pride. "Secret's in the thyme and a touch of rosemary. My mamma's recipe."

"She must have been an amazing cook."

"That she was." Lily glanced around the cafe, noting that the other tables were momentarily settled, then slid into the chair across from Sophie with the easy familiarity of someone accustomed to friendly conversation. "So, you're buying Luke's ranch?"

The direct question might have seemed intrusive coming from someone else, but Lily's manner was so genuinely warm that Sophie responded without hesitation.

"If all goes well with the paperwork," she confirmed between bites.

"Janet doesn't let paperwork go sideways," Lily assured her with confidence. "If she says you'll close tomorrow or the next day, you will." She studied Sophie with friendly curiosity. "What brings a Seattle veterinarian to our little corner of Montana?"

Sophie hesitated, uncertain how much to reveal to this friendly stranger. Yet something about Lily's open expression and genuine interest invited honesty.

"A fresh start," she said finally. "And a return to my roots, in a way. I grew up on a ranch in Colorado before moving to the city for school and work."

"Ah, so you're not a complete city slicker, then," Lily nodded approvingly. "That'll help with the adjustment. Though Ironwood Creek Ranch is a pretty big operation to take on single-handed, even for someone with experience."

"Luke's staying on for sixty days to teach me the specifics," Sophie explained, surprised at how easily the words flowed. "It was part of our agreement."

Lily's eyebrows shot up with unmistakable interest. "Is that so? Well, isn't that interesting?"

Something in her tone made Sophie look up sharply from her pot pie. "It's strictly a business arrangement," she clarified quickly. "I need to understand the ranch operations, and he's the expert."

"Of course it is," Lily agreed, though her eyes held a knowing gleam that made Sophie suddenly very interested in her food. "Luke Harding is certainly the expert when it comes to that ranch. Grew up there after his parents passed. His uncle Carter raised him from age ten."

Sophie hadn't known that detail. The information added another layer to her understanding of Luke's deep connection to the property. "He mentioned his uncle loved the ranch."

"Carter Harding built that place from practically nothing," Lily confirmed, her voice carrying the respect of someone who'd watched the transformation happen. "Started with a good-sized inheritance and a bigger dream. Man had a way with horses that bordered on magical, according to some. Luke has that same touch."

Sophie thought of how Thunder had responded to Luke's presence, the easy confidence with which he'd handled the magnificent stallion. "I can believe that."

"Carter's passing hit Luke harder than most folks realized," Lily continued, her voice softening with sympathy. "Two years ago this coming August. Heart attack while Luke was away fighting fires. By the time Luke made it back home, Carter was gone."

A pang of sympathy tightened Sophie's chest. "That's terrible. Losing someone you love when you're not there to say goodbye..."

"It was devastating," Lily agreed, her expression sad. "Luke blamed himself for not being there, though there wasn't anything he could have done. Carter was gone before the ambulance even arrived. But guilt isn't rational, is it?"

"No," Sophie murmured, thinking of her grandparents' sudden deaths during her second year of veterinary school. She'd been consumed with finals, too busy to call for nearly two weeks before the accident. The regret still lingered, a dull ache she'd learned to carry. "It really isn't."

Lily studied her face with the perceptiveness of someone who'd spent years reading people, seeming to recognize the shared understanding of loss. "Everyone in town figured Luke would settle into ranching full time after that. Carter always said the land was in Luke's blood, the same as his own. But I think losing Carter pushed Luke in the opposite direction."

"Back to firefighting," Sophie supplied, remembering what Luke had said about his Forest Service position.

Lily nodded sadly. "The sky calls to him, same as it did to Carter in his younger days. Though Carter found his peace on the ground eventually, with the horses and the land. Luke hasn't reached that point yet." She paused, choosing her words carefully. "I suspect Luke's selling the ranch because it reminds him too much of what he's lost. Some grief is easier to outrun than to face head-on."

Sophie absorbed this insight, thinking of her own hasty departure from Seattle. Wasn't she doing something similar in her own way? Running from the painful reminder of Marcus's betrayal rather than staying to fight for the recognition she deserved?

No, she decided. She wasn't running away; she was running toward something. This ranch, this opportunity, had been her dream long before Marcus Brennan entered her life. God had opened this door, and she was walking through it with purpose.

"You said his uncle was a pilot too?" she asked, steering the conversation back to safer ground.

"Crop duster," Lily confirmed with a nostalgic smile. "Flew for ranches and farms all over this part of Montana. Taught Luke to fly when he was a teenager." She smiled at some private memory. "Those two were thick as thieves, sharing the same passion for the sky and for horses. Different as could be in temperament, though. Carter was all bluff and bluster, the life of every party. Luke's always been the quieter, more serious type—thoughtful, you know?"

Sophie thought of Luke's intense focus during the foaling, the controlled urgency in his voice as he directed his ranch hands with calm authority. "I can see that."

"Don't let that serious exterior fool you, though," Lily cautioned with a meaningful look. "Still waters run deep, as my mama used to say. And Luke Harding's got depths not many people get to see."

Something about the way she said it made Sophie wonder if Lily was among those few who had glimpsed those hidden depths. The thought stirred an unexpected flutter of curiosity about the man.

"The ranch seems exceptionally well-run," she said. "The breeding program especially impressed me."

"Carter's pride and joy," Lily nodded. "And Luke's taken it to new levels since taking over management. That stallion of theirs—Thunder—has sired some of the finest horses in three counties."

"I met him briefly," Sophie said, unable to keep the admiration from her voice as she remembered the magnificent animal. "He's absolutely stunning."

"That he is," Lily agreed. "Worth a small fortune, too. I'm surprised Luke's including him in the sale, honestly."

"The entire breeding program stays with the ranch. It was a key factor in my decision to make an offer."

Lily's expression turned thoughtful, almost speculative. "Luke must see something special in you, then."

"What do you mean?" Sophie asked, though her pulse quickened inexplicably.

"Carter built that breeding program from the ground up, and Luke helped expand it from the time he was old enough to hold a lead rope. It's their legacy—more than just business, it's family history." She shrugged, but her eyes remained keen. "For Luke to entrust it to a newcomer... well, let's just say he doesn't give his trust easily, especially these days."

Sophie shifted uncomfortably. "I have extensive experience with equine medicine and breeding programs. My grandparents ran a smaller but similar operation in Colorado."

"I didn't mean to suggest otherwise," Lily assured her quickly, reaching across to pat Sophie's hand in a motherly gesture. "Just making an observation. Luke's particular about those horses—protective, even. The fact that he's willing to sell them all to you, and stay on to teach you personally... well, it speaks volumes about the impression you made."

Before Sophie could respond to this intriguing statement, a timer dinged from the kitchen.

"That'll be the cobbler," Lily said, rising from her chair with obvious reluctance to end their conversation.

Left alone, Sophie mulled over what she'd learned. Luke's connection to the ranch ran deeper than she'd initially understood. It wasn't just property to him; it was a legacy, a lifetime of memories both joyful and heartbreaking. His decision to sell—and to stay on to teach her personally—took on a new significance in that light.

Why would someone walk away from such a deep-rooted connection? And why entrust a stranger with continuing what he and his uncle had built with such love and dedication?

She recalled the moment in the barn when their eyes had met over Moonbeam's laboring form, that flash of understanding as they worked together to bring new life safely into the world. Had her instinctive response to the emergency somehow proven her worthy of taking on his uncle's precious legacy?

"Here we are," Lily announced, returning with a generous slice of golden-brown cobbler topped with a scoop of vanilla ice cream that was already beginning to melt around the edges.

The cobbler smelled of summer—ripe peaches, warm cinnamon, and buttery pastry that made Sophie's mouth water. She took a bite and closed her eyes in pure appreciation. "This is absolutely divine."

"The recipe's as old as the mountains," Lily said with a smile, settling back into her chair. "Some things don't need improving upon."

Sophie nodded her agreement, savoring another perfect bite. "So... Luke's returning to firefighting. What exactly does he do?"

"He's an aerial firefighter—flies those planes that drop water and fire retardant on wildfires. Used to pilot tankers all over the western states before his uncle's health started declining." Lily's expression grew serious. "He scaled back to local work those last few years so he could help Carter with the ranch, but word is he's taking a lead position with the Forest Service this season."

"Sounds incredibly dangerous," Sophie observed, thinking of the massive wildfires she'd seen on the news, the pilots who risked everything to protect communities and wilderness.

"It is," Lily confirmed soberly. "Luke lost his flying partner almost two years back—Jake Morrison. Terrible tragedy that shook our whole community. Left behind a young widow and two young children."

Sophie's fork paused halfway to her mouth. "How awful."

"The whole town grieved with Katie—that's Jake's widow. She's a teacher at the elementary school, sweetest thing you ever met, and one of the strongest women I know. But Luke took Jake's death especially hard." Lily lowered her voice, though the nearest occupied table was well out of earshot. "He was flying lead that day, you see. Blames himself, though the official investigation cleared him completely. Equipment failure on Jake's plane—nothing Luke could have prevented."

The information cast Luke in an entirely new light, adding layers of grief and guilt to what Sophie was beginning to understand was a deeply complex man.

"That must have been devastating," she said quietly, her heart aching for him.

Lily nodded sadly. "Nearly grounded him for good. He struggled terribly with Jake's death, questioning everything about his calling to fight fires. Then Carter passed just weeks after Jake and Luke quit firefighting entirely to step up and manage the ranch full time."

The picture emerging of Luke Harding was far more complex than Sophie had initially assumed. Not just a rancher selling his property, but a man navigating multiple layers of grief, guilt, and the difficult pull between two callings—the sky and the earth.

"What about family?" Sophie asked gently. "You mentioned his parents passed when he was young, but does he have siblings? Other relatives in the area?"

"None to speak of," Lily replied with obvious sadness. "His father was Carter's only sibling, and his mother was an only child. Luke's about as alone in the world as a person can be, at least in terms of blood relations." She brightened slightly, her natural optimism reasserting itself. "Though in Riverbend Valley, family isn't just about blood. We look after our own here."

"That's... really good to hear," Sophie said, meaning it more than she could express. The isolation of her life in Seattle—where colleagues were competitors and neighbors rarely exchanged more than polite nods—had worn on her more than she'd realized until this moment.

"Speaking of looking after our own," Lily continued, her tone shifting to something more businesslike, "if you're planning to establish any kind of veterinary practice here, you should know Dr. Patterson's been hoping to scale back his workload. Man's been covering multiple counties by himself for more years than is reasonable."

Sophie perked up at this information, though she was careful in her response. "Really? I'd been wondering about the local veterinary situation, though my focus will be entirely on the ranch."

"Jim Patterson's a good man and a fine vet, but he's fifty-eight and has a bad back from decades of large animal work. He's been praying for someone to take over some of his practice, especially the equine cases. His strengths have always leaned more toward cattle and the occasional exotic pet people insist on keeping out here."

"I'd love to meet him," Sophie said honestly. "Once I'm settled at the ranch, of course. It would be good to know the local veterinary resources."

"Well, you never know when an emergency might come up where your expertise could help," Lily said practically. "Maybe you could work out some kind of consulting arrangement with Jim—emergency calls, difficult cases, that sort of thing." She smiled warmly. "Jim comes in for breakfast most Tuesday mornings. Easy enough to make sure you two cross paths. I'll give him a call and let him know you're in the area."

The casual offer of connection—so freely given, with no expectation of return favor—touched Sophie deeply. In Seattle, networking had been a calculated game of advantages and leverage. Here, it seemed to be simply how neighbors helped each other.

"Thank you," she said sincerely, her voice thick with unexpected emotion. "For the meal, the information, and especially for the welcome. I can't tell you how much this means to me."

Lily waved away her gratitude. "Part of the service at the Bluebird. First meal's on the house for newcomers, by the way. Town tradition."

"Oh, I couldn't possibly—"

"Nonsense," Lily interrupted firmly, though her eyes twinkled with humor. "Town tradition, and I never break tradition."

Sophie conceded with a grateful smile. "Then I'll be sure to become a regular customer to make up for your generosity."

"I'll hold you to that promise," Lily said, rising from her chair as the bell over the door announced new customers. "Finish your cobbler before that ice cream turns to soup. Nothing worse than peachy milk, if you ask me."

As Lily moved to greet the young couple who had just entered, Sophie turned her attention back to her dessert, her mind processing everything she'd learned. The ranch, Luke, the community—all were more layered and interconnected than she'd anticipated when she'd made her impulsive decision to buy property sight unseen.

She'd come to Riverbend Valley seeking independence and a fresh start, imagining she would build something entirely new from the ground up. Instead, she was stepping into an existing web of relationships and history, and taking over a precious legacy rather than creating one from scratch.

The realization was both daunting and oddly comforting. In Seattle, she'd been adrift, her sense of self systematically eroded by Marcus's calculated manipulation. Here, she would have roots—not just in the land she was purchasing, but in a community that already seemed eager to welcome her with open arms.

Sophie finished her cobbler and drained the last of her coffee, watching as Lily moved effortlessly among her customers, refilling cups and exchanging news with the practiced ease of someone who genuinely cared about each person who walked through her door. The café hummed with the gentle rhythm of small-town life—unhurried conversations, the comfortable clink of silverware, and the welcoming hiss of the espresso machine behind the counter.

Tomorrow, she would sign the papers that would make Ironwood Creek Ranch officially hers. Sixty days after that, Luke would leave to pursue his calling in the dangerous skies, and she would be solely responsible for continuing what he and his uncle had built with such love and dedication.

It was a sobering thought, but as she gazed around the warm, welcoming café, Sophie felt a surge of certainty that had nothing to do with her own capabilities and everything to do with faith. She had made the right decision in coming here, in choosing this place for her fresh start. God had led her here for a reason, and she trusted Him to provide the wisdom and strength she would need.

Seattle and Marcus Brennan belonged firmly to her past. Riverbend Valley, with its majestic mountains and endless skies, its genuine people and unexpected connections, held her future—whatever form that future might take.

And for the first time in longer than she could remember, that future looked not just bright, but full of possibilities she hadn't even begun to imagine.

Chapter 5

Sophie drove the U-Haul up the gravel driveway of Ironwood Creek Ranch—her ranch now. The paperwork had been signed yesterday evening in Janet Myers' office, with minimal fuss but plenty of congratulatory handshakes and a prayer of blessing from Janet herself.

As the house came into view, morning sunlight bathed its weathered cedar siding in warm amber tones. Sophie exhaled slowly, allowing herself a moment to absorb the reality. She'd done it. Against all odds and Marcus's predictions of failure, she'd bought a ranch. In under a month, she'd quit her job, broken free from his shadow, driven a U-Haul towing her car across three states, and claimed something entirely her own.

"Home sweet home," she said aloud as she brought the truck to a stop in the circular drive.

She climbed down from the cab, her boots crunching on the gravel as she approached the front porch. Several cardboard boxes were stacked neatly by the door—Luke's remaining belongings, she assumed. The sight gave her an unexpected pang. This transition represented her triumph but his loss, regardless of how willingly he'd made the sale.

Sophie withdrew the keys from her pocket, the metal cool against her palm. The brass key with the ranch's brand stamped into its head slid smoothly into the lock. With a deep breath that tasted of pine and possibility, she turned it, pushed open the door, and stepped across the threshold.

"Mine," she murmured, the word both thrilling and terrifying. No Marcus to undermine her decisions or steal credit for her work. No noisy city pressures or concrete walls closing in around her. Just twelve hundred and forty acres of God's country, stretching toward mountains that seemed to touch heaven itself.

Sophie moved through the living room, trailing her fingers along the back of the leather sofa. The furniture remained, but the personal touches that had marked it as Luke's home were gone. The model airplanes she'd noticed during her first visit had been removed from the shelves, leaving only dust outlines on the wood.

In the kitchen, the coffee maker remained on the counter, though the surfaces had been cleared of whatever personal items Luke had kept there. Sophie opened cupboards and drawers with the careful reverence of someone exploring sacred space, finding practical dishes, sturdy cookware, and basic utensils—all clean and organized with military precision.

She continued her exploration, moving down the hallway to what would now be her bedroom. The master suite was larger than her entire Seattle apartment, with windows overlooking the creek and mountains beyond. The room had been stripped of personal effects, the king-sized bed made up with fresh linens that smelled faintly of lavender. Only the essential furniture remained—the bed, matching nightstands, a dresser, and a comfortable-looking armchair positioned to take advantage of the mountain view.

The adjoining bathroom featured a claw-foot tub she could already imagine soaking in after long days of ranch work. A separate shower stood in the corner, and twin sinks were set into a vanity of polished pine that gleamed in the morning light.

"This is really happening," Sophie said aloud, her voice echoing slightly in the empty space. "I'm really here."

She returned to the truck, pulling open the rear door to begin the daunting process of moving her entire life inside. She had just lifted the first box when a deep voice called from behind her.

"Need some help with that?"

Sophie turned to find Luke approaching from the direction of the barn, flanked by Ray and Gus. Two other men she hadn't met yet followed a few paces behind, their work-weathered faces curious but welcoming.

"I've got it," she replied automatically, then reconsidered as she registered the weight of the box in her arms. "Actually, yes, thank you. That would be wonderful."

Luke nodded, gesturing to the men behind him with easy authority. "You've met Ray and Gus. This is Ed Vance and Dan Miller, two of our other full-time hands. You'll meet Eric Thorne later—he's out mending fence in the north pasture."

Ed, a stocky man in his early forties with a neatly trimmed beard and kind eyes, touched the brim of his hat with old-fashioned courtesy. "Ma'am. Welcome to Ironwood Creek."

Dan, younger and leaner with a shock of red hair visible beneath his Stetson, gave a friendly nod. "Dr. Lawson. Heard you saved Moonbeam and her foal. That's some fine work."

"Sophie, please," she corrected, setting down the box she'd been holding. "And thank you. I appreciate the help—and the warm welcome. More hands will definitely make this go faster."

The men moved to the truck with the smooth efficiency of a well-practiced team, beginning to unload boxes and furniture with careful precision. Luke paused beside her, close enough that she caught the scent of his cologne.

"Car keys?" he asked, nodding toward the BMW still secured to the trailer.

Sophie dug in her pocket and handed him the key fob, their fingers brushing briefly in the exchange. The contact sent an unexpected flutter through her pulse. "Thanks."

Luke turned to Dan, seemingly unaffected by the moment that had left Sophie oddly breathless. "Give me a hand with the car and trailer, would you?"

As they moved toward the back of the U-Haul, Sophie heard Gus let out a low whistle of appreciation.

"That's some fine city car you've got there, Doc," he called over his shoulder, carrying a box labeled 'Kitchen,' toward the house. "Might want to think about getting yourself a truck, though. First heavy snow and that little beauty'll be buried up to its windows."

Sophie smiled. "That car was my first major purchase after I finished veterinary school. I have sentimental attachment to it, but I'll definitely look into something more practical for ranch work."

"Smart thinking," Ray agreed, hefting a box of books with surprising ease. "Though I'd pay good money to see you try to haul feed bags in that BMW."

"I'll spare you the entertainment," Sophie laughed, following him into the house.

For the next hour, they worked together with a rhythm that surprised Sophie in its natural flow. The initial awkwardness she'd anticipated didn't materialize; instead, there was a comfortable efficiency to their efforts, punctuated by occasional questions about where she wanted particular items placed and good-natured ribbing among the men.

Luke remained somewhat apart from the easy banter, not distant exactly, but more reserved than the others. He handled her belongings with careful respect, speaking little but watching everything with those thoughtful brown eyes. Sophie caught him glancing around the house once or twice, his expression unreadable but tinged with something that might have been loss.

When the last box had been carried in and her BMW freed from the trailer, they gathered in the kitchen. Sophie filled glasses with water from the tap, passing them around to the men who had just made her transition infinitely easier.

"So," Ray said after draining his glass and wiping his mouth with the back of his hand, "how does it feel to own a spread like this?"

"Overwhelming," Sophie admitted with characteristic honesty. "But in the best possible way. Like stepping into a dream I didn't know I was allowed to have."

Ed nodded thoughtfully, understanding flickering in his weathered features. "Takes time to settle into a new place, especially one with this much history. But the land has a way of claiming you, if you let it."

"That's what the next sixty days are for, right?" Sophie glanced at Luke, who leaned against the counter with his arms crossed over his chest. "Learning to let the land claim me?"

"About that," he said, straightening slightly. "I'll be committed to the Forest Service on Saturdays and Sundays, probably just on call the first few weeks, but I'm available the rest of the week to focus on getting you familiar with the ranch."

Sophie nodded, appreciating his directness. "When do you want to start? I'm eager to begin learning everything you can teach me."

"How about tomorrow morning? That'll give you the rest of today to get settled and make this place feel like home."

"That works perfectly for me," Sophie agreed readily. "What's the plan for tomorrow?"

"Not a hundred percent sure, really. Maybe a tour of the property. You'll need to know the boundaries, water sources, seasonal challenges, that sort of thing. After that, we could dive into the breeding program documentation."

It was a logical approach, practical and thorough. Sophie appreciated that he wasn't talking down to her or assuming she knew nothing, despite her obvious inexperience with an operation of this scale.

"Perfect," she said, meaning it. "I'll be ready whenever you think best to start."

"Seven o'clock works."

"Seven it is."

An awkward silence settled over the kitchen as the immediate task of moving in was completed, but the new dynamic between them all remained undefined. Sophie was acutely aware that the ranch hands had worked for Luke and his uncle for some time, following their lead and respecting their authority. Now they were technically her employees, and Luke himself occupied an unusual middle ground—no longer the boss, not quite an employee, but something altogether more complicated.

Ray cleared his throat, breaking the tension. "Well, we should let you get settled in. But before we go—" he hesitated, then continued with the kind of consideration that spoke to his character, "I put a pot roast in the slow cooker this morning. Made enough to feed an army, as usual. You're welcome to join us for dinner at the bunkhouse tonight if you'd like. Save you from having to cook after all this unpacking."

The invitation surprised Sophie with its genuine warmth. She glanced at Luke, uncertain whether accepting would cross some boundary in their new professional arrangement.

"Good idea," Luke said, his expression softening slightly for the first time that morning. "Ray pot roast is the best. And it would give you a chance to get to know everyone better."

Sophie looked between the faces of her new employees—Ray's weathered kindness, Gus's youthful enthusiasm, Ed and Dan's quiet assessment. These were the men who would help her transform her dream into reality, who knew this land with an intimacy born of years. Breaking bread with them seemed like the right foundation for everything that would follow.

"I'd love that," she said with a genuine smile that seemed to relax everyone in the room. "Thank you for the invitation. What time?"

"Six-thirty?" Ray suggested. "Gives everyone time to clean up after the day's work."

"I'll be there at six-thirty," Sophie promised. "Should I bring any-thing? A side dish or dessert?"

"Just yourself," Ray assured her with paternal kindness. "We've got everything covered."

As the men filed out, Sophie caught Luke's arm gently. "Wait—your boxes are still on the porch. Do you need help moving them to the bunkhouse?"

A flicker of something—embarrassment, perhaps, or reluc-tance—crossed his face. "I'll get those later. They're just the last odds and ends."

Sophie nodded, releasing his arm but noting the warmth that lingered where they'd touched. "Thanks for organizing the help today. And for... everything else. This transition could have been so much harder."

Luke held her gaze for a moment longer than necessary, something unspoken passing between them. "You're welcome. See you at dinner."

After they left, Sophie stood in the middle of her new home, surrounded by boxes that held the pieces of her former life. The enormity of what she'd done crashed over her with sudden, overwhelming force. She was alone in Montana, hundreds of miles from everything familiar, responsible for twelve hundred and forty acres and dependent on virtual strangers for guidance.

She sank onto the leather sofa, her confident facade cracking under the weight of reality. This was what she'd wanted—independence, a clean break, a chance at a new life. So why did it suddenly feel so terrifying?

Help me, Lord, she prayed, closing her eyes and drawing in a shaky breath. I know You led me here, but I feel so small compared to all of this. Give me wisdom and strength for what's ahead.

The panic receded gradually, replaced by the steady calm that always came when she remembered she wasn't facing this alone. God had brought her this far; He wouldn't abandon her now.

"One day at a time," she reminded herself aloud, the words carrying more conviction now. "One step at a time, with faith as my guide."

She'd survived Marcus's betrayal and the crushing realization that her professional reputation had been built on quicksand. She'd driven across three states alone, delivered a foal within minutes of arriving at an unknown ranch, and negotiated the purchase of her dream property. She could handle whatever came next.

Rising from the sofa with renewed determination, Sophie moved to the nearest box labeled "Bedroom" and headed down the hallway to begin truly making this house her home. With each item she put away—her grandmother's quilted throw across the foot of the bed, her grandfather's worn copy of "All Creatures Great and Small" on the nightstand, photos of her Colorado childhood on the dresser—the house began to feel less like Luke's former home and more like her own sanctuary.

In the kitchen, she arranged her collection of specialty teas and gourmet coffee beans, hung the copper measuring cups her grandmother had given her for her sixteenth birthday, and placed the ceramic rooster salt and pepper shakers that had always made her smile on the windowsill where they would catch the morning light.

By mid-afternoon, she'd made significant progress in the transformation. Most of her clothes hung in the spacious closet or nestled in the sturdy dresser drawers. Her books filled a previously empty shelf in the living room, adding life and personality to the space. Her laptop and veterinary reference texts were arranged on the desk in what had been Luke's office—her office now, though the thought still felt surreal.

The ranch's business records remained where Luke had left them, in leather-bound volumes neatly arranged on one of the built-in bookcases. Sophie ran her fingers along their spines, noting the meticulous labeling by year and category that spoke to generations of careful stewardship. Soon, she would begin learning their contents, understanding the heartbeat of this place that was now her responsibility. Tonight, she would break bread with the men who would help her write the next chapter of Ironwood Creek's story.

Sophie glanced at her watch. She had time for a shower and to choose her outfit carefully for this important first dinner. The prospect filled her with nervous anticipation mixed with genuine excitement. These men had worked this land for years; their acceptance would be crucial to her success. And Luke... his position in this new arrangement remained complicated in ways that made her pulse quicken whenever she thought about it too carefully.

She showered, letting the hot water wash away the dust and sweat of moving day along with the last of her anxieties. Afterward, she chose her outfit with deliberate care—dark jeans that fit well without being too fitted, a soft chambray shirt that brought out the color of her eyes, and her well-worn leather boots. Casual enough to show she wasn't putting on airs, but respectful enough to honor the occasion. She pulled her blonde hair back into a simple ponytail and applied minimal makeup, wanting to look like herself rather than some city version of what she thought a ranch owner should be.

At six twenty-five, Sophie stepped onto the porch, breathing in the crisp evening air that carried the scent of pine. The sky stretched endlessly above her, painted in broad strokes of orange and pink as the sun began its graceful descent behind the mountains. In Seattle, buildings had hemmed in the horizon, limiting her view to narrow slices of sky between glass and steel towers. Here, the vastness was almost overwhelming in its beauty, a constant reminder of God's infinite creativity.

The bunkhouse stood a distance from the main house, a sturdy structure that looked like it had been built to last for generations. As she approached, Sophie could hear male voices and easy laughter from within, the sounds of friendship and camaraderie that spoke of years of shared work and mutual respect. She hesitated at the bottom of the wooden steps, suddenly feeling like an intruder in their established world.

Before she could knock, the door swung open to reveal Gus, his lanky frame filling the doorway and his boyish face lit with genuine welcome.

"Right on time, Doc!" he exclaimed with characteristic enthusiasm. "Come on in. Ray's pot roast is about ready to fall off the bone, and the whole place smells like heaven."

Sophie climbed the steps, drawing strength from his infectious good humor as she crossed the threshold into what was clearly the heart of the ranch's social life. The interior was surprisingly comfortable and welcoming—a large common area with mismatched but well-maintained furniture, a dining table sturdy enough to seat eight comfortably, and a kitchen area where Ray stood stirring something on the stove with the concentration of a master chef. The walls were decorated with photographs that told the story of the ranch through various eras—horses and landscapes and groups of ranch hands spanning what looked like decades.

The mouth-watering aroma of slow-cooked beef, carrots, and onions filled the space, making Sophie's stomach respond with embarrassing enthusiasm.

"Welcome to our humble castle," Ed said with a courtly gesture, rising from his chair near the fireplace to offer her a seat at the dining table. "It's not fancy, but it's been home to a lot of good men over the years."

"It's wonderful," Sophie said genuinely, taking in the lived-in comfort of the space and the obvious care with which it was maintained.

Dan emerged from what appeared to be a hallway leading to the sleeping quarters, his red hair still damp from a recent shower and his face freshly shaved. "Evening, Sophie. Hope you're hungry—Ray always cooks like he's feeding a threshing crew."

"I'm definitely hungry," she said, settling into the chair Ed had pulled out for her with old-fashioned courtesy.

"So," Gus said, dropping into the chair across from her with his characteristic lack of ceremony, "how does it feel to be the new boss lady of Ironwood Creek?"

"That's going to take some getting used to," Sophie admitted with a laugh. "For all of us, I imagine. I've never been anyone's boss before."

"You'll do fine," Ray called from the kitchen. "Anyone who can save Moonbeam and her foal the way you did has already earned my respect."

Warmth spread through Sophie's chest at the simple validation from this man, whose opinion clearly mattered to everyone in the room. "How are they doing today? I've been thinking about them."

"Strong as young colts," Ed reported with obvious pleasure. "That little filly's got legs like springs—been bouncing around the paddock like she owns the place. Which I guess she does now, come to think of it."

The door opened again, bringing a cool evening breeze and Luke's familiar presence into the room. He'd changed since earlier in the day, now wearing a clean blue shirt with the sleeves rolled up to reveal tanned forearms corded with muscle from years of physical work. He carried a white paper bag in one hand, and Sophie noticed he'd taken time to shower and shave as well.

"Brought dessert," he announced, setting the bag on the kitchen counter. "Lily's famous apple pie... which she didn't even charge me for. She said to tell you to come visit her again soon, Sophie."

"That was incredibly thoughtful of her," Sophie said, touched by the gesture from a woman she'd only just met.

Luke shrugged, but she caught the pleased look that flickered across his features. "That's just Lily's way. Heart as big as the Montana sky."

Ray began bringing dishes to the table—the promised pot roast that looked like it belonged in a magazine, mashed potatoes with flecks of fresh herbs visible in their creamy perfection, green beans that had been cooked just until tender, and a basket of rolls still warm from the oven.

"Did you actually make all this?" Sophie asked, genuinely impressed by the spread before them.

"The rolls are from the bakery in town," Ray admitted. "Everything else is mine. Been cooking for these yahoos for so many years I could do it in my sleep. Figure they'd all starve to death otherwise."

"Hey now," Gus protested with mock indignation. "I make a mean scrambled egg when I put my mind to it."

"If by 'mean' you mean 'barely edible,'" Dan shot back with a grin, "then you're absolutely right."

The easy banter continued as they passed dishes around the table with the comfortable rhythm of long practice. Sophie noticed that despite the joking, there was a natural deference to Ray, who seemed to occupy the position of an unofficial leader among the ranch hands. She also noticed that while Luke participated in the conversation, he seemed slightly removed from it, as if part of him remained elsewhere.

"So, Sophie," Ed said as they began to eat, cutting his pot roast with obvious appreciation, "Luke tells us you're planning to start a therapeutic riding program here eventually."

Sophie nodded, swallowing a bite of the incredibly tender beef before responding. "Eventually, yes. My grandmother ran one in Colorado when I was growing up. I saw firsthand how powerful the connection between horses and humans can be for healing—physical, emotional, spiritual."

"My sister's boy went through something like that over in Hamilton," Dan said, his usual easy humor replaced by genuine emotion.

"Joshua has some learning difficulties, been struggling in school. That horse program worked wonders for him—gave him confidence he'd never had before."

"That's nice to hear," Sophie said, her heart warming at the story. "It never ceases to amaze me what horses can do for people facing all kinds of challenges. They seem to see right into people's hearts."

"The Morrison kids go to that same program in Hamilton," Ray mentioned, his eyes flicking briefly to Luke with obvious concern.

Sophie recalled what Lily had told her about Jake Morrison, Luke's wing man who had died in the aerial firefighting accident. The mention of his children created a momentary heaviness at the table, the easy conversation faltering slightly.

"Katie says it's been good for them," Luke said after a beat, his voice carefully controlled but tinged with something deeper. "Especially Michael. He was having a really tough time after Jake died—angry, acting out, not sleeping well. The horses seem to give him a way to work through some of that."

"They're good kids," Gus added quickly. "Emma's ten now, smart as a whip and pretty as her mama. Michael's twelve, full of energy and questions about everything."

"What's the program like in Hamilton? I'd love to visit sometime, maybe get some ideas for what might work here," Sophie said.

For the next several minutes, Dan described his nephew's experience with therapeutic riding in detail, while the others chimed in with what they knew about the Hamilton program's structure and approach. Sophie listened attentively, mentally cataloging the information for future reference while appreciating how the conversation had returned to more comfortable territory.

As dinner progressed, the atmosphere grew increasingly relaxed and natural. Sophie learned that Ray had worked at Ironwood Creek for over thirty years, having started as a green teenager under Carter Harding's patient tutelage. Ed had been there for fifteen years, coming from a ranch in Wyoming that had been sold for development—a loss that still pained him. Eric had been with the ranch for thirteen, coming from a ranch in Colorado. Dan and Gus were relatively newer additions, at six and four years respectively, but they'd been thoroughly adopted into the ranch's extended family.

"What about you?" Sophie asked Luke during a brief lull in the conversation. "You grew up here, right?"

Luke nodded, setting down his fork with deliberate care. "My parents passed away when I was ten. My Uncle Carter took me in without hesitation and taught me everything I know about ranching, about horses, and about what it means to be a steward of the land."

"You must miss him terribly," Sophie said softly, recognizing the weight of loss in his voice.

Luke met her gaze across the table, something vulnerable flickering briefly in his brown eyes before being carefully shuttered away. "Every day. He was more than an uncle—he was my father, my mentor, and my best friend. Losing him was like losing my anchor."

Sophie felt an unexpected surge of connection to this man whose life had been shaped by a profound loss, just as hers had been. "I understand that feeling. My grandparents raised me after my parents died. Then I lost them during veterinary school and it nearly broke me. Grief has a way of changing the entire landscape of your world."

The admission hung in the air between them, creating a moment of shared understanding that seemed to surprise them both with its intimacy.

Ray cleared his throat gently, his weathered face kind with understanding. "Well, who's ready for some of Lily's apple pie?"

Luke rose to help clear the table, the moment of vulnerability carefully packed away. Sophie moved to assist, but Gus waved her back to her seat with exaggerated authority.

"Guest of honor doesn't do dishes," he insisted with mock seriousness. "Official ranch rule."

"I don't think that's actually a rule," Sophie laughed, grateful for his efforts to restore the lighter mood.

"It is tonight," Ed confirmed with a theatrical wink. "And what the ranch hands say goes."

As the men moved around the kitchen with the comfortable efficiency of long practice—a choreographed dance of clearing, washing, and organizing that spoke of years of shared domestic responsibility—Sophie felt a surge of profound gratitude for their easy acceptance. They could have been standoffish or resentful of the newcomer, who had purchased their workplace and disrupted their established routines. Instead, they had welcomed her with genuine hospitality and warmth.

When the pie was served—golden-crusted and fragrant with cinnamon, nutmeg, and the promise of perfectly tender apples—conversation turned naturally to the practical aspects of ranch life.

"What's the irrigation situation like?" Sophie asked between bites of the spectacular dessert. "I noticed the creek runs through a good portion of the property, but what about the higher pastures and more distant fields?"

"We've got a solid system," Luke explained, slipping easily into teacher mode. "Carter installed a really efficient setup about ten years ago—combination of gravity feed from the upper springs and strategic pumping stations for the areas the natural flow can't reach. I can show you the whole network tomorrow during our tour."

"I'd appreciate that. What about the fence line on the northern boundary? I noticed during my initial drive around that it looked like it might need some attention."

"Already on the schedule for next week," Ray said with obvious pride in their organization. "We rotate maintenance and improvements through the seasons, trying to stay ahead of problems before they become emergencies. Luke's got it all documented in the ranch management system."

Sophie nodded, increasingly impressed with the level of organization and forethought that went into running an operation of this scale. "And the breeding program? How many mares are we expecting to foal next spring?"

The conversation continued in this productive vein, with Sophie asking informed questions and the men providing detailed, thoughtful answers. She was careful not to imply criticism of current practices or suggest immediate changes, focusing instead on understanding the existing operations and the reasoning behind various decisions. Luke, she noticed, watched her closely during these exchanges, his expression thoughtful and assessing.

As the evening drew toward its natural close, Sophie felt a growing confidence about the path ahead. These men clearly knew their jobs exceptionally well, took pride in their work, and cared deeply about the ranch's welfare. With their help and Luke's intensive guidance over the next sixty days, she could make this transition work.

"I should probably head back," she said finally, checking her watch and noting with surprise how late it had become. "It's been a long day, and we're starting bright and early tomorrow."

"We'll walk you back," Luke said, rising from his chair with easy grace.

"That's really not necessary," Sophie protested, though she was touched by the old-fashioned courtesy.

"Maybe not necessary," Ray agreed with a smile, "but it's proper. Besides, gives these boys a chance to walk off some of that pie before they try to sleep."

Outside, the night had settled fully over the ranch like a soft blanket. Stars blazed overhead in numbers Sophie had never imagined possible in her light-polluted city life, a dizzying array of celestial fire against the velvet darkness. The air had cooled significantly, carrying the clean scents of pine, grass, and the distant promise of mountain snow.

"It's absolutely breathtaking out here," she said, her voice soft with wonder as they walked slowly toward the main house.

"Wait until you see it in winter," Gus said with obvious affection for the land. "When the snow blankets everything and the mountains look like they're carved from silver and ice."

"Or spring," Ed added with equal enthusiasm. "When the wildflowers bloom in the high meadow and the whole world looks like God's own garden."

"Each season has its particular beauty," Luke said quietly. "And its own challenges. You'll learn to love them all, given time."

They reached the porch of the main house, where Sophie paused, turning to face the small group of men who had just given her such a precious gift of acceptance and belonging. The porch light illuminated their faces, revealing the genuine kindness and quiet strength that seemed to characterize everyone she'd met in this valley.

"Thank you," she said sincerely, meaning it more than she could express. "For dinner, for the help today, for making me feel so welcome. I know this transition isn't easy for any of us, but I'm grateful beyond words for your patience and support."

"That's just how we do things around here," Ray said simply. "We look after each other—that's what makes this place special."

"See you at seven," Luke reminded her, his voice carrying a note of anticipation for the day ahead. "We'll start with breakfast at the bunkhouse—Ray makes biscuits that'll spoil you for any other kind—then head out for your first real education about this place."

Sophie nodded, her heart lifting at the prospect. "You all certainly know how to treat a lady. I'll see you bright and early at the bunkhouse."

One by one, the men said their goodnights and turned back toward the bunkhouse, their easy camaraderie evident in their relaxed conversation as they walked away. Luke lingered a moment longer, something he seemed to want to say hovering in the space between them.

"You did well tonight," he said finally, his voice carrying a note of approval that warmed her more than it should have. "They respect that you're asking the right questions, listening more than talking, not coming in with preconceived notions about how things should be done."

"I have so much to learn. I'd be foolish to pretend otherwise, and even more foolish not to value the wisdom you all have to offer."

Luke studied her for a moment in the soft porch light, his expression unreadable but somehow intent, as if he were seeing her clearly for the first time. "Sixty days isn't very much time to transfer years of accumulated knowledge," he said finally. "But we'll make the most of every day."

"Yes," Sophie agreed, feeling something shift and settle in her chest—determination mixed with anticipation and something else she wasn't quite ready to name. "We will."

As Luke walked away, Sophie remained on the porch for a few minutes longer, looking up at the vast canopy of stars and breathing in the sweet night air. Tomorrow would begin her real education about this place that was now her responsibility and her home. Tonight, she would rest in the knowledge that God had not only provided her with the desire of her heart, but with good people to help her learn to be worthy of it.

Thank You, she prayed silently; the gratitude flowing as naturally as breath. For all of this. For bringing me home.

Chapter 6

Luke balanced his coffee mug on the bunkhouse porch railing, stretching muscles still stiff from a night on an unfamiliar mattress. He rolled his shoulders, working out the kinks while surveying the property in the pale light of early morning. The sunrise painted the mountains with brushstrokes of rose and gold, a masterpiece that spoke of God's artistry in ways no human hand could capture.

Two days.

That's how long he'd been living in the bunkhouse, and each morning brought the same disorienting moment upon waking—the split second of confusion when he opened his eyes to see wooden ceiling beams instead of the white ceiling of his former bedroom, the sounds of other men breathing and shifting in their bunks instead of the quiet solitude he'd grown accustomed to.

The coffee was good, though—Ray's special blend, strong enough to wake the dead. Luke took another sip, savoring the bitter warmth as it chased away the last vestiges of sleep. Beyond the porch steps,

Ironwood Creek Ranch spread out before him. His ranch, but not his ranch. Not anymore.

The door creaked open behind him, and Ray stepped out, wiping his hands on a dishcloth.

"Breakfast in fifteen," the foreman announced. "Hope the new boss likes bacon."

"Who doesn't like bacon?" Luke replied, not turning from his contemplation of the landscape.

Ray grunted agreement, then paused. "Sleep any better last night?"

Luke shook his head. "Dan snores like a freight train."

"Told you to take the bunk by the window," Ray said, no sympathy in his voice.

"Gus talks in his sleep near that window," Luke countered. "Trading one disturbance for another."

Ray chuckled. "Been a while since you shared sleeping quarters, boss. Might take some getting used to."

"I'm not the boss anymore," Luke reminded him, the words still strange on his tongue. "And it's temporary. My cabin should be ready in a few weeks."

Ray joined him at the railing, his weathered face thoughtful as he gazed at the land they both loved. "Strange how things work out, isn't it? A few days ago, you were settled in at the main house, running this place like you'd been born to it. Now you're bunking with the hands and getting ready to teach an adventurous gal how to be a rancher."

"She grew up on a ranch," Luke said, surprising himself with the quick defense. "I suspect she'll catch on quick."

"Mmm," Ray hummed noncommittally. "She's something, that's for sure. Never seen a woman walk into a crisis like that foaling and take charge so naturally."

Luke nodded, remembering Sophie's swift, confident movements as she'd saved Moonbeam and her foal. There had been no hesitation, no second-guessing—just pure competence and focus. The memory stirred something in his chest that he wasn't ready to examine too closely.

"Going to be an adjustment for all of us," Ray continued. "Taking orders from someone new after all these years."

"You took orders from me for just a couple of years after my uncle passed." Luke pointed out.

Ray snorted. "You grew up under my watch, boy. I was changing your diapers when Carter first brought you here."

"I was ten years old!"

"Figure of speech," Ray waved dismissively. "Point is, you were family. Dr. Lawson—Sophie—she's an unknown quantity."

Luke understood the concern beneath Ray's gruff exterior. These men had worked at Ironwood Creek for years, some for decades. The ranch was more than a job to them; it was home, purpose, and community.

"She'll do right by this place," Luke said with more certainty than he'd expected to feel. "And by all of you."

Ray studied him for a long moment. "You sound sure of that."

Luke turned his gaze back to the mountains. "I am."

"You've known her all of what... three days?" Ray's tone was carefully neutral, but the question carried weight.

"I've seen enough," Luke replied simply.

The truth was more complicated. Something about Sophie Lawson had resonated with him from that first moment in the barn—a determination, a quiet strength beneath her professional exterior. She handled the horses with instinctive understanding, asked intelligent questions about the ranch operations, and treated the men with respect rather than condescension. But there was more to it than that—a vulnerability beneath her confidence that Luke recognized because he carried his own.

He'd caught glimpses of her faith, too—the way she'd murmured a prayer before working on Moonbeam, her reference to God's timing when they'd discussed her arrival. That shared foundation meant more to Luke than he'd initially realized.

"Well," Ray said finally, pushing away from the railing, "I trust your judgment. Always have." He turned toward the door, then paused. "Biscuits are almost done. Better come in soon if you want them hot."

The door closed behind him, leaving Luke alone with his thoughts and the awakening ranch. He drained his coffee, letting his gaze drift to the main house. Lights glowed in the kitchen window—Sophie was awake, preparing for her first official day of ranch education. Yesterday had been consumed with her settling in and today the real work would begin.

Sixty days.

The agreement echoed in his mind. He'd committed to giving her sixty days' worth of knowledge, after which he would transition fully to his Forest Service position. The construction of his cabin was proceeding on schedule. Everything was going according to plan.

So why did he feel this strange reluctance?

The answer was simpler than he wanted to admit. For all his talk of returning to flying, of honoring Jake's memory through continued service, part of him ached at the thought of fully severing his connection to this land. The ranch represented more than property—it was the backdrop to every significant moment of his life since age ten. The place where Carter had taught him to ride, to rope, and to be a man of integrity. The refuge he'd sought after Jake's death when the sky no longer felt safe.

And now he'd sold it to a stranger.

Movement near the main house caught his attention. Sophie emerged onto the porch, pausing to pull on a light jacket against the morning chill. Even from this distance, Luke could make the purposeful set of her shoulders as she headed toward the bunkhouse. The early sunlight caught in her blond hair, turning it to spun gold.

He watched her approach, struck again by the contradiction she presented—city polish mixed with practical ranch sensibility. She wore jeans and boots with the ease of someone who'd grown up in them, but there was a crispness to her appearance that spoke of her professional background. She moved with confidence across the yard, her stride long and steady.

As she drew nearer, Luke raised a hand in greeting. "Morning."

"Good morning," Sophie called back, climbing the steps to join him on the porch. Her cheeks were flushed from the brisk walk, her blue eyes bright with anticipation. "Ready for day one?"

"That depends," Luke replied, the corner of his mouth quirking up. "Are you?"

Sophie laughed, the sound bright in the morning air. "As ready as I'll ever be. I already filled three pages of a notebook with questions."

"Only three?" Luke teased. "I expected at least ten."

"The day is young," Sophie countered with a smile that reached all the way to her eyes. "I'll have those other seven pages by lunchtime."

Luke's chest warmed with unexpected pleasure at their easy banter. "Ray's making breakfast inside. Fair warning—his biscuits are addictive. Once you've had them, store-bought will never taste right again."

"I'll risk it," Sophie said, her blue eyes bright with humor. "My jeans fit for now, but I make no promises for the full sixty days if everything's as good as that pot roast was last night."

The mention of their agreement—sixty days—sobered Luke slightly. A reminder of the temporary nature of their arrangement.

"How was your first night in the house?" he asked, changing the subject.

"It was fine."

"But?" Luke prompted, sensing the unspoken.

Sophie hesitated, then admitted, "It's very quiet. And big. I'm used to my apartment in Seattle, where I could hear my neighbors arguing about whose turn it was to take out the recycling."

Luke nodded, understanding. "It takes some getting used to. The quiet out here can be... profound."

"Exactly," Sophie agreed, seeming relieved he didn't find her admission strange. "There's a depth to the silence that's almost tangible." She looked out over the ranch, her expression softening. "But the stars I saw last night—I've never seen so many in my life. I sat on the porch steps for over an hour before going to bed, just looking up. It made me feel small in the best possible way, like I could actually see the vastness of God's creation."

"Wait until winter, when the air is crystal clear and the Milky Way looks close enough to touch," he said. "It's the kind of sight that reminds you of Psalm 19—'The heavens declare the glory of God.'"

Sophie's eyes lit up at the scripture reference.

"Do you miss it?" Sophie asked suddenly. "Living in the main house?"

The question caught Luke off guard. He considered it for a moment, looking toward the house that had been his home for most of his life.

"Some aspects," he admitted finally. "The privacy. The space." He shrugged, trying to downplay the emotion. "But the bunkhouse has its own charm."

"Such as?" Sophie prompted, genuinely interested.

"Ray's cooking available twenty-four seven," Luke replied with a half-smile. "And Gus's terrible jokes to wake you up in the morning. The bunkhouse has always been... lively."

"Sounds nice, actually," Sophie said, her voice softening. "Like having a built-in family."

The observation struck close to home for Luke. That was exactly what the ranch hands had become over the years—family. Not by blood, but by choice, circumstance, and shared purpose.

"It is," he agreed, meeting her understanding gaze. "Though Dan's snoring might change a person's mind about that."

Sophie laughed again, and Luke found himself wanting to draw out that sound, to see the way it brightened her features. Her laugh lightened something in his chest that had been heavy for too long.

The bunkhouse door swung open, and Ray's voice boomed out. "Breakfast is gonna get cold! You two planning to stand out there jawing all morning, or are you going to come eat?"

"We'd better go in," Luke said. "Ray takes his cooking seriously. Cold biscuits are considered a personal insult."

"Can't have that on my first official day," Sophie said, moving toward the door.

Luke followed, noticing the light scent of her shampoo as she passed—something floral but not overpowering. It was a distinctly feminine note in the otherwise masculine domain of the bunkhouse, and it struck him how much he enjoyed the contrast.

Inside, the main room was filled with the mouthwatering aromas of bacon, coffee, and freshly baked biscuits. The large wooden table that dominated the space had been set for seven, with mismatched plates and mugs arranged around platters of food.

"Morning, Boss—er, Sophie," Gus corrected himself, his cheeks flushing slightly at the slip.

"Good morning," Sophie replied easily, seeming not to notice the correction. "Something smells amazing."

"Ray's biscuits and gravy," Eric informed her. "Worth getting up at dawn for."

Ray gestured to an empty chair. "Sit yourself down, Sophie. Coffee's hot and food's ready."

Sophie took the offered seat, and Luke settled into the chair beside her, aware of the subtle warmth radiating from her even across the small space between them.

The meal proceeded with the comfortable rhythm of a long-established routine. The men discussed the day's tasks between bites, while Ray kept a watchful eye on empty plates, quick to offer seconds. Sophie integrated seamlessly into the conversation, asking informed questions about the pasture rotation and expressing interest in the breeding program documentation Luke had mentioned.

Luke observed her throughout the meal, noting how quickly she was winning over his former crew. Her questions were thoughtful, her attention genuine.

"I figured we'd start with the north section today," Luke said as the meal wound down. "Show you the water rights issues with the Peterson property, then work our way around to the breeding paddocks."

Sophie nodded, reaching for her coffee. "Perfect. I'm particularly interested in the water management system you mentioned yesterday."

"Carter was ahead of his time with irrigation," Ray commented. "He set up a system that conserves more water than most ranches half this size. He always said we were called to be good stewards of what God provided."

"That's the kind of knowledge I need," Sophie said. "Especially with climate patterns changing. Water management is only going to become more critical."

Luke felt a flicker of admiration at her foresight. Many ranchers he knew refused to acknowledge changing weather patterns, clinging to outdated practices even as drought conditions worsened.

"We'll take the ATVs," Luke decided. "Cover more ground that way."

"Sounds good," Sophie agreed, then hesitated. "Though I should warn you, it's been a while since I've driven one."

"Like riding a bike," Gus assured her. "It'll come back to you."

"Or Luke could ride double with you for the first tour," Ray suggested, the slightest twinkle in his eye.

Luke shot Ray a warning look, which the foreman pretended not to notice. The idea of sharing an ATV with Sophie—her seated in front of him, perhaps leaning back against his chest on the steeper sections of trail—stirred an unexpected warmth that Luke quickly tried to suppress.

"I'll be fine," Sophie said confidently. "I'll just need a quick refresher before we head out."

Breakfast concluded with the efficient cleanup that characterized the bunkhouse routine. Everyone handling a task, and within minutes, the table was cleared, and the kitchen restored to order.

"We'll head out in fifteen minutes," Luke told Sophie as the men dispersed to their various tasks. "Meet me by the equipment shed?"

"I'll be there," she promised, then turned to Ray. "Thank you for breakfast. Those really were the best biscuits I've ever had."

Ray's weathered face creased in a pleased smile. "Come by anytime. Always plenty to go around."

As Sophie headed back to the main house, Luke found himself watching her retreating figure. Ray sidled up beside him, drying his hands on a dish towel.

"She fits," the foreman observed quietly.

Luke nodded, knowing exactly what Ray meant. Some people never adjusted to ranch life, never synchronized with its rhythms and demands. Sophie, despite her city credentials, moved through this world as if she belonged in it.

"She does," Luke agreed.

"Bet those sixty days go by fast," Ray continued, his tone casual but his eyes shrewd.

Luke chose not to engage with the implication. "Better get the ATVs ready. Lot of ground to cover today."

Ray's knowing chuckle followed him out the door, and Luke couldn't entirely dismiss the thought that had taken root in his mind. Sixty days had seemed like a reasonable time frame when he'd agreed to Sophie's condition. Now, he knew for sure it wouldn't be enough—not just for her to learn what she needed to know about the ranch, but for him to understand the unexpected stirring in his heart whenever Sophie Lawson was near.

Chapter 7

Luke headed toward the equipment shed, his mind already organizing the route they would take, and the features of the ranch he needed to show Sophie. Sixty days wasn't much time to transfer generations of knowledge, but he was determined to give her everything she needed to succeed.

Because despite Ray's insinuations and his own complicated feelings about selling the ranch, Luke wanted Sophie to thrive here. He wanted Ironwood Creek to flourish under her care. Not just for his uncle's legacy, but for the ranch hands who depended on it, for the horses born and bred on this land, and for Sophie herself, who had risked everything on this fresh start.

At the equipment shed, Luke backed out two ATVs, checking the fuel levels and tires with practiced efficiency. As he worked, he found himself anticipating Sophie's reactions to the hidden gems of the property—the natural spring in the north pasture that never ran dry, the grove of aspens that turned gold in fall, and the high meadow where wildflowers created a carpet of color each spring. He wanted to share these places with her, to see them fresh through her eyes.

The realization pulled him up short. This wasn't supposed to be about connection or sharing; it was about transfer of knowledge, pure and simple. A business arrangement with a clear beginning and end.

Yet as he saw Sophie approaching across the yard, notebook in hand and determination in her stride, sunlight catching in her blonde hair, Luke knew the reality was already more complicated than he'd planned.

"Ready for Ranching 101?" he called as she drew near.

Sophie's smile was bright with anticipation. "Ready as I'll ever be. Lead the way, Professor Harding."

The teasing formality made Luke laugh despite himself. "Well then, Dr. Lawson, your first lesson awaits." He gestured to the ATV. "Let's see if we can get you reacquainted with this contraption before we tackle water rights and pasture management."

As he demonstrated the controls, Luke was acutely aware of Sophie beside him, her attention focused intently on his instructions, her questions precise and practical. The morning breeze carried the subtle scent of her shampoo—something floral and clean that contrasted pleasantly with the earthier smells of the ranch.

"I think I've got it," Sophie said confidently after a brief practice run around the yard. "Where to first?"

Luke swung onto his own ATV and started the engine. "North boundary," he called over the rumble. "Time to show you what you've really bought into, Sophie Lawson."

Her answering laugh carried on the morning breeze as they set off side by side, the ranch unfolding before them in the clear light of a Montana day.

The ATVs churned up small clouds of dust as they followed a well-worn path that curved around the main pasture. Sophie kept pace with Luke, her hands steady on the handlebars as they navigated the gentle rises and dips of the terrain. The morning air had a crispness that spoke of the mountains, carrying the mingled scents of pine resin and wild sage that grew in patches along the trail.

Luke led them through a stand of ponderosa pines, their rust-colored trunks rising like pillars on either side of the path. Sunlight filtered through the canopy, creating patterns on the needle-covered ground. The trail narrowed, forcing them to proceed single file, with Luke checking over his shoulder periodically to ensure Sophie was managing the increasingly rugged terrain.

They emerged from the trees onto a gentle slope that offered a sweeping view of the northern section of the ranch. Luke cut his engine and dismounted, waiting as Sophie pulled alongside him and did the same.

"This is Lookout Point," he said, gesturing toward the panorama before them. "One of the best views on the property."

Sophie moved to stand beside him, her expression one of quiet awe as she took in the vista. From this elevation, they could see the creek winding its silver path through the valley, the main house and outbuildings nestled against the backdrop of mountains, and the patchwork of pastures stretching toward the horizon.

"It's breathtaking," she said softly. "Like looking at a living canvas of God's handiwork."

Luke nodded, allowing himself to see the familiar landscape through her eyes. "My uncle used to come up here a lot. Said you could see the whole world from this spot, or at least the parts that mattered."

Sophie glanced at him, something softening in her expression. "He sounds like an interesting man."

"He was," Luke agreed, the familiar ache of loss tempered by the warmth of memory. "Stubborn as they come, but wise about the things that counted. He called this his 'perspective spot'—said when your problems seem big, you just need to see them against a bigger backdrop."

The wind rustled through the pines behind them, and hawks circled lazily overhead. Luke found himself wanting to linger, to share more about his uncle and his own history with this place. The impulse surprised him with its intensity.

"I can see why he'd come here," Sophie said, turning slowly to take in the full panorama. "It's the kind of place that reminds you of how small we are in the grand scheme, but also how we fit into something much larger than ourselves."

Her words resonated with Luke's own feelings about this spot, articulating something he'd felt but never expressed quite so clearly. Another unexpected connection between them that made his heart beat a little faster.

"Anyhow," he said, turning back to business. "From here, you can see the northern boundary." He pointed to a line of fencing that followed the natural contour of the land. "That ridge marks the edge of your property. Beyond that is National Forest land."

Sophie followed his gesture, shielding her eyes against the sun. "That explains the quality of the view. No development to spoil it."

"And none likely in the future," Luke confirmed. "The national forest designation means this vista stays protected."

Sophie made a note in her small notebook. "What about grazing rights on the forest land? Is there an agreement in place?"

Luke raised an eyebrow, impressed by the question. "There is. Renewed every five years. Current agreement runs for another three. It allows limited grazing in designated areas during the summer months.

The paperwork's in the office, but I'll show you the sections we have access to."

"That's valuable," Sophie observed. "Especially during drought years, I'd imagine."

"It is," Luke agreed. "My uncle was meticulous about maintaining good relations with the Forest Service. Made sure we never overgrazed our allotment."

"Something I'll need to continue," Sophie said, making another note. She glanced up at him, her blue eyes catching the sunlight. "I know those relationships are just as important as any legal document."

Luke nodded, struck by her understanding. She was treating this like the serious business it was, not some romantic fantasy about ranch life. Another quality that drew him to her.

"Ready to continue?" he asked after she'd finished writing.

"Lead on," Sophie replied, tucking the small notebook into her jacket pocket.

They remounted the ATVs and followed the trail as it descended toward the northern pastures. The path grew rocky in places, requiring careful navigation, but Sophie handled the terrain with increasing confidence. Luke found himself admiring the way she approached each challenge—cautious but not timid, learning with each passing minute.

Luke pulled to a stop near a clearing where a natural spring bubbled up from the ground, creating a small pool before flowing down to join the main creek. The water was crystal clear, reflecting the blue of the sky above.

"North Spring," Luke announced as Sophie parked beside him. "Feeds the northern pastures and never runs dry, even in the worst drought years."

Sophie dismounted and approached the spring, kneeling to touch the water. "It's ice cold," she remarked with surprise.

"Comes straight from the mountain aquifer," Luke explained, joining her at the edge of the pool. "Temperature stays constant year-round. Doesn't freeze in winter, either."

"That's remarkable," Sophie said, letting the water run through her fingers. "A consistent water source like this is incredibly valuable."

"More than that," Luke said, "it's sacred to some of the local Indian tribes that still live in the area. This spring was here long before the ranch, long before any of us. My uncle made sure it was respected, never polluted or altered."

Sophie looked up at him, her expression thoughtful. "I'll honor that tradition. There's wisdom in recognizing that we're stewards, not owners, of resources like this."

Luke nodded. "Good. Uncle Carter always said we were borrowing this land from future generations and from God Himself. The spring feeds a series of stock tanks through gravity flow. I'll show you the system as we go."

They spent the next hour exploring the northern section of the ranch, with Luke pointing out key features—the best grazing areas, problematic spots where erosion needed monitoring, and the infrastructure that kept water flowing to where it was needed.

Sophie was an attentive student, asking insightful questions and making frequent notes. She seemed particularly interested in the native grasses, often dismounting to examine different species up close.

"My grandfather was obsessive about pasture management," she explained when Luke commented on her interest. "He believed the health of the land determined the health of the animals. He said you could tell a good rancher by looking at their grass, not just their livestock."

"Your grandfather sounds a lot like my uncle," Luke remarked. "He used to say something similar—that we were grass farmers first, livestock ranchers second."

Sophie smiled at that. "My grandfather also said something similar. I remember being confused by that concept as a child. I kept looking for him to plant grass seeds, like in our vegetable garden."

The mental image of a young Sophie, puzzled by the ranching philosophy, brought a genuine smile to Luke's face. "What was it like, growing up on a ranch in Colorado?"

Sophie's expression turned reflective as they walked back to their ATVs. "It was... wonderful, in the ways that matter most to a child. Freedom to roam, animals to care for, and grandparents who let me be involved in everything."

"Sounds like they gave you a good foundation."

"The best," Sophie agreed. "Everything I know about horses and land came from them. Everything I know about faith and compassion, too." She looked at him with those clear blue eyes. "They taught me that God speaks through His creation if we're paying attention. I see that truth here at Ironwood Creek."

Her words resonated deeply with Luke, echoing Uncle Carter's own teachings. "That's exactly how uncle saw it," he said, surprised at how much it meant to find this shared perspective. "He'd point out how everything on the ranch—the seasons, the weather patterns, the animals—reflected bigger spiritual truths."

"Like what?" Sophie asked, genuine interest lighting her features.

"Like how new growth follows winter's barrenness," Luke explained, warming to the subject. "Or how the herd functions best when each animal knows its place but still looks out for the vulnerable. He saw parables everywhere."

Sophie nodded, understanding in her eyes. "My grandparents were the same way. Made faith tangible and practical, not just something confined to Sunday mornings."

She swung onto her ATV. "I'm curious... was it hard, coming to live with your uncle after your parents passed away?"

The question caught Luke off guard. Few people asked him directly about that transition, usually dancing around the subject of his parents' death. "It was... an adjustment," he said carefully. "I was angry for a long time. Angry at my parents for dying, angry at God for taking them. Which didn't make it easy for Uncle Carter."

"But he stuck with you," Sophie observed.

"He did," Luke confirmed, starting his engine to signal a shift back to their tour. "More than stuck with me—he gave me purpose and direction. Taught me about the ranch, and about flying. Showed me there was still good in the world, even after loss. He was a good father."

Sophie nodded, understanding in her eyes. "That's what my grandparents did for me, too."

Luke cleared his throat, feeling he'd revealed more than he'd intended. "We should head to the east pastures next. There's a section of fence that needs regular maintenance that I want to show you."

They continued their exploration, moving from the northern boundary toward the eastern sections of the ranch. The landscape changed subtly as they traveled, with more deciduous trees mixing with the pines and the terrain becoming less rugged.

"This whole eastern section is prime grazing land," Luke explained as they surveyed a broad meadow. "It's where we rotate the breeding mares during spring and summer."

"The grass looks exceptionally rich here," Sophie observed.

"It is. Something about the soil composition in this section. Uncle Carter had it analyzed years ago. The mineral content is good for lactating mares."

They rode along the eastern fence line, stopping periodically for Luke to point out landmarks or explain maintenance issues. At one point, they dismounted to inspect a section where the fence posts were showing signs of weathering.

"This stretch needs replacement every few years," Luke explained, testing one post with his hand. "Something about the soil moisture here rots the wood faster."

Sophie knelt to examine the ground around the post. "It's damp here," she noted. "Almost boggy. Might be an underground seep."

Luke nodded, impressed again by her observation. "That was Uncle Carter's theory, too. We've tried different materials for the posts in this section. Metal rusts too quickly, and the fancy composite posts are too expensive to use everywhere."

"What about locust wood?" Sophie suggested. "Naturally resistant to rot."

"Worth trying," Luke agreed.

As they worked their way around the property, the sun climbed higher in the sky. By midday, they had covered the entire eastern and southern sections of the ranch, with Luke explaining water rights, grazing rotations, and the breeding program's use of different pastures throughout the seasons.

"Ready for a break?" he asked as they approached a small rise topped by a lone oak tree, its sprawling branches offering shade from the increasingly warm sun.

"Definitely," Sophie agreed, wiping her brow. "I'm starting to understand why everyone around here wears a hat."

Luke grinned, reaching into the storage compartment of his ATV and pulling out a canvas bag. "Brought lunch. Hope you're hungry."

"Starving," Sophie admitted, following him to the shade of the oak tree.

They settled on the grass, and Luke unpacked the simple meal—sandwiches wrapped in waxed paper, apples, and a thermos of iced tea.

The oak branches swayed gently overhead, creating a shifting patchwork of shade and sunlight on the ground around them as they ate.

"This spot has a name too, I'm guessing?" Sophie asked, unwrapping her sandwich.

Luke nodded. "Carter's Oak. He said every ranch needed at least one good shade tree for lunch breaks."

Sophie smiled, taking a bite of her sandwich. "Smart man."

"He was full of little bits of wisdom like that," Luke said, leaning back against the trunk of the tree. "Some profound, some practical, and some just plain quirky."

"Like what?" Sophie prompted, genuine interest in her voice.

Luke thought for a moment, then smiled at a memory. "He used to say, 'Never trust a horse that doesn't spook at something now and then. The ones that never spook are just saving up for something spectacular.'"

Sophie laughed, the sound carrying across the open grassland. "That's actually good advice. The too-perfect ones are always hiding something."

"He had another one about people," Luke continued, warming to the subject. "'Judge a man by how he treats his animals when no one's watching.' That was practically his religion."

"I like that. It says a lot about character."

They ate in companionable silence for a few minutes, the only sounds the rustle of the oak's leaves and the distant call of meadowlarks. Luke found himself studying Sophie's profile as she gazed out over the ranch, struck by how at ease she seemed in this environment, how naturally she fit into the landscape.

"Can I ask you something?" Sophie said finally, setting aside her apple core.

Luke nodded, curious about her suddenly serious tone.

"Why aerial firefighting? Of all the ways to fly, why choose something so dangerous?"

The question was direct, but not accusatory. Genuine curiosity in her blue eyes. Luke considered how to answer, aware that his usual deflections wouldn't satisfy her.

"It's hard to explain to someone who hasn't experienced it," he began slowly. "There's a... clarity that comes with that kind of flying. Everything nonessential falls away. It's just you, the aircraft, and the fire."

Sophie listened intently, her expression thoughtful.

"And there's purpose in it," Luke continued. "Immediate, visible purpose. You drop water or retardant on a fire line, and you can see the difference it makes. You can save homes, livestock, wildlife, even entire communities sometimes."

"But the risk." Sophie's voice was soft, concerned rather than judgmental.

"The risk is part of it," he admitted. "We're trained to minimize risk, and to make calculated decisions. But yes, there's danger, and we accept that."

"Because the purpose outweighs the risk?"

"For me, it does," Luke said simply. "Or it did until..."

He trailed off, uncertain how much to reveal about the doubt that had plagued him since Jake's death, the questions he'd wrestled with about his calling, his faith, and his place in the world.

Sophie seemed to sense his internal struggle. "Until Jake's crash," she finished for him, her voice gentle.

Luke nodded, his gaze fixed on the distant mountains. "Everything got... complicated after that. I started questioning things I'd never questioned before. Why him and not me? What was the purpose of that loss? Where was God in that moment?"

The words came more freely than he'd expected, perhaps because Sophie was still new enough to be a neutral presence, someone who hadn't known Jake or witnessed Luke's struggle in the aftermath.

"Did you find answers?" she asked, her eyes holding his without judgment.

Luke shook his head. "Not the kind that fit neatly into a box. More like... a gradual acceptance that some questions don't have clear answers in this life." He looked at her directly. "Faith isn't about having all the answers I've learned. It's about trusting even when the answers aren't clear."

"More than you might think," Sophie replied, reaching out to touch his arm briefly in a gesture of understanding that sent warmth through his entire body. "When my grandparents died, I asked a lot of similar questions. Sometimes I think the questions themselves are part of the journey."

Luke wanted to ask more about her loss, about how she'd navigated her own grief, but something in her expression suggested the subject was still tender, just as Jake's death remained a raw spot for him. Still, the connection they'd just shared felt significant—a bridge across their different experiences.

"We should head to the southwestern pastures next," he said, gathering the remains of their lunch. "There's a section I want to show you before the afternoon gets away from us."

Sophie nodded, accepting the change of subject with a small smile. "Lead on, Professor."

They packed up and returned to their ATVs; the conversation shifting back to the practicalities of ranch management. As they rode toward the southwestern section of the property, Luke replayed their conversation under the oak tree. He'd revealed more than he'd intended and shared thoughts he rarely voiced aloud. Yet somehow, it had felt natural, even necessary—part of the knowledge transfer this arrangement was supposed to be about.

The southwestern pastures offered a different character than the areas they'd explored earlier. Here, the land rolled more dramatically, with small ravines cutting through the landscape and clusters of trees creating natural windbreaks. Elk Run Creek meandered through the lower sections, widening in places to create natural watering holes.

"This is where we keep the yearlings most of the year," Luke explained as they paused on a rise overlooking a group of young horses grazing in the distance. "The varied terrain helps develop their agility and surefootedness."

Sophie nodded in approval. "Natural obstacle course. Smart approach."

"Uncle Carter's idea," Luke acknowledged. "He believed in letting young horses develop as naturally as possible. Said too much flat ground made for lazy legs and dull minds."

"I can see that philosophy at work in Thunder," Sophie observed. "He moves with an exceptional awareness of his body. That comes from navigating varied terrain during development."

Luke glanced at her with renewed respect. "You've got a good eye."

"My grandfather drilled observation into me from an early age," Sophie said with a small smile. "He used to quiz me on horses' movement patterns, asking me to spot potential issues before they became problems."

"Sounds like a good teacher."

"The best," Sophie agreed, her expression warm with memory. "Though I didn't always appreciate his methods at the time. Especially the five A.M. lessons in winter."

Luke chuckled, imagining a young Sophie bundled against the Colorado cold, grudgingly absorbing lessons that would shape her future. "Early mornings are a universal ranch kid experience, I think."

"Along with frozen fingers and the smell of a horse's breath in winter," Sophie added with a laugh that made Luke's heart lighten unexpectedly.

They continued their exploration and Luke pointed out the seasonal variations in water flow, the areas prone to flooding during spring runoff, and the sections where wildlife corridors intersected with ranch operations.

"We get elk through here regularly," he explained as they paused near a game trail that cut across one pasture. "And occasionally moose. It's important to keep fencing wildlife-friendly."

"How do you balance that with keeping the horses contained?" Sophie asked, making another note in her book.

"Strategic placement," Luke replied. "We use different fence designs in different areas. Wildlife tends to follow established corridors, so we accommodate those while securing the rest of the perimeter."

As the afternoon progressed, they made their way toward the final section of their tour—Ironwood Creek and the special grove of trees that gave the ranch its name. The creek and distinctive stand of trees were visible from a distance, a vivid blue and a darker green against the lighter hues of the surrounding vegetation.

Luke felt a familiar tightening in his chest as they approached. The grove of ironwood trees was special—sacred, almost, in the memories it held. It was where Uncle Carter had taught him to identify birds by their calls, where they had talked about flying and loss and faith, where Luke had retreated after Jake's death when the walls of the house felt too confining.

They crossed the creek and parked the ATVs at the edge of the grove and proceeded on foot. The temperature dropped noticeably as they stepped beneath the canopy of the ironwoods, their dense foliage creating a natural cathedral overhead. The ground was carpeted with fallen leaves and small ferns, and the air carried the earthy scent of rich soil and growing things.

"This is beautiful," Sophie said, her voice naturally lowering in response to the grove's hush. "So different from the rest of the property."

"Uncle Carter started planting these trees the year he bought the ranch," Luke explained, leading her deeper into the Grove. "He added more each year."

"Why ironwoods specifically?" Sophie asked, running her hand along the smooth bark of one trunk.

"They're not native to Montana," Luke said. "Carter brought the first saplings from a trip back east. Said they reminded him of resilience—trees that bend but don't break easily, that grow steadily with incredible strength." He paused, resting his hand on a particularly impressive trunk. "He called them his 'faith trees'—reminders that the strongest things often grow through the toughest conditions."

They reached the center of the Grove, where an expansive clearing opened up, ringed by the oldest and largest of the ironwood trees. A simple wooden bench sat at one edge of the clearing, weathered but solid.

"This was his thinking spot," Luke said, gesturing to the bench. "Where he came to make the big decisions, talk to God, or just to find some peace."

Sophie approached the bench. "May I?" she asked, gesturing to the seat.

Luke nodded, watching as she sat down, her hands resting lightly on the worn wood. Something about seeing her there—in Uncle Carter's special place—stirred conflicting emotions in him. A protective instinct toward the memories the Grove contained, but also a sense of rightness, as if the place itself welcomed her presence.

"I can see why he loved it here," Sophie said after a moment. "There's a feeling of... sanctuary."

"That's exactly the word he used," Luke said, surprised. "He called it his sanctuary when the world got too noisy or complicated."

Sophie smiled up at him. "Your uncle and my grandfather would have gotten along well, I think. They seem to have shared a similar philosophy about the important things."

Luke moved to sit beside her, the bench solid and familiar beneath him.

They sat in silence for a few minutes, listening to the subtle sounds of the Grove—the whisper of leaves overhead, the occasional call of a bird, the distant murmur of the creek. Luke was acutely aware of Sophie beside him, her shoulder occasionally brushing his when she shifted position.

"I think I'd like to use this place for the therapeutic riding program," Sophie said finally. "If that's okay with you. It has the right... energy for healing work."

Luke considered this, trying to imagine the Grove filled with children, horses, and the activity of a therapeutic program. Surprisingly, the image didn't clash with his memories of the place's tranquility. Instead, he could almost see Uncle Carter nodding in approval at such a use for his sanctuary.

"I think that would honor his memory," Luke said honestly. "He believed in healing—for people, animals, land. Used to say that was our real job here."

Sophie's expression brightened. "Yes... the real work I envision happening here will not be about teaching riding skills, but about creating space for healing to happen."

"It's getting late," he said, glancing at the slanting sunlight filtering through the trees. "We should head back."

They rose from the bench and made their way back to the ATVs, the day's exploration drawing to a close. As they emerged from the Grove, Luke paused, looking back at the trees silhouetted against the afternoon sky.

"There's one more thing you should know about the Grove," he said.

Sophie turned to him, waiting.

"Uncle Carter's ashes are scattered there," Luke said simply. "He wanted to remain part of the ranch he loved."

Understanding filled Sophie's eyes, followed by a gentle respect. "Thank you for sharing that with me," she said softly, her hand briefly touching his arm in a gesture of compassion. "I'll make sure it's always treated with the reverence it deserves."

The simple promise, sincerely given, eased the tightness in Luke's chest. He nodded his thanks, unable to find the right words but deeply moved by her understanding.

They mounted their ATVs and headed back toward the ranch's main buildings. As they approached the house, Sophie cut her engine and turned to Luke, the late afternoon sun catching in her hair and turning it to gold.

"Thank you for today," she said, her blue eyes meeting his with warmth. "Not just for sharing the practical information, but for sharing the history and heart of this place. It means more to me than I can express."

"It's part of what you bought," he said simply. "Knowing the stories helps you understand the land."

Sophie nodded, her expression thoughtful. "Fifty-nine more days of stories to go," she said with a smile that quickened his pulse. "I'm looking forward to every one of them."

As she headed toward the house, Luke remained by the ATVs, watching her go.

Fifty-nine more days.

The number seemed both too many and not enough—too many days to maintain the professional distance he'd intended, and not enough to share all that Ironwood Creek Ranch was and could be.

This arrangement was going to change him in ways he couldn't even begin to imagine. The question was whether he would embrace the changes or resist them until the very end.

Chapter 8

S ophie flipped through another leather-bound ledger. Carter Harding had maintained meticulous records, his handwriting precise and unwavering even in the oldest volumes. Three ledgers lay open on the desk before her, spreadsheets detailing breeding records, profit margins, and operational expenses.

She'd been up since five, too excited to sleep, eager to immerse herself in the business side of her new ranch. The quiet of early morning had wrapped around her like a blanket as she'd made coffee and slipped into the office.

A firm knock at the front door interrupted her concentration. Sophie glanced at the clock on the wall—7:15 A.M.

Setting down her pen, she rose from the desk chair and made her way through the house. When she pulled open the front door, Luke stood on the porch, a leather portfolio tucked under his arm and two travel mugs in his hands. The morning sunlight caught in his dark hair, highlighting hints of auburn she hadn't noticed before.

"Morning," he said, extending one of the mugs toward her. "Thought you might enjoy some of Ray's strong coffee."

"Thanks," Sophie accepted the mug gratefully, their fingers brushing briefly in the exchange. "I was just going through some of the ledgers in the office. Your uncle was remarkably organized."

Luke's mouth quirked up in a half-smile that made her heart skip. "He was good about record keeping. Said a man should be able to account for his stewardship at any moment." He hesitated. "I apologize... I realized this morning that we never set a time to start today. I hope I'm not too early."

"Not at all," Sophie stepped back, gesturing him inside. "I've been up for a while. There's so much to learn. I figured I'd get a head start by browsing through ledgers."

Sophie caught the subtle scent of his musky cologne as he stepped inside.

"That was actually my plan for today—give you an education on the meat and bones of the ranch business. The financial side, especially."

"Perfect timing, then. I've just been scratching the surface."

They moved into the office, where Sophie's notes were spread across the desk alongside Carter's ledgers. Luke paused in the doorway, his expression shifting briefly as he took in the familiar space now occupied by someone else. The shadow of loss crossed his features, gone so quickly Sophie might have missed it if she hadn't been watching.

"Sorry about the mess," she said, gathering her papers to make room. "I got a bit carried away."

"No, it's good," he replied, setting his portfolio on the desk. "Shows you're taking this seriously." His tone carried genuine approval that warmed her more than it should have.

"I am," Sophie affirmed, returning to the chair she'd vacated minutes earlier. "This is the biggest investment I've ever made financially. I need to understand every aspect of it."

Luke settled into the chair opposite her, the leather creaking beneath his weight. He opened his portfolio and extracted several neatly organized documents.

"I've prepared a few summaries that should help you grasp the financial structure more quickly than going through years of ledgers," he explained, spreading the papers between them. "Though Carter's records are worth studying when you have time."

Sophie leaned forward, eyes scanning the first document—a comprehensive overview of the ranch's revenue streams and operating costs. The care he'd taken in preparing these materials touched her deeply. It would have been easy for him to provide cursory information. Instead, he'd clearly invested hours organizing this knowledge in an accessible format.

"Let's start with the basics," Luke began, his tone shifting subtly into teaching mode. "Ironwood Creek has three primary revenue sources: the breeding program, hay production, and grazing leases to neighboring ranches during specific seasons."

Sophie nodded, making notes as he spoke.

"The breeding program is the crown jewel," Luke continued, pointing to a detailed spreadsheet. "Thunder's stud fees alone brought in $187,000 last year."

Sophie's eyebrows shot up.

"He's got an impressive reputation. Quarter Horse and Arabian cross with proven offspring in competitive events. We turn down more breeding requests than we accept."

"Selective breeding maintains quality," Sophie observed.

Luke nodded. "Exactly. We currently have twenty-eight brood-mares of varying bloodlines. Twenty-two are our own, and six are boarding arrangements where we provide complete care through gestation and early training of the foals."

"And what percentage of foals do you keep versus sell?" Sophie asked, flipping to a fresh page in her notebook.

"We typically keep about twenty percent of the fillies for our own breeding program. The rest are sold, usually with contracts and waiting lists in place before they're even born."

For the next hour, Luke methodically walked Sophie through the financial intricacies of the breeding operation. He explained their pricing structure, breeding contracts, and the specific traits they selected for in their program. Sophie asked questions at each stage, comparing practices to what she'd learned from her grandfather and during her veterinary training.

What impressed her most was the integrity that was clear in every aspect of the operation. Carter—and later Luke—had built relationships based on trust and transparency, even when it meant turning down profitable opportunities that didn't align with their values.

"Now, the hay operation," Luke said, shifting to another spreadsheet. "We produce more than we need for our own stock. The surplus is sold to other ranches and equestrian facilities, generating about $205,000 annually."

"That's substantial," Sophie remarked. "What's your acreage allocation for hay?"

"About two hundred and eighty acres rotated through different fields each year. Carter invested in efficient irrigation systems that maximize yield while conserving water. The equipment's not cheap to maintain, but the ROI has been solid."

They delved into the specifics of the hay operation—equipment costs, seasonal timing, labor requirements, and quality control measures. Sophie was impressed by the operation's efficiency and the forward-thinking investments Carter had made.

"The third revenue stream is grazing leases," Luke continued, pulling out a map of the property with color-coded sections. "These sections," he indicated several areas along the eastern boundary, "are leased to the Henderson and Collins ranches during specific periods. It generates about $95,000 annually while giving our own pastures time to recover."

"Smart land management," Sophie commented. "Multiple income streams while promoting sustainable grazing."

Luke's expression warmed, a gentle pride evident in his eyes. "Carter was ahead of his time with rotation strategies. He always said we were stewards, not owners, even of private property. He believed that God entrusted us with the land for a season, and we'd be held accountable for how we tended it."

"I like that perspective. My grandfather said something similar—that our role was to leave the land healthier than we found it."

Their eyes met briefly across the desk, another small connection forming between them.

"There are smaller revenue sources too," Luke continued, moving to another document. "Trail riding experiences for tourists in summer, though we keep that limited. Some specialized training programs for young horses. Consulting fees when other ranches want advice on bloodlines or breeding programs."

"It's more diversified than I realized," Sophie admitted.

"Has to be in this business. Ranch operations have tight margins even in good years. Diversification provides stability when challenges come—and they always do." He ran a hand through his hair, the gesture unconsciously drawing Sophie's attention to the strong line of his jaw. "Carter used to quote Ecclesiastes—'If you wait for perfect conditions, you will never get anything done.' He believed in preparation rather than perfection."

"Wise man," Sophie said, impressed again by the faith foundation evident in the ranch's philosophy.

Luke turned to a different page, his expression becoming more serious. "Now for expenses."

For the next portion of the morning, they examined the cost structure of running Ironwood Creek Ranch. Feed costs, veterinary expenses, equipment maintenance, property taxes, insurance, and labor formed the bulk of regular expenditures. Sophie was particularly interested in the veterinary expenses, noting areas where her own expertise would reduce costs.

"This is comprehensive," she said, reviewing the final summary page. "The profit margins are better than I expected."

Luke nodded. "The breeding program makes the difference. Conventional cattle ranching or general horse boarding wouldn't generate these returns. It's the specialized breeding program with Thunder and our premium mares that creates the value."

"Speaking of the horses," Sophie said, turning to a fresh page, "can you walk me through exactly what stock I have? I know about Thunder and the broodmares, but I'd like to understand the full inventory."

Luke leaned back in his chair. "You have sixty-seven horses on the property currently. Twenty-eight broodmares, as I mentioned. Two younger stallions with promising bloodlines, but not yet in full breeding service."

"What are their names?" Sophie asked.

"Storm Runner—we call him Storm—is five, just starting limited breeding. Midnight Warrior—Warrior—is three, still in training. Then we have fifteen yearlings and two-year-olds in development."

Sophie jotted down the information. "And the rest?"

"Eleven foals born this spring, including Serendipity. Nine working horses—these aren't part of the breeding program, but horses Carter and I acquired over the years. Some are rescues, some caught our eye at auctions, others were trades."

"Tell me about them," Sophie prompted, genuinely interested in these horses that seemed to have personal rather than business value.

Luke's expression softened, the professional veneer falling away as he spoke of the animals he clearly loved. "There's Buck, which was my general riding horse—quarter horse gelding, fourteen years old, solid as they come. I've had him since he was three. Whisper is a paint mare Carter rescued from neglect about seven years ago. Gentle as they come now, but it took months to earn her trust."

As Luke continued describing each of the working horses, Sophie noticed how his typical reserve gave way to genuine warmth. These horses clearly held special meaning beyond their practical functions. His entire countenance changed when he spoke of them—his eyes brightened, his gestures became more animated, and a tender note entered his voice.

"Blue is our oldest at twenty-three. Appaloosa gelding, semi-retired but still helps with new rider training. Patient teacher, especially with children. Dakota and Cheyenne are matching mustangs we got from a BLM adoption event five years ago. Sierra's our mountain horse for more challenging terrain. Diesel, Misty, and Eagle round out the group."

"They sound like characters," Sophie said with a smile, charmed by his evident affection.

"Each one's got their own personality," Luke agreed, a genuine smile lighting his features. "Horses are like people—the more you learn about them individually, the more you appreciate God's creativity. You'll get to know them over time. Most of the hands have their preferred mounts, but they're all technically ranch horses."

Sophie sat back, processing the scope of what she'd learned. Sixty-seven horses, each with specific needs, traits, and purposes. Three revenue streams creating a sustainable business model. Five ranch hands plus Luke to manage it all. The numbers aligned with her vision, yet exceeded her expectations in many ways.

"It's a lot to take in," Luke acknowledged, reading her expression. "But you've got a solid foundation here. Carter built something special, and I've tried to maintain it. With your veterinary background, you bring additional expertise that could enhance this ranch's operations further, and also reduce overhead costs significantly."

"This is exactly what I dreamed of owning for most of my life, just... bigger." Sophie said, her confidence mingling with the weight of responsibility. "Sometimes I wonder if I'm up to the task."

The admission of vulnerability slipped out before she could stop it. In Seattle, she'd learned to hide any sign of uncertainty from Marcus, who treated doubt as a weakness to exploit.

But Luke's response held no judgment, only understanding. "That feeling never entirely goes away," he said. "At least it never did for me. Carter once told me that's actually a good thing—when you stop questioning whether you're doing right by the land and animals, that's when you need to worry."

His candor steadied her. "Thank you for that. It helps to know I'm not the only one who's felt this immense weight of responsibility."

Luke nodded, then continued, "Speaking of responsibility, there's one more financial aspect we should discuss—the therapeutic riding program you want to establish."

Sophie straightened in her chair. "Yes, that's a priority for me. Not immediately, but within the first year or two."

"I've put together some projections based on similar programs here in Montana," Luke said, extracting a final document. "Initial investment will be substantial—specialized equipment, additional insurance, possibly hiring certified instructors, depending on your qualifications."

Sophie reviewed the numbers, noting the startup costs and projected timeline. "This is incredibly helpful, Luke. I was planning to research all this myself."

"Consider it a head start. I made some calls to programs in Hamilton and Missoula. They were willing to share basic financial models, though, understand every operation is different."

The thoughtfulness of his preparation touched Sophie deeply. He didn't have to go to such lengths, yet he had—reaching out to other programs, creating detailed projections, organizing everything in a way that made the overwhelming task seem manageable.

"I appreciate this," she said simply, holding his gaze to convey her genuine appreciation. "This gives me a solid foundation to build from."

Luke nodded, seeming slightly uncomfortable with her gratitude. "Just part of the sixty days," he said, though his eyes suggested it meant more.

Sophie's stomach growled audibly, interrupting the moment. She laughed, checking her watch. "I didn't realize it was already past noon. Time flies when you're buried in spreadsheets."

"Let's take a break," Luke said, closing his portfolio. "Give you a little time to process what we've covered before moving on."

"How about lunch?" Sophie suggested. "I can make sandwiches."

Luke hesitated only briefly. "Sounds good. I need to call the Forest Service anyway and check in about tomorrow's schedule."

While Luke stepped outside to make his call, Sophie worked in the kitchen, pulling ingredients from the refrigerator. She assembled simple roast beef sandwiches with sharp cheddar, adding lettuce and sliced tomatoes from the grocery store in town. The domestic activity felt grounding after the morning of intensive financial discussion.

By the time Luke returned, she had set the dining table with sandwiches, chips, and glasses of sweet tea.

"Nothing fancy," she said as he entered, "but it'll keep us going for the rest of the afternoon."

"Looks perfect," Luke replied, taking a seat across from her. "The call went well—my training session tomorrow has been moved to the afternoon, so we can get in some work in the morning if you'd like."

"Absolutely," Sophie said, passing him a plate. "What exactly are you training for tomorrow?"

"Refresher course on the Super Scooper—the amphibious aircraft we use for water drops," he explained after swallowing. "The training is just a state formality, but a refresh is a good thing."

"Amphibious?" Sophie asked, intrigued despite herself. "It lands on water?"

Luke nodded, his expression brightening with genuine enthusiasm. "That's what makes it so effective. We can scoop up 1,600 gallons of water in 12 seconds from a lake or river, then drop it precisely on a fire line. No need to return to an airport between drops."

"That sounds..." Sophie searched for the right word, "exhilarating."

"It is," Luke confirmed, animation transforming his usually re-served demeanor. "Challenging flying—low altitude, often poor vis-ibility with smoke, variable wind conditions. But when you make a drop that saves a fire crew on the ground or protects a family's home..." He trailed off, then added more quietly, "There's nothing like it."

The passion in his voice was unmistakable. Flying clearly ignited something vital within him. His eyes brightened, his gestures became more expansive, and a vibrant energy radiated from him that Sophie found captivating.

"How did you get interested in flying?" Sophie asked, genuinely curious about this side of him.

Luke set down his sandwich, his expression turning reflective. "Uncle Carter. He was a crop duster along with being a rancher. Some of my earliest memories are of watching his plane from the fence line, this tiny yellow speck against the sky, making these perfect, precise passes over fields."

Sophie smiled at the image of a young Luke, wide-eyed and watch-ing his uncle's aerial acrobatics.

"He took me up for the first time when I was eleven," Luke con-tinued, his voice softening with the cherished memory. "Said I was old enough not to 'fidget and crash us.' That first flight... the perspective it gave me, seeing the ranch from above, the mountains, everything looking so different yet somehow more connected. I was hooked."

"When did you learn how to fly?" Sophie asked, fascinated by this glimpse into his past.

"When I was sixteen. Carter bought me lessons for my birthday. Said I was getting my driver's license anyway, might as well aim higher." Luke smiled at the memory, a genuine, unguarded expression that transformed his features. "I soloed when I was eighteen and got my license a few months later. I worked as Carter's co-pilot for a while before branching into firefighting."

"That's a beautiful gift he gave you," Sophie observed. "Not just the skill, but the perspective."

Luke nodded. "Flying gave me freedom when I needed it most. After my parents died, I felt... trapped by grief, by anger, and by questions I couldn't answer. In the sky, I could breathe again." He looked at her, seeming surprised by his own candor. "What about you? What drew you to veterinary medicine?"

"A chestnut mare named Copper," she answered. "She was my grandmother's favorite broodmare. When I was nine, she had a difficult foaling—not unlike Moonbeam's situation. I'll never forget how amazingly calm my grandfather was during that crisis. He saved both mare and foal, and I just remember thinking he was the most powerful person I'd ever seen."

"Because he saved the horses?" Luke asked.

"Partly that," Sophie acknowledged. "But more because of how he did it—this perfect balance of knowledge and intuitive connection with the animals. He explained everything he was doing and never talked down to me, even though I was just a kid. After it was over, he knelt beside me and said, 'Sophie, God gives different gifts to each of us. I think He's given you special eyes for seeing when animals are hurting.' By the end of the day, I knew exactly what I wanted to be."

"And your grandparents supported that dream?"

"Completely. Grandpa started teaching me everything he knew about horse anatomy and behavior the very next day. Grandma drove me to the local clinic every Saturday so I could observe and help with small tasks. In my teenage years, I started volunteering at the clinic regularly on weekends." Sophie smiled at the memory. "They never once suggested it wasn't practical or achievable, even though veterinary school is incredibly competitive."

"They sound like remarkable people."

"They were," Sophie agreed, a familiar pang of loss tempering her smile. "I wish they could see this place. They would have loved it."

"I think they would be proud of you," Luke said. "Taking this leap, building something of your own... it's remarkable."

The simple affirmation touched Sophie deeply. She found herself wanting to know more about him—not just as the former owner of her ranch or her temporary teacher, but as the man whose passion came alive when he spoke of flying.

"What's the most beautiful thing you've ever seen while in the air?" she asked.

"Sunrise over Glacier National Park. I was flying back from a fire in northern Montana. The light hit the mountains just right, turning the glaciers into rivers of gold against the rock. The lakes below were still dark, reflecting the peaks like mirrors." He paused, his voice softening. "It's the kind of beauty that makes you believe in something bigger than yourself."

"That sounds breathtaking."

"It was. Almost made me miss my landing approach because I was so distracted," he admitted with a self-deprecating smile that made Sophie's heart flutter. "What about you? What's the most beautiful thing you've ever seen?"

Sophie thought about it. "The birth of a foal, maybe. That moment when new life takes its first breath, and you can actually see awareness enter its eyes. Or..." she hesitated, then continued, "there was this moment in Colorado, high up between the mountains on my grand-parents' ranch. A summer thunderstorm had just passed, and a double rainbow appeared over this valley filled with wildflowers. The light was doing something impossible, making everything look simultaneously sharper and softer. I remember thinking it was like seeing the world the way it was meant to be seen."

Luke nodded, understanding in his eyes. "Those king of moments stay with you."

"They do," Sophie agreed. "They remind you why all the hard parts about living are worth it."

"My uncle called those 'thin places,'" Luke said. "Said they were moments when the veil between heaven and earth gets transparent, and you catch a glimpse of how things are meant to be."

"I like that description," Sophie replied softly. "It fits exactly what I felt."

The conversation shifted to lighter topics as they finished their lunch. Sophie shared amusing stories from veterinary school, while Luke recounted the ranch mishaps that had become legendary among the ranch hands. Despite their different backgrounds, Sophie was struck by how easily conversation flowed between them.

As they cleared the table together, Sophie was reluctant for the business portion of the day to resume. There was something refreshing about connecting with Luke as a person rather than just as her ranch mentor. When their hands brushed as she passed him a plate to dry, the brief contact sent a ripple of awareness through her that she tried to dismiss.

"What's next on the agenda?" she asked.

"Let's switch things up a little... how about we take a tour of the main barn, go over the feed and supplement programs for the Mares? The breeding program has specific nutritional requirements that differ from conventional horse management," he said as he dried his hands on a kitchen towel.

"That sounds perfect," Sophie replied, tucking a loose strand of hair behind her ear. "One of my specialties was reproductive health, so I'm interested in your protocols for pregnant and nursing mares."

"Uncle Carter developed some custom feed mixes based on our soil composition and mineral needs," Luke explained as they headed toward the door. "He was always tweaking formulas based on blood work results."

"Progressive approach," Sophie noted approvingly. "Most ranchers just follow standard protocols without considering local soil conditions."

"My uncle believed in being attentive to the specific needs of this land and these animals," Luke said. "He always said cookie-cutter approaches rarely work in ranching or in life."

They headed toward the door, their brief personal interlude giving way once more to the business of the ranch. Yet, Sophie felt a subtle shift between them—a growing ease, the foundation of what might become genuine friendship beneath their formal arrangement.

As they stepped onto the porch, the afternoon sun warmed Sophie's face. The ranch spread before them, alive with activity—horses grazing in distant pastures, Ray directing Dan as they repaired a section of fence, the windmill turning lazily against the backdrop of mountains. A red-tailed hawk circled overhead, its wings barely moving as it rode the thermal currents rising from the warmed earth.

"I still can't quite believe this is mine," Sophie admitted.

Luke glanced at her, something unreadable flickering in his eyes. "It suits you," he said. Then, after a pause that held more meaning than Sophie dared analyze, he added, "The ranch has been waiting for someone like you."

Chapter 9

"Here, feel this," Luke said, placing a handful of grain mixture into Sophie's palm. The blend was warm from the afternoon sun streaming through the barn windows, with varying textures against her skin.

Sophie brought it to her nose, inhaling deeply. The rich aroma of molasses mingled with the earthy scent of oats and a hint of something medicinal.

"Smells interesting." She sifted through the mixture with her finger, identifying components. "What's the red supplement?"

"Iron and vitamin E complex," Luke explained, leading her deeper into the feed room. Metal bins lined the walls, each labeled with precise handwriting. "My uncle developed this formula specifically for the pregnant mares. The soil here runs slightly deficient in certain minerals, so we compensate through their feed."

Sophie nodded, impressed by the meticulous approach. "Smart."

Luke opened another bin, revealing a unique mixture. "This one's for the stallions. Higher protein content, different vitamin profile."

A crash from the main aisle interrupted them. Luke's mouth quirked in a half-smile that made Sophie's heart do an unexpected little flip.

"That would probably be Gus," he said, his eyes warm with affection. "The man has two left feet when he's in a hurry."

They emerged from the feed room to find Gus scrambling to pick up scattered curry combs, brushes, and hoof picks that had apparently fallen from a supply shelf.

"Sorry 'bout that," he called, his face flushing when he spotted Sophie. "Just proving I'm as graceful as ever."

"Need a hand?" Sophie asked, already moving to help gather the grooming supplies.

"Wouldn't say no," Gus admitted. "Though it's hardly fitting for the boss to be picking up after me."

Sophie knelt beside him, collecting brushes. "I stopped believing in hierarchy the first time a thousand-pound patient tried to use me as a doormat. We're all equal in the eyes of a horse."

Gus laughed, relaxing visibly. "Can't argue with that logic."

Luke leaned against the wall, watching their easy interaction. "Gus here is our resident expert on looking busy while creating more work."

"Hey now," Gus protested good-naturedly. "I'll have you know I was multitasking. Ray wanted these supplies moved for the yearling check-ups tomorrow."

"And how's that working out for you?" Luke asked dryly.

Gus grinned as he and Sophie placed the last items back in the caddy. "Just taking the scenic route to efficiency."

Sophie straightened, brushing dust from her jeans. "Yearling check-ups tomorrow?"

"Routine stuff," Gus explained. "Feet, teeth, general condition. We rotate them through quarterly assessments."

"I'd love to participate," Sophie said. "If that's alright with everyone."

"Be glad to have you. Between you and me, Doc Patterson's eyesight isn't what it used to be. Man missed a developing abscess last time." Gus said with a grin. "You enjoying your education with Luke, Sophie?"

"Sophie's getting the full barn tour this afternoon. Feed programs, supplement schedules, the works," Luke said.

"Better you than me," Gus said with an exaggerated shudder. "Luke's barn tours are legendary for their..." he searched for the right word, "thoroughness."

"Hey now... thoroughness is the foundation of good horse management," Luke countered with a grin that transformed his face, bringing a youthful playfulness to his usually serious features.

"And the foundation of putting ranch hands to sleep," Gus stage-whispered to Sophie.

She laughed, enjoying their banter. There was a comfort in their teasing that spoke of deep bonds and shared history.

"I'll try to stay awake," she promised. "Though I can't make any guarantees if he starts listing feed protein percentages."

Luke's eyebrows rose. "I'll have you know protein percentages are critically important to—"

"Oh no, I've started it now," Sophie groaned, exchanging a conspiratorial look with Gus.

"Good luck, Doc," Gus said, hoisting the caddy and backing away. "If you need rescuing, just fake a sneeze. I'll create another disaster as a distraction."

As Gus disappeared down the barn aisle, Sophie turned back to Luke. The laughter still lingered in his eyes, softening his features in a way that made her breath catch slightly.

"You're good with the hands," he observed. "They respect that."

"They're good men, I can tell," Sophie replied. "And this is their home as much as it's mine now. I want them to know I value that."

Luke studied her for a moment, something warm flickering in his gaze. "That attitude will serve you well here. The best leaders understand they're really servants... compliments of my uncle's wisdom."

The mention of Carter's wisdom resonated with Sophie's own faith principles. "'The first shall be last, and the last shall be first.' Not just scripture, but practical ranch wisdom, too."

Luke nodded in agreement as he gestured toward the opposite end of the barn. "Let's continue. The supplement schedules are posted in the tack room."

The barn itself was immaculately organized, reflecting the same precision Sophie had observed in Carter's ledgers. The central aisle stretched the building's length, with stalls lining both sides. The concrete floor was swept clean, and each stall's nameplate included the occupant's lineage and birth date.

In the tack room, leather saddles gleamed from regular oiling, arranged by size and purpose on custom racks. Bridles hung from pegs, bits polished to a shine. A glass-fronted cabinet contained specialized equipment—training aids, show tack, and ceremonial gear for special occasions.

"This place is better organized than most vet clinics I've seen in the past," Sophie remarked, running her hand over a hand-tooled western saddle.

"Carter was military before ranching," Luke explained, removing a binder from a shelf. "The organization stuck with him. He often reminded me that a messy barn leads to missed details and missed details lead to sick horses."

"Smart man."

"That he was." A gentle sadness crossed Luke's features, quickly replaced by focused attention as he opened the binder, revealing color-coded charts detailing feeding and supplement schedules for each horse on the property. "These are updated weekly. Each horse has individualized nutrition based on workload, age, and breeding status."

Sophie leaned closer, their shoulders touching as she examined the detailed records. The faint warmth from his body and the subtle scent of his cologne made it momentarily difficult to focus on the charts before her. "This is impressive. Moonbeam's calcium supplement increased after foaling, I see."

"Milk production was depleting her reserves. We adjusted when her last blood work showed slight deficiency."

"And Thunder gets a joint supplement?" Sophie tapped a notation on the stallion's chart.

"Preventative. He's at a prime breeding age, but we always tried thinking long term."

Sophie nodded her approval. "Forward-thinking. Many operations run stallions hard until problems develop, then scramble for solutions."

"Carter's philosophy was to think a few years ahead with every decision." Luke turned a page, revealing more detailed charts. "These track seasonal adjustments. Winter requires higher caloric intake, summer brings heat stress considerations."

As Luke continued explaining the nutrition program, Sophie found herself impressed not just by the system itself, but by the depth of his knowledge. He spoke with quiet authority about metabolic rates, mineral interactions, and fiber requirements, occasionally referencing studies that had informed their approach. His passion for the well-being of the animals shone through his typically reserved demeanor.

"You've put a lot of thought into this," she observed during a brief pause.

Luke looked up from the binder, his eyes meeting hers. "Carter started it. I just refined the system after taking some equine nutrition courses at Montana State."

"You took college courses specifically for the ranch?"

He shrugged, seemingly uncomfortable with her implied praise. "Made sense. Good nutrition prevents most health problems. Cheaper to feed them right than treat them later."

"Practical and compassionate," Sophie said softly. "A rare combination."

"Just good stewardship," he replied. "These animals depend on us. That's a responsibility I've never taken lightly."

The quiet conviction in his voice touched Sophie deeply. Here was a man who understood that caring for God's creation was both a blessing and an obligation.

Before Luke could continue, Ray appeared in the tack room doorway, his face creased with amusement.

"Giving our new boss the full lecture, I see," he said to Luke. "Poor woman. Has she tried to escape yet?"

"I'm actually finding it fascinating," Sophie replied truthfully. "The attention to detail is impressive."

Ray chuckled. "That's because you haven't gotten to the part where he breaks down hay protein content by cutting and field rotation."

"You're just in time," Luke told Ray with feigned seriousness. "I was about to show her the spreadsheets tracking crude protein percentages over the last five years."

Sophie laughed at Ray's mock horror. "Now I know you're teasing. Even I'm not that interested in hay analysis."

"Don't encourage him," Ray warned. "The man's got charts going back to the Reagan administration."

"Carter started those records," Luke pointed out. "I'm just continuing them."

"And adding color-coding," Ray countered. "Don't forget the color-coding."

Sophie glanced between them, enjoying their easy rapport. These moments revealed the family-like bonds that connected everyone at Ironwood Creek. It was the kind of atmosphere she'd hoped to find—where work and relationships blended seamlessly, where faith and daily life weren't compartmentalized but woven together into something beautiful.

"Actually," Ray continued, "I came to ask if you want the new mineral blocks put out today, or should we wait?"

Luke considered this. "Better do it today. The yearlings have been licking the old ones pretty aggressively."

Ray nodded. "That's what I figured. Sophie, any input on mineral block placement? You being a vet and all."

The casual inclusion in the decision-making warmed Sophie unexpectedly. "I'd suggest rotating the placement a distance away from the previous blocks. Encourages more movement across the pasture, prevents overgrazing in one area."

"Good thinking," Ray approved, his eyes crinkling with genuine respect. "We'll shift them about thirty yards from the current spots."

As Ray turned to leave, Luke called after him, "Tell Dan to check for any standing water near the placement sites."

"Will do, boss—" Ray caught himself with a rueful smile. "Sorry, old habit. Will do, Sophie's ranch consultant, who is definitely not the boss anymore."

Luke rolled his eyes. "Just go move the mineral blocks, old man."

Ray departed with a chuckle, leaving them alone in the tack room once more.

"They still see you as the authority," Sophie observed.

Luke closed the nutrition binder, returning it to its shelf. "It'll take time. The transition won't happen overnight."

"I'm not bothered by it," Sophie assured him. "Actually, I'm grateful they respect you so much. Makes my job easier when I eventually take over completely."

Luke nodded, though something flickered briefly across his features—perhaps regret or uncertainty. For a moment, Sophie wondered what it must be like for him—teaching someone else to run the ranch and preparing to step away from a place that was clearly entwined with his identity.

"Is it difficult?" she asked, before she could stop herself. "Watching someone else learn to run what you've managed for so long?"

Luke stilled, his hand still on the shelf. For a moment, Sophie thought he might deflect the question or offer a polite non-answer. Instead, he turned to face her fully.

"Sometimes," he admitted, his voice low. "Carter poured his life into this place. I did too. There are moments when it feels like..." He paused, searching for words.

"Like you're giving away part of yourself," Sophie finished for him.

Their eyes met, a moment of genuine understanding passing between them.

"Yes," Luke acknowledged. "But then I remember that everything we have is just on loan, anyway. We're stewards, not owners."

The simple acknowledgment of faith principles touched Sophie deeply. Here was a man who didn't just talk about beliefs but lived them, even when it cost him something precious.

"Thank you for trusting me with it. I promise to honor what you and Carter built."

Luke held her gaze as he gestured toward the door. "Let's continue to the breeding records. They're kept in a separate office near the foaling stalls."

As they walked, they passed stalls where curious equine faces peered over half-doors. Sophie greeted each horse by name, having memorized them from the records Luke had shown her earlier. The animals responded with pricked ears and soft nickering, sensing her affinity for their kind.

"You remember all their names already," Luke observed, watching as she stopped to scratch a chestnut mare's forehead.

"I've always had a good memory for animal names," Sophie replied. "People, not so much."

Luke's smile reached his eyes. "My uncle was the same way. He could remember every horse he'd ever bred, but would call me by three wrong names before landing on the right one."

The breeding office was larger than the tack room, but equally organized. A desk dominated the space, with file cabinets lining one wall and framed photographs of notable foals decorating another. A veterinary examination table stood in one corner, equipped with modern diagnostic equipment.

"This is impressive," Sophie said, examining an ultrasound machine that was newer than what many dedicated vet clinics possessed. "Carter spared no expense."

"He believed in having the right tools on-site," Luke explained, opening a drawer to extract more binders. "Especially for breeding management. These contain complete reproductive histories for every mare and detailed records for every breeding program."

Sophie accepted the binder he handed her, their fingers brushing briefly. The contact, though fleeting, sent a small shiver up her arm that she tried to ignore. Opening the binder, she found meticulous notes. The level of detail surpassed standard breeding records, including observations about behavioral changes and subtle physical indicators that might escape less observant caretakers.

"This is remarkable," she said, turning pages with growing appreciation. "These observations about early pregnancy behavior could form the basis for a research paper."

"Carter always said God put His signature in the details," Luke replied, leaning against the desk. "He believed that the more carefully you observed His creation, the more you understood the Creator."

Sophie looked up. "That's beautiful. And true."

"He was a better theologian than most preachers I've known," Luke said with a soft smile. "Found sermons in horse behavior and weather patterns."

"I wish I could have met him," she said sincerely.

"He would have liked you," Luke replied, his voice warm with certainty. "Your passion for the animals, your attention to detail, your willingness to learn—these were all qualities he respected."

Sophie looked up from the binder again to find Luke watching her, his expression more open than usual. The moment stretched between them, unexpectedly intimate in the small office. There was something in his eyes—appreciation, connection, and something deeper—that made her breath catch.

A sharp buzzing broke the silence as Luke's phone vibrated in his pocket. He extracted it, glancing at the screen with a slight frown.

"Everything okay?" Sophie asked.

"It's Mike from my construction crew," Luke explained, typing a quick response. "They want me to come look at the helipad foundation they poured yesterday out by my cabin."

"A helipad?"

"Practical necessity for emergency response," Luke explained, pocketing his phone. "If I'm on call with the Forest Service, sometimes they need to pick up personnel directly rather than waiting for me to drive to the airfield."

He hesitated, then added, "I should head over there now. Would you... like to come see my place?"

The invitation seemed to surprise even him, as though the words had escaped before he'd fully considered them. Yet he didn't retract them, watching her with an expectant gaze that held a hint of vulnerability.

Sophie felt a flutter of anticipation. She'd been wondering about Luke's new home—this place he'd chosen to build while selling the ranch he'd grown up on. The invitation seemed significant somehow, a small opening in the professional boundary he maintained.

"I'd love to. If you're sure you don't mind the company."

"Wouldn't have asked if I minded," Luke replied with that almost-smile that was becoming familiar—and increasingly disarming. "We can take Buck and Sierra. They could use the exercise, anyway."

Chapter 10

Twenty minutes later, they were mounted and heading west across the property. Buck, Luke's steady quarter horse gelding, moved with the confident stride of an animal who knew every inch of the land beneath his hooves. Sierra, the mountain horse Luke had chosen for Sophie, was equally sure-footed but more alert, her ears constantly swiveling to catch sounds from the surrounding countryside.

"She's lovely," Sophie commented, appreciating the mare's responsive movement and comfortable gait. "Spanish Mustang cross?"

Luke glanced over, eyebrows raised slightly in appreciation of her knowledge. His eyes, a warm brown in the sunlight, held a spark of admiration that sent a flutter through Sophie's chest.

"Good eye. She's mostly Spanish Mustang with some Quarter Horse about three generations back. Carter got her from a ranch in Wyoming that specializes in preserving old bloodlines."

"She moves beautifully." Sophie patted the mare's sleek neck. "Like she's dancing with the earth rather than just walking on it."

Luke's mouth curved into that half-smile she was beginning to look forward to. "That she does."

They rode at a comfortable pace, following a trail that wound through groves of aspen and pine before opening into rolling grassland. The afternoon sun warmed Sophie's shoulders, and the rhythmic motion of horseback riding—so familiar yet recently absent from her daily life—brought a deep contentment she'd been missing.

"So your cabin," Sophie began as they crested a small rise. "How long have you been planning it?"

Luke adjusted his hat against the sun, the gesture unconsciously drawing her attention to the strong line of his jaw. "A little over a year. I started the design process when I realized the main ranch was just too much for me... more space than I needed. Plus, I wanted a place separate from the ranch. Somewhere I could live nearby but apart, if that makes sense. Then, after I seriously started to think about selling the ranch, I hired a crew and we broke ground three months ago."

"Was it difficult? Deciding to sell, I mean."

Luke was quiet for several strides, his gaze fixed on the horizon. When he finally answered, his voice carried a thoughtfulness that suggested he was still processing the decision himself.

"Yes and no," he said. "After Carter died, staying at the ranch felt... complicated. Every room, every barn, and every pasture held memories. Some good, some painful. The ranch was his dream, not mine, though I loved it." He paused, his expression softening with a vulnerability that made Sophie's heart ache. "But flying has always been my true calling."

"But you still wanted to keep a connection to the land," Sophie observed. "Hence the thirty acres."

Luke nodded. "I couldn't imagine being completely disconnected from this place. It shaped me. But I needed... I don't know. A fresh perspective, I guess. Something that was mine, not Carter's legacy I was trying to live up to."

The honesty of his answer touched Sophie deeply. In that moment, she saw beyond the capable rancher to the man beneath—someone wrestling with grief, identity, and the weight of inherited purpose. She understood the complex emotions of inherited legacies and the struggle to honor them while finding one's own path.

"I get that," she said. "After my grandparents died, I sold their ranch. It was in their will that I had the choice to take over the ranch or sell it, with the profits being added to a trust fund they had created for me. I was young and still in college with several years to go." Her throat tightened with the familiar ache of old loss. "I decided to sell, and it's always felt like a piece of me went with it. Having something of your own while staying connected to the larger property seems like a wise choice on your part."

Luke glanced at her with that penetrating look that made her feel thoroughly seen. "You understand, then." It wasn't a question, but a recognition—another bridge forming between them.

Their horses walked side by side now, close enough that Sophie could have reached out and touched Luke's arm if she'd dared.

"I think God gives us these connections to places for a reason," she ventured. "They shape us, become part of who we are. But sometimes He also calls us to new beginnings without asking us to completely let go of what came before."

Luke studied her for a long moment, something shifting in his expression. "That's... remarkably insightful... and comforting."

The trail descended slightly into a shallow valley before rising toward a stand of ponderosa pines in the distance. As they approached, the outline of a structure became visible among the trees.

"There it is," Luke said, gesturing ahead. "Still under construction, but it's getting closer to being finished."

As they drew closer, Sophie could see the cabin emerging from the landscape. It was larger than she'd expected—not a small hunting cabin, but a proper home designed to blend harmoniously with its surroundings. The foundation and exterior walls were complete, finished in a combination of local stone and rich cedar siding. Large windows faced the valley, promising spectacular views.

A team of seven men worked at various points around the structure. One group was focused on a concrete pad some distance from the main building—presumably the helipad.

"Luke, it's beautiful," Sophie said as they dismounted near a temporary hitching post. "The way it's positioned to capture the valley view while nestled among the trees... it feels like it belongs here, like it's growing from the land itself."

A hint of color touched Luke's cheeks at her praise. "That was the goal," he replied, seeming genuinely pleased by her observation.

He secured Buck to the hitching rail, then helped Sophie with Sierra's reins. Though she hardly needed assistance, she appreciated the warmth of his hand briefly covering hers, the unspoken care in the gesture.

"Luke! Perfect timing!" A stocky man in his fifties approached, wiping concrete dust from his hands onto already-stained jeans.

"Mike, this is Dr. Sophie Lawson, the new owner of Ironwood Creek Ranch," Luke introduced. "Sophie, Mike Donovan. Best builder in the area, though his ego doesn't need to hear that."

Mike grinned, offering a dusty hand to Sophie. "Pleasure to meet you, Doc. Heard you saved a valuable mare and foal your first day here and made quite an impression."

Sophie shook his hand, surprised by the reference. "Word travels fast."

"Always does," Mike replied cheerfully. "Though good news travels faster than bad, contrary to popular belief."

"Mike's grandfather built the original sections of the main house on your ranch," Luke explained, his hand coming to rest lightly on Sophie's lower back as he spoke. The casual contact sent a wave of awareness through her. "Donovan Construction has been working this valley for three generations."

"Four now," Mike corrected, his keen eyes missing nothing as they flickered between Sophie and Luke. "My son just joined the business last year. He's over there wrestling with the stone facing." He nodded toward a young man carefully setting river rock against the cabin's foundation.

"The craftsmanship is impressive," Sophie said sincerely, trying to ignore the lingering warmth where Luke's hand had been. "That stonework pattern is amazing!"

Mike beamed with pride. "That's my boy's touch. Studied architecture before deciding he preferred getting his hands dirty. Brings that design eye to everything we build."

Luke cleared his throat. "You mentioned questions?"

"Right. Come, take a look at the helipad." Mike said as he walked toward the concrete pad.

Sophie took the opportunity to wander closer to the cabin itself. The structure was clearly designed with both functionality and beauty in mind. Peering through the windows from the front porch, she could see the main living space featured vaulted ceilings with exposed beams. Large windows would offer views of mountains to the west and the valley to the east. The covered porch wrapped around the entire cabin, offering sheltered outdoor living space.

The home revealed much about the man having it built—thoughtful, appreciative of beauty, valuing both tradition and practicality. It was a home designed for solitude as a sanctuary rather than an escape.

"It's going to be something when it's finished," a voice commented beside her.

Sophie turned to find Mike's son had approached, his hands still dusty from the stonework.

"Jason Donovan," he introduced himself. "Sorry, I can't offer a handshake. Mortar's still wet on my hands."

"Sophie Lawson," she replied with a smile. "And no apology needed. I've had my hands covered in worse things as a veterinarian."

Jason laughed. "Fair point. So you're the new owner of Ironwood Creek? That's a beautiful property."

"It is," Sophie agreed. "I'm still pinching myself that it's mine."

"This cabin Luke's had us build has some of the best views in the valley, including your new ranch off in the distance," Jason commented, gesturing toward the panoramic view.. "Especially at sunset. Those mountains turn all shades of purple and red. The first time I saw it, I understood why he was so particular about the window placement."

Sophie nodded. Even now, in the afternoon light, the view was breathtaking. "It feels peaceful here. Like a place where a soul could breathe."

"That's what Luke said he wanted." Jason's perceptive gaze studied her for a moment. "A place of his own that offered peace but kept him close to the land he grew up on." He nodded toward where Luke and Mike were still deep in conversation. "He was pretty particular about the design. Wanted it to honor the tradition of the area and the land, but with modern efficiency. Geothermal heating, solar backup... the works."

"Forward-thinking," Sophie observed, impressed again by Luke's thoughtful approach to creating his new home.

"Luke's always struck me as a man with one foot in tradition and one in innovation," Jason agreed. "Makes for good building clients—they respect craftsmanship but aren't afraid of new methods." He paused, then added with casual deliberation, "It's a home meant for putting down roots."

Luke approached, having apparently concluded his helipad discussion with Mike. His eyes sought Sophie's immediately, a subtle smile warming his features when he found her. "Giving her the tour, Jason?"

"Nah... that's your job," Jason replied with a grin. "I've just been explaining why we've got the best crew for the job, naturally."

"Naturally," Luke said as he grinned. "Your subtlety rivals your father's."

Jason laughed. "I'll leave you two to explore. Need to finish that stone section before the light changes." He nodded to Sophie. "Nice meeting you, Dr. Lawson."

As Jason returned to his work, Luke turned to Sophie. "Want to see the inside? It's rough still, but you can get the general idea."

"I'd love to."

They stepped through the doorway into the main living area. The open concept design allowed the kitchen, dining, and living spaces to flow together while maintaining distinct areas. Large windows captured light and views from multiple angles. Sophie could imagine this space filled with warmth and life—morning coffee by eastern windows, evenings spent watching sunset paint the mountains.

"The kitchen is just about finished. They have an island to build yet," Luke explained. "The living room here, and I added built-in bookcases on either side of the fireplace. They're supposed to install those within the next few days."

"This is beautiful," Sophie said, turning slowly to take in the entire space. "Spacious without feeling cavernous. It feels... welcoming."

"I wanted room to move around, but not so much space it felt empty for one person."

"Bedrooms through there?" she asked, indicating a hallway extending from the main area.

Luke nodded. "Master and a guest room. Office space as well."

They moved through the partially finished rooms, with Luke explaining features and design choices. Sophie was struck by the clarity of his vision for the space—practical yet beautiful, with thoughtful details that revealed his character. Built-in bookshelves for his collection of aviation and Western history volumes in the office. A mudroom designed for easy transition from outdoor work to indoor living. Windows positioned to capture sunrise in the kitchen and sunset in the living room.

In the master bedroom, Sophie paused by the large window that framed a perfect view of distant mountains. The space was unfinished, but already possessed a peaceful quality.

"This room... complete bliss with that view," she said softly. "Like a sanctuary."

Luke moved to stand beside her at the window, close enough that she could feel the warmth radiating from him. "That's exactly what I wanted. A place to rest and end each day in peace while enjoying the view."

"You've thought of everything," Sophie remarked as they returned to the main living area.

"I tried to," Luke admitted, running his hand along an unfinished wall. "I figured if I'm building from scratch, might as well get it right."

They stepped back outside onto the covered front porch. The afternoon was beginning to wane, with lengthening shadows stretching across the clearing. In the distance, Ironwood Creek Ranch spread beneath them, a patchwork of pastures and woodlands culminating in the main house and various outbuildings.

"What a view," Sophie said quietly, leaning against an unfinished railing. "You can see almost the entire ranch from here."

Luke moved to stand beside her. "One of the reasons I chose this spot. It feels connected without being... immersed. I always want to remember the place that shaped me into who I am today."

Sophie understood the distinction he was making. This place allowed him to maintain his connection to Ironwood Creek while establishing physical and emotional separation—room to breathe, to be his own person rather than merely Carter's successor.

"It's perfect," she said simply.

Luke turned slightly, studying her profile with an intensity that made her pulse quicken. The late afternoon light gilded his features, softening his expression. "Thanks for coming out here today. I realize touring an unfinished cabin wasn't on our official training agenda."

Sophie smiled, meeting his gaze. "I'm glad you invited me. It helps me understand... the bigger picture."

"The bigger picture is important," he agreed, his voice low and intimate. "Sometimes we get so caught up in details that we miss what God might be trying to show us."

The unspoken connection between them hummed like electricity in the air. Sophie found herself wondering what might happen if she took one step closer to him, if she acknowledged the growing awareness between them.

Mike's voice calling from the helipad broke the moment. "Luke! One more question before you go."

Luke straightened, the professional mask sliding back into place, though his eyes lingered on hers a moment longer. "Be right there," he called back.

"Feel free to explore more if you'd like. I'll try to make this quick."

As Luke strode toward the helipad, Sophie remained on the porch, her heart still beating a little faster than normal. She turned her gaze back to the panoramic view, trying to collect her thoughts. From this vantage point, she could see the full scope of what she'd purchased—the rich tapestry of land and life that was now her responsibility. The magnitude of it struck her anew, both exhilarating and daunting.

She hadn't come to Montana looking for anything but a fresh start, a place to rebuild her life. Yet standing here on this porch, Sophie couldn't help but wonder if God had plans that extended beyond her wildest imagination.

The thought both thrilled and terrified her.

Chapter 11

"Hold him steady now!" Ray called as the yearling colt reared back, hooves striking the air inches from Gus's face. "He's feeling frisky this morning!"

Sophie ducked under the round pen railing, rushing to join the three men struggling with the dappled gray yearling. The young horse snorted, white-rimmed eyes rolling as he fought against the restraints.

"Easy there," Sophie said, keeping her voice low and steady as she approached from the side, making sure the colt saw her coming.

Ray shot her an appreciative glance as she moved in smoothly. "Lucky here is being difficult. Nearly took Dan's hat off earlier."

"Teenage rebellion," Sophie replied, slowly raising her hand to the colt's neck. She stroked firmly rather than tentatively, her touch confident. "Dr. Patterson running late?"

"Always is," Luke said, maintaining his grip on the lead rope while giving the colt enough slack to prevent panic. "Saturday mornings can be hectic for him."

The yearling trembled beneath Sophie's touch, but gradually relaxed his stance. She continued the steady, rhythmic strokes, her other hand coming up to massage the tense muscles along his jawline.

"That's a good boy," she murmured. "Just a check-up today. Nothing scary."

Luke watched her work, admiration warming his gaze. The wordless connection between them seemed to strengthen the calm bubble forming around the nervous horse.

"You've got that magic touch," Ray observed. "Took us twenty minutes to get this halter on him. You walk up and he's butter."

"Horses respect confidence," Sophie replied, continuing her methodical stroking. "And I suspect he's picking up on your frustration."

"I believe you're correct," Luke acknowledged, adjusting his grip on the lead rope. Their eyes met briefly over the yearling's withers.

Sophie held his gaze a beat longer than necessary. "Where do you want to set up for the exams?" she asked, glancing around the round pen.

"Usually do it right here," Luke answered. "Open space, good light, fewer things for them to hurt themselves on if they get spooked."

Sophie nodded. "Perfect. Dr. Patterson bringing his own equipment?"

"Some," Ray said. "We've got most of what he needs in the medical shed. Gus, go fetch those things, will you?"

The young ranch hand, clearly relieved to escape Lucky's vicinity, ducked under the pens rails.

"What's on the agenda for these check-ups?" Sophie asked, gradually releasing the colt's neck but maintaining contact with her fingertips.

"Standard quarterly assessment," Luke explained, shifting his weight to maintain the yearling's attention. "Weight, height, legs, feet, teeth, eyes, and general condition. These yearlings are all potential breeding stock, so we're particularly looking at development patterns."

"Making sure none of them have issues that would disqualify them from the program," Ray added.

Sophie nodded, mentally cataloging what she'd want to examine. "How many are we checking today?"

"Eight," Luke said. "The cream of last year's crop. Four colts, four fillies."

"And Lucky here is apparently the troublemaker of the bunch," Sophie said with a smile, patting the now-calmer colt.

"Got his sire's temperament," Luke agreed, his expression softening. "Thunder was just as opinionated at this age."

"Good conformation, though," Sophie observed, her professional eye assessing the yearling's structure. "Strong hindquarters, good shoulder angle."

"That's why we tolerate his attitude," Ray said dryly. "His bloodline's too valuable to give up on because he's got a temper."

"Sometimes the most challenging spirits have the most to offer," Sophie remarked thoughtfully, looking directly at Luke. "God puts extra fire in the ones destined for greatness."

Luke's eyes met hers. "Couldn't agree more."

The sound of a vehicle approaching drew their attention as an aging blue pickup truck pulled to a stop.

"That'll be Doc Patterson," Luke said. "Always announces himself with that muffler."

Sure enough, a tall, lanky man in his mid-fifties emerged from the truck, medical bag in hand. He wore faded jeans, a plaid shirt with the sleeves rolled up, and a straw cowboy hat that had seen better days. His gait had the slight hitch of someone who'd spent decades bending over large animals.

"Mornin' folks!" he called, his voice carrying across the yard.

"Jim," Luke acknowledged with a nod. "Thanks for coming."

Dr. Patterson approached the round pen, his experienced eyes already assessing the young horse. "Is this the troublemaker you were telling me about, Ray?"

"One and the same," Ray confirmed. "Nearly took my head off earlier."

Dr. Patterson's weathered face creased in a smile as he spotted Sophie. "And you must be Dr. Lawson. Lily at the Bluebird wouldn't stop talking about you yesterday. Said you saved a foaling mare your first day here."

Sophie extended her hand over the railing. "Call me Sophie, please. And yes, fortunate timing with Moonbeam."

"Jim Patterson." His handshake was firm, but not overbearing. "Always good to have another vet in the valley. Been stretching myself thin for years now."

"I've heard," Sophie replied. "Though I should clarify, I'm focused on running the ranch for now, not establishing a practice."

Patterson raised an eyebrow. "Shame. We could use your expertise. But I understand the ranch is a full-time job itself." He hefted his bag. "Shall we get started with this young rebel?"

Gus returned with items he'd retrieved, setting them out on a nearby folding table. Lucky eyed it all suspiciously, nostrils flaring.

"I'll stay with his head if you like," Sophie offered.

The older vet studied her for a moment, then nodded. "Appreciate it. Let's see what we've got here."

For the next forty minutes, Sophie assisted as Doc Patterson conducted a thorough examination of the yearling. His methods were old-school but effective, his hands moving with the confidence of decades of experience. Sophie admired his knowledge and expertise, even as she noted a few areas where more modern approaches might yield better results.

Throughout the examination, she was acutely aware of Luke's presence—his steady hands holding the lead rope, the quiet authority in his voice when giving instructions, and the way his eyes occasionally sought hers.

"Teeth look good," Patterson announced. "No wolf teeth yet, but they'll probably come in soon. Might want to consider removing them before they cause trouble."

"I can handle that," Sophie said without thinking.

Patterson shot her an appraising look. "Dental work's your specialty?"

"One of them," Sophie replied. "I did my residency focusing on equine dentistry and reproductive health."

"Well now. That's a useful combination."

The examination continued, with Doc Patterson checking joints, hooves, and overall condition. Throughout, Sophie provided assistance, anticipating needs and offering observations that complemented the older vet's assessment. Occasionally, she would catch Luke watching her, an unreadable expression in his eyes that made her pulse quicken.

"Well," Patterson announced finally, "despite his attitude, this one's developing nicely. Good bone structure, proper growth rate, no joint issues I can detect. He'll need that right front hoof watched—a slight imbalance that could lead to issues if not corrected early."

"I noticed that too," Sophie agreed. "The lateral wall is growing faster than the medial."

Patterson's eyebrows rose slightly. "Good eye. Most folks wouldn't catch that until it became more pronounced."

"My grandfather was obsessive about hoof balance," Sophie explained. "Drilled it into me from childhood."

"Good man," Patterson replied. "Feet are the foundation. Everything else follows."

As they finished with the first yearling, Ray and Gus led Lucky out and brought in the next—a chestnut filly with a calm demeanor that contrasted sharply with her predecessor.

"This is Penny," Luke introduced, running a hand along the filly's glossy neck. "Sweet temperament, but we've been watching her right hock. Had some swelling last month."

The morning progressed in this fashion, with each yearling brought in for examination. Sophie fell into an easy rhythm with Patterson, their professional strengths complementing each other. Luke remained present throughout, his quiet authority ensuring the process moved efficiently. She found herself increasingly aware of his presence—the competent way he handled each horse, the respectful attention he gave to both veterinarians' observations, and the occasional glances he sent her way.

By mid-morning, they had examined six of the eight yearlings. The sun had risen higher, burning off the morning chill and bringing warmth to the round pen. Sophie wiped her brow as they finished with a particularly muscular bay colt.

"I need a hydration break," Patterson announced, heading for the water dispenser Ray had set up nearby. "These old bones need occasional mercy."

Sophie joined him, accepting the paper cup of water he offered. "Thanks for letting me assist today," she said.

Patterson studied her over the rim of his cup. "You've got exceptional skills, Dr. Lawson. Wouldn't mind picking your brain about some of those dental techniques I saw you using."

"Happy to share," Sophie replied. "And I'd value your insights on a few things as well."

"Quid pro quo, eh?" Patterson's eyes crinkled with amusement. "I like your style." He lowered his voice slightly. "Between us, I've been looking to scale back for years. My wife's been after me to consider semi-retirement, spend more time with the grandkids."

Sophie recognized the opening for what it was. "I'm focused on getting the ranch established first," she said carefully. "But I wouldn't rule out limited veterinary work in the future."

Patterson nodded, satisfaction evident in his expression. "Good enough for now. Let's finish these youngsters, then maybe we can talk more specifically later."

Across the round pen, Luke was deep in conversation with Ray, their heads bent close as they consulted a clipboard. Something in Luke's posture—the straight line of his shoulders, the attentive tilt of his head—drew Sophie's eye. There was an inherent grace to his movements, economy, and purpose in every gesture. The morning light caught the dark waves of his hair and highlighted the strong planes of his face. He was classically handsome and compelling in a way that made it difficult to look away.

As if sensing her attention, Luke glanced up, meeting her gaze across the distance with a smile.

"Interesting dynamic," Patterson commented quietly beside her.

Sophie turned, finding the older vet watching her with shrewd eyes. "What do you mean?"

"Carter Harding built this place from nothing," Patterson said. "Luke's been running it successfully since Carter passed. Now he's sold it to you—a stranger—and stayed on to teach you the ropes." He shrugged. "Not the typical succession plan for a family ranch."

Sophie considered this. "Luke's calling is in the air, not on the ground. At least, that's my understanding."

Patterson nodded slowly. "Maybe so. But a man doesn't walk away from a legacy like this without good reason." He drained his water cup, then added softly, "Or a good feeling about who's taking it over."

His words settled in Sophie's chest, warming her from within. Before she could respond, Luke approached, checking his watch.

"Ready for the last two?" he asked, his voice carrying a hint of regret. "I've got to head out for Forest Service training by noon."

"Let's do it," Patterson agreed, crumpling his cup. "Sophie's been making this go twice as fast, anyway."

The final two yearlings—both fillies with promising conformation—went through their examinations without incident. Sophie continued to assist, though she found her attention occasionally drifting to Luke, noting the increasing frequency with which he checked the time. His duty to the Forest Service was clearly important to him, yet she sensed his reluctance to leave the ranch work unfinished.

"That's our roster," Ray announced as they released the final filly. "Clean bills of health all around, with just a few watch items."

"I'll write up my notes and send them over Monday," Patterson said, packing his equipment. "Though I suspect Dr. Lawson here could provide a more detailed assessment than mine."

"We appreciate your time, Jim," Luke said, extending his hand. "Your experience with these bloodlines is invaluable."

"Been caring for Ironwood Creek horses since before you were born," Patterson replied with a wry smile. "Hard to replace that history."

As the men exchanged handshakes, Sophie helped Gus gather the supplies. "Thanks for your help this morning," the young ranch hand said. "Usually takes us twice as long."

Sophie grinned. "Glad to help. That's what community is about, right? Bearing one another's burdens."

Gus nodded. "Exactly. Ray says a ranch runs on cooperation and prayer, in that order."

"Dr. Patterson," Luke called. "Why don't you join the ranch hands for lunch before you head back to town? Ray's making his famous chili."

"Famous for causing indigestion," Gus muttered, earning a light cuff from Ray.

Patterson checked his watch. "Wish I could, but I've got appointments starting at one. Another time?" He turned to Sophie. "And I'd like to schedule that chat with you, Dr. Lawson. Give me a call when you have time?"

"I will," Sophie agreed.

As Patterson gathered his things and headed for his truck, Sophie stood beside Luke at the round pen railing. The morning's work had been satisfying—the kind of hands-on involvement with the horses that had drawn her to veterinary medicine in the first place.

"You impressed him," Luke said. "Patterson doesn't give praise easily."

"He impressed me, too. He knows his stuff. Old-school methods, but solid skills and advice."

"He's been caring for the valley animals for years. Delivered some of the ranchers themselves back when he was doing mixed practice."

Sophie smiled at the image. "A true country doctor."

Luke checked his watch again, his expression conflicted. "I need to head out soon. Forest Service training starts at one, and I need to change before driving to the airfield."

"Don't worry about us," Sophie assured him. "We managed to survive the morning without disaster and I assume the rest of the day will go the same."

"More than survived," Luke corrected, his eyes meeting hers. "You're fitting in just fine around here. You were meant to be here."

"Thank you. That means a lot coming from you." She tucked a strand of hair behind her ear.

"Will you be alright on your own this afternoon?" Luke asked, concern evident in his voice.

"I'll be fine," Sophie assured him, touched by his consideration. "I thought I might take Sierra out for a ride later, explore a little on my own. Get to know the lay of the land better."

"Good idea," Luke nodded. "Just let Ray know your route before you head out. Standard safety protocol."

"Will do."

"And if you have any questions—"

"Ray will be here," Sophie finished for him, smiling. "Go do your firefighter training. The ranch won't fall apart in your absence."

Luke's mouth quirked in that almost-smile. "Guess I'm being a bit overprotective of the place."

"Understandable," Sophie said softly. "It's been your responsibility for a long time."

"Still is, in a way," Luke replied, his expression turning more serious. "At least for fifty-six more days."

The reminder of their arrangement—the countdown of days remaining in their agreement—sobered Sophie slightly. The numbers seemed to hang between them, a reminder of the temporary nature of their current relationship.

"I should go," Luke said, straightening from the railing.

"Don't let me keep you. Good luck today with your training."

Luke hesitated, then asked, "Do you have plans for tomorrow?"

"I thought I'd check out the church in town," Sophie replied. "Morning service, then maybe explore Riverbend Valley a bit more.."

"Riverbend Valley Community Church is good people," Luke nodded. "Pastor Sam's sermons actually make you think instead of putting you to sleep."

"High praise," Sophie laughed. "Will you be there?"

"Planning on it, if there are no emergency call-outs," Luke confirmed. "Service starts at ten." He hesitated briefly, then added, "I could save you a seat if you want."

"That would be nice," she replied, trying to match his casual tone despite the thrill that shot through her. "Thanks."

Ray approached, wiping his hands on a bandana. "Chili's on the stove, folks. Luke, you heading out soon?"

"Need to change first," Luke confirmed. "Sophie might take a ride this afternoon. Can you make sure she has a radio?"

"I can do that," Ray assured him. "Don't worry, city girl won't get lost on my watch."

Sophie rolled her eyes good-naturedly. "This 'city girl' grew up navigating mountain trails in Colorado. I think I can handle your gentle rolling hills."

"Ouch," Ray clutched his chest in mock pain. "She's got teeth, this one."

Luke chuckled. "You're in good hands," he told her. "Ray knows this land better than anyone except maybe me."

"Thirty some odd years will do that," Ray agreed. "Now go on and get to your flying fix. We've got things covered here."

With a final nod to Sophie, Luke jogged toward the bunkhouse to change. She watched him go, struck by the easy athleticism in his movement.

"He's a good man," Ray said quietly beside her. "Better than he gives himself credit for."

Sophie glanced at the foreman, surprised by the comment.

Ray's weathered face softened slightly. "Carter would approve, you know. Of you taking over. He believed in stewardship over ownership—that the right person for the land isn't always the one you'd expect." He looked toward the horizon, his voice taking on a reflective quality. "He used to say God doesn't always send us blessings in the packaging we anticipate. Sometimes they come in surprising forms."

The unexpected validation touched Sophie deeply. "Thank you for saying that."

"Just speaking the truth," Ray replied matter-of-factly. He studied her face for a moment, then added with gentle directness, "Luke's happier with you here than he's been in a long time. More at peace, somehow. That's worth noting."

Before Sophie could process this revelation, Ray changed the subject. "Now, how about some lunch before you head out exploring? Can't have the boss going hungry on my watch."

"The boss appreciates your concern," Sophie smiled, falling into step beside him as they headed toward the bunkhouse. But her mind lingered on Ray's words, turning them over like precious stones, examining their facets and implications.

Fifty-six more days of her and Luke's arrangement remained. What might those days bring, beyond the practical knowledge of ranch management? The question filled her with both anticipation and uncertainty as she followed Ray toward the promise of lunch and the afternoon's exploration that awaited.

Chapter 12

Sophie slipped into the back of Riverbend Valley Community Church, the heavy wooden door closing behind her with a soft thud. The morning sunshine filtered through stained-glass windows, casting jewel-toned patterns across the pews and wooden floors. The church hummed with pre-service conversations, pews already filled with families and individuals dressed in their Sunday best.

She viewed the century-old architecture with appreciation. Exposed beams arched overhead, their rich mahogany tones deepened by decades of candle smoke and faithful gatherings. The walls, painted a warm cream, displayed framed photographs of church events stretching back generations—picnics, baptisms, weddings, and community gatherings that told the story of Riverbend Valley's spiritual heart.

"You must be Dr. Lawson!"

Sophie turned to find a tall man with salt-and-pepper hair and kind blue eyes extending his hand. His smile was warm and genuine.

"I'm Pastor Sam Harlow," he introduced himself. "Welcome to Riverbend Valley Community Church."

Sophie smiled, accepting his handshake. "Please, call me Sophie."

"Welcome, dear," a petite woman with brown hair highlighted with silver threads and twinkling eyes stepped forward. "I'm Virginia Harlow, Sam's better half. We're so pleased you've joined us this morning."

"Thank you," Sophie replied, instantly warming to the couple. "I've been looking forward to visiting."

Virginia patted her arm. "We don't want to monopolize you. Please, make yourself comfortable. We're having our monthly potluck on the church grounds after service, and I hope you'll join us."

"I'd love to stay for that," Sophie said.

"Wonderful! Now go on in and find a seat," Virginia encouraged.

Sophie smiled as they moved away to greet the other arrivals. She turned toward the sanctuary, scanning the gathered congregation. Most pews were already filled with families and groups, their conversations creating a gentle murmur beneath the piano prelude being played at the front.

She didn't see Luke among the attendees. Perhaps he'd been delayed, or maybe his firefighting duties had kept him away. The thought brought an unexpected twinge of disappointment that surprised her with its intensity. She'd been looking forward to seeing him in this context, sharing in worship together—a dimension of connection beyond the ranch.

"Sophie! Over here!"

Lily Hawthorne waved enthusiastically from a pew about halfway up the left side. The café owner's bright smile was impossible to miss, and Sophie felt a rush of gratitude for the familiar face.

She made her way through the congregation, returning nods and smiles from curious but friendly faces. By the time she reached Lily's pew, she'd received at least a dozen welcomes from people she'd never met.

"I saved you a spot," Lily said, patting the space beside her. "Figured you might not know many folks yet."

"Thank you," Sophie replied with genuine appreciation, sliding into the offered seat. "I wasn't sure where to sit."

"Church seating is serious business in small towns," Lily whispered conspiratorially. "Some families have occupied the same pews for generations. Sit in the wrong spot, and you might accidentally start a feud."

Sophie laughed. "Thanks for the warning."

"I'm kidding. Mostly." Lily's eyes sparkled with mischief. "Though the Henderson's and the Wilson's did have words once when someone sat in the wrong place."

Sophie glanced around, taking in the diverse gathering. Young families with squirming children, elderly couples with weathered hands clasped together, teenagers trying to look disinterested while sneaking glances at their phones—the typical Sunday morning tapestry of community.

"Luke not with you?" Lily asked, her tone carefully casual though her eyes held a knowing gleam.

"No, I came alone. He mentioned he might come, but I haven't seen him." Sophie tried to keep her voice neutral, though the disappointment she felt seemed to color her words despite her efforts.

"He usually sits with Ray and some of the ranch hands," Lily said, nodding toward a row near the back.

As if summoned by their conversation, the back door opened, and Luke stepped inside. He wore dark jeans, polished boots, and a crisp white button-down shirt that emphasized the breadth of his shoulders and the lean strength of his frame. His hair was neatly combed, and he'd clearly shaved that morning, accentuating the strong line of his jaw.

Sophie smiled at the sight of him.

"Speaking of," Lily murmured, following Sophie's gaze. "Luke cleans up nice, doesn't he?"

Sophie felt her cheeks warm slightly. "He does."

Luke scanned the sanctuary, nodding to several people who greeted him. His searching gaze eventually found Sophie, and when their eyes met across the distance, a smile lifted the corners of his mouth—warmer and more genuine than his usual reserved expression. After a brief hesitation, he made his way toward them, weaving between people with quiet purpose.

"Morning," he greeted, stopping at their pew. "Mind if I join you?"

"Not at all," Lily replied, scooting over to make room. "We were just talking about you."

Luke raised an eyebrow as he settled in beside Sophie, close enough that she could catch the clean scent of his aftershave mingled with something uniquely him. "Should I be concerned?"

"Always," Lily quipped, then leaned forward to address Sophie. "Luke and I have known each other since he was a little thing. I have stories that would make your hair curl."

"None of which are appropriate for church," Luke countered good-naturedly, his shoulder brushing against Sophie's as he shifted in the pew.

The casual contact sent a ripple of awareness through her that seemed disproportionate to the simple touch. She noticed the black radio clipped to his belt, its presence a reminder of his other responsibilities.

"On call today?" she asked quietly.

Luke nodded, his expression turning more serious. "It's always busier on weekends. More campers, more campfires, more potential for trouble."

The piano music swelled, and Pastor Sam approached the pulpit. The congregation rose for the opening hymn, a traditional song about God's faithfulness that Sophie knew from childhood. The familiar melody wrapped around her like a warm blanket, connecting her past with her present.

Luke's voice beside her was unexpectedly rich and pleasant—a warm baritone that harmonized naturally with the congregation. Another layer of the man revealed. Another piece of the puzzle that was Luke Harding.

As the service progressed, Sophie found herself increasingly aware of Luke's presence beside her—the subtle shift of his weight during prayers, the warmth radiating from him, the way his fingers followed along in the Bible during scripture readings.

Pastor Sam's message focused on new beginnings, drawing parallels between spring's renewal and the fresh starts God offers in life. The sermon seemed particularly relevant to her current situation, and Sophie wondered if it was divine timing.

"God rarely takes us from one mountaintop directly to another," Pastor Sam was saying, his voice resonating through the sanctuary. "The valleys between—those places of transition and sometimes uncertainty—that's where growth happens. That's where we learn to trust not just in our own abilities, but in God's guidance and provision."

Sophie felt the words resonate deep within her. Her decision to leave Seattle and purchase Ironwood Creek Ranch had been driven by desperation as much as aspiration—a leap of faith into unknown territory.

Beside her, Luke shifted slightly in his seat, his arm pressing gently against hers. She glanced at him and found his expression thoughtful, almost vulnerable, as if the message had pierced something carefully guarded within him.

Pastor Sam's voice grew more impassioned. "When God closes one door, He often opens another. But it's in that hallway between—that sometimes uncomfortable space of waiting and wondering—where our faith is refined. Where we learn that His timing is perfect, even when it doesn't match our preferred schedule."

Sophie glanced at Luke and found him already looking at her, his brown eyes holding a question and something else—a recognition, perhaps, that they were both standing in that hallway between, waiting for God's timing to unfold. The moment stretched between them, laden with unspoken thoughts and unexpected connection.

Luke's radio vibrated softly against his hip, breaking the moment. He checked the display discreetly, his expression shifting to one of focused concentration as he read the message there.

Leaning closer to Sophie, he whispered, "Fire call. Northwest of here. Gotta go."

His breath was warm against her ear, sending a shiver down her spine despite the seriousness of the moment.

She nodded her understanding. "Be safe," she whispered back, the words carrying more emotion than she'd intended.

Luke hesitated, then reached for her hand. His fingers wrapped around hers and squeezed gently, the touch conveying what words couldn't in that moment—gratitude for her concern, reassurance of his competence, and something more tentative that neither was ready to name.

"I will," he promised softly, his eyes holding hers for a heartbeat longer before he slipped out of the pew and made his way quietly toward the exit.

Sophie watched him go, her hand still warm from his touch, her heart beating a little faster than it had moments before.

Lily leaned close. "He'll be fine," she whispered. "Luke's the best at what he does."

The remainder of the service passed in a blur of hymns and announcements. Pastor Sam closed with a prayer for protection over their community, including specific mention of the firefighters and emergency personnel who served the valley. Sophie added her own silent "amen," Luke's face vivid in her mind.

As the congregation filed out into the brilliant Montana sunshine, the church grounds transformed into a bustling social gathering. Long tables covered with checkered cloths had been set up beneath ancient oak trees, filling quickly with covered dishes and desserts that promised a feast.

"Come on," Lily said, linking her arm through Sophie's. "Time for the real Riverbend Valley welcome—feeding you until you can't move."

Sophie laughed, allowing herself to be guided toward the food tables. "This looks impressive."

"Rural church potlucks are serious business," Lily confided. "People have been known to change denominations over particularly good casseroles."

They joined the line forming at the buffet tables, where the aromas of home cooking mingled enticingly—fried chicken, potato salad, baked beans, and countless casseroles whose contents remained delightfully mysterious beneath their cheese-topped crusts.

"Dr. Lawson! So pleased you could join us today."

Sophie turned to find a woman with silver-streaked auburn hair and keen hazel eyes approaching, a warm smile on her face.

"Please, call me Sophie," she replied warmly.

"I'm Abigail Whitaker. I own the Rusty Spur Feed Store. Stop by sometime, and we can chat about what supplies you might need for the ranch."

"I'd like that," Sophie said sincerely.

"Abigail makes the best seven-layer dip this side of the Rockies and serves it daily in her store," Lily informed Sophie. "It's worth the trip just for that."

"Family secret recipe," Abigail confirmed with a wink. "Speaking of food, you'd better fill your plate before the Henderson boys get to the fried chicken. Those teenagers can clear a table faster than a plague of locusts."

As they progressed through the line, Sophie was introduced to what felt like half the town. Phil Needham, the bootmaker, who insisted she stop by for a proper fitting. Kathryn Gillman from the grocery store, who promised to set aside fresh produce when it arrived, if she'd like. Lauren Gillman, Kathryn's daughter who ran the bookstore, enthused about a new horse reference book she'd ordered that Sophie might find useful.

Each introduction came with a warm welcome, but Sophie couldn't help noticing how many people mentioned Luke in their conversations with her.

"Luke says you're a miracle worker with horses," from the elderly gentleman who raised quarter horses.

"Luke told me you're going to implement some of the latest breeding techniques at Ironwood Creek," from the owner of a neighboring ranch.

"Luke mentioned you might be interested in community outreach with your therapeutic riding program," from a local schoolteacher.

By the time Sophie settled at a table with Lily and several others, her head was spinning with names and connections—and the realization that Luke had been speaking about her, about her plans and abilities, in ways that reflected not just professional respect but genuine admiration.

"Don't worry about remembering everyone," Lily assured her, passing a basket of fresh rolls. "I've lived here all my life and still get the Wilson siblings confused. There are twelve of them, and they all look alike."

"It's the eyebrows," Phil Needham confirmed from across the table. "The Wilson eyebrows are like their family crest."

Sophie laughed, finding herself relaxing into the easy camaraderie. "Everyone's been so welcoming. I wasn't sure what to expect, being an outsider."

"Riverbend Valley's always been good about welcoming folks," said an elderly woman Sophie had been introduced to as Edith Stevens, her bright eyes twinkling in a face lined with decades of smiles. "Course, buying Ironwood Creek helps. That ranch is the heart of this valley's economy. Everyone's just relieved Luke sold to someone who plans to keep it operating, instead of some developer wanting to build vacation homes."

Sophie nodded, understanding the sentiment. "I'm committed to maintaining it as a working ranch. I grew up on one in Colorado—it's in my blood."

"That's what Luke said," Phil remarked, buttering a roll. "Said you had the right instincts for the place and that Carter would've approved of you taking over. High praise coming from Luke."

The casual comment thrilled Sophie.

"So Colorado, huh?" Abigail joined their table, settling beside Sophie. "What brought you all the way to our little corner of Montana?"

Sophie hesitated, unsure how much of her Seattle experience to share. "I was working at a veterinary practice in Seattle, but I'd always dreamed of having my own ranch. When I saw the listing for Ironwood Creek, it felt like the right opportunity at the right time."

"Quite a leap of faith," Edith observed, her wise eyes suggesting she sensed there was more to the story. "But sometimes those are the best kind. Most good stories start with someone brave enough to take a chance."

"I agree," Sophie said, touched by the woman's insight. "I'm so grateful for Luke's help during the transition. There's so much to learn about ranch."

"Luke Harding is a good man," Edith said. "Been through more than his share of hardship, but it never hardened his heart. Just made him more careful with it." She fixed Sophie with a meaningful look. "Takes someone special to earn his trust."

Sophie felt warmth rise to her cheeks under Edith's knowing gaze. "I respect him greatly. He's been incredibly generous with his knowledge."

"Knowledge isn't all a person can share," Edith remarked cryptically, before turning her attention to her plate.

The conversation shifted to general community news—upcoming events, local gossip, and the persistent question of whether Sheriff Wilson would ever retire. Sophie found herself laughing at Lily's dramatic retelling of a mishap at the café involving a traveling salesman and a mislabeled bottle of hot sauce.

As the afternoon progressed, the gathering took on the feel of a family reunion rather than a church potluck. Children played tag between the tables, teenagers clustered near the dessert section, and various groups formed and reformed as people moved between conversations.

"So, what do you think of our little community?" Pastor Sam asked, joining Sophie as she helped clear away empty plates.

"It's wonderful," she replied honestly.

He nodded, his eyes kind but perceptive. "Small towns can be insular sometimes, but Riverbend Valley has always had a gift for recognizing when someone belongs, even before they know it themselves."

Sophie considered this. "And you think I belong?"

"I think you're exactly where you're meant to be," he replied simply. "And I'm not the only one who sees it."

Before Sophie could press him on what he meant, Pastor Sam was called away to settle a good-natured dispute over whose pie should win the unofficial "best dessert" title. She watched him go, turning his words over in her mind.

Exactly where you're meant to be. The phrase resonated with a truth she felt but hadn't fully acknowledged. Despite the challenges ahead—the enormous responsibility of the ranch, the learning curve, the uncertainty of her future—there was a rightness to being here that Sophie couldn't deny.

"Penny for your thoughts?" Virginia Harlow approached, carrying a fresh glass of lemonade that she offered to Sophie.

"Thank you," Sophie accepted the drink gratefully. "I was just thinking about how different this town is from Seattle."

Virginia smiled. "Different rhythms of life. Neither better nor worse, just different." She gestured toward the scattered groups of conversing townspeople. "These connections, they're what carry people through the hard times. When winter storms knock out power or summer fires threaten homes, it's knowing your neighbor that makes all the difference."

Sophie thought of Luke out there battling a wildfire while the community enjoyed their Sunday gathering. The image of him facing danger sent a ripple of worry through her that felt surprisingly personal. "Speaking of fires, have you heard anything about the situation Luke was called to?"

Virginia's eyes softened with understanding. "No, but Sam usually gets updates. First responder communications are important out here, where cell service can be spotty." She patted Sophie's arm reassuringly. "Luke knows what he's doing. He's been fighting fires since he was old enough to join up."

"I know," Sophie said, her concern showing despite her efforts to sound casual. "It's just... different, knowing someone who's actually out there."

Virginia studied her for a moment, a gentle knowing in her expression. "It takes some getting used to. The waiting, the wondering." She glanced toward where her husband was engaged in animated conversation with several parishioners. "Sam was a military chaplain for a time. Those deployments taught me a lot about faith during uncertainty."

"How did you manage?" Sophie asked, genuinely curious.

"Prayer helps," Virginia answered simply. "And staying busy. And remembering that worrying adds no time to anyone's life—it just robs today of its joy. We can't control everything that goes on in this world. Remember that." She smiled softly. "I've known Luke for several years. He's careful and skilled."

Virginia glanced up at the sky, where afternoon clouds were beginning to gather.

"Speaking of control, I should help organize the cleanup just in case those clouds decide to open up," she said, squeezing Sophie's arm gently before moving away.

As the afternoon continued, Sophie was drawn into the collective effort of clearing tables and packing up leftover food. The cooperative spirit reminded her of community gatherings at her grandparents' ranch—everyone pitching in without being asked, work becoming fellowship through shared purpose.

By late afternoon, the church grounds had been restored to order, and people began dispersing to their homes. Sophie helped Lily load her remaining casserole dishes into her car.

"This was lovely," Sophie said sincerely. "Thank you for making me feel so welcome."

"That's what we do in a small town," Lily replied with a warm smile. "Besides, it's not entirely selfless. We're all hoping you'll stick around."

"Planning on it," Sophie assured her.

Lily's expression turned thoughtful. "You know, when Luke first announced he was selling, people worried. That ranch has been one of the backbones of our local economy for generations. But seeing you today, watching you meet everyone, and hearing your plans... I think those worries can be put to rest."

The vote of confidence warmed Sophie. "I'm here for the long haul, I promise."

"I believe that," Lily said, closing her trunk. "And for what it's worth, I think Luke believes it, too. Sometimes God sends the right people into our lives at just the right moment—and not always for the reasons we initially think."

Chapter 13

Ray tapped his pencil against the clipboard, the rhythmic sound punctuating the early morning quiet of the barn. "South pasture rotation needs to happen today. Those yearlings have about picked that section clean."

Sophie studied the ranch map spread across the wooden feed barrel they were using as an impromptu table. The morning light slanted through the barn doors, illuminating the colorful sections Ray had marked with different grazing schedules. She tucked a strand of blonde hair behind her ear, focusing intently on the details before her.

"What about moving them to the northeast section instead of the northwest?" Sophie suggested, pointing to an area shaded in green. "If we shift them to the northeast first, it gives the northwest another two weeks to develop deeper root systems before grazing."

Ray's weathered face broke into an approving smile. "That's actually a good call. The northeast section does have better shade, too, which they'll appreciate with this heat we've been having."

"My thoughts exactly," Sophie agreed, feeling a quiet satisfaction at Ray's approval.

Dan scratched his chin thoughtfully. "Might need to check those water troughs first. Last time I rode through, the float valve on the main trough was sticking. I fixed it then, but better safe than sorry... might want to check it again."

The barn door creaked open, drawing everyone's attention. Luke stepped inside, dressed in fresh work clothes, his hair still damp from a recent shower. Despite the clean appearance, subtle shadows beneath his eyes suggested a long night. The morning sunlight caught the dark waves of his hair, highlighting the strong angles of his face.

Sophie's heart quickened unexpectedly at the sight of him. She'd been worried since he left for the fire yesterday, though she'd tried not to dwell on it.

"Morning," he said, voice carrying a hint of gravel that spoke of too little sleep.

"Luke!" Ray straightened. "Glad to see you back. Fire contained?"

"Mostly." Luke rolled his shoulders, working out what looked like lingering stiffness. "Mop-up crews are handling it now. All quiet."

Sophie studied him, noting the careful way he held himself. Fighting fires clearly took a physical toll, though he seemed determined not to show it.

"You look like you could use some coffee," she said, gesturing to the thermos on the barrel.

A ghost of a smile crossed Luke's features, warming his tired eyes. "Already had two cups, but I won't turn down a third." His gaze met hers for a moment longer than necessary.

While Luke poured himself coffee, Ray continued outlining the day's tasks, efficiently dividing responsibilities among the men. Sophie listened attentively, mentally noting which activities she wanted to observe more closely, though she found her attention drifting to Luke more often than she cared to admit.

"I've been thinking, Ray," Sophie said as Ray began wrapping up the meeting. "I'd like to spend time shadowing the ranch hands this week, really getting into the specifics of their daily routines and responsibilities."

Ray nodded, looking slightly surprised but willing. "Sure thing. I think that's a great idea. Dan can take you up to check the northeast pasture before we move the yearlings."

"Actually," Luke interjected, setting down his mug, "Ray, how about you just consider me one of the ranch hands this week, and since I'm supposed to be showing Sophie the ropes... we could team up together." He turned to Sophie, his expression carefully neutral, though his eyes held something warmer.

Sophie felt an unexpected warmth bloom in her chest at his offer. Their eyes met briefly, and something unspoken passed between them—an acknowledgment of the growing connection that neither had openly addressed.

"That works for me," she agreed, hoping her voice sounded more casual than it felt.

Ray studied his clipboard, the corner of his mouth twitching with poorly concealed amusement. "The western portion of the ranch, near where your cabin is, Luke—there are some downed trees near the fence line after that last windstorm. That needs to be taken care of.."

Luke nodded. "I know the spot."

"And," Ray continued, a knowing glint in his eye, "the spring-fed trough up in Hidden Meadow needs checking; it can get clogged with debris this time of year. Since you know that area best, Luke, you two can take the ATVs and cover that." He turned to Dan. "You can focus on the north pastures with Eric."

"Works for me."

As the meeting broke up, the men dispersing to their various tasks, Sophie caught Ray watching her and Luke with an expression that seemed just a little too knowing. He caught her gaze and winked before turning away, leaving Sophie to wonder how transparent her growing feelings for Luke might be.

***

Twenty minutes later, they were navigating the western trails, ATVs rumbling beneath them as they climbed toward the higher elevations of the ranch. The morning air carried the sweet scent of wild grasses and pine, growing stronger as they ascended into more forested terrain.

Luke led the way, occasionally glancing back to ensure Sophie was managing the increasingly rugged trail. She followed confidently, appreciating his concern but determined to show her competence.

They crossed a shallow stream, water splashing against their tires, before the trail curved upward through a stand of ponderosa pines. Sunlight filtered through the branches, creating shifting patterns on the needle-covered ground.

Luke pulled to a stop in a small clearing and cut his engine. Sophie followed suit, the sudden silence emphasizing the surrounding wildness.

"Fence line is just through those trees," Luke said, dismounting.

Sophie joined him, adjusting her hat against the dappled sunlight.

"This is actually part of the acreage I kept, though the fence separates it from my actual building site," Luke said as he retrieved tools from the storage compartment of his ATV—a chainsaw, heavy gloves, and various fencing supplies.

"So we're technically on your property now?" Sophie asked, helping gather equipment.

Luke nodded. "For another fifty yards or so, then we cross back onto Ironwood Creek land." His voice softened slightly. "Feels different somehow, knowing where the boundaries are now."

As they made their way through the trees, the damage became visible as they approached the fence line. Two medium-sized pines had fallen across the wire fencing, bending the posts and stretching the wire to its breaking point. One section had snapped completely, leaving a gap large enough for animals to pass through.

"Definitely some elk took advantage of this," Luke observed, pointing to distinctive tracks in the soft earth. "See those prints? Probably came through in the past couple of days."

Sophie knelt beside him to examine the tracks. "At least three different animals, from the pattern. Do they cause problems with the horses?"

"Not usually. They tend to keep to themselves. The issue is more about pasture management—we need to control where and when grazing happens." Luke set down the equipment and surveyed the damage more closely, his arm brushing against hers as he pointed to the broken wire. "This will take some work. We'll need to clear the trees first, then repair the fence."

For the next hour, they worked together to address the damage. Luke operated the chainsaw with ease, cutting the fallen pines into manageable sections. Sophie helped drag the cleared pieces away from the fence line, then assisted as they began repairs.

Despite the physical demands, Sophie enjoyed the work. There was something deeply satisfying about the immediate, tangible progress they made. And working alongside Luke created an unexpected rhythm—they quickly learned to anticipate each other's movements, passing tools and holding sections of wire without needing to exchange many words.

"Hold this taut," Luke instructed as they stretched a new wire between posts.

Sophie gripped the wire firmly, maintaining tension, while Luke secured it with heavy staples.

"You're doing a good thing wanting to work alongside the ranch hands," Luke commented, glancing at her as he hammered the last staple. "Most new ranch owners would be directing from a distance, not getting their hands dirty."

Sophie laughed, the sound carrying across the quiet forest. "My grandfather would roll over in his grave if I stood back and just directed everyone. He made sure I could handle every aspect of ranch work by the time I was eighteen."

"You're not what I expected when I decided to sell the ranch."

"Is that good or bad?"

"Definitely good. Better than I could have hoped for."

The simple statement, delivered with quiet sincerity, warmed Sophie from within. She ducked her head, focusing on coiling excess wire to hide the flush she could feel spreading across her cheeks. With the fence repaired, they packed up the tools and headed back to the ATVs.

"Ready to check that spring-fed trough?" Luke asked, securing the equipment. "It's about fifteen minutes further up, in Hidden Meadow."

"Hidden Meadow?" Sophie repeated, intrigued by the name. "Sounds mysterious."

"It is, in its way. You'll see why."

They remounted their ATVs and continued up the trail, climbing higher into the western section of the ranch. The forest gradually opened up as they ascended, pines giving way to scattered stands with increasing views of the valley below.

The trail narrowed as it curved around a rocky outcropping, then suddenly opened into a sight that made Sophie gasp.

Hidden Meadow deserved its name—a perfect, secluded meadow nestled between protective ridges, invisible from below. Wildflowers carpeted the open space in swaths of purple lupine, yellow balsam root, and delicate white yarrow. Sunlight bathed everything in clear, golden warmth, and the surrounding mountains created a natural amphitheater of stone and forest.

Sophie cut her engine, momentarily speechless.

"Worth the trip?" Luke asked, dismounting beside her. His expression held a mixture of pride and pleasure at her reaction.

"It's incredible," she breathed, turning slowly to take in the panoramic beauty. "How is this even part of the ranch?"

"Carter was strategic when he bought adjoining parcels over the years," Luke explained, moving to stand beside her. "He always said the meadows were Ironwood Creek's crown jewels—a place where heaven touches earth."

Sophie could see why. The meadow had an almost sacred quality—peaceful and removed from the world below, yet vibrantly alive with color and movement. Standing there with Luke, surrounded by such beauty, created an intimacy that felt both natural and profound.

"The trough is on the far side," Luke said, his voice gentler than usual. He gestured toward a stand of aspens at the meadow's edge. "Fed by a natural spring that comes right out of the mountain."

They walked across the meadow, boots swishing through knee-high grasses and wildflowers. Sophie found herself walking more slowly, reluctant to rush through such beauty. Luke matched her pace, seemingly content to savor the moment with her.

"I can't believe I own this," she said quietly, almost to herself.

Luke glanced at her. "It has a way of owning you, if you let it."

They reached the trough—a substantial concrete basin fed by a pipe emerging from the rocky hillside. Clear mountain water bubbled continuously from the pipe, but the trough itself was partially clogged with fallen leaves, pine needles, and other debris.

"This happens seasonally," Luke explained, rolling up his sleeves. "Wind blows debris in, then it gets waterlogged and sinks. If we don't clear it regularly, it can clog the drainage overflow."

Sophie found herself momentarily distracted by the sight of his forearms—tanned and strong from years of outdoor work. She quickly refocused on the task at hand, kneeling beside the trough.

They set to work cleaning the trough, scooping out handfuls of soggy material and clearing the drainage system.

"So," Sophie said as they worked, deciding to take advantage of this moment of privacy, "tell me something about yourself that I don't already know."

Luke considered the question while clearing a particularly stubborn mass of pine needles. "Well... let's see. My parents were missionaries."

"Missionaries?" Sophie looked up, surprised by this revelation.

Luke nodded. "They left on their last mission when I was ten. They were headed to a small village in South America. Their plane went down in a storm."

"I'm so sorry, Luke," Sophie said softly, instinctively reaching out to touch his arm.

Luke's hand briefly covered hers, accepting the comfort she offered. "It was a long time ago. Carter became my family after that." He paused, eyes distant with memory. "The sad thing is, I barely remember them now. I'm thankful I have a few pictures."

Sophie understood loss—the way it shaped you and became part of your story without defining it completely. Her heart ached for the ten-year-old boy who'd lost everything, only to build himself into the steadfast man beside her.

They worked in silence for a few moments. The only sounds was the splash of water and distant birdsong.

"It was good to see you at church yesterday," Sophie said gently, changing the subject. "Pastor Sam's message… it really resonated with me."

Luke looked up, his hands stilling momentarily, his eyes meeting hers with an unexpected openness. "Yeah, he has a way of hitting home. 'Valleys between mountaintops'…" He shook his head slightly. "Felt like he was talking straight to me."

"Me too," Sophie admitted. "I've been in quite a valley myself lately."

Luke straightened, wiping his hands on his jeans. "I think we both have. Ready to take a break?"

They moved to a sun-warmed rock near the spring's source, setting out the water bottles and protein bars Luke had packed. The meadow stretched before them, alive with butterflies dancing among the wildflowers and the gentle sway of grasses in the mountain breeze.

"So Seattle… moving here wasn't just a career move for you, was it?" Luke asked after they'd settled, his voice gentle but direct.

The question caught Sophie by surprise. She studied her water bottle, weighing how much to share. Something about this place—the beauty, the isolation, the man beside her—made honesty feel both safe and necessary.

"No," she admitted, lifting her gaze to meet his. "It was an escape." Sophie took a deep breath, the mountain air filling her lungs with courage. "I was dating my boss at the veterinary practice I worked at—Dr. Marcus Brennan. He was…" She paused, searching for the right words. "Controlling. Manipulative. And in the end, cold and uncaring. He took credit for my research and innovative techniques, blocked my promotion, and managed to make me believe I was worth less than I am."

Luke's expression darkened. "Sounds like a real piece of work."

"That's one way to put it," Sophie said, a humorless laugh escaping her. "It took me a while to see through the manipulation. By then, I'd nearly lost myself. When I finally broke things off, he threatened to ruin my professional reputation."

"So you came to Montana," Luke concluded, his voice gentler now.

"So I came to Montana," she confirmed. "Bought a ranch sight unseen with my trust fund. It was the most impulsive thing I've ever done."

"Brave," Luke countered immediately, reaching out to touch her hand. "Not impulsive. Brave."

The quiet affirmation, delivered with such conviction, touched Sophie deeply. His hand over hers felt right—warm and steady.

"Thank you for saying that," she said. "I've had a lot of time to think about my relationship with Marcus. I've realized I fell out of love with him a long time ago, if I was ever truly in love at all. I was just going through the motions, working beside him day after day. Slowly, over time, it became just a working relationship with none of the heart that should exist in a true partnership."

"He didn't deserve you," Luke said simply, his thumb tracing a small circle on the back of her hand. "Some men don't know how to value what's right in front of them."

They sat in silence for a moment, the peaceful meadow creating a natural sanctuary for difficult conversations. Luke's hand remained over hers, neither advancing nor retreating—just present, like the man himself.

"What about you?" Sophie asked. "Your valley—was it after Jake's accident?"

Luke's shoulders tensed slightly, but he nodded, his hand remaining on hers. "Jake was… more than my wingman. He was like a brother. We flew together for six years. Knew each other's moves before we made them." He stared out across the meadow, his gaze distant. "The day he went down, we were working a fire in the Cabinet Mountains. Bad conditions—shifting winds, poor visibility. He was making a drop on a fire line that was threatening a crew on the ground."

Sophie listened quietly, sensing that Luke rarely shared these details. She turned her hand beneath his so their palms met, fingers intertwining in silent support.

"His plane caught a downdraft. He tried to pull up, but…" Luke's voice faltered slightly, his grip on her hand tightening unconsciously. "I watched it happen. Couldn't do anything but call it in."

"I'm so sorry, Luke," Sophie said, the inadequacy of words striking her even as she spoke them.

"After that, I had a hard time getting back in the cockpit," Luke continued, his thumb absently stroking the side of her hand. "Took a leave of absence. Came back to the ranch. Told myself I was done with flying forever."

"What changed?"

Luke's expression softened slightly. "Pastor Sam, partly. He has a way of asking questions that make you confront what you're really afraid of." He picked up a small stone with his free hand, turning it over in his fingers. "I realized I wasn't honoring Jake by grounding myself. He loved flying as much as I did. He would have hated seeing me walk away from it."

"So now you're back to flying," Sophie said, admiration coloring her voice.

"Yes. I know now that flying is what I'm meant to do. But it took a lot of conversations with Sam and many prayers that felt like they went nowhere." Luke smiled. "Turns out God answers on His timeline, not ours."

"My grandmother used to say... God's never late, but He sure does like to arrive at the last minute."

Luke laughed, the sound warm and genuine, echoing across the meadow. "I like that. It's true."

They finished their water, still holding hands, the conversation shifting to lighter topics—amusing stories about ranch mishaps, Sophie's veterinary school adventures, Luke's early flying lessons with his uncle. There was an ease between them now, a comfortable intimacy born of shared vulnerability.

"We should probably get back to work," Luke said eventually, reluctantly releasing her hand as he gathered their empty water bottles.

They returned to the trough, finishing the cleaning process and checking that water flowed freely through the system.

"There," Luke said with satisfaction as clear water bubbled into the newly cleaned basin. "Good for now."

As Sophie turned, her boot slipped on the wet rocks near the trough. Luke reacted instantly, reaching out to steady her. His hands caught her waist, strong and sure, preventing what would have been an ungraceful fall.

"Careful," he murmured, his voice unexpectedly close.

Sophie looked up to thank him and found his face inches from hers. Their eyes locked, and the air between them seemed to change—charged suddenly with something that had been building since that first day in the barn with Moonbeam.

For a heartbeat, neither moved. Sophie was acutely aware of his hands at her waist, the warmth of them seeping through her shirt. His eyes held a question she wasn't sure she was ready to answer.

Luke's gaze dropped briefly to her lips, then back to her eyes. The moment stretched, suspended in the mountain air, the only sounds their breathing and the gentle splash of water from the spring.

"Sophie," he said, her name a question and a prayer on his lips.

Her heart thundered in her chest. Here in this beautiful meadow, with this good man who had shared his pain and listened to hers, the walls she'd built after Marcus seemed to crumble like dust.

Luke slowly, giving her every chance to pull away, leaned closer. Then he stopped, uncertainty flickering in his eyes.

"I don't want to presume..." he began.

Sophie found herself leaning forward slightly, drawn by something stronger than caution. But at the last moment, reason reasserted itself.

Luke seemed to read her hesitation. He cleared his throat and released her waist, taking a step back. The cool mountain air rushed between them, breaking the spell of the moment.

"We should, uh—we should check that other section of fence," he said, his voice slightly rougher than usual.

Sophie nodded, ignoring the flutter in her chest and the lingering warmth where his hands had been. "Lead the way."

The remaining fence inspection passed without incident, though Sophie was conscious of a new awareness between them that had been carefully contained until now. They worked efficiently, but the easy conversation of earlier had been replaced by a charged silence, punctuated by brief, necessary exchanges.

By early afternoon, they had completed their tasks and were heading back toward the main ranch buildings. The descent was quicker than the climb had been, and they arrived at the equipment shed just as Ray and Ed were returning from their hay delivery.

"Perfect timing," Ray called as they parked the ATVs. "How'd it go up at Hidden Meadow?"

"Trough is clear, the fence is repaired," Luke reported. "No issues other than what we expected."

Ray nodded approvingly, though his keen eyes moved between them, missing nothing. "Good work. We're about to have a quick lunch at the bunkhouse if you two want to join."

"I should check on some paperwork," Sophie said, needing a moment of space to process the day's unexpected emotional terrain. "Rain check?"

"Sure thing," Ray agreed easily. "Luke?"

"I'll be there in a few," Luke said. "I need to put away these tools first."

As Ray and Ed headed toward the bunkhouse, Sophie helped Luke unload the equipment from the ATVs.

"I appreciate your help today," Sophie said as they finished.

"Happy to help," Luke replied, his tone carefully casual though his eyes told a different story. "It's a big place. Takes time to really know it."

They stood for a moment in the equipment shed, neither quite ready to part ways. The almost-kiss in the meadow hovered between them, unacknowledged but impossible to forget.

"I was thinking," Luke began, then paused, seeming to reconsider his words. "That is—if you're not too busy—"

Sophie waited, her heart picking up speed despite her best efforts to remain calm.

Luke ran a hand through his hair, a gesture she was beginning to recognize as a sign of uncertainty. "There's a good steakhouse in town. The Branding Iron Grill. Nothing fancy, but the food's excellent. I thought maybe—if you wanted—we could have dinner there. Tonight."

Sophie studied him, noting the careful neutrality he was trying to maintain despite the hint of vulnerability in his eyes.

"It took you long enough to ask," she said.

Luke's composure slipped momentarily, a flash of surprise crossing his features before his mouth curved into that half-smile that made her pulse race. "I guess it did."

Sophie considered their current arrangement—him teaching her to run the ranch, the temporary nature of his stay, the boundaries that seemed sensible when they'd first met.

But she also thought about the man she'd come to know over the past few days. His integrity. His quiet strength. The way he spoke about faith and loss with hard-earned wisdom. The connection they seemed to share. The way her heart lifted whenever he entered a room.

"You know, after my experience with Marcus, I promised myself I wouldn't date anyone for a long time," she said finally, watching his expression carefully.

"I understand."

"But," Sophie continued, taking a step closer to him, "I think dinner would be nice. Not a date—just dinner. Between..." she hesitated, searching for the right word, "friends."

"Friends," he repeated. "I'd like that."

"What time?"

"Six? I can pick you up at the main house."

"Six it is."

As Sophie walked back toward the house, she couldn't quite dismiss the flutter of anticipation in her stomach, or the memory of Luke's eyes when they'd stood so close by the mountain spring.

Just dinner between friends, she reminded herself firmly. *Nothing more.*

Yet somewhere inside, a voice whispered that she wasn't being entirely honest—with Luke, or with herself. Because friends didn't notice the way sunlight caught in each other's hair, or feel electricity at the brush of fingertips, or wonder about the taste of each other's lips.

Friends didn't make your heart race with a single look.

And friends certainly didn't leave you counting the hours until you saw them again.

Chapter 14

Sophie tugged at the sleeve of her dress, smoothing an imaginary wrinkle as she waited on the front porch. In the distance, she spotted a cloud of dust rising from the driveway.

Her pulse quickened. "Not a date," she reminded herself. "Just dinner between friends."

But the navy blue wrap dress she'd chosen—the one that brought out the color of her eyes and draped softly over her curves—suggested she wasn't entirely convinced by her own assertion. She'd even applied mascara and a touch of lip gloss, something she hadn't bothered much with since arriving in Montana.

Luke's truck slowed as it approached the house. As he pulled to a stop, Sophie took a steadying breath and stood, running her suddenly damp palms down the sides of her dress.

Luke emerged from the truck in a crisp blue button-down shirt and dark jeans, his usual work boots replaced by polished brown leather. The sight of him sent a flutter through her stomach that she immediately tried to suppress.

"Evening," he called, climbing the porch steps with an easy grace that belied his size. He paused at the top, his eyes meeting hers with a warmth that made her heartbeat quicken. "You look beautiful."

The simple compliment, delivered with such genuine appreciation, brought warmth to her cheeks. "Thanks. You clean up pretty well yourself."

"Special occasion," he said simply. "Not every day I get to take the boss out to dinner."

"Well... this boss is looking forward to it."

Luke moved to the porch railing, leaning against it rather than immediately suggesting they leave. "How'd the paperwork go this afternoon?"

"Fine. Just updating some breeding records and reviewing the up-coming schedule." Sophie hesitated, then added with a smile, "Actually, I may have spent more time choosing what to wear this evening than working on paperwork."

"Well, it was time well spent," he replied, his voice dropping slightly. "Shall we?" he asked, gesturing toward his truck, offering his arm with a gentlemanly flourish that seemed both playful and sincere.

Sophie's heart fluttered as she placed her hand on his forearm, feeling the solid strength beneath the crisp fabric of his shirt. "Lead the way."

They descended the porch steps together. At the truck, Luke opened the passenger door for her.

"Thank you," Sophie said, sliding into the seat.

As Luke walked around to the driver's side, Sophie took in the interior of his truck—meticulously clean, with a small wooden cross hanging from the rear-view mirror. A well-worn aviation manual peeked out from the side pocket of the door, and a forestry ser-vice radio was mounted beneath the dashboard. These little details—glimpses into his personal space—felt significant somehow, another layer of understanding of this complex man.

Luke settled behind the wheel, starting the engine with a rumble that vibrated through the cab. "Ready?" he asked.

"Absolutely," Sophie replied, certain she meant it on multiple levels.

They drove down the long driveway and turned onto the main road toward town; the mountains silhouetted against the early evening sky in hues of purple, rose, and gold. The conversation flowed easily between them—observations about the day's work, a discussion of the yearlings they'd examined with Dr. Patterson, and plans for the coming week's ranch activities.

"So the Branding Iron Grill," Sophie said as they neared town.

"Best steaks around," Luke said, his profile strong and defined against the sunset-painted landscape outside his window. "Madison Blake runs it—her family's been raising beef in this valley for years. She knows her cuts."

"Madison," Sophie repeated, placing the name. "She was at church yesterday, right? Blonde, energetic?"

"That's her. Runs line dancing events on Friday nights too. It's quite the local institution." Luke's eyes drifted briefly to Sophie. "Maybe we could check that out sometime... if you're interested."

The casual invitation hung between them, another small step across the boundary between professional and personal. "I'd like that," Sophie replied, surprised by how much she meant it. "Fair warning though—I have two left feet when it comes to dancing."

Luke chuckled, the sound warming something deep inside her. "That makes two of us. We can stumble around together."

They drove down Main Street; the buildings glowing warm in the evening light. Riverbend Valley took on a different character in the evening—storefronts illuminated from within, porch lights flickering on at homes, the mountains rising like silent guardians around the town.

Luke parked in front of a rustic building with a hand-carved wooden sign depicting a branding iron. The restaurant's wide windows glowed with welcoming light, and country music drifted softly from inside.

"Here we are," Luke said, cutting the engine. He reached across the center console, his hand briefly touching hers. "Thanks for coming with me tonight."

"I'm glad you asked."

Luke came around to open her door, offering his hand to help her down from the truck. His palm was warm against hers, strong and calloused from years of physical work, yet gentle in the way he held her fingers. Sophie found herself reluctant to let go when her feet touched the ground.

Inside, the Branding Iron lived up to its name. Western décor dominated the space—branding irons mounted on the walls, saddles repurposed as chairs at the bar, wagon wheel chandeliers hanging from the ceiling. The scent of grilled meat and fresh-baked bread permeated the air, making Sophie's stomach rumble appreciatively.

A woman with wavy blonde hair and bright blue eyes spotted them from behind the hostess stand. "Luke Harding!" she called, her face lighting up, eyes darting between them.

"Evening, Madison," Luke greeted as they approached. "Table for two?"

Madison's gaze shifted to Sophie, curiosity and warm welcome mingling in her expression. "Nice to see you again, Sophie."

Madison grabbed two menus from behind the counter. She led them to a corner booth near a stone fireplace, currently unlit due to the warm evening. The table offered a measure of privacy while still allowing a view of the restaurant's rustic interior.

"Can I start you with drinks?" Madison asked as they settled into the booth.

"I'll have iced tea, please," Sophie requested.

"Same for me," Luke added.

Madison smiled knowingly. "Two iced teas coming right up. Take your time with the menus—I'll check back in a few." She hesitated, then added with a wink, "So nice to see you out and about, Luke. It's been too long."

As she walked away, Sophie took in the restaurant more fully. Several tables were occupied—an elderly couple sharing a dessert, a family with teenage children, and a few pairs of ranchers still in their work clothes.

"This place has character," Sophie observed. "Feels like it's been here forever."

"Since 1932," Luke confirmed. "It was a trading post originally, then a general store, and then a bar and grill owned by a man who just never took care of the place. It was pretty run down when Madison bought it a few years ago and brought it back to life."

"You know everyone's history, don't you?"

"Hazard of growing up here," Luke replied with a shrug, his eyes warm with affection as they held hers. "Everyone knows everyone's business—the good and the bad."

"And what do they know about Luke Harding?" Sophie asked, curious about how the community viewed him. She found herself leaning slightly closer, drawn by a desire to understand this man, who was gradually claiming more of her thoughts with each passing day.

Luke's expression turned thoughtful, his eyes searching hers as if weighing how much to reveal. "Depends who you ask. To some, I'm

Carter's nephew, who took over the ranch. To others, I'm the pilot who fights fires. To the old-timers, I'm still the ten-year-old boy who came to live with Carter after his parents died."

"And to you?" Sophie pressed gently, her voice softening. "Who is Luke Harding to himself?"

He considered it for a moment, his fingers absently tracing the grain of the wooden table, occasionally brushing against hers in a way that felt both accidental and deliberate.

"Still figuring that out," he admitted finally, his voice low enough that she had to lean closer to hear. "For a long time, I defined myself by what I did—rancher, pilot. Then by what I'd lost—Jake, Uncle Carter. Lately..." He paused, his eyes meeting hers. "Lately, I've been wondering if there's more to me than either of those things."

Madison returned with their drinks. "Two iced teas," she announced, setting them down. "Have you decided, or do you need more time?"

"I'll have the ribeye," Luke said without looking at the menu. "Medium rare."

"And for you?" Madison turned to Sophie.

"The same, please," Sophie decided. "Medium well."

"Excellent choice," Madison approved. "Loaded baked potatoes for both?"

They nodded, and Madison collected their menus. "I'll get this right in. Holler if you need anything before then."

As she left, a comfortable quiet settled between them. Sophie sipped her tea, appreciating the fresh mint leaves floating among the ice cubes.

"So," Luke said, his eyes holding hers with gentle intensity. "Now that we've established who I am—or who I'm trying to figure out I am—what about you? Who is Sophie Lawson beneath the veterinarian and ranch owner titles?"

Sophie considered the question, stirring her tea absently, touched by his genuine interest. "I'm not entirely sure anymore either," she admitted. "I used to know. Growing up with my grandparents, I had such a clear sense of myself—who I was, what I wanted, where God was leading me. But the last few years in Seattle..." She trailed off, her expression clouding slightly.

"It changed you," Luke observed, his voice gentle with understanding.

"It did," Sophie agreed, meeting his gaze with newfound openness. "And not for the better. I lost sight of myself somewhere along the way. Lost my connection to what matters most."

Luke reached across the table, his fingers brushing hers in a touch that felt both casual and profound. "And here you are, finding yourself again."

"I believe I am," Sophie replied, not pulling away from his touch. "Originally, though, when I was planning to leave Seattle, it was more about escape than discovery. But God seems to have had bigger plans."

Luke's fingers interlaced with hers, the gesture offering comfort and connection. "Sometimes running away and running toward something look similar from the outside. But the heart knows the difference."

Sophie nodded, appreciating his insight.

Luke's thumb traced a gentle pattern on the back of her hand. "Would it be overstepping if I asked more about what happened in Seattle? With Marcus?"

Sophie felt a momentary tightening in her chest at the mention of Marcus's name. But looking at Luke's expression—open, concerned, without a trace of judgment—she felt comfortable talking about one of the lowest points of her life. Here, in this warm restaurant far from Seattle, with this man who had shown her nothing but respect, the weight of Marcus's manipulation seemed less overwhelming.

"It's not overstepping," she said finally, turning her hand to fully clasp his. "Actually, it might be good to talk about it. I haven't talked about that time in my life with anyone."

Luke waited, giving her space to collect her thoughts. His patience, the way he simply listened without pushing, created a safety Sophie hadn't expected.

"I met Marcus during my residency," she began, drawing strength from Luke's steady presence. "He was brilliant, charismatic, respected in the field. When he offered me a position at his practice in Seattle, it felt like winning the lottery. The perfect and logical next step."

She took a sip of tea, organizing her thoughts. "At first, everything was wonderful. Professionally challenging, personally exciting. He mentored me, encouraged my research. He made me feel special, chosen."

Luke listened attentively, his focus entirely on her, his hand a warm anchor in hers.

"The relationship evolved gradually," Sophie continued. "Looking back, I can see how calculated it was—how he created situations where I depended on him, and sought his approval. But at the time, it just felt... natural. Like we were equals building something together."

"When did things change?" Luke asked quietly, his thumb continuing its gentle caress against her skin.

Sophie's fingers tightened around his. "About a year ago. I developed a new technique during surgery. The results were remarkable. When I suggested publishing the findings, Marcus insisted we present it as collaborative work, with him as lead author."

"He took credit for your innovation," Luke said, a note of controlled anger in his voice.

"That was just the beginning," Sophie continued, finding it easier to speak now that she'd started. "He started presenting my ideas as his own at conferences. Scheduled me for routine cases while he handled the more difficult procedures. Then he began taking credit for things I had done. When clients praised my work, he'd redirect it, subtly at first, then more blatantly."

Madison approached with their salads, pausing when she sensed the serious conversation. She placed them down quietly with a gentle smile and withdrew without interrupting.

"The worst part wasn't the professional undermining," Sophie said after a moment, her voice lower now. "It was how he made me doubt myself. He'd praise me lavishly in private, then question my judgment in front of colleagues. He'd encourage me to take risks, then criticize the outcome, regardless of the result. It was... destabilizing."

"Manipulative," Luke supplied, his jaw tightening, his hand squeezing hers gently in silent support.

Sophie nodded, drawing strength from his understanding. "The last straw came when I was being considered for partnership in the practice. I'd met every benchmark, exceeded every expectation. Then suddenly, Marcus was telling the board I wasn't ready, that I needed more seasoning, more supervision. That my judgment was questionable in high-pressure situations."

She paused, the memory still sharp enough to sting. "When I confronted him privately, he acted like he was protecting me. Said I should be grateful for his guidance, that I'd be nothing without him. That no one would believe in my abilities if he didn't vouch for me."

Luke's eyes darkened with protective anger, his grip on her hand tightening. "That's gas-lighting, plain and simple," he said, his voice low and controlled.

"I know that now," Sophie agreed. "But then... for a short time, I believed him. That's what scares me most when I look back—how completely I bought into his version of reality. How I let him define my worth."

"What changed?" Luke asked, his thumb resuming its gentle circles on her hand. "What made you see through it?"

Sophie's expression softened slightly. "A horse named Midnight. Severe colic case, that needed immediate surgery. Marcus was at a conference, and I was alone at the clinic. I performed the procedure—using the technique I had developed. The horse recovered beautifully."

She took a breath, drawing comfort from Luke's steady gaze. "When Marcus returned, he was furious. Not because I'd done something wrong—the outcome was perfect—but because I'd acted independently. Made a decision without consulting him. Taken 'unnecessary risks.' That's when I finally saw it clearly—this wasn't about my skills or judgment. It was about control."

"That took courage," Luke said quietly, his voice warm with admiration.

"Once I saw it, I couldn't unsee it. I started noticing all the ways he'd manipulated situations, isolated me from colleagues, undermined my confidence. When I tried to assert boundaries, he escalated—threatened to damage my professional reputation if I left the practice. He actually said no one would hire me without his recommendation."

"So you came to Montana."

Sophie nodded, squeezing his hand. "Buying the ranch was impulsive and terrifying, but I knew I had to get away completely. I basically stopped and took control of my own life and followed the dream I've had since I was a little girl... I bought a ranch."

"It wasn't impulsive," Luke countered, his voice firm with conviction. "It was brave. It was faith. And from what I've seen, it was exactly right. You're a gifted veterinarian and a natural with the ranching lifestyle." His eyes held hers, steady and sure. "And Marcus was wrong about you. Completely wrong."

They fell silent as Madison delivered their steaks—perfectly cooked ribeyes accompanied by loaded baked potatoes and seasonal vegetables.

"Enjoy," Madison said with a smile, seeming to sense the importance of their conversation. "I'll check back in a bit."

When she'd gone, Sophie picked up her fork but paused before eating. "The strangest part is, looking back, I realize I fell out of love with Marcus a long time before I left. Maybe I never really loved him at all—just the idea of him, or what I thought we could be together."

Luke nodded thoughtfully, reluctantly releasing her hand so they could eat. "Sometimes we see what we want to see in people."

"I honestly don't think he ever loved me," Sophie confessed, cutting into her steak. "I was just... useful to him? Another tool for his advancement?"

Luke considered her words carefully, his expression serious. "I can't speak to what he felt," he said finally. "But I can say this—anyone who truly loves someone wants them to shine, not to diminish them so they can shine brighter themselves."

"That's... profoundly true," she said.

They ate in silence for a few minutes, the rich flavors of the perfectly prepared meal a welcome reprieve from the emotional intensity of their conversation.

"What about you?" she asked after a while, genuinely curious about his past. "You mentioned before you haven't dated in a few years. Why is that?"

Luke set down his fork, his expression turning reflective. "After Jake and Uncle Carter died, I wasn't in a good place. I was dating a woman, Laurel, at the time—elementary school teacher, kind, patient. We'd been together about a year."

He took a sip of his tea before continuing, his gaze occasionally meeting Sophie's. "When I took leave from flying... I just shut down emotionally. I couldn't process what had happened. I couldn't talk about it, and I couldn't move forward. Laurel tried, but I wasn't available—not really. Not where it counted."

"That must have been hard for both of you," Sophie observed quietly, understanding the struggle to remain present when grief overwhelms.

"It was," Luke agreed. "She deserved better than what I could give her then. Eventually, I broke it off. Told her it wasn't fair to either of us to continue when I was so... broken."

"Was that the real reason?" Sophie asked gently, sensing there was more beneath his words.

Luke looked up, meeting her gaze. "Partly. But if I'm honest, I was also afraid. Afraid of caring too much, of being responsible for someone else's happiness when I couldn't even manage my own. Afraid of the risk of more loss."

"I can understand that."

Luke turned his hand to capture hers, their fingers intertwining naturally. "When Jake died, then Uncle Carter a few weeks later," he continued, his voice lower, meant only for her ears. "It was like the ground disappeared beneath me. The two people who had anchored my life were just... gone. I was stuck in a dark hole, trying to make sense of it all. I focused on the ranch after that, on practical things I could control. I see clearly now that I was isolating myself from getting close to anyone."

"And now?" Sophie asked.

"Now... it's time for me to live again." His thumb traced the sensitive skin of her inner wrist, sending a pleasant shiver up her arm.

The implication in his words sent a flutter through Sophie's chest. Their hands remained joined as they continued eating, the conversation shifting to lighter topics—amusing stories from Sophie's veterinary school days, Luke's tales of Carter's more eccentric ranching experiments. Yet beneath the casual conversation flowed a current of growing connection, of walls carefully lowered.

As they finished their meal, Madison approached with dessert menus. "Room for something sweet? The apple pie is fresh out of the oven."

"I couldn't possibly," Sophie demurred, though the mention of apple pie was tempting.

"We could share a slice."

Sophie smiled, relenting. "Alright, one slice with two forks."

"Coming right up," Madison said with a wink that made Sophie blush slightly.

When she'd gone, Luke leaned forward slightly, his expression turning more serious. "Sophie, can I ask you something?"

"Of course."

He hesitated, then said, "What is this thing between us?"

The directness of the question made Sophie pause.

"I don't know," she admitted finally, her voice soft with vulnerability. "I didn't come to Montana looking for... this. Whatever it is. But I can't deny there's something going on between the two of us."

Luke nodded, his eyes never leaving hers. "Selling the ranch and returning to firefighting full-time—finding someone special wasn't part of my plan, either."

"And yet," Sophie said, her pulse quickening as she held his gaze.

"And yet," he echoed, his voice dropping to a near whisper. "Here we are."

Madison returned with their pie, and two forks, setting it between them with a flourish. "Enjoy, you two. On the house—consider it a welcome to Riverbend Valley gift for our newest resident."

"That's so kind," Sophie protested. "But you don't have to—"

"My restaurant, my rules," Madison insisted with a smile. "Besides, it does my heart good to see Luke out enjoying himself for a change... with such lovely company."

As Madison walked away, Luke shook his head with a rueful smile. "And that's small-town life for you—everyone invested in everyone else's business."

"It's sweet," Sophie said, picking up a fork. "They care about you."

"They'll care about you too, before long," Luke replied, his eyes warm as they held hers. "You're the kind of person people can't help caring about."

The simple compliment touched her deeply, and Sophie ducked her head, focusing on the pie to hide the emotion welling in her eyes.

They shared the dessert, which was indeed delicious—warm cinnamon-spiced apples in a flaky crust, topped with vanilla ice cream slowly melting into the filling. Luke insisted she take the first bite, watching her reaction with obvious pleasure as she closed her eyes in appreciation of the flavors.

"Back to your question," Sophie said after they'd finished the last bite. "I'm not sure what this is, but I know it scares me... this instant attraction between us... but at the same time, it feels right in a way I can't explain. I'm not ready to define this... and really, do we have to label it?"

"No. We've both got baggage that we're still unpacking. And this—" he gestured between them, "—is worth taking slow. Worth doing right."

"Plus, there's the whole sixty-day arrangement to consider," Sophie added. "You're technically working for me, at least for now... and it's an odd situation."

"Fifty-five more days," Luke acknowledged, his thumb tracing patterns on her palm. "And then what?"

"I don't know," Sophie said truthfully. "Let's just roll with it and see where God leads us."

Luke smiled, his eyes crinkling at the corners. "Roll with it? I like that. Trust the journey."

"That's my new outlook on life," she said, returning his smile. "Take a chance and see where it leads me... roll with it."

Chapter 15

Sophie gripped the fence post with one hand and kept tension on the wire with the other, as Luke hammered the barbed wire into place. The late morning sun beat down on her shoulders, and perspiration trickled down her spine beneath her work shirt.

"Almost there," Luke called, his voice carrying over the rhythmic pounding of the hammer. "Just need to secure this last section."

Sophie adjusted her grip, maintaining tension on the wire. "Whoever said ranching is glamorous clearly never spent a morning wrestling barbed wire in ninety-degree heat."

Luke's laugh rumbled low as he drove the final staple home. "I think that's written in the fine print of every ranch deed. 'Buyer acknowledges glamour is not included in the purchase price.'"

"Now you tell me," Sophie quipped, relaxing her hold as Luke tested the wire's tension with a satisfied nod.

They'd spent the morning on horseback, riding the perimeter of the high north pasture to check on a small group of broodmares. The fence repair had been an unexpected addition to their task list when they'd discovered a section damaged by what appeared to be elk migration.

Luke wiped his brow with his forearm, leaving a smudge of dirt across his tanned skin. "That should hold. Unless those elk decide to stage another break-in."

"Maybe they just appreciate our premium grass," Sophie suggested, flexing her fingers to restore circulation.

"Can't blame them for good taste." Luke collected the tools, sliding them into the leather saddlebags draped over his horse's withers. "How are your hands? Barbed wire isn't forgiving."

Sophie glanced down at her palms—reddened but intact. "I've had worse."

"The first time I repaired fence with Uncle Carter, I was eleven. I looked like I'd tangled with a bobcat."

The mention of his uncle brought a nostalgic warmth to Luke's eyes, and Sophie studied his profile—the powerful line of his jaw, the slight crinkles at the corners of his eyes that deepened when he smiled. Since their dinner at the Branding Iron two days ago, something had shifted between them. Not dramatically, but noticeably—a new ease, a deeper current of understanding that made her pulse quicken whenever he was near.

"Ready to check on those mares?" Luke asked, untying Buck's reins from a nearby sapling.

"Lead the way," Sophie replied, moving toward Sierra, who was contentedly cropping grass a few yards away.

They mounted up and continued along the ridgeline, following a well-worn trail. The slight elevation provided a spectacular view of Ironwood Creek Ranch spreading below them—patchwork fields of green and gold, the silver ribbon of the creek winding through the property, and the cluster of buildings at its heart that now represented home.

"I still can't believe this is all mine," Sophie said, taking in the vista with wonder that hadn't diminished despite daily exposure to such beauty.

"It suits you," Luke replied, his gaze resting on her rather than the view.

She turned, catching his eyes. Something in his expression—admiration mixed with something deeper—made her heart flutter. "What makes you say that?"

"The way you approach it," he said simply. "Not as a possession, but as a responsibility. A living thing that needs care and stewardship."

The compliment warmed her more than the Montana sun, settling in her chest like a blessing.

They rode in silence for several minutes, the only sounds the rhythmic hoofbeats and the occasional call of a red-tailed hawk circling overhead. The trail curved around an outcropping of rock, opening onto a sheltered meadow where a dozen broodmares grazed in the dappled shade of scattered cottonwoods.

"There they are," Luke said, slowing Buck to a walk. "Looking healthy from here."

Sophie surveyed the group with a professional eye, noting their relaxed postures and glossy coats. "Good weight on all of them. That chestnut on the far side—that's Ember, right? She looks closer than the others."

Luke nodded. "She's due about two weeks before the rest. We should probably move her down to the foaling barn soon."

They dismounted at the edge of the meadow, ground-tying their horses to allow them to graze while they checked the mares. Sophie moved among the pregnant horses with practiced ease, running her hands along flanks, checking udders, and gauging overall condition. Luke worked alongside her, noting observations in a small notebook he'd pulled from his shirt pocket.

"Clover's got some thrush starting in her back left," Sophie observed, examining the hoof of a copper-colored mare with a white blaze. "Nothing serious yet, but worth treating before it progresses."

"I'll have Dan bring up the medication later today," Luke said, making a note.

"I can take care of it," Sophie offered.

They continued their examinations, moving efficiently through the small herd. There was something deeply satisfying about working alongside someone who matched her pace and understood her process, who valued the same things she did.

As they checked the final mare, a leggy bay with a gentle disposition, Luke chuckled quietly.

"What?" Sophie asked, glancing up from her examination.

"Just thinking about how Carter would react to all this," he said, his voice carrying fondness and a touch of melancholy. "He was always trying to get me more interested in the breeding program. Said I had the knowledge, but not the passion for it." His eyes met hers across the mare's back. "He would have appreciated your expertise. And your enthusiasm."

"I wish I could have met him," Sophie said sincerely, her heart aching for the grandfather figure Luke had lost.

"I wish that, too. He would have liked you. Probably would have told me I was a fool for selling the ranch, though."

The reminder of their temporary arrangement sent a familiar pang through Sophie's chest. Fifty-three more days, she thought, the countdown ever-present in her mind like a ticking clock measuring something precious and finite.

They finished their work and walked back to where Buck and Sierra waited; the horses lifting their heads expectantly as they approached. They mounted and turned their horses back toward the trail, but instead of immediately heading down, Luke hesitated at the meadow's edge, his expression thoughtful.

"We could take the long way back," he suggested, nodding toward a different trail that curved along the ridgeline. "There's a viewpoint about half a mile from here that gives you a different perspective of the entire property. Might be useful for you to see."

"Lead on."

The trail Luke chose was less defined than their ascent route, winding through taller grass and occasional rocky outcroppings. It followed the natural contour of the ridgeline, offering increasingly spectacular views of the valley below. Sierra seemed to sense Sophie's relaxed mood, tossing her head playfully as they rode.

"Someone's feeling spirited," Luke observed as the mare danced sideways for a few steps.

Sophie laughed, patting the horse's arched neck. "She's been cooped up in the paddock too much lately. All this open space is going to her head." She leaned forward slightly, whispering loudly enough for Luke to hear, "Ready to show this Montana boy what a Colorado girl can do?"

Luke's eyebrow rose in challenge, a spark of mischief transforming his usually serious expression. "Is that right? You think that fancy Colorado upbringing of yours can outrun a seasoned Montana cowboy?"

Sophie straightened in the saddle, her eyes sparkling with delighted mischief. "Care to find out?"

Luke's serious expression cracked into a grin that transformed his entire face, revealing the playful man beneath his reserved exterior. "You're on, Dr. Lawson."

He pointed ahead to where the trail widened into a broad, grassy stretch that ran along the ridge for several hundred yards. "From that juniper to the lightning-struck pine. Fair race, no tricks."

"Stakes?" Sophie asked, already gathering her reins in anticipation, her competitive spirit rising to match his challenge.

Luke considered for a moment, his eyes twinkling. "Winner chooses the dinner menu for the next ranch barbecue."

"Deal," Sophie agreed immediately, her confidence infectious. "I hope you like five-alarm chili."

"Now I'm worried," Luke said with mock concern. "Maybe we should have discussed the stakes more thoroughly."

They lined up their horses at the juniper; the animals sensing the impending run and tensing beneath them like coiled springs. Buck pawed the ground impatiently while Sierra's ears pricked forward, her entire body radiating anticipation.

"Ready?" Luke asked, his voice rich with excitement that made Sophie's heart race.

"Set," Sophie replied, leaning forward slightly in the saddle, feeling Sierra gather herself beneath her.

"Go!" they called in unison.

The horses leapt forward as if released from invisible restraints, surging along the ridgeline in a thunder of hoofbeats that seemed to echo the rhythm of Sophie's heart. Her hair whipped behind her from beneath her hat as Sierra stretched into a full gallop, her powerful strides eating up the ground with fluid grace. Beside them, Buck matched their pace, his longer legs compensating for Sierra's quicker acceleration.

Sophie's laughter bubbled up unbidden, pure exhilaration filling her chest as they raced across the ridge. The wind rushed past her ears, carrying away all thoughts except the sheer joy of speed and freedom.

She glanced sideways to see Luke urging Buck forward, his face alight with the same unrestrained pleasure, all traces of his usual reserved demeanor swept away by the moment.

This was how God meant them to live, she thought fleetingly—with joy, with abandon, with trust in His goodness.

They thundered neck-and-neck down the grassy stretch, neither gaining a clear advantage. Sophie could feel Sierra's determination beneath her, the mare's competitive spirit matching her own. As the lightning-struck pine approached, she gave Sierra the slightest encouragement, and the mare surged forward with a last burst of speed that spoke of heart as much as ability.

They flashed past the finish marker mere inches ahead of Buck, Sophie's whoop of triumph blending with Luke's shout of good natured protest. The horses gradually slowed from their headlong pace, sides heaving, nostrils flared as they gulped the thin mountain air.

"I demand a rematch!" Luke called, his voice carrying laughter that made Sophie's heart sing. "Buck was carrying more weight!"

"Excuses, excuses," Sophie teased, her cheeks flushed with victory and exertion. "Just admit you've been outrun by a Colorado girl and her superior horsemanship."

They guided their mounts to a halt side by side, both breathing nearly as hard as their horses from the excitement of the race. Sophie pushed back her hat, which had somehow stayed on throughout their wild ride, and turned to find Luke watching her with an expression that stole what remained of her breath.

"What?" she asked, suddenly self-conscious under the intensity of his gaze.

"Nothing," he said, his voice softer than before, touched with wonder. "I don't think I've laughed like that in years."

They dismounted, loosening their horses' girths and leading them at a walk along the ridgeline. The exhilaration of the race gradually mellowed into a comfortable quiet, though Sophie remained acutely aware of Luke beside her—his easy stride, the way his sleeve occasionally brushed hers as they walked, and the contentment that seemed to radiate from him.

"This view," Luke said, gesturing ahead as they approached a rocky outcropping. "This is what I wanted to show you."

Sophie followed his gaze and caught her breath. The outcropping offered a panoramic vista of Ironwood Creek Ranch in its entirety. The ranch house and barns looked like miniatures from this height, the creek a silver thread binding it all together in perfect harmony.

"It's spectacular," she breathed, feeling small and blessed in the face of such magnificence.

"This is Eagle's Rest," Luke explained. "My uncle once told me that a man needed to see his work from above sometimes, to remember the bigger picture. To remember that we're part of something larger than ourselves."

"I like that wisdom. It's easy to get lost in the daily details and forget the greater purpose."

"He was a man who saw things clearly. Not just the land, but people too. God's handiwork in all of it."

They stood side by side, letting the horses graze nearby while they absorbed the vast landscape spread before them. The perspective was humbling and inspiring at the same time.

"I've been thinking," Luke said after several minutes of contemplative silence, his voice carrying a fresh note of hesitation that drew her attention.

Sophie turned to look at him, struck by the slight uncertainty in his expression—so different from his usual confidence.

"About?"

"I was wondering… would you be willing to take a day off from the ranch?"

The request caught Sophie by surprise. "A day off?" she echoed, her brow furrowing slightly. "Why? What did you have in mind?"

Luke turned to face her fully. "Well… I haven't mentioned it before, but I own a small plane. I keep it at the airfield just outside Riverbend Valley." He gestured vaguely toward the west, where the town lay beyond the visible horizon. "I'd like to take you up. Show you the ranch from the sky."

"A plane," she repeated, her voice reflecting her surprise. "You own a plane."

Luke nodded. "It was Carter's originally. A Cessna 182." A brief smile touched his lips, warming his features.

"I would love to!"

"Really?"

"Really," she confirmed, touched by his vulnerability. "Though I should warn you, I've never been in a small plane before."

"It's perfectly safe," he assured her. "And the views…" He shook his head slightly, as if words were inadequate. "There's nothing like seeing this land from above. It changes your perspective on everything."

Sophie looked out over the vast expanse of Ironwood Creek Ranch, trying to imagine how it might appear from even higher—from Luke's element, the sky that called to his soul.

"What time tomorrow?"

"How about we leave the ranch around eleven? That'll give us good light and calm air."

"It's a date," Sophie said.

Luke's eyes met hers, a smile spreading slowly across his face like a sunrise. "A date."

"Roll with it, remember?" Sophie said, her heart beating faster as she held his gaze.

"Roll with it," he agreed.

Chapter 16

"This is it," Luke said, cutting the engine as he parked at the Riverbend Valley Airfield. The modest facility stretched before them—a single asphalt runway flanked by open grassland, a weathered control tower, and a row of hangars. Morning sunlight glinted off small aircraft scattered across the tarmac, their metal surfaces catching the light against the backdrop of mountain ranges that encircled the valley like protective arms.

Sophie's stomach fluttered with anticipation as she unbuckled her seatbelt. The moment felt significant somehow—another threshold to cross, another layer of Luke's world he was willing to share.

Luke reached behind the seat and retrieved a wicker picnic basket. "Courtesy of Lily at the Bluebird Café. I called in a special order this morning."

"You thought of everything," Sophie said

"I try." He patted the thermos strapped to the side of the basket, his eyes warm with anticipation. "Coffee included. Lily insisted we couldn't have a proper picnic without it."

They climbed out of the truck, and Sophie inhaled deeply. The air carried the distinctive scent of aviation fuel mingled with wild grasses—an unexpected combination that spoke of adventure and possibility.

Luke led the way across the tarmac, nodding to a weathered man in coveralls who waved from the open door of a maintenance hangar.

"Morning, Charlie!" Luke called.

"Luke Harding, good to see ya," the mechanic shouted back with obvious delight. "Special occasion?"

Luke's ears reddened slightly as he lifted the picnic basket in acknowledgment. "Perfect day for flying."

Charlie's keen gaze shifted to Sophie, and his weathered face split into a knowing grin. "I'd say so. You two have a good flight!"

They continued toward a hangar at the far end of the row. Luke punched a code into a keypad, and the side door unlocked with a metallic click.

Sophie's eyes adjusted to the dimmer light as she stepped inside. The single-engine plane was smaller than she'd imagined but immaculately maintained—its white body accented with navy blue stripes that curved elegantly from nose to tail. "N7219C" was painted in precise lettering near the vertical stabilizer.

"She's beautiful," Sophie said sincerely, moving closer to examine the sleek lines of the aircraft.

"Cessna 182 Skylane," Luke said, unmistakable pride warming his voice. "Carter bought her new in 1987. I've updated the avionics and interior, but she's mostly original." He ran his hand along the smooth metal of the wing with the reverence of a horseman for a cherished mount. "Over 1,900 hours of flying memories with this plane."

Sophie moved closer, noticing the name painted in script beneath the pilot's window: Sky Dancer.

"Carter named her," Luke explained, following her gaze. "Said she responded to air currents like a dancer follows music." His expression softened with memory. "First time he took me up, when I was eleven, he sat me on a cushion so I could see over the dashboard. I was hooked from that moment."

Sophie touched the cool metal surface, understanding that she was in the presence of something sacred. "So this is where it all began."

Luke nodded. "This plane is... she's family, in a way. My connection to Carter."

The simple admission moved Sophie deeply. She understood then that bringing her here wasn't just about showing her the ranch from above—it was Luke sharing his history, his heart, and one of the most essential part of himself.

"Let's get her ready to fly. Want to help with the pre-flight check?"

"I wouldn't miss it," Sophie replied, eager to take part.

Luke set the picnic basket on a workbench and grabbed a clipboard hanging on the wall. "Pre-flight checklist. I'm military-strict about this—no exceptions, no shortcuts. Even on a perfect day like today."

For the next twenty minutes, Luke guided Sophie through the methodical inspection of the aircraft. He explained each step in clear, patient terms, showing her how to check control surfaces, inspect the propeller, examine fuel quality, and assess every critical component. His hands moved with practiced confidence, and Sophie found herself as fascinated by his expertise as by the aircraft itself.

"Aviation has its own language," Luke said as they circled the plane, "but the principles are simple. Know your aircraft, respect the physics, and plan for contingencies."

Sophie appreciated his thoroughness, recognizing it as the same careful attention he brought to every aspect of ranch operations. "Not so different from veterinary medicine," she observed. "Assessment, diagnosis, and careful procedure."

"Never thought of it that way, but you're absolutely right."

With the exterior inspection complete, Luke helped Sophie climb aboard through the passenger-side door. The interior was surprisingly spacious, with two leather seats up front and additional seating behind. The instrument panel was a fascinating mix of traditional round gauges and modern digital displays that glowed to life as Luke settled into the pilot's seat and began flipping switches with practiced efficiency.

"Nervous?" he asked, glancing at her with gentle concern.

"Excited," Sophie corrected, fastening her seatbelt with steady hands. "It feels like I'm about to see a whole new world."

"You are." Luke handed her a headset, his fingers brushing hers in the exchange. "Put this on. It protects your hearing and lets us talk without shouting over the engine."

Sophie adjusted the headset over her ears, immediately noticing the reduction in ambient noise. When Luke spoke next, his voice came through clearly in the earpieces, intimate and reassuring.

"Can you hear me, okay?"

"Perfectly," she replied, surprised at how close his voice sounded, as if he were whispering directly into her ear.

Luke worked through his startup checklist, explaining key steps as he went. "Each aircraft has its own personality," he said, his hands moving confidently across the controls. "Sky Dancer likes her oil temperature just so before takeoff, and she prefers a gentle touch on the throttle."

The propeller began to turn, slowly at first, then faster until it blurred into a silvery disc. The engine's vibration traveled through the air, a mechanical heartbeat that signaled life and infinite possibility.

"Ready?" Luke asked, his eyes meeting hers with excitement.

"Ready," Sophie confirmed, surprised by the calm certainty she felt. With Luke at the controls, she felt completely safe.

Luke taxied the plane from the hangar onto the runway, communicating briefly with the control tower in the crisp, professional language of aviation. With permission granted, he advanced the throttle, and Sky Dancer accelerated down the asphalt strip, gathering speed with surprising swiftness.

"Here we go," Luke said, his voice steady and reassuring in her headset.

The nose lifted, and suddenly, they were airborne; the earth falling away beneath them in a rush of exhilaration. Sophie's stomach dipped momentarily with the sensation of ascent, then settled as the plane climbed smoothly into the limitless Montana sky.

"Oh!" The exclamation escaped her involuntarily as Riverbend Valley expanded beneath them, the town quickly becoming a cluster of miniature buildings nestled in the broader tapestry of the landscape.

Luke glanced at her, his expression brightening at her reaction. "First impressions?"

"It's... Luke, it's incredible." Sophie pressed her face closer to the window as they banked gently, gaining altitude. "Everything looks so different from up here. So... connected."

"From up here, you see how everything fits together—the patterns, the relationships between landscape features that aren't obvious from the ground. It's like seeing from Heaven's perspective."

They climbed to 6,500 feet, leveling off above the patchwork of ranches, farms, and wilderness that made up the valley. Mountains rose around them like ancient sentinels, their forested slopes giving way to rocky peaks that seemed close enough to touch. The morning light cast long shadows across the terrain, emphasizing every contour and texture in stunning detail.

"I fly this route often," Luke said, banking the plane gently to the east. "Different seasons, different times of day. It never looks exactly the same twice. God's artistry never repeats itself."

"It's like seeing with new eyes," Sophie replied, trying to absorb every detail of the panorama below. "I feel so small, but also... significant. Part of something magnificent."

Luke guided the plane in a wide arc, following the curve of the valley. "There's Sapphire Lake," he pointed to a jewel-blue expanse of water nestled between pine-covered slopes. "And there—see that meadow with the distinctive horseshoe shape that hugs the river? That's where the valley got its name. Early settlers named this town after the bend in the river."

Sophie nodded, appreciating how each landmark Luke identified added another layer to her understanding of the region she now called home. Every story deepened her connection to this place, and to the man sharing it with her.

"And now," Luke said, banking the plane again with fluid grace, "let's go see your ranch from above."

They flew southwest, crossing over forest and stream until the distinctive boundaries of Ironwood Creek Ranch came into view. Sophie's breath caught as the full expanse of her property unfolded beneath them, more magnificent than she'd ever imagined.

"That's... that's all Ironwood Creek?" she asked, the scale suddenly more apparent than it had ever been from ground level.

"Every acre," Luke confirmed, his voice carrying a note of pride that touched her heart. "See the way the creek forms the spine of the property? Carter planned it that way—water as the lifeline connecting every section."

He brought the plane lower, pointing out features as they passed overhead. "There's the main house and barns. The Ironwood Grove stands out from above—see how the trees form that distinctive arc? And there's Hidden Meadow, where we raced yesterday."

Sophie leaned closer to the window, captivated by this new perspective on her land. From above, the organization of the ranch made perfect sense—the relationship between grazing areas, water sources, and natural boundaries revealed a thoughtful design that honored the land's natural contours while maximizing its potential.

"It's breathtaking," she said softly, emotion thickening in her voice. "I knew it was special, but seeing it like this..."

"This view helped me make peace with selling," Luke admitted, his voice quieter now. "Seeing it as a whole, understanding that it would continue regardless of who owned the deed—as long as that person truly understood what it is."

Sophie turned from the window to look at him, struck by the openness in his expression. Here, in the sky, Luke seemed freer somehow—the guarded quality that sometimes shadowed his features on the ground lifted away, replaced by a calm certainty that made her heart flutter.

"I promise to honor it always," she said simply, meaning every word. "To be worthy of the trust you've placed in me."

His eyes met hers briefly, something profound passing between them. "I knew from the moment I met you... the ranch belonged in your hands."

Luke returned his attention to flying, banking the plane to circle the ranch in a graceful arc that showcased every corner of the property.

"I want to show you something special," he said, his voice taking on an almost reverent quality. "There's another meadow in the northern section. It's only accessible on horseback or on foot, but it's perfect for landing."

"You can land there? On the grass?" Sophie asked, surprised and intrigued.

Luke nodded, his eyes sparkling with anticipation. "The Cessna's designed for unimproved airstrips. This meadow is one of the reasons Carter bought this particular model—he loved flying in for picnic lunches when the weather was perfect."

"And that's where we're headed?"

"If you're game," Luke confirmed, already adjusting their course. "It's the most beautiful view on the entire property. Carter called it his cathedral."

"Let's do it," Sophie said, excitement bubbling through her at the adventure ahead.

They flew north, following the gentle rise of the land toward the foothills. Below, Sophie spotted a group of elk moving through a stand of aspens, their movements graceful and unhurried. Red-tailed hawks soared around them below, riding thermals with lazy circles that spoke of absolute mastery of their domain.

"There," Luke said, pointing ahead to where the forest opened into a natural clearing. "Carter's Meadow."

The meadow stretched before them, a perfectly flat expanse of emerald grass bordered by pine forest on three sides and opening to a stunning valley view on the fourth. A small pond glittered at one end like a jewel, fed by a stream that emerged from the tree line in a ribbon of silver.

"Luke," Sophie breathed, overwhelmed by the sheer beauty of the hidden sanctuary.

"Wind conditions look perfect," Luke said, his voice shifting to the focused tone she was learning to recognize as his pilot mode. "We'll come in from the east, using that line of trees as our final approach marker."

Sophie watched, fascinated, as Luke transformed before her eyes—his movements precise, his attention absolute as he guided the plane through a careful descent. He narrated his process calmly, explaining how he assessed wind direction, calculated glide slope, and chose his touchdown point.

The meadow grew larger as they descended, details emerging like a painting coming into focus—wildflowers dotting the grass in splashes of color, and the mirror-smooth surface of the pond reflecting the endless sky.

The wheels touched down with barely a whisper; the plane rolling smoothly across the natural landing strip before coming to a gentle stop near the pond. Luke powered down the engine, and suddenly the cockpit was filled with the sound of their breathing and the faint tick of cooling metal.

"Welcome to Carter's Meadow," Luke said, removing his headset with a smile that transformed his entire face. "Population: currently two."

Sophie laughed, unbuckling her seatbelt with hands that trembled slightly from excitement. "That was amazing! The landing was so smooth I barely felt it."

"Good ground," Luke explained, reaching behind their seats for the picnic basket. "Nature's perfect runway, carved by God's own hand."

They climbed out of the plane, and Sophie was immediately struck by the profound quiet of the meadow—a silence deeper and more complete than she'd experienced anywhere else. The subtle sounds that did exist—the whisper of a breeze through tree leaves, the distant call of birds, the gentle lapping of water at the pond's edge—seemed amplified and sacred in the stillness.

"This is incredible," she said, her voice instinctively lowered to match the reverent atmosphere.

Luke nodded, understanding flickering in his eyes. "My uncle felt the same way. He'd fly up here once a week during good weather, just to sit and think and pray. Said he always felt closest to God in this place." He gestured toward a flat-topped boulder near the pond. "That was his thinking rock, as he called it."

Sophie followed Luke to the boulder, which proved large enough to serve as a natural table. He spread a checkered cloth from the basket and began unpacking Lily's provisions—thick sandwiches on homemade bread, mason jars of potato salad, sliced fruit that gleamed like jewels, and cookies wrapped in waxed paper.

"This is perfect," Sophie said, settling beside him on the sun-warmed stone. "I had no idea this meadow even existed on the property."

Luke poured steaming coffee from the thermos into two enamel mugs, the familiar aroma mingling with the scent of wild grass and mountain air. "Carter considered this place his private retreat. Only showed it to people who truly mattered to him." He passed her a mug, their fingers brushing in the exchange. "I've only brought two people here before—Jake, and later Jake and Katie when he was planning to propose to her."

"What a beautiful place for a proposal."

They ate in comfortable silence for a few minutes, the beauty of their surroundings making conversation seem almost unnecessary. The view from the boulder encompassed miles of Montana wilderness—layered mountain ranges receding into blue distance, forests giving way to rocky highlands, and the silver thread of a river winding through the valley far below like a ribbon dropped from heaven.

"So," Sophie said finally, turning toward Luke, "I have to ask—how did Carter discover this place? It seems so hidden, so perfectly secret."

Luke's face lit up with the memory. "Pure accident, and God's providence. Early days of his flying, he had engine trouble and needed to make an emergency landing. He spotted this meadow and put down safely. While waiting for help, he fell in love with the place." Luke gestured toward the surrounding forest. "Later, when he started building the ranch, he made sure to acquire this parcel—said it was non-negotiable."

"I would have done exactly the same thing."

"My uncle had vision," Luke agreed, his voice warm with admiration for his uncle. "He could see potential where others just saw obstacles or worthless land."

Sophie bit into her sandwich thoughtfully. "You're like him that way."

Luke looked genuinely surprised. "You think so?"

"I do. The way you approach problems, the way you see beyond immediate circumstances to longer-term solutions." She gestured toward the plane. "The way you fly—it's all about seeing the bigger picture, trusting in something greater than yourself, isn't it?"

"No one's ever made that connection before." He was quiet for a moment, then added with quiet honesty, "After Jake died, I thought I'd lost that ability—to see beyond the immediate pain, to trust in a future I couldn't yet envision."

Sophie set down her coffee, giving him her full attention. "What helped you find it again?"

"Prayer," Luke said simply, without embarrassment. "Not the asking kind, but the listening kind. Coming to places like this and just... being still before God." He glanced toward the distant mountains. "I think sometimes God speaks loudest in silence, when we finally stop talking long enough to hear Him."

"'Be still and know that I am God,'" Sophie quoted softly. "My grandmother used to say God's whispers are easier to hear when we stop shouting our own demands."

"Wise woman, your grandmother."

"The wisest." Sophie hesitated, then added, "I still talk to her sometimes, in my prayers. Ask what she would do in certain situations."

"What would she think of all this?" Luke asked, gesturing to encompass the meadow, the plane, the picnic—perhaps even the two of them together.

Sophie considered the question honestly. "She'd love it. The ranch, the community, and the purpose of it all." She met his eyes directly. "She would have liked you to, I believe."

They finished their meal, conversation flowing easily between topics—from ranch matters to childhood memories, from flying adventures to dreams for the future. Luke described a particularly challenging wildfire flight from the previous season, his hands unconsciously illustrating the story. Sophie shared a humorous tale about a stubborn mule she'd treated in veterinary school that had outsmarted three experienced professors.

When the food was gone, they walked along the pond's edge, discovering a family of ducks nestled in the reeds and a patch of wild strawberries growing in a sunny spot near the water.

"These are perfectly ripe," Sophie exclaimed, kneeling to examine the tiny red fruits.

Luke joined her, and they gathered a handful each. The sweet-tart burst of flavor on their tongues. A perfect natural dessert. Sophie laughed as juice stained her fingers red, and Luke pulled a clean handkerchief from his pocket to offer her.

"Very gallant," she teased, accepting it with a smile. "Do all pilots carry handkerchiefs, or just the especially courteous ones?"

"Carter's influence," Luke admitted with a self-deprecating smile. "He insisted a gentleman always carries one. Said you never know when a lady might need it, or when you'll find wild strawberries that demand immediate attention."

"Smart man, your uncle," Sophie said, carefully cleaning her fingers.

"In most things," Luke agreed, his expression turning more thoughtful. "Though he once told me his biggest regret was that he never married and never had children of his own." He looked toward the plane. "Said he got so caught up in building the ranch and flying that he let love pass him by."

The confession carried weight beyond the simple words. Sophie sensed Luke wasn't just sharing Carter's regret, but acknowledging a path he himself might have been following..

"What about you?" she asked gently. "Any regrets so far?"

Luke was quiet for a long moment, his eyes on the distant mountains. "I think my biggest regret so far has been letting fear keep me from taking chances that matter. From trusting what God might be offering me."

The air between them seemed to shimmer with unspoken possibility. Sophie was acutely aware of their solitude in this hidden meadow, and of the way Luke's eyes held hers with growing intensity.

"Sophie," he said, her name carrying the weight of a question and a prayer.

"Yes?" Her pulse thrummed so loudly she was certain he could hear it.

Luke's hand rose to gently brush a strand of hair from her face, his touch whisper-light against her skin. "I know we said we'd just roll with this, see where God leads us. But I think we both know He's leading us somewhere... significant."

Sophie nodded, not trusting her voice for a moment.

"And that scares you," he observed, his hand still cupping her cheek with infinite tenderness.

"Not in the way you might think. I'm not afraid of you." She took a steadying breath. "I'm afraid of how right this feels. How natural and yet how unreal this all seems?"

"Sophie," Luke said softly, understanding flooding his expression.

"I promised myself I'd be more cautious, more guarded in my life," she continued. "But with you..."

"With me?" Luke prompted gently when she hesitated.

"With you, I feel safe enough to not be guarded," Sophie finished. "And that's terrifying and wonderful all at once."

Luke's smile bloomed slowly, transforming his features with joy. "I know exactly what you mean."

He leaned forward slowly, pausing just before their lips met—a silent question, a request for permission. Sophie answered by closing the final distance between them, her heart soaring as their lips touched for the first time.

The kiss was gentle at first, a tentative exploration that quickly deepened as Sophie's hand rose to rest against his chest, feeling his heartbeat accelerate beneath her palm. Luke's arm circled her waist, drawing her closer as the kiss continued. Neither was willing to break this first, perfect connection that felt like both discovery and home-coming.

When they finally parted, Sophie kept her eyes closed for an extra moment, memorizing the sensation—the softness of his lips, the warmth of his breath, the security of his embrace, the rightness of it all.

"That was…" Luke began, then chuckled softly. "I'm not sure there are words for what that was."

Sophie opened her eyes to find him watching her with such tenderness it made her heart flip in her chest. "I don't think we need words for everything."

He rested his forehead against hers, their breath mingling in the small space between them. "I've wanted to do that since the day I met you in the barn."

Sophie laughed softly, joy bubbling up from deep within her chest. "Even when I was barking orders at you?"

"Especially then," Luke confirmed, his eyes crinkling at the corners. "You were magnificent with Moonbeam. Fearless. Completely in your element. It was the moment I knew you were special."

"So are you," Sophie replied, glancing toward the plane. "Up here, flying, sharing this sacred place. I've never seen a person more at peace with who they are."

Luke nodded, acknowledging the truth in her observation. "Flying grounds me, as contradictory as that sounds. Helps me remember what matters." His arms tightened slightly around her. "What matters most isn't always what I thought it would be."

In the distance, a cloud shadow raced across the valley, followed by golden light that illuminated the meadow in waves of beauty that took Sophie's breath away. The wind picked up slightly, carrying the scent of pine and wild grass around them like a blessing.

"Weather's shifting," Luke noted, his pilot's instincts never fully dormant. "We should probably head back in case those clouds build into something more serious."

Sophie nodded, though she was reluctant to leave this perfect, private moment suspended between earth and sky. "Can we come back here? Soon?"

"Whenever you'd like," Luke agreed, his smile promising future adventures. "Carter's Meadow isn't going anywhere. And neither am I."

"And one other thing... no more counting down the days either," Sophie said firmly. "It feels like we're putting an artificial end to something that's just beginning to bloom."

"Agreed," Luke said, his eyes warm with promise. "Now let's pack up. I want to show you what a Montana sunset looks like from the air."

They gathered their picnic items and returned to the plane, working together to secure everything for the flight home. As Luke conducted his pre-flight checks, Sophie watched him with new eyes—appreciating the competent movements of his hands, the focus in his expression, and the quiet confidence that defined him in this element.

When they were seated and buckled in, headsets in place, Luke turned to her before starting the engine.

"Ready?" he asked.

Sophie smiled, reaching across the space between their seats to briefly squeeze his hand. "Ready for whatever God has planned for us."

Chapter 17

"Twenty pounds of the protein supplement," Sophie called out, marking the clipboard with a quick check. "That'll last what—two weeks for the broodmares?"

Luke nodded, hefting a bag of electrolytes onto the stack they'd been inventorying. "About that. Though with the heat we've been having, they go through electrolytes faster."

"Better add another bag to be safe," Ray suggested from where he was counting medical supplies. The ranch foreman squinted at a nearly empty bottle of injectable antibiotic. "And we're running low on penicillin."

Sophie added it to her growing list. The three of them had been working for the past hour, taking inventory of everything from feed supplements to fencing materials—a task that felt both mundane and essential to her growing understanding of ranch operations.

"Copper supplement?" she asked, moving to the next bin. "Levels look low."

"Good catch," Luke said, coming to stand beside her. His shoulder brushed against hers as he peered into the bin, and Sophie felt a small jolt of awareness at the contact. Even after their kiss yesterday at Carter's Meadow, every touch still carried that electric current of newness.

"The soil in the north pastures is copper deficient," Luke continued, his voice professional, but his eyes warming when they met hers. "I always supplement to prevent deficiencies. Twenty pounds should do it. Abigail usually carries the brand we prefer at the Rusty Spur, but if she's out, we may have to drive to the next town over."

"Speaking of which," Ray interjected, closing the medical cabinet with a metallic clang, "when are you two heading into town?"

"I was thinking we could leave around ten? That would give us time to finish up here and still get back before the afternoon chores."

"Works for me," Luke agreed, moving to count the remaining boxes of fence staples in a nearby bin. "We can grab lunch at the Bluebird after we hit the feed store. Lily's Friday special is worth the stop."

"The roast beef sandwich?" Ray asked, perking up with obvious interest. "I might have to tag along just for that."

Sophie laughed, enjoying the easy camaraderie between them. "Come with us, Ray. An extra set of hands will make loading all this faster."

Luke came over to review her clipboard, standing close enough that she could smell the clean scent of his soap mingled with leather and hay. "Let me see what we've got so far." His finger traced down the list, pausing occasionally. "Looks thorough. Abigail will be impressed with your first official supply run."

"Is there a secret handshake I should know about?" Sophie teased, acutely aware of his proximity and the way the morning light caught the flecks of gold in his brown eyes. "Some special rancher code to earn my official Riverbend Valley supply buyer badge?"

"Just don't let her upsell you on the deluxe horse brushes," Luke advised with mock seriousness that made her heart flutter. "They're the same as the regular ones, just with fancier packaging."

"Noted," Sophie replied, treasuring these moments of playful intimacy. "Any other insider tips?"

"Her seven-layer dip," Ray chimed in with religious fervor. "Sample it. It's not optional."

"That's actually legitimate advice," Luke agreed, his eyes crinkling at the corners in the way that made Sophie's pulse quicken. "She keeps it in a crock pot near the register. Local legend has it that three marriages and five business partnerships have resulted from conversations over that dip."

Sophie raised an eyebrow, charmed by the small-town folklore. "That's quite a dip."

"Magical properties," Ray insisted with complete seriousness. "My theory is she puts something special in it."

"Like what? Love potion?" Sophie asked, amused by his earnestness.

"Nah," Ray replied with a dismissive wave. "MSG, probably."

Their laughter echoed in the barn, startling a barn swallow that had been nesting in the rafters. The bird swooped low over their heads before darting out the open door into the bright morning.

Sophie finished counting the remaining bags of senior feed, making a note of the quantity. "Almost done here. Just need to check the horse treats, and then I think we'll have everything on the—"

A sharp electronic crackle cut through the air like a blade, followed by a static voice from the radio clipped to Luke's belt. *"All available units, we have a new start reported in Blacktail Canyon, east of Miller's*

Ridge. Coordinates to follow. Looks to be approximately five acres, moderate rate of spread in mixed conifer."

Luke unclipped the radio immediately, his entire demeanor shifting with practiced efficiency. The relaxed rancher vanished, replaced by the focused firefighter as he pressed the transmit button. "Dispatch, this is Harding. What's the resource status?"

The radio crackled again with urgency. "Engine crews responding, but air resources are limited. Palmer called in sick. Chief Roberts requesting you report to base ASAP for possible deployment."

"Copy that. ETA forty-five minutes. Harding out." Luke clipped the radio back to his belt and turned to Sophie, his expression apologetic but resolute. "They need me."

The abrupt shift left Sophie momentarily off-balance, the warm bubble of their morning routine suddenly shattered. One moment they'd been laughing about the magical dip, the next Luke was mentally already gone, preparing to fly into danger. The whiplash was jarring.

"Of course," she said, working to keep her voice even despite the sudden hollow feeling in her stomach. "Duty calls."

"I'm sorry about the supply run," Luke said, his eyes holding hers with genuine regret. "Rain check? I promise I'll make it up to you."

"Don't worry about it," Sophie assured him, forcing a smile that felt only slightly strained. "Fighting fires is slightly more important than buying supplies."

Luke's phone rang—a different ringtone than his usual one, sharp and urgent. He glanced at the screen with the focused attention she was learning to recognize as his emergency response mode. "It's Chief Roberts."

"Go. We've got things handled here." Sophie said, gesturing toward the door while fighting the urge to reach for his hand.

Luke answered the phone as he headed for the door, his voice shifting to that calm, professional tone she was starting to recognize as his "firefighter voice." "Chief... Understood... How bad is it?... He's out sick? Right, I see... Yes, sir, I can be there... Copy that. I'm on my way."

He ended the call and turned back to them.

"Be safe out there," Sophie said.

Luke's gaze lingered on her face for a moment longer than necessary. "I'll call when I get a chance."

He turned to Ray with the efficiency of a man accustomed to sudden departures. "Keep an eye on things."

"Always do," Ray replied with a nod that conveyed more than the casual words—an understanding between men who had worked together for years, who knew what was at stake when duty called.

Then he was gone. Sophie walked to the barn doorway, and watched as he climbed in, started the engine, and drove away, a plume of dust rising behind him like a miniature smoke column that somehow felt ominous.

"Well," Ray said, his voice gentle with understanding as he stood beside her, "duty calls. It's the life he's chosen. And a good thing for the rest of us that he answers it."

Sophie nodded, trying to process the whiplash of emotions coursing through her. She'd known Luke was a firefighter, of course. She'd known his job would take him away suddenly, put him in danger. But knowing it intellectually was different from experiencing it—the abrupt shift, the immediate prioritization of duty over personal plans, the uncertainty of when he'd return.

Is this what a future with him would look like? The thought whispered through her mind unbidden. Plans constantly interrupted, moments of connection severed by the call of duty, the underlying current of worry every time he left?

The pattern felt uncomfortably familiar, though she recognized immediately that this was different from Marcus's manipulations. Luke's reasons were noble, selfless, necessary. But the disruption to normal life, the sudden re-prioritizing of everything else...

"You okay there?" Ray asked quietly, his weathered face creased with concern.

Sophie straightened, pushing aside the spiral of worry. "Fine. Just... adjusting to the realities of his work, I guess."

"Takes some getting used to," Ray acknowledged. "That supply list won't fill itself. I'll go with you, if you like."

"That would be great, Ray. Thank you." Sophie drew a steadying breath, grateful for his practical support. "I appreciate it."

"Meet me by the ranch truck in twenty minutes," Ray said, his tone matter-of-fact and reassuring. "I need to check in with Gus about the irrigation schedule first."

As Ray headed toward the fields where Gus was working, Sophie took a moment to center herself. This was part of ranch life too—adapting to changing circumstances, carrying on with necessary tasks regardless of personal feelings, and finding strength in routine when emotions threatened to overwhelm.

She glanced in the direction Luke had driven, the dust already settled back to earth. *Lord, keep him safe,* she prayed silently; the words coming as naturally as breathing. *And help me trust in Your plan, even when I can't see where it's leading.*

Gathering her purse and the supply list from the tack room, Sophie pushed aside her disappointment and focused on the task ahead. The ranch needed supplies, and she was perfectly capable of handling the responsibility.

Even if she'd rather be doing it with Luke beside her.

****

"Sorry about that," Ray said, swerving to avoid another crater in the gravel road that led toward town. "County keeps promising to grade this stretch, but they're always behind schedule."

"No problem," Sophie replied, bracing herself against the dashboard as they hit another pothole. "It adds character to the journey."

Ray chuckled, his weathered hands steady on the steering wheel. "That's one way of looking at it. Luke usually takes the county road instead—smoother, but fifteen minutes longer."

They'd been on the road for about twenty minutes, the ranch buildings long since disappeared behind them. The landscape rolled by in a parade of golden fields punctuated by stands of pine, distant mountains framing the horizon like a picture postcard.

"Mind if I ask you something?" Ray said, breaking a comfortable silence that had allowed Sophie's mind to wander back to Luke's abrupt departure.

"Go ahead."

"You settling in, okay? Really settling in, I mean—not just the polite answer you'd give anyone who asked."

Sophie considered the question. "I am. It's been a learning curve, but a good one. Every day I feel more confident about what I'm doing."

Ray nodded, satisfied with her honesty. "Good. The boys and I were talking about it yesterday. You've got a natural way about you—with the animals, with the business side, and with all of us. Different from Luke's style, but effective in your own right. You seem to be fitting in just fine."

The compliment warmed her more than she'd expected. "That means a lot, coming from you. From all of you, really."

"Just calling it like I see it." Ray adjusted his grip on the steering wheel. "Carter would have approved, you know. He had an eye for character, and he would have seen what Luke saw in you right from the start."

Sophie glanced at Ray's weathered profile, struck by the affection in his voice. "You miss him."

"Every day," Ray admitted without embarrassment. "He was more than a boss. He was my friend and mentor. Taught me most of what I know about ranching and about being a man worth respecting. Luke too." He paused, his expression growing more serious. "It was hard on him when Carter passed. He lost Jake just a few weeks before Carter."

At the mention of Jake, Sophie's thoughts turned inevitably to Luke, out there right now fighting fire from the sky—the same element that had claimed his partner's life. "It shaped him, didn't it? Those losses."

"Shaped but didn't break him," Ray corrected with quiet conviction. "There's a difference. Some men get broken by loss and stay there. Turn bitter. Mean-spirited. Close themselves off completely. Not Luke. He just... went deeper into himself for a while. More careful with who he let in, more cautious about letting himself care too much."

The observation aligned with what Sophie had seen in Luke—his initial reserve; the gradual opening up, the careful way he'd approached their growing connection, as if he were handling something precious and fragile.

"He's different with you," Ray added, his tone casual but his words deliberate. "Lighter. More like his old self—the man he was before loss taught him to be so careful with his heart."

Sophie felt her cheeks warm, unsure how to respond to such direct insight. "I'm not sure what you mean."

Ray's knowing glance suggested he wasn't fooled by her diplomatic deflection. "Sure you do. And it's a good thing, in my book. That boy's been alone too long, carrying burdens that were never meant to be carried in alone." He paused, then added with gentle gruffness, "Just don't tell him I said so. Man's got enough of an ego when it comes to his flying."

The gentle teasing broke the emotional tension, and Sophie laughed despite her worries. "Your secret's safe with me."

"Speaking of secrets... when we get to the Rusty Spur, let me do the talking first. Abigail's known for interrogating newcomers, and you'll want to establish the right relationship from the start."

"I met her briefly at church," Sophie said, remembering the kind but sharp-eyed woman. "What kind of interrogation are we talking about?"

"Nothing sinister," Ray assured her quickly. "Just thorough. The woman's like a living newspaper. Wants to know everything about everybody, but not in a malicious way. She just... cares deeply about everyone in this valley. Problem is, she can be overwhelming if you're not prepared for the full Abigail experience."

Ray slowed as they approached the outskirts of Riverbend Valley, the scattered houses giving way to the more concentrated buildings of the town center. "Almost there. You ready for your official introduction to the real heart of ranching operations?"

"The feed store?" Sophie asked, amused by his dramatic buildup.

"Yes. Forget the land, the cattle, and the equipment. It's the feed store where the real business of ranching happens. Half gossip mill, half supply chain, all essential to making ranch life work."

Sophie laughed at his theatrical delivery, grateful for the distraction from her worry about Luke. "Lead on, then. I'm ready to be initiated into the mysteries of proper feed store etiquette."

They drove down Main Street, the small-town bustling with mid-morning activity. Unlike her previous visits, Sophie found herself noticing details with a more proprietary eye—mental notes about businesses she might frequent, community bulletin boards advertising events, the rhythm of small-town life that was becoming increasingly familiar and welcoming.

The Rusty Spur occupied a large metal building at the western end of Main Street, its wide loading doors propped open to the warm day. The parking lot contained a mix of trucks, many with horse trailers or flatbeds loaded with hay bales. A hand-painted sign above the entrance depicted a weathered spur, the name written in stylized western lettering that spoke of tradition and authenticity.

Ray parked the ranch truck near the entrance and turned to Sophie with a solemn expression that was only partially feigned. "Remember, let me introduce you properly. First impressions with Abigail set the tone for years to come."

"You're making me nervous," Sophie admitted, half-joking but aware that she genuinely wanted to make a good impression on this woman who was clearly a cornerstone of the community.

Ray climbed out of the truck with deliberate ceremony, and Sophie followed, smoothing her shirt and tucking the supply list into her pocket.

The interior of the Rusty Spur was a marvel of organized chaos that somehow made perfect sense. Aisles packed with feed bags, tack, fencing supplies, and ranching equipment created a maze that the locals navigated with easy familiarity. The air smelled of leather, grain, molasses-based feeds, and the distinctive rubber odor of new boots. Country music played softly from speakers mounted near the ceiling.

Behind a broad counter that dominated the front of the store, Abigail was deep in conversation with a customer about mineral block options for goats. She looked up as they approached, recognition lighting her intelligent face.

"Ray Jenkins. To what do I owe the pleasure?" Her gaze shifted to Sophie, shrewd but welcoming. "And Dr. Lawson. Welcome to my humble establishment."

Ray removed his hat with a courtly gesture that made Sophie smile. "Abigail Whitaker, I'd like to properly introduce Dr. Sophie Lawson, the new owner of Ironwood Creek Ranch. I believe you both met at church. Sophie, this is Abigail, proprietor of the finest feed and tack store in the area and keeper of all knowledge worth having in Riverbend Valley."

Abigail came around the counter with energetic strides, hand extended. Her grip was firm, her smile genuine and evaluating in equal measure. "This is your first visit to the Rusty Spur, Dr. Lawson, and that deserves special recognition."

"Call me Sophie, please."

"Where's Luke?" Abigail asked, glancing toward the door as if expecting him to materialize. "I thought he'd be the one showing you the ropes today."

"Fire call," Ray explained succinctly, his tone conveying both the routine nature of such interruptions and their inherent seriousness. "Got summoned just as we were finishing inventory this morning."

Understanding and concern flickered across Abigail's features. "I see. Well, we'll make do without him. Though he's better at reaching the high shelves than Ray here."

"I heard that," Ray protested.

Abigail winked at Sophie with conspiratorial warmth. "Come on back to my office. We need to set up your account properly. Ray, you know where everything is—go fetch whatever's on that list of yours while we handle some paperwork."

Ray nodded. "I'll be over in the agricultural supplies section if you need me, Sophie."

Abigail led Sophie to a small office tucked behind the counter. Unlike the organized chaos of the store, the office was meticulously arranged—files labeled with precise handwriting, a computer setup that looked surprisingly modern, and walls covered with framed photographs of local ranchers, community events, and landscapes that told the story of Riverbend Valley's history.

"Have a seat," Abigail offered, gesturing to a comfortable chair across from her desk. "Can I get you something to drink? Coffee? Water? Fresh lemonade?"

"I'm fine, thank you," Sophie replied, taking the offered seat.

"Well, I'm having coffee. It's my third cup, and I make no apologies for it." Abigail poured herself a mug from a pot that sat on a small table near her desk. "Now, then, let's get your account set up properly. Carter had excellent credit with us—never late, always ordered sensibly, treated our relationship as a true partnership. I assume you'll be continuing with the same purchasing patterns?"

"For the most part," Sophie confirmed, appreciating the implicit trust in the arrangement. "Though I might adjust some things as I learn more about what works best for the ranch."

"Sensible approach." Abigail pulled a form from a desk drawer with efficient movements. "I'll need some basic information. Business legal structure, tax ID, preferred payment methods. The usual boring but necessary details."

As Sophie provided the information, Abigail filled out the form with quick, neat handwriting. Despite the businesslike procedure, the older woman managed to weave in questions that went well beyond the paperwork's requirements.

"And how are you finding Riverbend Valley so far? Getting truly settled in, not just surviving the adjustment?"

"Yes, everyone's been incredibly welcoming," Sophie replied honestly. "It already feels more like home than Seattle ever did."

"Seattle..." Abigail repeated thoughtfully, her pen pausing momentarily. "That's quite an adjustment, coming from a city that size to our little corner of Montana."

"In the best possible way," Sophie assured her. "I grew up on a ranch in Colorado, so this feels more like coming home than starting over. The city never really suited me."

"Colorado? Whereabouts?"

"Near Durango. My grandparents owned a ranch there—nothing as large as Ironwood Creek, but similar in spirit."

They finished the paperwork, and Abigail stood with purposeful energy. "Now, let's get to the fun part—your first official Rusty Spur shopping expedition. You have a list too, I presume?"

Sophie produced the inventory list from her pocket, noting how it had become slightly crumpled during the morning's events. "Right here. Pretty comprehensive, I think."

Abigail scanned it quickly with experienced eyes. "Good, thorough. Luke's influence, I imagine. That boy never misses a detail when it comes to animal care." She handed it back with an approving nod. "Well, let's get started. And while we shop, you can tell me how you're adjusting to ranch life. And to Luke's teaching style. He can be quite... intense when he's explaining things he cares about."

The knowing glint in Abigail's eye suggested she might be fishing for more information than her casual inquiry implied. Sophie felt a momentary flush, but kept her expression diplomatically neutral. "He's been an excellent teacher. Very thorough and patient."

"Mmm-hmm," Abigail hummed, clearly unconvinced by Sophie's carefully neutral response. "I've known that boy since he was a little thing... following Carter all over this store. Watched him grow up, suffer through losses that would break most people, and somehow keep his faith and his heart intact. He deserves happiness, that one."

The directness of the statement caught Sophie completely off guard. "I—yes, he does."

Abigail patted her arm with maternal warmth. "Don't worry, dear. I'm not prying. Much. It's just my way—ask anyone in town. I meddle because I care, and because I'm surprisingly good at it." Her expression softened with genuine affection. "And because I've seen too many good people miss opportunities for joy because they were afraid to reach for it."

Before Sophie could formulate a response to such a pointed observation, Abigail was moving briskly toward the aisles with renewed purpose. "Now, let's start with your feed supplements. I've got that copper supplement Luke prefers over here. And while we're at it, let me show you the new joint supplement that's working wonders for aging performance horses. Might be perfect for some of those older broodmares on your ranch..."

For the next hour, Sophie followed Abigail through the store, filling her cart with items from the list while being introduced to every product line, specialty item, and new arrival that might benefit Ironwood Creek. The older woman's knowledge was encyclopedic, her recommendations thoughtful and specifically tailored to Sophie's needs and circumstances.

Along the way, they encountered other ranchers and townspeople, each of whom Abigail introduced to Sophie with genuine warmth and obvious pride. "This is Sophie Lawson, the new owner of Ironwood Creek Ranch—and yes, she's every bit as competent as she looks, so don't try to pull any fast ones on her."

The introductions were invariably followed by comments about how pleased everyone was that Ironwood Creek would continue as a working ranch, and sometimes subtle inquiries about Luke that Sophie deflected with growing skill and good humor.

As they approached the counter with the loaded cart, Abigail gestured to a slow cooker set up on a small table nearby, surrounded by a basket of tortilla chips. "Take yourself a bite... its sacred tradition around here."

Sophie laughed, remembering Ray's earlier comments about the dip's legendary properties. "I've heard about this famous creation. Apparently, it has magical properties?"

"Complete nonsense," Abigail dismissed with a theatrical wave, though her eyes twinkled with mischief. "Just good seasoning and fresh ingredients. Nothing magical about bringing people together over excellent food."

She handed Sophie a tortilla chip laden with the aromatic dip. Sophie took a bite and immediately understood the reputation—the flavors melded perfectly, savory and rich without being overwhelming, with layers of taste that revealed themselves gradually.

"This is incredible," she admitted with genuine appreciation. "What's your secret?"

"Family recipe," Abigail replied with exaggerated primness. "Though I might be persuaded to share it someday, under the right circumstances."

Before Sophie could ask what those circumstances might be, the store's door opened and Ray entered, carrying a clipboard. "The boys on the loading dock are gathering the feed bags. You about finished here, Sophie?"

"Almost," she replied. "Just need to check out and load everything up."

As Abigail rang up their purchases, Sophie's phone buzzed with an incoming text. Her heart jumped when she saw Luke's name on the screen, relief flooding through her.

Should be back by evening. How's Abigail treating you?

Sophie smiled.

Learning all about the magical seven-layer dip. Stay safe out there.

His response came quickly: *Good. And Sophie? Rain check on our supply run. Promise I'll make it up to you. Lunch definitely included.*

"Good news?" Abigail asked, noting Sophie's expression as she put the phone away.

"Just Luke checking in," Sophie replied. "He's on the fire line now."

Abigail nodded. "He'll be careful. He always is. Carter raised him right." She finished bagging the smaller items with efficient movements. "Now, Ray, you go on and back the truck up to the loading dock for those feed bags. Sophie, while he's doing that, let me show you our new veterinary supplies that just came in."

As Ray headed out to move the truck, Abigail led Sophie to a well-organized display of equine medical supplies. "Luke mentioned you might be thinking of establishing a limited practice alongside running the ranch. These new portable ultrasound units are game-changers for field work."

"He talked to you about that?" Sophie asked, touched and slightly surprised that he'd shared her professional aspirations.

"Not directly. I overheard him telling Rex Webster about your skills. He was quite impressed with your expertise." Abigail's expression grew more serious and businesslike. "This valley desperately needs a good large animal vet, especially one who understands ranch economics. Dr. Patterson is looking to retire within the next few years, and we've all been worried about who might step in."

Sophie examined the ultrasound unit, considering the possibilities. "I hadn't planned on jumping right back into practice immediately, but I have been talking with Dr. Patterson about maybe working with him one day a week, eventually."

"Smart approach," Abigail approved with obvious satisfaction. "And for what it's worth, having diverse income streams makes for a more stable ranch operation. Carter understood that principle. It's one of the reasons Ironwood Creek weathered economic downturns that sank other operations."

The practical advice resonated with Sophie's own thinking and planning. "Thanks, Abigail. I really appreciate the insight and the honesty."

"That's what the Rusty Spur is for," Abigail replied with a warm wink. "Feed, supplies, community gossip, and free advice—some of which is actually worth what you pay for it."

By the time they'd loaded the last of the supplies into the ranch truck, Sophie felt she'd passed some unspoken but important test. Abigail's parting words confirmed her impression.

"You come back anytime you need anything, Sophie Lawson. You're family around here now, and family takes care of family. My doors always open."

As Ray drove them back toward the ranch, Sophie gazed out at the Montana landscape rolling past—so different from Seattle's urban sprawl, yet increasingly familiar and beloved.

"Penny for your thoughts?" Ray asked, breaking the comfortable silence that had settled between them.

Sophie smiled, surprising herself with the certainty in her voice. "Just thinking that I made the right choice, moving here."

Ray nodded sagely, his weathered hands steady on the steering wheel. He glanced at the thin column of smoke visible on the distant horizon. "Luke will be back before dark, I expect. That fire doesn't look too ambitious from here."

"I'm not worried," Sophie said, surprising herself with the truth of it. Concerned, yes. But not the paralyzing worry she might have expected.

"Good," Ray replied with simple approval. "That's the first lesson in learning to love someone with a dangerous calling—worry just burns energy you can't spare. Better to put that energy into faith and useful work."

Chapter 18

"So you're sure about vaccinating and rotating the yearlings tomorrow instead of Monday?" Sophie asked, scraping the last bit of peach cobbler from her bowl. The sweet cinnamon aroma lingered in the evening air, mixing with the rich scent of coffee and the earthy fragrance of the ranch settling down for the night.

Ray nodded. "We've got a busy week ahead. It just makes sense to go ahead and get it done."

"Sounds good," Sophie agreed, making a note in her planner. "What about the vet check for Ember? Should we schedule that with Dr. Patterson, or would you prefer I handle it?"

"Keep Doc Patterson on for now," Ray advised thoughtfully. "You've got enough on your plate learning the ranch operations. Besides, he knows each of these animals personally."

The porch swing creaked gently as Sophie shifted, stretching her legs out before her. After the busy day and Luke's abrupt departure that morning, the evening quiet felt both well-earned and slightly hollow. Crickets had begun their nightly chorus, and in the distance, an owl called into the gathering twilight. The mountains stood as purple silhouettes against the darkening sky, the last light fading from their peaks like a benediction.

"This cobbler was really something," Ray said, patting his stomach contentedly. "My compliments to the chef."

"It's one of my grandmother's recipes," Sophie replied, pride warming her voice. "Pure comfort food, though I think I might have been heavy-handed with the cinnamon."

"No such thing as too much cinnamon," Ray countered, reaching for his coffee mug. "It's like bacon—always improves whatever it's added to."

Sophie laughed, then paused as the distinctive rumble of an approaching vehicle caught her attention. Headlights swept across the yard as a truck turned into the driveway, cutting through the settling darkness.

Her heart quickened, though she tried to maintain a casual demeanor for Ray's benefit. Relief flooded through her—he was safely home. "Looks like our firefighter's back."

Ray glanced toward the approaching vehicle, satisfaction evident in his weathered features. "Good. Means that fire's under control."

Luke parked near the house and cut the engine. When he stepped out, Sophie could see the evidence of his day written across his entire bearing, a bone-deep weariness in the set of his shoulders that hadn't been there that morning. Despite this, he smiled as he approached the porch.

"Evening, folks," he said, climbing the steps with movements that spoke of physical and emotional exhaustion. "Something smells good."

"Peach cobbler," Ray supplied with barely concealed glee. "But you're too late—we finished it off."

"That's just cruel," Luke replied good-naturedly, lowering himself into the empty seat beside Sophie with a soft groan of tired muscles. "Spent the day smelling nothing but smoke, and I come back to find you've eaten all the good stuff."

Sophie stood. "I saved you some. Let me grab it."

"You're a saint," Luke called after her as she headed inside.

Through the screen door, Sophie heard Ray asking about the fire as she moved to the kitchen. She retrieved the covered dish of cobbler from the counter, scooping out a generous portion into a fresh bowl, adding a dollop of vanilla ice cream. After a moment's thought, she poured a tall glass of cold milk as well—something told her Luke needed comfort as much as sustenance.

When she returned with the dessert and drink, Luke was describing the day's firefighting efforts to Ray with the methodical precision of someone who'd learned to compartmentalize danger.

"...wasn't massive, but the terrain made it tricky. Steep ravine, heavy fuel load, shifting winds that kept changing the game plan. We managed to establish a solid containment line before it could spread, though."

"Anyone else fly with you today?" Ray asked.

"Jenny Walsh was in the other SEAT plane. She's solid—a former Air Force pilot with nerves of steel. We worked well together." Luke accepted the bowl from Sophie with a grateful smile that made her heart flutter. "Thank you for this. And the milk—you read my mind."

"You're welcome." She said as she settled back into her spot on the swing.

"Oh man," he groaned, closing his eyes briefly in appreciation. "This is exactly what I needed. Like a hug in dessert form."

Sophie felt warmth bloom in her chest at his genuine pleasure in something she'd made. "My grandmother always said food was love made visible."

"Smart woman," Luke said, taking another bite with obvious relish. "This definitely qualifies as love."

"So you're on standby this weekend?" Ray asked, steering the conversation back to practical matters.

Luke nodded, washing down the cobbler with a long drink of milk. "Yeah, the fire danger's moderate right now—not extreme yet."

"Good to know," Ray said, satisfaction evident in his voice. "We could use your help with the yearling rotation tomorrow. Those young ones can be a handful when they get riled up."

"Count me in," Luke agreed without hesitation, scraping his bowl clean with the thoroughness of a genuinely hungry man. "What time?"

"First light," Ray answered, standing and stretching with the careful movements of someone whose joints had earned their protests. "Which means I should turn in. Morning comes early around here, and it waits for no one."

"That it does," Luke agreed, setting his empty bowl aside.

"Thanks for the cobbler, Sophie. The best I've had since my mama's, and that's saying something." He nodded to Luke. "Glad you made it back safe. See you both at sunrise."

As Ray descended the porch steps and headed toward the bunkhouse, his silhouette gradually swallowed by the darkness, Luke settled more comfortably in his chair.

"How was your day?" he asked, genuine interest in his voice.

"Abigail is... quite an interesting person," Sophie said, searching for the right words.

Luke chuckled, the sound rich and warm in the evening air. "That's putting it diplomatically. Did she interrogate you thoroughly?"

"Oh yes. Very thoroughly. I believe I passed inspection."

"If she fed you the seven-layer dip, you definitely passed," Luke assured her with obvious amusement.

"She did," Sophie laughed, remembering the older woman's knowing smile. "It was absolutely delicious."

"Told you." Luke leaned back in his chair, stretching out his long legs with a quiet sigh of relief. "Sorry again for abandoning you."

"It's fine. Really. I understand," Sophie said gently.

He studied her, the porch light casting shadows across his thoughtful expression. "Do you? Most people say that, but they don't really understand—the unpredictability, the dropped plans, the missed moments. The way duty has to come first, even when your heart's somewhere else."

Sophie paused, weighing her response, aware this wasn't just small talk.

"I'm learning," she said, holding his gaze. "Today was... eye-opening."

Luke's mouth curved into a half-smile. "That's one way to put it."

"I mean it," she said, setting her coffee mug on the table between them. "I've been thinking about it all day. Understanding something in theory is nothing like living it. I knew you were a firefighter. I knew it meant risk and uncertainty. But knowing and feeling—that's not the same."

He nodded slowly, a flicker of appreciation in his eyes. "Most people don't realize that until it's too late."

Sophie leaned forward slightly. Her voice was quiet, but steady. "I'm still learning. But I want to understand, Luke. I need to." She hesitated, then asked the question that had weighed on her all day.

"What will it actually look like—when you go full time with the Forest Service? How often will you be gone?"

Luke seemed to understand immediately that this wasn't idle curiosity. She was trying to glimpse the shape of a future with him, to understand what loving him would truly require.

"The position I've accepted is based in Kalispell. During fire season—May through October—I'll be on a seven-day rotation. Five days on, two off. On those five days, I'll be in Kalispell for twelve-hour shifts, ready to deploy at a moment's notice."

Sophie's brow furrowed. "Would you stay overnight at the base?"

He shook his head. "Not unless we're called out to a major fire in another region. That happens now and then. If we're deployed out of the area, I could be gone anywhere from a few days to a couple of weeks."

"Weeks," Sophie echoed softly, her mind already counting the cost.

"But those longer stints are rare," he added quickly, picking up on her worry. "Maybe once or twice a season—usually during the worst fire years."

"And the rest of the year? Outside of fire season?"

He nodded. "Much quieter. There's maintenance, training flights, and the occasional prescribed burn when conditions are right. Predictable hours. Fewer emergencies." He paused, then added with quiet honesty, "I'd have a lot more control over my schedule during those months."

Sophie nodded slowly, absorbing the reality he'd laid out—half the year lived on a knife's edge of constant readiness, danger, and sudden departures; the other half spent in quieter rhythms and steadier routines. It reminded her of ranch life in a way—seasonal demands, just with different stakes.

"Is it worth it to you?" she asked, her voice quiet but earnest. "The disruption, the risk, the toll it takes on relationships—what makes it worth that kind of sacrifice?"

Luke's expression shifted, the weariness in his features replaced by something sharper, more alive. His eyes held a quiet fire as he answered.

"When you're up there, fighting to keep a fire from swallowing someone's home—or their livestock, or their life—there's a clarity that's hard to put into words. Everything else falls away. In that moment, I know I'm doing exactly what God put me here to do." He paused, searching for words deeper than instinct. "That sense of purpose—of using every skill you've been given to protect what truly matters—it's... overwhelming, in the best way."

Sophie watched him closely, the conviction in his voice transforming his tired face. This wasn't just work to him—it was a calling. Woven into his bones. Essential.

"I understand that," she said softly, the truth of it settling in her chest. "It's how I feel about veterinary work. When you're in that moment—life or death—and you know what to do, and you can do it... there's nothing else like it."

Luke's face lit with recognition, his smile more real than it had been all night. "Exactly. You get it."

"That sense of calling—knowing you're doing what you were made to do—it's hard to explain."

"It is," he agreed. "After Jake died, and then Uncle Carter, I thought maybe I could settle into ranching. Stay grounded. Stay safe. But that pull... to serve, to be there when I'm needed most—it's part of me. I can't turn it off. It's as much a part of me as my faith."

"And the risk?" she said quietly. "How do you ask the people who love you to live with that fear, day after day?"

Luke didn't answer right away. He turned his gaze to the stars scattered above them like diamonds flung across black velvet. When he finally spoke, his voice was low, and full of the kind of truth that only comes from lived pain.

"I had to come to terms with the truth that safety's never guaranteed," Luke said at last. "Jake could've died crossing the street or falling off a horse. What I do is dangerous, yes. But hiding from risk isn't really living—it's just surviving in fear."

He turned back to her then, his eyes steady in the soft glow of the porch light, open in a way that made her breath catch.

"I fly as safely as I possibly can. I respect every protocol, follow every weather advisory, and take care of my aircraft like my life depends on it—because it does. I don't take foolish risks. I don't let pride get in the way of good judgment. But at the end of the day, Sophie... we're not in control. None of us are. We do our best and trust God with the rest."

His words struck something deep inside her, resonating with more than just logic. Wasn't that the heart of faith? Not blind trust, but deliberate surrender—loving deeply, preparing wisely, yet still placing the outcome in hands far greater than her own?

"That's a hard thing to live out," she admitted, her voice low. "Trusting like that. Letting go of control."

Luke nodded. "I'm still learning."

A quiet stretched between them, not awkward, but weighty. The porch swing creaked gently beneath them, and the soft chorus of crickets and wind through the trees filled the space with a grounded hush.

Sophie cleared her throat, her heart still catching up. "Your cabin's almost finished, right?"

Luke's face brightened, clearly grateful for the shift in topic. "Final inspections are Monday. If all goes well, I can start moving in on Tuesday."

"I'm willing to help you move your things."

"I'll take you up on that, and I appreciate the offer."

"Are you looking forward to having your own space again?"

"More than you know." His chuckle was filled with relief. "The guys at the bunkhouse have been great, but sharing a bathroom with five cowboys? I'm officially over it. Ray sheds more than a border collie."

Sophie laughed, the mental picture both horrifying and hilarious. "I really didn't need that image."

"Sorry," he said, not sounding sorry at all. "Anyway, Tuesday, if all goes well, I'll have my own place again. I only have a couple of truckloads of things to move. It shouldn't take long, and I'll make dinner. I can't promise anything fancy, but I grill a decent steak."

"I'd like that," she said, heart skipping.

"It's a date, then." His smile held a warmth that reached his eyes. "Speaking of which, I still owe you a rain check for our supply run. Want to try again next Friday? Morning at the feed store, lunch at the Bluebird, maybe even a movie in Kalispell?"

Sophie tilted her head, teasing. "Are you asking me on another official date, Luke Harding?"

"I believe I am, Dr. Lawson," he replied, the hint of nerves behind his charm only making it sweeter. "Though I can't promise my radio won't interrupt us again."

"I'll take that chance."

"I should probably head to the bunkhouse," Luke said, reluctant but practical. "Early morning with the yearlings—and I'm running on fumes."

He stood, then reached for Sophie's hand, gently drawing her to her feet. With unhurried tenderness, he cupped her cheek, his thumb brushing a quiet path across her skin.

"Thank you," he said softly.

Her breath caught. "For what?"

"For trying to understand this wild life I lead. For making me feel like coming home... is the best part of my day."

Luke leaned in and pressed a slow, reverent kiss to her forehead. The warmth of his breath lingered as he whispered, "Goodnight, Sophie."

She barely found her voice. "Goodnight, Luke."

She released his hand only when he stepped back, and she watched as he descended the porch steps. He paused once, halfway to his truck, glancing back at her through the hush of evening before disappearing into the dark.

Sophie remained on the porch, eyes fixed on the red glow of his taillights as they disappeared. Her fingers lifted, almost unconsciously, to the place where his lips had touched her skin—light as a promise, lasting as a prayer.

She sank slowly into the swing, the wooden slats creaking beneath her, her heart full of both wonder and worry. She was falling—deeply—for a man whose life would always carry the weight of risk, whose devotion to duty might sometimes pull him away, and whose steadfast faith in God's plan humbled and inspired her.

Chapter 19

"Hold him! Hold him there!" Luke called, his voice carrying across the morning air as the yearling reared, front hooves pawing skyward.

Sophie braced herself, tightening her grip on the lead rope while pressing her body against the corral fence. The young colt's eyes rolled white with alarm, nostrils flaring as he fought against the unfamiliar restraint.

"Easy, Thunder Junior," she murmured, keeping her voice steady despite the surge of adrenaline. "Nobody's going to hurt you."

Luke approached from the side, his movements deliberate and unhurried. "That's it. Keep him distracted."

The yearling snorted, stomping his front hoof against the packed earth as his attention swiveled between Sophie and Luke. Sweat darkened his chestnut coat along his neck and flanks, evidence of the twenty minutes they'd already spent trying to get him into position for Ray to check his hooves.

"Some days I think we should've named him Rebel instead of T.J.," Ray grumbled. "Takes after his daddy in all the wrong ways."

"He just needs to learn trust," Sophie countered, maintaining eye contact with the agitated colt. "Don't you, buddy? You just need to figure out we're on your side."

Luke had nearly reached the yearling's shoulder when his phone chimed with an incoming text. The unexpected sound sent T.J. surging backward, yanking the lead rope through Sophie's hands before she could regain her grip. The rough hemp burned her palms as the colt broke free, trotting triumphantly to the far side of the corral.

"Sorry about that," Luke said, grimacing as he pulled his phone from his pocket. "Should've silenced it."

Sophie flexed her stinging hands. "No harm done. We'll try again in a minute."

Luke glanced at his phone screen, his expression shifting to one of surprise and then dismay. "Oh no. I completely forgot."

"Forgot what?" Sophie asked, watching as T.J. settled into prancing circles around the perimeter of the corral, periodically tossing his head as if mocking their failed attempt.

"Katie and the kids are coming today." Luke ran a hand through his hair, leaving dusty streaks. "I can't believe I forgot. They come out to the ranch once a month—it's a standing thing we've done since Jake died."

"Katie? Jake's widow?" Sophie asked, processing this new information.

Luke nodded, his expression apologetic. "They'll be here around eleven. I completely lost track of the date with everything else going on."

Sophie glanced at her watch—just past eight. "That's fine. We have plenty of time to finish with the yearlings before they arrive."

"You don't mind?" Luke asked, studying her face.

"Why would I mind?" Sophie replied, though a small flutter of uncertainty stirred in her chest.

"It's just... I should have mentioned it earlier. They usually stay for lunch and the afternoon." Luke tucked his phone away, his eyes still on her.

"I think it's wonderful that you've stayed close with them. I'm excited to meet them."

The tension in his shoulders eased visibly. "Good, that's a relief. Katie's great, and the kids... well, they're special to me."

Ray cleared his throat from the fence line. "Not to interrupt, but we've still got four yearlings to check, including our escape artist, over there." He nodded toward T.J., who was now contentedly ripping at tufts of grass near the fence.

"Right," Luke said, refocusing. "Let's try a different approach. Sophie offer him the apple pieces. I'll come from behind while he's distracted."

They resumed their work, moving methodically through the yearling examinations. By ten-thirty, they'd successfully checked all five colts on schedule for today, administered their vaccines, and returned them to the pasture. The morning sun had intensified, bringing with it the distinctive heat of high summer, and Sophie's shirt clung to her back as they walked toward the ranch house.

"We should have time to clean up before they arrive," Luke said, checking his watch. "Katie always brings lunch, but I usually provide drinks and dessert."

"I have chocolate chip cookies in the freezer. I'll pull them out and defrost them in the microwave," Sophie offered. "There's plenty if you think the kids would like them."

"They'd love them," Luke replied with a grateful smile. "Emma has a serious sweet tooth. Michael's more reserved about everything, but he never turns down cookies."

"How old are they?"

"Emma's ten, going on thirty," Luke said with clear affection. "Full of energy and questions. Michael's twelve. Quieter, thoughtful. Looks more like Jake every time I see him." A flicker of sadness crossed his features before he continued. "They're good kids. Katie's done a wonderful job with them."

As they approached the house, Luke hesitated on the porch steps. "I should warn you... I don't know what to expect with this visit. Katie mentioned last month when she was here that she's started dating someone. A deacon from her church. It took me by surprise, and she was a nervous wreck about it."

"That's a big step."

Luke nodded. "It is. I think it's good, though. She deserves to be happy." He paused. "It's been two years since Jake died. Long enough that... well, life goes on, doesn't it?"

The question seemed directed as much at himself as at Sophie. She touched his arm lightly. "Yes, it does. And that's as it should be."

"Jake would want her to be happy," Luke said with quiet certainty.

They parted to shower and change before the visitors arrived. Sophie selected a light blue blouse that brought out her eyes and a pair of well-worn jeans, brushing her hair into loose waves that framed her face.

She joined Jake on her front porch as a blue SUV pulled up to the house. The driver's door opened, and a woman emerged—petite with honey-blonde hair pulled back in a simple ponytail, wearing jeans and a green top that complemented her hazel eyes. Even from a distance,

Sophie could see the warm smile that lit up her features as she spotted Luke.

The back doors of the SUV flew open, and two children tumbled out. Emma raced toward Luke with unrestrained enthusiasm, her blonde pigtails bouncing with each step. Michael followed more sedately, his dark hair and measured movements creating a striking contrast to his sister's exuberance.

"Uncle Luke!" Emma squealed, launching herself at him.

Luke caught her with ease, swinging her in a circle before setting her down. "There's my favorite cowgirl! You've grown at least a foot since last month."

"Only an inch," Emma corrected seriously. "Mom measured me on my birthday."

"Still growing like a weed," Luke replied, turning to the boy. "Hey, Michael. How's it going, buddy?"

Michael offered a small smile and a half-hug, his expression brightening slightly despite his reserved demeanor. "Good. I made the travel baseball team."

"That's fantastic!" Luke's enthusiasm was genuine. "Your dad would be so proud of that arm you're developing."

At the mention of his father, Michael's expression flickered between pride and sadness before settling on something more neutral. "Thanks."

Katie approached last, giving Luke a warm hug. "Sorry we're a few minutes late. Someone," she gave a pointed look at Emma, "couldn't decide which boots to wear."

"It's important, mom," Emma defended, crossing her arms.

Luke laughed, then turned toward Sophie, who had remained on the porch steps. "I want you all to meet someone special. This is Dr.

Sophie Lawson, the new owner of Ironwood Creek Ranch. Sophie, this is Katie Morrison and her children, Emma and Michael."

Sophie descended the steps, extending her hand to Katie. "It's wonderful to meet you."

Instead of taking her hand, Katie pulled her into a surprisingly strong hug. "So you're the famous Dr. Lawson! I'm so glad to finally get to meet you."

Warmth flooded Sophie's cheeks. "Nothing famous about me, I'm afraid."

"Are you really a horse doctor?" Emma piped up, regarding Sophie with undisguised curiosity.

"I am," Sophie confirmed. "I work with all kinds of large animals, but horses are my specialty."

Emma's eyes widened. "That's what I want to be when I grow up! A horse doctor. Or maybe an astronaut. I haven't decided yet."

"Both excellent choices," Sophie replied seriously, charmed by the girl's enthusiasm.

Michael hung back slightly, observing the exchange with watchful eyes. She turned to him with a gentle smile. "And you're a baseball player, Michael?"

The boy straightened slightly. "I'm a pitcher, mostly. Sometimes I play first base."

"Impressive," Sophie said. "I know nothing about baseball except that pitchers have the most important job on the field."

A glimmer of a smile touched Michael's lips. "Third basemen might disagree with you."

"Then they'd be wrong," Sophie replied with a conspiratorial wink that earned her a fuller smile.

Luke, who had been watching this exchange with clear pleasure, clapped his hands together. "How about we all head inside Sophie's house? Katie, what's for lunch?"

"Chicken salad sandwiches, pasta salad, and fresh strawberries," Katie confirmed. "Nothing fancy, but it travels well."

"I'll help you bring it in," Luke offered, and the two of them moved toward the car while Sophie led the children into the house.

Emma chattered continuously, asking questions about the ranch and the animals without waiting for complete answers before moving on to the next topic. Michael remained quieter but took everything in, his eyes lingering on the photographs of the ranch that decorated the walls.

"You live here now, with Uncle Luke?" Michael asked suddenly, turning to Sophie.

"No, this is my house now," Sophie explained. "I bought the ranch from Luke. He's living in the bunkhouse for now, but his cabin is almost done."

"Why? Why did Uncle Luke sell the ranch" Michael's direct question carried a hint of confusion.

Sophie considered her answer carefully. "I think... sometimes people need different things at different times in their lives. Luke wants to focus on his firefighting career, and I was looking for a place to build a new life. The timing worked out for both of us."

Michael absorbed this, his boyish face thoughtful. "Dad was a firefighter too. He flew planes like Uncle Luke."

"I know," Sophie said gently. "Luke has told me all about your dad. He sounds like he was an amazing person."

"He was," Michael said simply, his eyes dropping to the floor.

Emma, who had been exploring the living room, called out from across the room. "Is that a real saddle? Can I sit on it?"

Grateful for the interruption, Sophie moved to join Emma, who was pointing at an ornate western saddle displayed on a stand in the corner. "That was my grandfather's parade saddle. I think it would be okay for you to sit on it as long as you're careful."

Luke and Katie entered with a cooler just as Sophie was helping Emma into the saddle, the girl's face alight with delight.

"Already corrupting my daughter with horse fever," Katie observed with a laugh. "Be careful, Sophie. Once she gets started on horses, she doesn't stop."

"I think it's already too late for that," Luke commented. "Emma's been horse-crazy since she could walk."

"Just like her father," Katie said, a fond smile touching her lips.

They prepared lunch together, falling into a peaceful rhythm. Katie organized the food while Luke poured drinks and Sophie set the table. The children helped in their own ways—Emma enthusiastically but haphazardly arranging napkins, and Michael carefully placing silverware at each setting with precise movements.

When they gathered around the table, Luke bowed his head to offer grace. "Lord, we thank You for this food and the hands that prepared it. We're grateful for friendship, for memories that sustain us, and for new beginnings. Guide us today and always. Amen."

"Amen," the others echoed.

Conversation flowed easily over lunch, skimming across topics from church activities to ranch updates. Sophie found herself drawn into the familiar dynamic between Luke and the Morrison family, included naturally, as if she had always been part of these monthly gatherings.

"So, Emma," Sophie said as they finished their strawberries, "would you like to see a new foal? Moonbeam's baby is only a couple of weeks old now."

Emma's eyes widened. "Can I really? Mom, can I?"

Katie laughed. "Of course."

"Michael, you're welcome to join us," Sophie added, not wanting the boy to feel excluded.

Michael hesitated, glancing at Luke. "Actually... I wondered if we could throw the baseball around first. I brought my glove."

"Absolutely," Luke replied, his face lighting up. "I've been working on my catching. You'll probably strike me out in no time."

The natural division into pairs happened organically—Sophie and Emma heading toward the paddock to visit the horses, while Luke and Michael retrieved a baseball and gloves from the SUV.

As they walked through the sunlight-dappled barnyard, Emma skipping slightly ahead, Katie fell into step beside Sophie.

"Thank you for being so welcoming," Katie said. "This is a special tradition for the kids coming to the ranch. I wasn't sure how it would work with the change in ownership."

"I'm happy to continue it," Sophie assured her. "They seem like wonderful children, and it's obvious how much they mean to Luke."

Katie nodded, watching her daughter dart ahead toward the paddock fence. "Luke's been a godsend since Jake died. He's always there for birthdays, school events, whenever we've needed him. I don't know how we would have managed without him."

"I'm glad he could be someone special for you," Sophie said, a swell of admiration rising in her chest.

"It hasn't been easy for him either," Katie continued. "Losing Jake was like losing a brother. I think, in some ways, he's carried even more guilt than grief."

Sophie glanced toward where Luke and Michael were visible in the distance, tossing a baseball back and forth in the open area near the bunkhouse. "Because he survived?"

"Yes. Classic survivor's guilt." Katie sighed. "It's better now than it was, but for a long time, I think he felt he owed Jake something—as if being there for us was paying a debt."

"And now?" Sophie asked.

A small smile touched Katie's lips. "Now I think he's finally understanding that life isn't a zero-sum game. That finding happiness doesn't dishonor Jake's memory." She gave Sophie a meaningful glance. "You've been good for him."

Sophie felt her cheeks warm. "We haven't known each other very long."

"Sometimes time isn't the most important measure," Katie replied with quiet certainty.

They reached the paddock where Moonbeam and her foal were enjoying the morning sun; the mare grazing contentedly while her gangly offspring explored the perimeter of their enclosure.

Emma had pressed herself against the fence rails, eyes wide with wonder.

"She's beautiful," Emma breathed. "What's her name?"

"Serendipity, but we call her Sera for short."

"Can I pet her?"

"Let's see if they'll come over," Sophie suggested, reaching into her pocket for a couple of apple slices she'd brought along. She whistled softly, and Moonbeam's head lifted, ears pricking forward in recognition.

The mare ambled toward them, her foal trailing behind. Sophie handed an apple slice to Emma. "Hold it flat on your palm, like this."

Emma followed the instruction perfectly, her small hand steady as Moonbeam delicately took the treat from her palm. The girl's face blazed with joy at the contact.

"She likes me!" Emma whispered, as if afraid to break the spell.

"She does," Sophie said, offering an apple to the curious foal.

For the next twenty minutes, Sophie guided Emma through proper greeting and handling of the horses, impressed by the girl's natural affinity and careful attention to instructions.

"Emma has Jake's way with animals," Katie commented as the girl gently stroked Sera's neck. "Fearless but respectful."

"She's a natural," Sophie agreed. "Has she had much experience with horses?"

Katie shook her head. "Just these monthly visits and a few birthday pony rides. We live in a subdivision on the other side of town—no room for horses. But she's horse-crazy. Has been since she could talk."

"You know," Sophie said, an idea forming, "I'm planning to start a therapeutic riding program here at the ranch. Once it's established, I could always use volunteers who have a way with horses."

Emma overheard this and spun around, eyes wide. "Me? I could help with real horses?"

"I'm sure I could find something you would enjoy doing," Sophie said, laughing at the girl's exuberance. "If your mom approves, of course."

"Please, Mom!" Emma clasped her hands together in exaggerated pleading.

Katie smiled. "We'll see when the time comes. For now, let's just enjoy today's visit."

Luke and Michael approached from across the yard, the boy's face flushed with exertion and sporting a wider smile than Sophie had yet seen from him.

"How's the baseball star?" Katie called.

"Mom, I struck out Uncle Luke three times!" Michael announced proudly.

"My pitching arm isn't what it used to be," Luke added with a theatrical groan, rubbing his shoulder. "This kid's got a fastball that would make the pros jealous."

Michael beamed at the praise. "Can we go riding now? You promised last time we could try the north trail."

"Sure thing," Luke agreed, then glanced at Sophie. "Will you join us?"

"Of course," Sophie replied. "Sweetie would be perfect for Emma, and maybe Rusty for Michael?"

Luke nodded. "Good choices. Katie?"

Katie shook her head. "You know me and horses—mutual suspicion, at best. I'll stay behind and enjoy some quiet time on the porch with a book, if that's alright."

"The porch swing is all yours," Sophie assured her. "Make yourself at home. There's sweet tea and lemonade in the refrigerator. Coffee grounds are in the cabinet above the coffeemaker."

They spent the next half hour preparing for the ride—Luke and Sophie helping the children brush and saddle their mounts. Sophie was impressed by Michael's quiet competence around the horses, his initial reserve gradually melting as he focused on the task.

"You're good at this," she observed as he checked Rusty's girth strap with careful attention.

"Uncle Luke taught me," Michael replied, a note of pride in his voice. "He says always check twice because a loose saddle means a sore backside."

Sophie laughed. "He's absolutely right about that."

When they were ready, the four of them set out from the barn area, Luke leading on Buck with Michael beside him on Rusty, while Sophie and Emma followed on Sierra and Sweetie. The arrangement happened naturally—Michael gravitating toward Luke, Emma staying close to Sophie with continuous questions about the horses and ranch.

They rode at a leisurely pace, following a well-established trail that wound through a portion of the ranch property. The day had warmed considerably, but a gentle breeze kept the heat from becoming oppressive.

"Dr. Sophie?" Emma called from beside her. "Why are you a horse doctor?"

"I grew up on a ranch like this one," Sophie explained. "When I was about your age, there was a horse—a beautiful palomino mare—who wasn't feeling well. My grandfather, who was a veterinarian, helped her. I knew right then that's what I wanted to do."

"Did the horse get better?" Emma asked, eyes wide.

"She did. She lived another twelve years." Sophie smiled at the memory.

Emma's expression grew more serious. "Dad used to tell me stories about the horses he grew up with. He said animals know things people don't—like when storms are coming or when someone needs extra love." She patted Sweetie's neck affectionately. "I want to help horses the way they help us."

"That's a wonderful reason."

Ahead of them, Luke had stopped to point out something to Michael—a hawk's nest high in a pine tree. The boy watched intently as Luke explained about the different birds of prey that called the ranch home.

"Uncle Luke knows everything about the ranch," Emma commented proudly.

"He does," Sophie agreed. "He's teaching me all about it, too."

Emma studied her curiously. "Do you like Uncle Luke?"

The directness of the question made Sophie smile. "Yes, I like him very much."

"Good." Emma nodded decisively. "Mom says he's been sad for too long."

They followed the trail as it wound upward, eventually opening onto a natural plateau that provided a sweeping view of the valley below. The ranch buildings looked like a miniature scene from this height, nestled against the backdrop of distant mountains and azure sky.

"Wow," Michael breathed, the view momentarily breaking through his reserved demeanor.

"Pretty impressive, isn't it?" Luke said, dismounting and helping Michael down from Rusty. "Your dad and I used to race our horses to this spot when we were teenagers."

Michael walked to the edge of the plateau, gazing out at the panorama. "Dad talked about this place. He said it was where he decided he wanted to fly helicopters and planes."

Luke joined him, placing a gentle hand on the boy's shoulder. "That's right. We were about fifteen, and my Uncle Carter flew over while we were up here. Your dad watched it until it disappeared over those mountains, then turned to me and said, 'That's what I want to do—see everything from above.'"

Michael absorbed this piece of his father's history, his expression a mixture of sadness and pride. "I remember when he'd take me flying in the little plane. He let me hold the controls sometimes."

"He was a good pilot," Luke said. "The best I've ever known."

Sophie and Emma joined them at the viewpoint, the four of them standing in a line gazing out at the landscape spread before them. They stayed for nearly half an hour, Luke pointing out landmarks to the children while Sophie took photos of them with her cell phone against the spectacular backdrop. When they finally remounted and headed back toward the ranch, the conversation had shifted to lighter topics—summer activities, favorite movies, and Emma's upcoming dance recital.

Katie was waiting on the porch when they returned, a glass of lemonade beside her and a novel in her lap. She waved as they approached, marking her place in the book before coming to meet them at the corral.

"How was the ride?" she asked as Michael slid from Rusty's back.

"Awesome!" Emma exclaimed. "Dr. Sophie let me trot by myself, and I didn't even bounce!"

"Very impressive," Katie replied, helping her daughter remove her helmet. "Michael?"

"It was cool," the boy admitted with uncharacteristic animation. "We saw a hawk's nest and Uncle Luke showed us where Dad decided to learn how to fly."

A flash of surprise crossed Katie's face, followed by a warm smile directed at Luke. "Wow... well, it sounds like you all had a good time."

"We did," Luke confirmed.

Once the horses were brushed and turned out to their paddocks, they returned to the house for cookies and lemonade on the porch. The children settled on the steps with their treats. Emma regaling Michael with plans for what they would do on their next visit to the ranch.

"So," Katie said, her voice lowered, so the children couldn't overhear, "the therapeutic riding program you mentioned, Sophie... is that something you two are planning together?"

"It's Sophie's project," Luke clarified. "Part of her vision for the ranch's future, and I'll support her in whatever she does."

"But you think it's a good idea?" Katie pressed.

"I do," Luke admitted. "It fits the ranch perfectly, and Sophie has the skills to make it successful."

Katie smiled knowingly. "That's good. When you first told me you were selling the ranch, Luke, I worried you were cutting ties with everything here."

"Not everything," Luke said quietly, his eyes meeting Sophie's briefly. "Sophie owns the ranch. I'll help her whenever she needs me."

A comfortable lull fell in the conversation as they watched the children, who had moved to the grass, where Emma was attempting to teach Michael a complicated clapping game.

"I should tell you, Luke," Katie said finally, "that things with James—the man I mentioned I've been seeing—they're going well. Very well, actually." She twisted her hands slightly in her lap. "He's asked me to dinner this Sunday to meet his parents."

"That's wonderful, Katie," Luke said immediately, his expression genuinely pleased.

Katie nodded, a mixture of happiness and lingering uncertainty in her eyes. "He's a good man. Kind, patient with the kids, and his faith is strong. It's just..." She paused. "Sometimes I still feel guilty, like I'm betraying Jake by moving forward."

"You're not," Luke said firmly. "Jake would want you to be happy, Katie. You know that better than anyone."

"I do know it," she agreed. "Intellectually, at least. The heart takes longer to catch up sometimes." She looked directly at Luke. "You understand that better than most."

The knowing look that passed between them spoke volumes about shared grief and the complicated journey toward healing. Sophie felt privileged to witness this moment of honest vulnerability between two people bound by loss and love.

"Life has to be lived forward," Katie continued, her gaze encompassing both Luke and Sophie now. "Jake used to say that. 'You can look back to learn, but you have to live forward.'"

"Practical wisdom wrapped in a simple phrase," Luke said.

"I think he would be happy to see us all finding our way," Katie added.

Luke didn't respond directly, but his hand found Sophie's between their chairs, a gentle squeeze conveying what words could not.

The afternoon began to wane, shadows lengthening across the yard as the sun dipped toward the western mountains. Emma approached the porch, her energy finally flagging after the day's excitement.

"Mom, can Dr. Sophie show me her veterinary stuff?" she asked hopefully.

Katie checked her watch. "We should probably head home, sweetie."

"Please?" Emma persisted.

Sophie intervened gently. "I tell you what, Emma. Next time you visit, I'll have everything ready to show you. Maybe you can even help me with a check-up on one of the horses."

Emma's disappointment transformed instantly to excitement. "Really?"

"Really. If that's okay with your mom?"

Katie nodded. "That sounds like a perfect plan for next month's visit."

"Uncle Luke, will you still be here next month? Sophie said you're moving to a cabin."

"I'll absolutely be here," Luke assured him. "My new cabin is just on the other side of the ranch. You'll still see me every time you visit." He exchanged a quick glance with Sophie. "It's just a change in where I sleep."

The answer seemed to satisfy Michael, who nodded seriously. "Good. Because I want to show you my curveball next time."

They began the preparations for departure—gathering Emma's discarded sweater, Michael's baseball glove, and the empty containers from lunch.

Near the SUV, the goodbyes were warmly affectionate. Emma threw her arms around Sophie's waist in an impulsive hug. "Thank you for letting me ride Sweetie and meet the baby horse."

"You're very welcome," Sophie replied, touched by the child's open-hearted embrace. "I'll see you next month, okay?"

Michael offered his hand to Sophie with an endearing formality. "Thank you for having us at your ranch, Dr. Lawson."

"Sophie," she corrected gently, shaking his hand. "And this ranch will always welcome you, Michael."

The boy's solemn expression lightened slightly. "See you next time... Sophie."

Luke helped the children into the SUV, while Katie drew Sophie aside. "Thank you for today," she said quietly. "The kids had a wonderful time, and it means a lot to see Luke so... happy."

"He's a special man," Sophie said simply.

"Yes, he is." Katie squeezed her arm gently. "And he deserves someone who sees that. I'm glad he's found you, Sophie."

Katie moved to give Luke a hug. "Take care of yourself," she told him. "And don't be a stranger. You're always welcome to stop by our house. The kids miss their Uncle Luke when too much time passes."

"I'll come by for Michael's baseball game next week," Luke promised.

With the last waves and calls of goodbye, the Morrison family departed, the SUV kicking up a small cloud of dust as it moved down the driveway toward the main road. Luke and Sophie stood side by side, watching until the vehicle disappeared from view.

"They're wonderful," Sophie said as they turned back toward the house.

"They are," Luke agreed, his expression thoughtful. "I appreciate what you did today. For making them feel so welcome."

"It was my pleasure," Sophie replied honestly. "Emma's enthusiasm is contagious, and Michael—he reminds me of you, actually. Observing everything, taking it all in before he trusts."

Luke smiled at the comparison. "He's a lot like Jake was at that age, too. Careful and thoughtful. Emma's more like Katie—all energy and heart right on the surface."

They settled on the porch swing, the evening air cooling as the sun continued its descent. The day's activities had left a pleasant tiredness in Sophie's muscles, and the gentle motion of the swing was soothing.

"I'm sorry. I forgot they were coming today. I've gotten so caught up in everything going on around here, and their visit slipped my mind."

"I understand. Honestly... no harm done," Sophie assured him.

Luke nodded. "After Jake died, I promised myself I'd always be there for them." He paused. "It wasn't just for them, though. It was for me, too. A way to keep part of Jake alive."

"I get that. The kids love you, that's obvious, and Katie seems to be doing well," Sophie said. "Moving forward."

"She is. It's been a long road for her." Luke's hand found Sophie's, their fingers intertwining naturally. "Seeing her ready to open her heart again... it's encouraging. Life really has to be lived forward, like she said."

Sophie thought about her own journey—the painful ending in Seattle, the leap of faith in coming to Ironwood Creek, and the unexpected connection she'd found with Luke. Each step had been necessary, moving her forward even when the path ahead wasn't clear.

"What are you thinking?" Luke asked, watching her expression.

"About paths forward," Sophie replied. "How they're rarely straight or clear, but they lead where we need to go, anyway."

Luke squeezed her hand gently. "Deep thoughts for a Saturday evening."

"Blame it on the company I've been keeping," Sophie teased.

Luke's radio chirped from where it sat on the porch railing.

"Forecasting alert for all field personnel," came the static voice. *"Extended dry conditions predicted for the next ten days. Fire danger elevated to high across the north and western sectors. All units maintain readiness."*

The intrusion of reality didn't break the moment so much as frame it—a reminder of the life Luke had chosen, the responsibilities he carried, the larger world beyond the peaceful and happy bubble of the ranch.

"Always on call," Sophie said, not as a complaint but as an observation.

"Part of the job."

His radio silent once more. They remained on the porch as twilight deepened around them, the first stars appearing in the darkening sky.

Chapter 20

Sophie nearly dropped the box marked "Kitchen" when her hip bumped against the counter, sending glasses clinking against each other inside their newspaper wrappings.

"Everything okay in there?" Luke called from the front porch, where he was directing the furniture delivery men.

"All good," Sophie replied, exhaling. "Your glasses survived their first brush with danger."

She set the box on the granite countertop and took a moment to absorb the reality of Luke's finished cabin. Just a week ago, the place had been crawling with contractors, littered with construction materials, and echoing with the sounds of power tools. Now, the cabin stood complete.

The rumble of heavy footsteps announced the return of the delivery men, maneuvering a piece of the leather sectional sofa through the front door.

"A little to the left," Luke instructed, gesturing toward the wall opposite the fireplace. "That's perfect, right there."

Sophie watched as Luke navigated the furniture placement with the same precision he brought to everything—thoughtful, deliberate, with an eye for both function and harmony. The broad-shouldered delivery man and his wiry partner positioned the sofa pieces exactly where Luke indicated and connected each piece easily, having done this many times before.

"Coffee table... just set it here for now... I'll figure out where I want it later," Luke continued, as he read the delivery form.

"You've got quite the view here," one of the deliveryman commented, pausing to look through the picture window at the mountains rising majestically beyond the property. "Perfect spot for a home, that's for sure."

"That it is," Luke agreed, his eyes finding Sophie's across the room. The quiet pride in his expression made her heart flutter.

She turned back to washing and drying dishes, silverware, and glasses as she unpacked them. Then arranged everything on the open shelving above the sink. Through the kitchen window, her attention caught on something in the distance—a thin gray thread of smoke rising against the clear blue sky to the north.

When the delivery men headed back to their truck for the dining table, Sophie stepped out onto the front porch, where Luke stood reviewing the delivery manifest.

"Is that smoke?" she asked, nodding toward the horizon.

Luke followed her gaze. "Yeah. Started yesterday—dry lightning strike. My radio was active with updates most of the night."

"Should we be worried?" The thread of smoke seemed insignificant against the vast Montana sky, but Sophie had learned that wildfires were unpredictable and fast-moving.

"They've got crews on it. Nothing to worry about right now, but I'll keep monitoring." He squeezed her shoulder reassuringly.

For the next hour, he directed the placement of the rest of his new furniture—the reclaimed wood dining table and chairs, a chair and desk for the small office nook, a king-sized bed and matching nightstands for the bedroom, and a dresser that the delivery men nearly scratched maneuvering through the doorway.

"Sign here, please," the deliveryman said, offering Luke a digital tablet after they'd positioned the final piece. "Everything to your satisfaction?"

"Looks great," Luke confirmed, scrawling his signature. "Thanks for your help."

As the delivery truck rumbled down the gravel driveway, Sophie and Luke stood in the center of the living room, surveying the transformation. The furniture brought the space to life, making it feel more like a home.

"Now for the personal touches," Luke said, moving toward a stack of boxes near the door. "Though I'm realizing I don't have much in the way of decorations."

"Minimalist by nature?" Sophie teased.

"Practical," Luke corrected with a smile. "Never saw much point in collecting things just to dust them."

Sophie picked up a box labeled "Photos" and carried it to the coffee table. "Mind if I help with these?"

"Go ahead," Luke replied, already arranging books on the built-in shelves flanking the fireplace. "There's not many, but they're important ones."

Sophie opened the box. Inside, picture frames were wrapped in bubble wrap and old t-shirts for protection. She unwrapped the first frame, revealing a formal portrait of an older man wearing a bolo tie, his weathered face serious yet kind beneath a western hat. The resemblance to Luke was striking around the eyes.

"Is this your Uncle Carter?" She asked, holding up the photo.

Luke crossed to her side, taking the frame. "His official ranch portrait. Complained the whole time about having to wear that tie." He positioned the photo carefully on the mantel. "He said that no self-respecting rancher had any business wearing a tie of any kind, but the photographer insisted on it."

The next photo showed Luke and another man—Jake, she realized—standing before a small firefighting aircraft, both in flight suits with their arms slung around each other's shoulders. Their grins were wide, their posture relaxed but proud.

"Our first season as a team," Luke explained, his voice softening. "Jake had just qualified on the SEAT. I was technically his training officer, but we became partners almost immediately."

"You both look so young," Sophie observed, noting the lack of lines around Luke's eyes, and the unguarded joy in his expression.

"We were," Luke agreed, placing the photo beside Carter's on the mantel. "I think we were both around twenty-four in this picture."

The third frame contained a newspaper clipping and photo, protected under glass. "AERIAL FIREFIGHTER SAVES THREE IN JEFFERSON VALLEY BLAZE," the headline proclaimed. A younger Luke stood accepting an award, his expression uncomfortable with the recognition.

"They made a bigger deal of it than it was," Luke said, taking the frame from her hands. "Right place, right time."

"Three people might disagree," Sophie countered gently.

The last item wasn't a photograph, but a framed piece of calligraphy on parchment-colored paper. Sophie recognized the Bible verse immediately: "Have I not commanded you? Be strong and courageous. Do not be afraid; do not be discouraged, for the LORD your God will be with you wherever you go. Joshua 1:9."

The lettering was beautiful and clearly done by hand. Small ink flourishes decorated the corners, and the signature at the bottom read, "With love, Mom."

"This is beautiful," Sophie said, running her finger along the frame's edge.

Luke smiled as he took it from her. "Uncle Carter's mother, my grandmother, made this and gave it to him when he graduated from high school. He kept it in his office."

"Where will you put it?"

Luke considered the question. "Bedroom, I think. Good to see it first thing in the morning and last thing at night."

As they continued unpacking, Sophie felt privileged to witness these pieces of Luke's life finding their places in his new home—not leaving his past behind, but carrying forward what mattered most.

"Books go alphabetically by author?" she asked, kneeling beside a box of hardcovers.

"Actually, by subject," Luke replied. "Aviation on the top shelf, theology in the middle, history, and biography on the bottom. Then all the fiction in the bookcases in my bedroom."

Sophie raised an eyebrow. "Theology?"

"Carter's influence," Luke explained. "He was big on understanding what you believe and why. C.S. Lewis, Bonhoeffer, and more contemporary stuff too."

This glimpse into Luke's intellectual life added another layer to her understanding of him. The man who could fly through smoke and fire with steady nerves also spent quiet evenings pondering deeper questions of faith and meaning.

By late afternoon, they'd made significant progress. Books lined the shelves of the built-in bookcases in the living room, office, and bedroom. Kitchen essentials were organized in cabinets, and Luke's clothes hung in the bedroom closet. Empty boxes were flattened and stacked by the door.

"Enough unpacking for one day," Luke declared, surveying their work with satisfaction. "How about dinner? I picked up steaks yesterday."

"Sounds perfect," Sophie agreed, suddenly aware of her growling stomach. "What can I do to help?"

"The stove won't be delivered until Thursday, but I can grill steaks outside. There's a brand-new grill on the back deck calling my name. I've got potatoes, we can microwave, and maybe a salad?"

"Let's make this happen, Chef Harding, before I faint of hunger," Sophie replied with a smile.

They moved around the kitchen with surprising ease for the space being so new to both of them. Luke retrieved steaks from the refrigerator while Sophie washed potatoes and located the few utensils she'd already unpacked.

Sophie wrapped the potatoes in paper towels and placed them in the microwave, while Luke stepped onto the back porch to start the grill. Through the window, she watched him glance again toward the northern horizon. The smoke plume had widened since morning, though it still seemed distant.

When the potatoes were humming in the microwave, she joined him outside. The back porch offered an even more spectacular view than the front—miles of Montana wilderness stretching toward distant mountains.

Luke stood at the grill, his attention divided between the steaks and the northern horizon.

"Wind's shifted," he noted, his voice casual despite the slight furrow in his brow. "Coming more from the northeast now."

Sophie felt a chill. "Is that bad?"

"Not necessarily," Luke said, flipping a steak with practiced ease. "Just means the fire behavior might change. They've got good crews on it... no worries."

Sophie nodded, as her eyes lingered on the smoke. The life she was beginning to envision—with this man, in this place—came with built-in uncertainty. The wildfire on the horizon served as both a literal threat and a metaphor for the risks inherent in loving someone with such a dangerous calling.

When the steaks were ready, they brought them inside to the new dining table, which Luke had positioned to capture the mountain view through the window. The steaks were perfectly cooked. They ate with gusto, the physical work of moving and unpacking having sharpened their appetites.

"I was thinking about curtains for the bedroom," Luke said between bites. "Something that blocks the morning sun but isn't too heavy."

"Practical," Sophie teased. "Not even moved in a day and already solving problems."

"Occupational hazard," Luke replied with a smile.

The quiet domesticity of the moment—discussing curtains while sharing a meal—wrapped around Sophie like a warm quilt. This felt right. It felt like possibility.

The fire radio on the counter crackled to life.

"All available units, Blackwood Canyon fire has jumped containment lines on the northern perimeter. I repeat, fire has jumped containment. Immediate air support requested. Wind shift pushing toward Riverbend Creek watershed. Resources being diverted from the eastern sector. All off-duty pilots standby for immediate recall."

Luke was on his feet before the transmission ended, his expression completely transformed. The calm, teasing man of moments ago was replaced by the focused firefighter, already calculating and assessing.

His phone rang seconds later. "Harding," he answered, voice clipped. "Yes, sir. Understood. ETA on the helicopter? Copy that. I'll be ready."

He ended the call and turned to Sophie, his eyes apologetic but his movements already efficient. "Chief Roberts. The fire's broken containment, and it's moving fast. They need all available pilots. A helicopter is en route to pick me up—should be here in about ten minutes."

Sophie stood frozen, her mind struggling to process the abrupt shift. One minute they were discussing curtains, the next he was being deployed to fight a wildfire that had been a mere thread of smoke that morning.

"What can I do?" she asked, finding her voice.

"Nothing to do," Luke replied, already moving toward the door. "I have a go-bag in my truck. I always keep it ready."

Sophie followed him outside, watching as he retrieved a duffel bag and what appeared to be a flight suit from behind the truck seat. The efficiency of his movements spoke of long practice—this wasn't the first time he'd been called away suddenly, and it wouldn't be the last.

"How long will you be gone?" she asked.

Luke paused, his expression softening briefly as he looked at her. "Hard to say. It depends on the fire behavior and available resources. It could be overnight, could be a few days."

The distant thrum of helicopter rotors reached them, growing louder by the second.

"That's my ride," Luke said, zipping the duffel. "Earlier than expected."

The reality of the situation crashed over Sophie—the half-eaten dinner on the table, the boxes still waiting to be unpacked, and the plans for the evening dissolved in an instant.

"I'm sorry about dinner," Luke said, genuine regret in his voice. "And leaving you like this?"

"Don't apologize," Sophie replied. "This is your job. This is who you are. Don't worry, I'll put the food away and lock the house when I leave."

The helicopter sound grew louder, the wind from its approach already stirring the leaves in the surrounding trees.

Luke descended the porch steps. Sophie's heart hammered against her ribs.

He paused at the bottom step, turning back to her. In his eyes, she saw regret mingled with purpose—the look of a man torn between duty and desire.

"Sophie," he said, her name almost lost beneath the growing roar of the helicopter.

She closed the distance between them, wrapping her arms around his neck and pressing her lips to his. His free arm encircled her waist, holding her close for precious seconds before they separated.

"Be careful," she said, her eyes locked with his.

"Always am," he promised. "I'll call or text when I can."

Then he was running toward the helipad. The helicopter, painted Forest Service green, settled onto the concrete pad in a swirl of wind and noise. Luke ducked low, tossed his bag and uniform inside, and climbed aboard.

Within moments, the aircraft lifted, banked sharply north, and sped up toward the plume of smoke on the horizon. Sophie stood on the porch long after it disappeared from view.

Inside, their half-eaten dinner sat abandoned. Boxes waited to be unpacked. Life interrupted.

Sophie moved through the cabin, covering the leftover food and putting in the refrigerator. She washed and put away the dishes they had used. Her movements were mechanical, her mind elsewhere—following that helicopter, imagining Luke preparing to confront a wall of flames from the air.

Returning to the porch, Sophie sank onto one of the Adirondack chairs and gazed toward the north. The smoke was distinctly visible now, an ominous smudge against the twilight sky. The wind carried the faintest hint of burning pine.

The realization settled over her with quiet certainty, neither sudden nor surprising, but simply true: *I've fallen in love with him.*

It should have terrified her—falling for a man whose duty could summon him away at any moment, whose calling placed him in danger's path. After Marcus's betrayal, she'd promised herself caution and independence. Yet here she was, her heart already invested in a future that came with built-in uncertainty.

Chapter 21

"**S**teady...." Sophie said calmly, as she grappled with the agitated stallion, who snorted and sidled sideways in the barn aisle. His dark eyes rolled white with alarm, nostrils flaring at the scent of smoke that hung in the morning air.

Ray appeared at her side, quickly taking the lead rope. "Easy, Thunder. Easy now," he murmured.

Sophie stepped back as Ray guided the horse back to a stall. The animal's muscles quivered beneath his sleek coat, tension clear in every line of his body.

"He's not the only one on edge," Ray said, securing the stall door. "That smoke's got 'em all jumpy this morning."

Sophie nodded, pushing a stray lock of hair from her face. She'd been up since before dawn, feeling similar. The distant smoke plume had grown overnight, a gray-brown smudge marring the otherwise clear Montana sky. And no word from Luke since his abrupt departure yesterday.

"Ray," she said as the other ranch hands began filtering into the barn for the morning meeting, "assign me to work with the ranch hands today. I need to work. I need to keep busy."

Ray nodded. "Don't you worry. You stick with me today. We'll keep those hands of yours and your mind plenty busy."

"I appreciate it."

The other ranch hands gathered around, their faces showed varying degrees of alertness at the early hour, but all turned attentive as Ray cleared his throat.

"Morning, boys," Ray began, his voice carrying on the barn's acoustics. "As you might've noticed, we've got smoke coming in from the north. That Blackwood Canyon fire's grown overnight."

"Heard it jumped containment," Gus offered, sipping his coffee. "Radio said they're calling in crews from Idaho."

Ray nodded. "Luke got called up yesterday. The Forest Service sent a helicopter for him, so it's serious business. Which means we've got extra responsibility today. The smoke's likely to keep the horses on edge, and we need to make sure everything runs smooth... it's business as usual here on the ranch."

"Now, for today's assignments," Ray continued. "Gus and Ed, I want you to check those irrigation lines in the north pasture. That pump was making a noise yesterday, and with this heat and the fire to the north, we can't risk any field drying out or having any pumps not working. After that, you boys make rounds and keep checking the other pumps around the ranch. Keep all the water troughs filled. Dan, you're on fence patrol—ride the perimeter of the property and especially the northern edge, keep an eye on the smoke and if it seems to keep getting closer, radio me, and we'll start moving all the horses out of the northern pastures. Eric, you ride the pastures today. If any horses seem agitated or out of sorts... just bring them to one of the corrals or barns."

The men nodded, taking mental notes of their tasks.

"Doc, you'll be with me," Ray concluded, using the nickname the hands had begun applying to Sophie. "We've got stalls to clean, horses to groom, and that delivery of medical supplies coming later today."

The meeting broke up, men dispersing to their assigned tasks with minimal chatter. As they filed out, Ray moved to a shelf near the tack room and pulled down a dusty radio, brushing it off before setting it on a hay bale.

"Luke usually keeps this on during fire season," he explained, adjusting the dial until static gave way to a clear transmission. "Forest Service channel. It'll keep us in the loop while he's out there."

"Will we be able to hear what's happening at the fire?"

"Some... not specific enough to know exactly what Luke's doing, but general updates on the situation. Helps to know what we're dealing with here at home."

The radio crackled, then a female voice emerged with clinical precision: *"Blackwood Canyon Fire update, 0700 hours. Fire now estimated at 12,500 acres, forty percent contained. Sustained winds from northwest at 12 mph. Type 1 Incident Management Team, assuming command at 0800 hours."*

Ray adjusted the volume, leaving it as background while he gathered mucking tools. "Let's get to those stalls. Standing around won't make the day go any faster."

Sophie followed his lead, grateful for the physical work ahead. She pulled on work gloves and grabbed a pitchfork, following Ray down the center aisle to the first stall.

For the next two hours, they worked methodically through the barn, cleaning stalls and refreshing bedding. The repetitive labor provided exactly what Sophie needed—physical exertion that required focus but allowed her mind enough freedom to process her swirling emotions.

"You're quiet this morning," Ray observed as they moved to their sixth stall.

Sophie paused, leaning on her pitchfork. "Just worried, I guess. It happened so fast yesterday—one minute we were eating, the next he was gone."

"That's the nature of the job. Fire waits for no one."

"I know that in my head," Sophie admitted. "But experiencing... how fast everything happened yesterday. Ray... I'm talking about minutes from the time the radio call came in... the next thing I know, I'm watching a helicopter disappear with him in it."

"I'll never forget the day Katie experienced her first emergency call out," Ray said. "Back then, she and Jake were living here in the ranch house with Carter and Luke while their house was being built. The first time Jake got called out, she was a nervous wreck. We all watched that helicopter swoop in and pick Jake and Luke both up. Carter and I took the rest of the day off to sit with Miss Katie and keep her mind busy. We sat on the front porch listening to this very radio, while the kids toddled around in the yard. That was a tough day for her. She was a ball of nerves."

"But over time, it got easier on her?"

Ray straightened, considering. "I believe it did... somewhat. She developed routines. Ways to keep busy. Prayer helped her a lot. And having the kids to focus on." He tossed another forkful of hay. "Eventually, she learned to trust his training and experience. And to trust God with what she couldn't control."

The radio crackled again, drawing their attention: *"Aerial resources now operating on all divisions. VLAT requested for Division Charlie. Spot fires reported one mile south of the primary containment line."*

Sophie's hand tightened on the pitchfork. "What's VLAT?"

"Very Large Air Tanker," Ray explained. "Biggest planes they've got. Means the fire's making a serious push somewhere."

A knot formed in her stomach. "And Luke?"

"He'd be in a smaller plane—what they call a SEAT. Single Engine Air Tanker. More maneuverable in tight canyons." Ray's expression softened at her obvious concern. "Luke's good at what he does, Sophie. One of the best."

"Jake was good too," she said quietly.

Ray's movements stilled. After a moment, he set down his tools and turned to face her fully. "Yes, he was. And what happened to Jake was a terrible tragedy. But it was also extremely rare. The safety protocols they have—" He stopped, seeming to recognize the futility of statistics against fear. "Look, I've known Luke nearly his whole life. He's careful. Methodical. He respects the fire, and that's half the battle right there."

"I don't mean to be morbid. It's just... yesterday, seeing that helicopter come for him. That... that helicopter made it all real... really real."

"It's a lot to process," Ray acknowledged. "But you strike me as someone with a strong backbone. You'll find your way through this, same as Katie did. Same as all of us who care about someone with a dangerous calling. But if it makes you feel any better... I still get a bit worried every time they call Luke out. I consider him my son. There's nothing wrong with worry... just don't let it consume you."

"Now, come on," he continued, picking up his pitchfork again. "We got work to do. Rusty's stall looks like he hosted a party in there."

Sophie laughed as she followed Ray to the next stall. The gelding in question nickered a greeting, seemingly oblivious to his reputation as the messiest resident of the barn.

They fell back into their rhythm, the physical labor grounding Sophie as the morning progressed. Occasionally, the radio would offer updates—technical information about fire lines, resource deployments, and weather conditions that meant little to Sophie.

By late morning, they'd finished the stalls and moved on to grooming the horses kept in the main barn. Sophie worked methodically on Sierra, the mare standing patiently as the curry comb moved in circular motions across her coat.

"Fire behavior increasing on the east flank," the radio announced. *"All air operations temporarily suspended in Divisions Alpha and Bravo due to visibility issues. Ground crews establishing contingency lines."*

Sophie's hand faltered mid-stroke. "Suspended operations... is that bad?"

"Not unusual," Ray assured her, though his brow furrowed slightly. "Sometimes the smoke gets too thick for safe flying. They'll wait for a window of better visibility."

Sierra sensed Sophie's tension, shifting restlessly. Sophie forced herself to breathe deeply, resuming the rhythmic grooming. "Sorry, girl," she murmured to the mare. "Not your fault. I'm on edge today."

Ray finished with Buck, patting the gelding's neck before leading him back to his stall. "Why don't we head up to the bunkhouse? I put fixin's' for chili in the crock pot this morning."

"Sounds good."

In the bunkhouse kitchen, the rich aroma of beef, beans, and spices filled the air, momentarily displacing the faint smell of smoke that had permeated everything outdoors.

"Want to eat on the porch?" Ray suggested, ladling generous portions into bowls. "We can bring a radio out there."

Sophie nodded, grabbing a sleeve of crackers and two glasses of iced tea. They settled on the porch, the radio placed on the small table between them. The view from the bunkhouse porch encompassed a good portion of the ranch—fields stretching toward distant tree lines, horses grazing in the nearest paddock, and to the north, that persistent smudge of smoke, now darker and more defined against the blue sky.

"Looks bigger," Sophie observed between bites of chili.

Ray nodded, following her gaze. "The wind shifted more in our direction. That's mostly what we're seeing—the column being pushed this way. Doesn't necessarily mean the fire itself is growing toward us."

"All units be advised, rapid crown fire behavior observed in Division Delta. Immediate pullback of all ground personnel to safety zones. Air attack, requesting additional resources for structure protection along County Road 27."

Ray's spoon paused halfway to his mouth. He set his bowl down, giving the radio his full attention.

"What does that mean?" Sophie asked, tension crawling up her spine at Ray's reaction.

"Crown fire means it's running through the tops of the trees, not just along the ground," Ray explained, his expression grave. "Much more dangerous, harder to control. And they're pulling crews back, which means the fire's moving faster than expected."

Sophie set her bowl aside, appetite vanishing. "And Luke? Would he be in Division Delta?"

"No way to know," Ray admitted. "But if they're asking for more air resources for structure protection, he could be involved in that."

The thought of Luke flying through smoke-filled skies toward advancing flames sent a chill through Sophie despite the warm day. She tried to picture it—the small plane navigating through turbulent air, precision drops of fire retardant, and split-second decisions with lives and homes at stake.

"You're thinking too much. Eat. The day's only half done, and you need the energy."

Sophie made an effort to take another spoonful of chili, though it tasted like ash in her mouth. "I don't like this waiting, and the not knowing?"

Ray's eyes held a lifetime of understanding. "You'll get better at carrying it. Faith is stronger than fear... remember that."

Chapter 22

"*Mayday, Mayday, Mayday. SEAT Tango-Seven-Four declaring emergency. Engine failure, preparing for emergency landing approximately two miles east of Division Charlie. Coordinates to follow.*"

Ray's face drained of color. Sophie's heart seemed to stop mid-beat.

"Is that—" she began, unable to complete the question.

Ray was already on his feet, moving closer to the radio as if proximity might yield more information. "I don't know Luke's call sign," he admitted, voice tight.

For several agonizing moments, they waited, the radio silent after the mayday call. Sophie's mind raced with terrifying images—a plane falling from the sky, smoke and flames, wreckage in remote terrain.

When the radio finally crackled again, it was with clinical efficiency: "*All units, SEAT Tango-Seven-Four down. Visual confirmation of intact aircraft. Ground team en route to landing site. Pilot status unknown at this time.*"

"Unknown," Sophie repeated, the word hollow in her mouth. She gripped the porch railing, suddenly needing its support.

Ray placed a steadying hand on her shoulder. "Easy now. 'Intact aircraft' is good news. It means it's down in one piece."

"But we don't even know if it's Luke," Sophie said. "And even if it's not, someone is down out there. Someone's family is going to get that call."

Ray nodded gravely. "Nature of the job. All we can do now is wait for more information and pray."

Prayer.

Throughout the morning, she'd been so focused on her fear, on practical details, and on distracting herself, that she'd neglected the one thing that might actually help.

She closed her eyes and prayed. "Lord, keep them safe. Guide them home. Give us all strength for whatever comes."

When she opened her eyes, Ray was watching her. "Faith looks good on you, Doc."

A small smile touched her lips, despite the circumstances. "My grandmother used to say prayer isn't about changing God's mind—it's about changing our hearts to align with His."

"My mama used to say worrying is like rocking in a rocking chair—gives you something to do, but doesn't get you anywhere. Pray about it—that's the only way to set the worry down."

The homespun wisdom brought a genuine smile to Sophie's face. She glanced at her watch, surprised to find it was already past one o'clock. "We should probably get back to work. Those medical supplies will be arriving soon."

Ray nodded, gathering their lunch dishes. "Best thing for worry is keeping those hands busy, Doc."

They returned to the barn and worked side by side on saddle maintenance. The radio offered no further information about the downed aircraft, though regular fire updates continued—technical details about equipment deployments, weather conditions, and containment strategies. Each time the static broke, Sophie's heart would jump, hoping for news.

Mid-afternoon, the delivery truck arrived with the veterinary supplies. Sophie welcomed the distraction, carefully checking each item against her order form—vaccines, antibiotics, bandaging materials, and the specialized supplements for the broodmares.

As she organized the new supplies in the medical cabinet, she nearly dropped the bottle of iodine she was holding when Ray appeared in the doorway, radio in hand.

"—confirmation that SEAT Tango-Seven-Four pilot is conscious and communicating with ground crew. Extraction team at the landing site. No fire activity in the immediate vicinity at this time."

Relief flooded through Sophie. "Conscious and communicating," she repeated. "That's good."

"Very good," Ray confirmed, his own relief evident. "Means whoever it is, they're alive and alert enough to talk."

Around four o'clock, the radio announced that the downed pilot had been successfully extracted and was being transported to a medical facility for evaluation. Still, no identification was provided.

By five, with evening chores beginning, Sophie's nerves were frayed from the prolonged uncertainty. She had just finished medicating Clover's hoof when her phone rang—not a text this time, but an actual call.

She fumbled it from her pocket, not recognizing the number on the screen. "Hello?"

"Sophie?" Luke's voice, slightly rough but unmistakably his, filled her ear.

"Luke!" She gripped the phone tighter, closing her eyes in overwhelming relief. "Are you okay? We heard about a plane going down. Was that you?"

"No, not me," he assured her quickly. "It was Jenny Walsh—she's a SEAT pilot too. Engine failure over the eastern section. She managed an incredible landing in a small clearing. She's going to be fine—some bruising from the harness, a possible concussion. She's one tough pilot."

Sophie sagged against the stall door, knees weak with relief. "Thank God," she breathed. "We've been worried sick all day."

"I couldn't get to a phone until now. The fire's pushing hard on multiple fronts, and we've been flying non-stop since dawn."

"Are you safe?" Sophie asked, the question encompassing far more than the immediate moment.

"I'm safe," Luke assured her. "Tired, but safe. I'm at the incident command post. Grounded for right now, ordered to take a 4-hour rest."

"How bad is it? The fire?"

Luke sighed, the sound conveying exhaustion beyond mere physical fatigue. "It's serious. About 14,000 acres now, and the containment percentage is rising. They've evacuated a one small community as a precaution. The weather's not helping—hot, dry, and the wind keeps shifting. They're bringing in more resources, but with Jenny's plane down, we're short on air support, so more out-of-state help is being brought in. I'll be here at least through tomorrow, possibly longer."

The reality of his dangerous profession settled more firmly around Sophie's shoulders.

"Are you okay?" He asked.

"Yes… yes, I'm fine. Ray and I have been working together all day. We've been listening to the radio as well."

"Ray's a good man," Luke said, warmth in his voice despite his evident fatigue. "Sophie, I need to go—they're calling a briefing for tonight's operations, and then I need to sleep for a few hours. But I wanted you to know I'm okay, and I'm thinking of you."

"I'm thinking of you, too. Be careful up there, Luke."

"Always am. I'll call when I can. And Sophie?"

"Yes?"

"All you can do is pray. Remember that."

"I can do that… stay safe."

"I promise, I'll do my best."

After they disconnected, Sophie stood for a moment in the quiet barn, phone still clutched in her hand. The relief of hearing Luke's voice warred with the continued concern for his safety in the days ahead.

Ray appeared in the doorway, his look questioning.

"It wasn't Luke's plane that went down," she told him. "It was another pilot—Jenny Walsh. Luke says she'll be okay."

"Good news. And Luke, how's he holdin' up?"

"He's going to rest for a few hours. He expects to be there at least through tomorrow, probably longer." She slipped her phone back into her pocket.

"We'll keep that radio on," Ray said simply. "And we'll keep praying."

As the evening progressed, Sophie found herself settling into a strange new normal—concern humming beneath everyday actions, prayers interspersed with practical tasks, and one ear always alert for the radio.

After the evening chores were complete, Sophie returned to the quiet of the main house. The day's emotional roller coaster had left her physically and mentally drained. She made a simple sandwich for dinner, lacking the energy for anything more elaborate, and carried it to the porch along with the radio, which Ray had insisted she take for the night.

Chapter 23

"Easy there, Doc! You're gonna wear out that pitchfork before lunchtime." Ray called from across the barn aisle, watching as Sophie attacked the straw bedding in Sweetie's stall with unnecessary force.

Sophie paused mid-jab, realizing she'd been driving the pitchfork into the packed bedding as if it had personally wronged her. Sweat trickled down her temple despite the relative coolness of the morning. "Sorry. Just being thorough."

"Thorough is one thing. Trying to stab straight through to China is another." Ray's weathered face softened with understanding.

Sophie exhaled, consciously loosening her white-knuckled grip on the wooden handle. The physical labor had provided a distraction, but even mucking stalls couldn't fully quiet her mind.

The Forest Service radio, positioned on a hay bale between their stalls, crackled to life, instantly capturing their attention.

"Blackwood Canyon Fire: Containment now at fifty-five percent. Acreage holding at approximately ten thousand. Favorable overnight

humidity recovery aided suppression efforts. Crews continuing to re-inforce lines on Division Charlie and mop-up operations on Division Alpha..."

A small measure of relief worked through Sophie's tense shoulders. The news wasn't bad—containment increasing, no growth in the fire's size. Still, every update reminded her that Luke was out there, flying through smoke and danger.

"Better than yesterday," Ray commented, leaning on his pitchfork.

"Yes." Sophie nodded, resuming her work with slightly less ferocity. "But still a lot of fire to fight."

"They're making progress. That's what matters."

They fell back into their rhythm, the repetitive motion of lifting soiled bedding and replacing it with fresh straw, providing a grounding routine. Sophie checked her phone for the third time that hour—no messages from Luke. His last text, sent just after dawn, had been brief: Morning briefing. Flying today. Will update when I can.

"Weather forecast for the fire zone today calls for—" The radio suddenly cut to silence.

Sophie froze mid-motion, her eyes meeting Ray's across the barn aisle. They both moved toward the radio at the same moment.

"Battery might be—" Ray began, but stopped short.

Three women stood in the barn's center aisle. Virginia Harlow's hand was still on the radio's volume knob, a gentle smile on her face. Beside her, Abigail Whitaker stood with arms crossed, looking like a woman on a mission, while Lily Hawthorne beamed brightly, holding an enormous picnic basket.

"Morning, Ray, Sophie," Virginia greeted warmly. "Hope we didn't startle you."

Lily stepped forward, lifting her basket slightly. "We come bearing sustenance and support!" She pulled back a checkered cloth to reveal containers packed with what appeared to be a complete meal.

"Ladies," Ray said, a smile creasing his face. "What brings you out to the ranch this morning?"

"You two," Abigail stated directly, her no-nonsense tone belied by the kindness in her eyes. "Working yourselves to the bone, by the looks of it."

Virginia's perceptive gaze settled on Sophie's face, noting the shadows beneath her eyes and the tension around her mouth. "We thought you could use some company, Sophie. And a lunch break."

"And some girl talk!" Lily added cheerfully.

Sophie blinked, momentarily overwhelmed by their unexpected appearance and obvious concern. "That's very kind, but—"

"No 'buts' about it," Abigail interrupted firmly. "When the menfolk are off being heroes, the women need to stick together. That's just how it is."

Ray set his pitchfork against the stall door. "The ladies are right, Doc. You've been at it since dawn. Take a break." He nodded toward the trio of women. "I'll finish up here."

"Are you sure?" Sophie asked, feeling guilty about abandoning the work.

"Positive. Besides," he added with a wink, "turning down Lily's cooking would be a crime in these parts."

"It certainly would!" Lily agreed, patting her basket proudly.

Sophie surrendered to their collective concern. The prospect of stepping away from the barn and the constant updates on the radio that kept her anxiety simmering held an undeniable appeal.

"Well, when you put it that way," she conceded, setting her pitchfork aside and brushing straw from her jeans.

"Smart girl," Abigail approved. "Now, let's head up to the house and get you fed properly."

As they walked toward the ranch house, Sophie was struck by the visible determination in her visitors' demeanor. Virginia moved with quiet grace, her presence somehow both calming and authoritative. Abigail strode purposefully, like a woman who'd never wasted a step in her life. Lily practically bounced alongside them, her natural exuberance clear.

"We've been keeping up with the fire reports," Virginia explained as they climbed the porch steps. "The whole town is concerned, of course, but we thought you might need a little female support."

"Pastor Sam wanted to come too," Lily added, setting her basket on the porch table, "but Abigail told him this was women's business."

Abigail shrugged unapologetically. "Men mean well, but some conversations need a woman's touch."

"I appreciate you thinking of me."

"That's what friends do," Virginia replied, helping Lily unpack the basket.

The porch table soon overflowed with Lily's offerings: thick chicken salad sandwiches on homemade bread, containers of pasta salad studded with vegetables, mason jars of fresh fruit, and, of course, Lily's delicious homemade cookies. A gallon-sized glass jar of sweet tea completed the spread, droplets of condensation gathering on its surface in the warm afternoon air.

"This is a feast," Sophie marveled as they settled around the table.

"Food nourishes more than just the body," Lily said, passing Styrofoam plates around. "Mama always said a good meal shared is medicine for the soul."

"Your mama was a smart woman," Abigail commented, accepting a plate.

They served themselves, the simple act of sharing food creating an immediate sense of camaraderie. They ate and chatted, while birds called to one another from nearby trees and horses whinnied.

"So," Lily said, "did you hear about Phil Needham's new puppy? It's the smallest German Shepherd I've ever seen. It got loose yesterday and chased Rex Webster's cat up a tree. Rex had to get the ladder out—not for the cat, mind you, but for Phil, who climbed up after it and then couldn't get down!"

Sophie couldn't help but smile at the mental image. "Is Rex's cat okay?"

"That cat?" Lily waved dismissively. "Meanest creature in the county. It was probably enjoying watching Phil suffer."

"Rex has the scratches to prove it," Abigail added dryly. "Came into the store yesterday looking like he'd tangled with barbed wire."

The conversation flowed easily between the women with town gossip, updates on various community members, and amusing anecdotes that had Sophie laughing. There was a deliberate lightness to their talk, a gentle distraction that Sophie found soothing.

"The summer festival committee is in an uproar," Lily continued, refilling their tea glasses. "Janet Myers wants to change the parade route this year, and you'd think she'd suggested painting the church purple!"

"Change doesn't come easy in Riverbend Valley," Virginia explained to Sophie. "Especially when it involves traditions."

"Speaking of change," Abigail said, her tone shifting slightly as she turned to Sophie, "Tell us more about this therapeutic riding program you'll be opening."

"It's still in the planning stages. My grandmother ran something similar on our ranch in Colorado. I've always wanted to continue that work."

"Carter would be pleased," Virginia said warmly. "He had such a heart for helping others."

The conversation continued, weaving through topics both light and meaningful. Sophie felt the tight knot of anxiety in her chest gradually loosening as she listened and shared. These women weren't just distracting her—they were integrating her into the fabric of their community, helping her see beyond the immediate crisis to the life she was building here.

As they finished their meal and moved to a more comfortable seating area on the porch, Virginia's expression grew more thoughtful. She settled beside Sophie on the porch swing, the gentle rocking motion adding to the peaceful atmosphere.

"Sophie, dear," she began gently, "it's clear that Luke means a great deal to you. I imagine it's difficult, with him being gone like this, especially when things are so new between you."

The direct acknowledgment of what had been hovering beneath the surface of their conversation made Sophie pause. She looked down at her hands, fingers twisting together in her lap.

"Yes. It is."

"It's the not knowing that's hardest," Abigail said knowingly. "When Jed was in the National Guard and got deployed, I nearly wore a path in my kitchen floor from pacing."

Lily nodded in agreement. "And my Frank was a volunteer firefighter for thirty years. Every time that alarm went off, my heart would just about stop."

Virginia patted Sophie's hand. "Would it help to talk about it? Sometimes naming our fears takes away some of their power."

The simple kindness in the gesture, the genuine understanding in their eyes, broke something open in Sophie's heart. These women weren't just being neighborly—they truly cared, and more importantly, they understood.

"It's more than just the fire," she confessed, her voice soft but steady. "It's... How much I feel for him already... it's just happened too fast."

She took a deep breath; the words tumbling out now. "I've known Luke for what—a few weeks? That's nothing. But the way I feel..." She shook her head, struggling to articulate the depth of her emotions. "It doesn't make sense to feel this much, this fast. After what happened with my ex, I promised myself I'd be so careful. That I'd never let myself be that vulnerable again."

Her voice dropped, almost to a whisper. "But with Luke, it's like all those protective layers I built just... disappeared. And now he's out there, in danger, and I'm terrified. How can I feel this deeply about him already? Is this even real, or am I just... wanting it to be?"

Sophie's cheeks warmed at her transparency. But instead of the awkwardness she feared, she was met with knowing looks and gentle smiles.

"Oh, honey," Virginia said, her voice warm with understanding. "The heart has its own timetable, and it rarely consults with our carefully laid plans."

"Ain't that the truth," Lily agreed fervently.

Virginia's eyes grew distant with memory. "Sam and I, we knew each other from church for years. He was Pastor Sam, and I was just Virginia, the ranch owner, in the third pew. We respected each other, of course, and exchanged pleasantries every Sunday. But then, one evening after a particularly trying church council meeting, we ended up talking for hours, truly seeing each other for the first time."

A smile touched her lips. "After that one conversation, that one real connection... I knew. It was as if a switch had been flipped. We started dating and a few months later, he proposed. We were married just weeks later."

She turned to Sophie, her expression gentle but certain. "When the Lord brings two hearts together, Sophie, sometimes He doesn't see the need for a long, drawn-out process. Sometimes, His 'yes' is swift and clear."

"Oh, that's nothing!" Lily interjected, her eyes sparkling with enthusiasm. "I was barely eighteen when I met my Frank. He walked into the grocery store where I was working—bold as brass, with a smile that could melt snow in January. Our eyes met across the produce section, and that was it! Lightning bolt, the whole nine yards!"

She laughed, the sound bright and infectious. "We were married three months later, scandalized half the town, I tell you! But we had thirty wonderful years before the Lord called him home. Thirty years of a love that started instantly and never faded."

Her expression grew more serious, though her eyes remained warm. "Don't let anyone tell you that love at first sight, or a love that blooms fast, isn't real or lasting. When your soul recognizes its match, time just... catches up."

Abigail, who had been listening thoughtfully, leaned forward in her chair. "Now, my story with Jed wasn't quite a lightning bolt like Lily's. No, sir. I thought he was a stubborn, opinionated know-it-all when I first met him at a cattle auction." She chuckled, the sound rich with remembered affection. "And he thought I was too bossy for my own good."

"Imagine that," Lily teased, earning a mock glare from Abigail.

"As I was saying," Abigail continued pointedly, "we kept finding ourselves working together on community projects, farm bureau meetings, and that sort of thing. And the more I saw him—how he treated his animals, how he helped his neighbors without expecting anything back, how his word was his bond—the more I knew. It wasn't a sudden flash, but a steady dawning. Within six months, I knew that stubborn, opinionated man was the only one I wanted by my side." Her voice softened. "And I was right."

She fixed Sophie with a direct look. "Sometimes, Sophie, God doesn't shout. He whispers. And it's in the quiet knowing, the recognizing of good character and a steadfast heart, that you find His will. You've seen Luke's character. Trust that."

Sophie absorbed their stories, a sense of relief washing through her. "I thought I was going crazy," she admitted. "Feeling all this so intensely, so quickly."

"There's nothing crazy about recognizing a good man when you see one," Abigail stated firmly.

"And Luke Harding is certainly that," Virginia added. "I've known that boy since he was knee high to a grasshopper. Watched him grow into a man of integrity, faith, and purpose. The way he stepped up after Carter died, how he's stayed connected to Jake's family... those aren't the actions of a man who runs from commitment or responsibility."

"But that's part of what scares me," Sophie confessed. "His sense of duty, his calling. The danger of it." She gestured vaguely toward the north, where smoke still stained the distant sky. "This won't be the last time he flies into danger. It's who he is."

Lily reached across to touch Sophie's arm. "That fear will never completely go away," she said, unusual solemnity in her typically cheerful voice. "Every time Frank answered a fire call, I felt it. But you learn to live alongside it, not let it consume you."

"How?" Sophie asked.

"Prayer," Virginia answered immediately. "Constant, honest prayer. Not just for his safety, but for peace in your own heart."

"Community," Abigail added. "Surrounding yourself with people who understand and support you. People like us."

"And purpose," Lily concluded. "Having meaningful work that keeps your hands busy, and your heart engaged, even when worry tries to take over."

Virginia slipped her arm around Sophie's shoulders in a gentle half-embrace. "The question isn't whether loving Luke comes with risk—all love does. The question is whether you'll let fear rob you of the joy that love brings."

"And whether you'll trust God with the parts you can't control," Abigail added.

Sophie thought about Luke—his quiet strength, his dedication, and the way his eyes crinkled when he smiled. The unexpected connection they'd found, as if they'd known each other for years instead of weeks. The way she felt completely herself with him, in a way she never had with anyone else.

"I want to trust this," she admitted. "I want to trust him. And myself."

"That's a start," Virginia said encouragingly. "And trust grows stronger with time, just like love does."

"Speaking of trust," Lily said, a mischievous glint returning to her eyes, "do you trust us enough to let us help you with chores this afternoon? I'm no stranger to ranch work, you know. Grew up on one myself."

"Me too," Abigail added. "Haven't lost my touch, either."

Virginia chuckled. "I may be a pastor's wife now, but I can still muck a stall with the best of them. I owned a ranch before marrying Sam, now my daughter, and son-in-law own it."

Sophie looked at the three women, so different in personality but united in their offer of support, and felt a surge of gratitude that brought unexpected tears to her eyes.

"I'd like that," she said, her voice slightly husky with emotion. "Thank you. For lunch, for sharing your stories, for... everything. You've made me feel not so alone... it's trying being the only female on this ranch."

"That's what friends do," Virginia said simply.

"And that's what you are now, Sophie Lawson," Lily declared. "Our friend. Whether you like it or not!"

"I like it very much," Sophie assured her with a laugh.

They gathered the lunch things, working together with the easy coordination of women accustomed to practical tasks. As they prepared to head back to the barn, Sophie found herself walking with a lighter step, the burden of her worry not eliminated but somehow more manageable.

Virginia fell into step beside her as they crossed the yard. "You know," she said conversationally, "when Sam and I were first married, I worried constantly about everything—whether we'd have enough money, if we'd be good grandparents someday, if I was cut out to be a pastor's wife. Then, I remembered some advice my mama gave me years ago."

"What was that?" Sophie asked.

"She always told me, 'Virginia, worry's like trying to sweep the porch in a windstorm—it keeps you busy, but it don't change a thing.' Then she'd pat my hand and say, 'Now prayer—that's the real work. That's what steadies the storm.'"

Sophie nodded, the simple wisdom resonating. "Oh... I love that. I bet she was a wonderful person."

"She was," Virginia agreed.

As they approached the barn, Ray emerged from the doorway, looking pleasantly surprised to see the entire group returning.

"Well now," he said, tipping his hat to the ladies. "Looks like I've got more help than I bargained for."

"Put us to work, Ray," Abigail instructed. "These hands aren't just for show."

Ray grinned. "Yes, ma'am. I know better than to argue with you."

They entered the barn together, and Sophie glanced toward the hay bale where the radio sat silent, wondering what updates they'd missed during lunch.

As if reading her thoughts, Ray said, "Fire's holding steady. No news is good news... how about we just leave that contraption off for a little while?"

Sophie nodded. "I'd like that very much."

"Alright, ladies," Abigail announced, her tone brisk but her eyes twinkling. "Let's show these men on this ranch how ranch work really gets done."

Lily laughed, already rolling up her sleeves. "I hope you're taking notes, Ray. This is going to be educational."

Chapter 24

Sophie pulled the cinch tight, tightening Sierra's saddle. The mare snorted, sidling slightly in protest against the sudden pressure. "Sorry, girl," Sophie murmured, patting the horse's neck.

The barn hummed with morning activity around her. Eric and Dan were visible through the open doorway, loading fence repair supplies onto the flatbed truck. The rhythmic scrape of Ray's pitchfork came from a nearby stall, punctuated by his occasional hum of an old country tune. Somewhere outside, a tractor engine rumbled to life, its sound fading as it moved toward the east pastures.

Three days had passed since the wildfire had shifted—three days of waiting, working, and watching the northern sky. The smoke had thinned considerably, and Luke's texts had grown more optimistic about containment progress, though they remained frustratingly brief and sporadic.

Sophie checked Sierra's bridle, adjusting the bit so it sat properly in the mare's mouth. The familiar scent of worn leather and sweet hay surrounded her, mingling with the earthy smell of the horses, calming her instantly.

"Headed out for a ride, Doc? Good day for it," Ray said, appearing in the center aisle of the barn. He wiped his face on a faded red bandana and then tucked it back into his pocket.

"Thought I would." Sophie nodded. "Sierra could use a good stretch, and honestly, so could I."

Ray nodded as he crossed to a shelf near the tack room, retrieving a small walkie-talkie. "Take this with you. Never know when you might need to reach out, or us, to you. Especially riding solo."

"Thanks, Ray." She said as she clipped the device to her belt.

"Want me to update you if anything about the fire comes over the radio?"

"No, Ray. Thank you, but not today. I think... I just need a little time away from it all. Some peace and quiet."

"Understood, Doc. Some days, the quiet is the best medicine. You go on and find some."

She led Sierra from the stall, the mare's hooves making hollow sounds against the concrete flooring. Outside, the morning had blossomed into full glory—brilliant blue skies stretched overhead, the air fresh with the scent of pine and sage carried on a gentle breeze. Only the faintest hint of smoke lingered.

Sophie mounted with ease, settling into the saddle and gathering the reins. Sierra shifted beneath her, eager to move. Powerful muscles bunched and released as the mare stepped forward, responding to the gentle pressure of Sophie's legs.

"Let's go, girl," Sophie said, directing Sierra away from the barn and toward the trails.

As they left the immediate ranch grounds, Sophie allowed Sierra to pick up her pace. The mare transitioned smoothly into a canter;

her stride lengthening across the open pasture. Wind rushed past Sophie's face, tugging tendrils of hair loose from her ponytail. She leaned forward slightly, moving in rhythm with the horse, feeling the exhilaration of speed and freedom wash through her.

The repetitive beat of hooves against earth created a soothing cadence, blending with the creak of saddle leather and Sierra's steady breathing. Sophie inhaled deeply, filling her lungs with the clean Montana air—so different from Seattle's urban scents, so reminiscent of her childhood home in Colorado.

They followed the trail through a stand of pines, where fallen needles cushioned Sierra's hooves and the air cooled beneath the canopy of branches. Occasionally, the mare would flick an ear at a rustling in the underbrush or the call of a bird overhead, but she maintained her forward momentum, seemingly enjoying the excursion as much as Sophie.

The trail climbed steadily, winding around rocky outcroppings and through small clearings dappled with wildflowers. Sophie relaxed more with each passing minute, the persistent knot of worry in her chest loosening as she focused on the simple joy of riding through this beautiful landscape.

When they reached the ridge that marked the approach to Hidden Meadow, Sophie slowed Sierra to a walk. The mare's sides heaved slightly from the exertion, her coat darkened with sweat along her neck and flanks. Sophie patted her neck appreciatively.

"Almost there, girl. Then you can rest and graze for a while."

They rounded the last bend in the trail, and Hidden Meadow opened before them, even more breathtaking than Sophie remembered. Summer was in full bloom—lupine and Indian paintbrush created vivid splashes of purple and red among the green grasses. Butterflies danced between flower heads, their wings catching the sunlight.

Sophie guided Sierra to the spring-fed trough, allowing the mare to drink deeply after their climb. The water bubbled continuously from the pipe emerging from the hillside, clear and cold from the mountain depths. Sophie dismounted, her boots sinking slightly into the lush grass.

She loosened Sierra's cinch to allow the mare more comfort while grazing, then slipped the bit from her mouth, leaving the bridle in place with the reins draped loosely to allow freedom.

"Enjoy yourself, Sierra. You've earned it," Sophie said.

While Sierra set to grazing contentedly, Sophie wandered to a particularly inviting patch of grass near a lone aspen tree. Its leaves trembled in the slight breeze, creating a gentle, whispering music. She settled onto the ground, stretching out her legs and leaning back on her elbows, face tilted toward the sun.

The peaceful isolation of the meadow enveloped her—no ranch chores demanding attention, no radio updates to monitor, no well-meaning friends offering support that required gracious acknowledgment. Just sky, grass, and quiet.

Sophie lay back fully, using her arms as a cushion beneath her head. Above her, cotton-white clouds drifted across the vast blue expanse, their shapes slowly morphing as they traveled. A hawk circled lazily on a thermal, its silhouette tiny against the immensity of the sky.

She closed her eyes, feeling the warmth of the sun on her face, listening to the subtle symphony of the meadow—Sierra's rhythmic tearing of grass, the faint gurgle of the spring, a chorus of insects humming in the wildflowers, and the whisper of a breeze through aspen leaves. The tension she'd been carrying since Luke's departure continued to melt away, replaced by a profound sense of peace.

After several minutes of quiet contemplation, Sophie opened her eyes again, gazing up at the endless sky. A feeling of smallness washed over her, not frightening but somehow comforting—a reminder that her worries were just a tiny piece of a much larger picture.

"Lord…" she began softly, her voice barely audible. "Lord, it's me, Sophie. It's so beautiful out here today. Thank You for this. For this quiet, for this… feeling of peace. I really needed this."

She sighed contentedly, watching a butterfly float past on delicate wings.

"When I first came to Montana, to Ironwood Creek, I was running. Running from so much pain, so much… betrayal. I thought I was just buying a ranch, a fresh start, and following my dream. But You knew, didn't You? You were leading me here, to this exact place, for reasons so much bigger than I could see."

A gentle breeze stirred the surrounding grasses, carrying the sweet scent of wildflowers.

"This ranch… it feels like it's breathing life back into parts of me I thought were gone for good. And the people here… Lily, Virginia, Abigail… they've been such a gift. Thank you for them."

Sophie's voice softened, becoming more vulnerable as she addressed the deepest part of her heart.

"And Luke… Oh, Father, Luke. My heart feels so… full when I think of him. It's a feeling I have never experienced. My feelings have come so fast and so strong. It scares me. After Marcus trusting someone with my heart… it's an enormous leap. But with Luke… it doesn't feel like a leap into darkness. It feels like… coming home."

Sierra lifted her head from grazing, ears pricked forward as if listening to Sophie's confession. The mare blinked long-lashed eyes before returning to the sweet grass.

"I love him, Lord. I truly do. And I see so much good in him—his strength, his kindness, that quiet integrity he carries. The way he loves this land, the way he looks out for Katie and the kids…"

A shadow of her earlier anxiety flickered across her features.

"His job... fighting those fires... that part still twists my stomach into knots. The not knowing, and the danger. But I'm trying, Lord. I'm trying to give that fear to You. Trying to trust that You're with him, that You'll bring him back safe if it's Your will."

Sophie reached out, running her fingers through the soft grass beside her.

"I guess what I'm trying to say is... thank You. For leading me through the brokenness to this. For showing me that my heart could heal, and showing me a love that is very real... so real. I've never experienced a love this strong with a man before. I don't know what Your full plan is, but I'm here. I'm listening. I want to follow where You lead, even if it's scary. Help me to be brave, Lord. Help me to trust You, and to trust this love You've put in my heart."

The breeze stilled, as if the meadow itself were listening.

"Help me be the partner Luke deserves and help me build a life here that honors You. Amen."

A profound calm settled over Sophie as she lay in the grass, listening to the sounds of the meadow—the buzz of insects, the whisper of wind, and Sierra's contented munching.

A buzzing sound interrupted the tranquil moment. Sophie's phone, placed on the grass beside her, vibrated with an incoming message. The intrusion was jarring in the meadow's quiet.

She sat up, reaching for the device. A small smile played on her lips as she saw Luke's name on the screen, and that familiar flutter of anticipation stirred in her chest. She opened the message, holding her breath slightly.

Just finished the final debrief. Got some paperwork to sign off on and need to run a quick system check on my gear. They're arranging a chopper back to the cabin. ETA roughly 4 hours. Can't wait to see you, Sophie.

Sophie read the message twice, savoring each word. She could almost hear the weariness in his voice, but beneath it, that warmth and eagerness that made her heart swell. Four hours. After days of separation and worry, just four more hours.

A radiant smile spread across her face, lighting her eyes as she quickly typed a reply: *See you soon!*

She slipped the phone into her pocket and looked up at the vast Montana sky again, the sun warm on her face. The peace from her prayer mingled with the joy of Luke's imminent return, creating a profound sense of gratitude that filled every corner of her being.

Sophie took a deep, cleansing breath, feeling centered and ready in a way she hadn't since the moment that helicopter had carried Luke away. She understood now—the waiting wasn't over, not really. Life with Luke would always include periods of separation and moments of worry. But she had found her footing again, her faith, and her strength to face those times.

And in just four hours, she would see him again.

"Come on, Sierra," she called, rising to her feet with renewed energy. "We should head back. Someone's coming home today."

Chapter 25

Sophie rode Sierra towards Luke's cabin. Behind her, tethered by a lead rope, Buck followed willingly. The steady rhythm of hooves against the earth created a vibrant cadence that matched the excited beating of her heart.

She'd left the ranch a little early, needing the ride, the movement, the sense of heading toward him after days of waiting and worrying. Luke's text message still echoed in her mind: *"ETA, roughly 4 hours. Can't wait to see you, Sophie."*

The trail curved around a stand of ponderosa pines, their scent sharp and clean in the summer air. She had left the ranch earlier than necessary, driven by a restlessness she couldn't shake. Luke's text earlier had sent a thrill of anticipation through her that made routine ranch tasks nearly impossible to focus on.

The trail widened as they approached the clearing where Luke's cabin stood. Sophie slowed Sierra to a walk, taking in the sight of the sturdy structure nestled against the tree line.

She dismounted at the edge of the clearing, her boots making a soft thud on the earth. After tethering both horses where they could graze on the tufts of grass nearby, she pulled a collapsible bucket from her saddlebag and filled it with the outdoor spigot.

"Drink up," she murmured as Sierra dipped her muzzle into the water.

With the horses settled, Sophie climbed the steps to the porch. Not having a key, she settled into one of the Adirondack chairs Luke had positioned facing the view, her gaze automatically lifting to the northern sky where, just days ago, smoke had billowed ominously. Now, only the faintest haze remained.

The wilderness sounds surrounded her—a woodpecker's distant rat-a-tat-tat, the whisper of wind through the tree leaves, and the occasional soft nickering of the horses. Sophie closed her eyes, allowing the peacefulness to wash over her. The waiting was almost over. Soon, he would be here, and the thought sent a flutter through her chest.

A faint vibration hummed through the air, so subtle she might have imagined it. Sophie opened her eyes, sitting straighter in the chair, listening intently.

Rising from the chair, she moved to the edge of the porch, her eyes scanning the sky. The sound grew steadily louder, transforming from a distant whisper to a distinctive beat. Then she saw it—a dark shape against the deep blue sky, blinking lights marking its approach.

The Forest Service helicopter made a wide, practiced circle over the clearing where the helipad sat. Sophie shielded her eyes, watching as it descended with a powerful roar that filled the evening air. The downdraft created a small cyclone of dust and tiny leaves.

With precision, the helicopter touched down, its skids settling onto the concrete pad with a slight bounce. The engine continued its high-pitched whine as the side door slid open.

And there he was.

Luke emerged from the helicopter, flight suit bundled under one arm, duffel bag slung over his shoulder. Even from this distance, she could see the proud set of his shoulders, and the competence in his movements. He looked tired—the way a man does after days of intense, focused effort—but he also looked magnificent.

He ducked instinctively, jogging clear of the aircraft with ease. The helicopter's engines throttled higher, the blades swishing faster as it prepared to depart. As soon as Luke was at a safe distance, it began to lift; the sound swelling again before banking sharply and heading north, leaving a sudden, ringing quiet in its wake.

Luke spotted her on the porch, and his entire posture changed—straightening, lightening. A smile broke across his face, transforming his exhaustion into something luminous that made her heart turn over in her chest.

Sophie descended the porch steps and hurried across the intervening space with determined strides. Without hesitation, he dropped the duffel bag and his bundled flight suit to the ground and opened his arms.

When she reached him, his arms crushed her to his chest. It wasn't a gentle hug; it was a reunion, a claiming. He lifted her clean off her feet, her arms instinctively going around his neck, her face buried against his shoulder. She breathed in the scent of him, that unique musky cologne essence that was purely Luke. He held her suspended for a long moment, as if anchoring himself through the physical connection.

He set her down gently, but his hands stayed on her arms, holding her steady as he stepped back just enough to see her face. His eyes—those serious brown eyes that had haunted her dreams—were full of so much exhaustion, relief, and a deep, tender emotion that made her breath catch.

"Miss me?" he asked, a smile playing on his lips.

"More than you know," Sophie replied, her smile tremulous. "Are you okay?"

"Better now." His thumbs stroked her arms gently. "A lot better now."

She studied his face, noting the shadows beneath his eyes, the lines of fatigue etched around his mouth. "You look tired."

"I haven't slept much," he admitted. "It's been a long few days."

Sophie reached up, her fingers gently tracing the stubble along his jaw. "You're here now. That's all that matters."

Luke leaned into her touch for a moment, his eyes closing briefly. Then he straightened, retrieving his bag and bundled flight suit from the ground. "I see you brought Sierra and Buck."

"I thought you might enjoy a horseback ride this evening," Sophie explained, falling into step beside him as they walked toward the cabin.

Luke's hand found hers, their fingers intertwining naturally. "Sounds perfect."

They walked in silence, just the sound of their footsteps and the chirping of early evening crickets. The distant roar of the helicopter had faded entirely, leaving only wilderness sounds.

At the cabin door, Luke released her hand to dig into his pocket for the keys. The metallic jingle seemed loud in the quiet evening. He unlocked the door with a definitive click, pushed it open, and stepped inside. After flicking on a light, he dropped his gear just inside the doorway.

"It's a bit warm inside, but the porch... the view's pretty good this evening," he said, gesturing toward the outdoor space. "Your choice."

Sophie smiled. "The porch sounds perfect."

They settled onto the wide porch swing, its chains creaking softly as they adjusted their weight. Luke leaned back with a weary sigh, stretching his long legs and draping his arm across the back of the swing behind her shoulders. Sophie sat close enough to feel the warmth of him along her side.

For several minutes, they simply sat together, gently swaying. The horses shifted occasionally, contented with their grazing. A pair of birds called to each other from nearby trees, their voices sweet in the cooling air.

"Tell me about it, Luke. What was it like?"

Luke didn't respond immediately. His gaze remained fixed on the distant horizon, where the last light of day painted the mountains in deepening purple shadows.

"Hot," he finally said, his voice low. "The kind of heat that feels alive, like it's breathing. And the smoke—it gets into everything. Your clothes, your hair, your lungs."

Sophie listened attentively, watching his profile as he spoke. The lines of his face seemed deeper, etched by experience and responsibility.

"We lost some acreage when the wind shifted that second day," he continued. "Had to pull ground crews back, watch as the fire crowned through a section of forest. There's this sound it makes when it's moving through the treetops—like a freight train, but more... alive. Hungry." He shook his head slightly. "Moments like that. You feel so small against the power of it."

His hand found hers, fingers interlacing. "Jenny Walsh—the pilot who went down—she's one of the best. Engine failure is the thing we all dread. She managed an incredible landing in a tiny clearing, barely bigger than her wingspan. When I heard that Mayday call..." His voice tightened. "Those moments before we knew she was okay... they're one of the hardest parts of the job."

Sophie squeezed his hand, offering silent support.

"But there were good moments too," Luke added, his tone lightening slightly. "The coordination between crews, the way everyone just... clicks into place during a crisis. The sunrise over Bear Creek valley on the third morning—the light filtering through the smoke, turning everything into this surreal orange-gold. Beautiful, in its own strange way."

He described the precise patterns of air drops; the skill required to navigate smoke-filled canyons with unpredictable updrafts, and the bone-deep fatigue that set in after hours of intense concentration.

"By the last day, containment was up to eighty percent. They'll keep crews on it for a while yet, mopping up hot spots, but the immediate danger has passed." He exhaled slowly. "No structures lost, no serious injuries. That's a win in this business."

Sophie absorbed his words, feeling a more profound understanding of what his calling entailed—the danger, yes, but also the purpose, the skill, the brotherhood of those who faced the flames together.

Luke fell silent again, leaning his head back against the swing. He closed his eyes briefly, exhaling a long breath that seemed to carry the weight of the past days.

"But it's over now. And I'm here." He opened his eyes, turning to her with an intensity that made her heart skip. "When I was headed home earlier in the helicopter... I was hoping you would be here waiting... and you were. Just the thought of you these past few days... you kept me going, believe it or not."

The naked honesty in his voice, the vulnerability in his eyes—it cracked something open inside Sophie's chest. This was her moment.

The words she'd rehearsed in her mind during those quiet moments in Hidden Meadow rose to her lips.

"Luke…" Her voice wavered slightly, but her resolve remained firm. "There's something I need to tell you. Something I figured out while you were gone." She took his hand between both of hers, her fingers tracing the callouses on his palm. "I know… I know we haven't known each other long, not in terms of weeks or months. But sometimes… sometimes the heart knows what it wants, what it needs, long before the mind catches up."

She lifted her gaze to meet his, her eyes clear and honest. "Luke, you're different from any man I've ever known. You've shown me what real strength, real kindness, and real integrity look like. Being with you… feels so natural. It feels like… like I've come home, like I'm meant to be right here in this moment with you. I believe God led me to you."

Sophie took a tremulous breath, her heart pounding. "I'm in love with you, Luke. I'm so completely, terrifyingly, wonderfully in love with you. And it's the realest thing I've ever felt."

Luke stared at her, his weariness momentarily forgotten, his eyes wide with raw emotion. A slow smile, full of wonder and relief, spread across his face. He brought her hand to his lips, kissing her knuckles tenderly.

"You have no idea how long I've wanted to hear you say that," he said, his voice thick with emotion, "or how scared I was that I never would."

He shifted on the swing, turning fully toward her, taking both her hands in his larger ones. "Soph, from that very first day… when you marched onto my ranch and took charge of that foaling like you were born to it, covered in sweat and determination… I think my heart just… stopped. And then it started again, but it was beating for you."

Luke's grip tightened, his eyes never leaving hers. "I've loved you since that first day, Sophie. Every cynical part of me that fought against loving someone ever again... it just melted away when I was with you. There's never been a moment's doubt in my mind or my heart." His voice dropped to a near-whisper. "You, Sophie Lawson, are the one. The only one."

The sincerity in his declaration stole Sophie's breath.

He leaned forward, one hand coming up to cradle her cheek. His lips met hers in a kiss that was everything—tender, passionate, full of relief and bursting with the promise of their declared love. It was a long, slow kiss that spoke volumes, erasing the exhaustion and the fear, leaving only the pure, undeniable truth of their connection.

When they finally broke apart, they remained close, foreheads resting together, breathing a little unsteadily.

"We are meant to be," Sophie whispered, the words not a question but a statement of profound certainty.

"We are," Luke agreed, his voice still thick with emotion. He kissed her forehead, her temple, and the tip of her nose. "God knew what He was doing when He brought you to Ironwood Creek."

Sophie smiled, nestling closer to him as the porch swing continued its gentle motion. The first stars had appeared in the deepening twilight, pinpricks of light against the darkening canvas of the sky.

"I prayed for you," she confessed softly. "Every day you were gone. I asked God to keep you safe, to bring you home."

"And He did just that," Luke murmured against her hair.

They sat together for several minutes, simply savoring the closeness, the shared understanding, the newly declared love that hummed between them like a tangible force.

Eventually, Luke straightened, a new light in his eyes despite the lingering fatigue. "The horses are getting restless," he observed, nodding toward where Sierra and Buck stood at the railing.

"They've been patient."

Luke stood, pulling her up with him. "Come on. Let's take that ride while there's still light. I want to feel solid ground beneath me for a change."

Hand in hand, they descended the porch steps. Buck nickered softly in greeting, pushing his muzzle against Luke's chest in welcome.

"Hey, buddy," Luke murmured, stroking the gelding's face. "Miss me?"

"He did," Sophie confirmed, untying Sierra's lead rope. "He looked for you every morning."

Luke smiled, checking Buck's cinch and adjusting the stirrups. "He's loyal, this one." He patted the horse's neck appreciatively.

They mounted in unison, settling into their saddles with ease. Luke looked at home on horseback, his posture relaxing visibly as Buck shifted beneath him.

"Where to?" Sophie asked, gathering Sierra's reins.

Luke considered for a moment, his gaze sweeping the surrounding landscape. "There's a trail in the woods behind the cabin that follows a ridgeline. Not too strenuous, but the view's worth it. We can make it to the ranch before it's fully dark."

"Lead the way," Sophie said, gesturing forward with a smile.

Luke nudged Buck into a walk, and Sophie fell in beside him. They rode through the woods and joined a narrow trail, forcing them to ride single file for a while, with Luke leading the way.

"Almost there," he called over his shoulder as the trail began a gentle climb.

The trees thinned, and suddenly, they emerged onto an open ridge top. Sophie drew Sierra to a halt beside Buck, her breath catching at the vista spread before them.

The valley stretched away to the east, Ironwood Creek Ranch visible as a collection of buildings nestled among fields and pastures. Beyond it, the lights of Riverbend Valley twinkled in the distance like earthbound stars. The mountains formed a dark silhouette against the twilight sky, their peaks etched in sharp relief.

"Wow," Sophie breathed, taking in the panoramic view.

"Worth the climb?" Luke asked, his eyes on her face rather than the scenery.

"Always."

Luke dismounted, tying Buck's reins loosely to a small pine. He moved to help Sophie down, his hands spanning her waist as she slid from the saddle. They stood close, reluctant to separate even after her boots touched the ground.

"Thank you," Luke said quietly.

Sophie looked up at him questioningly. "For what?"

"For being here. For waiting. For..." He struggled to find the words. "For loving me. Even with everything that comes with it... the danger... the uncertainty."

Sophie's hand came up to rest against his chest, feeling the steady beat of his heart beneath her palm. "Loving you isn't hard, Luke. It's the most natural thing I've ever done."

"Even knowing I'll be called away again? That there will be more fires, more absences?"

She nodded, her gaze steady. "I learned something while you were gone. With help from Virginia, Abigail, and Lily, actually."

"Oh?" Luke's eyebrow quirked upward. "The Riverbend welcoming committee paid you a visit?"

Sophie laughed softly. "They did. They brought lunch and wisdom in equal measure." Her expression grew more serious. "They helped me see that loving someone with a dangerous calling doesn't mean constant fear. It means finding strength in faith, in community, in purpose."

Luke's arms slipped around her waist, drawing her closer. "Smart women."

"They are," Sophie agreed. "And they helped me understand that what we have... it's worth any risk, and any uncertainty." She looked up into his face, memorizing every line, every plane in the deepening twilight. "I'd rather have this—us—with all its complications, than play it safe and miss out on the best thing that's ever happened to me."

Luke's eyes shone with emotion. "I don't deserve you."

"Yes, you do," Sophie corrected firmly. "We deserve each other. We deserve this chance at happiness."

His answer was a kiss—deep and thorough, full of promise and certainty.

"I love you, Sophie Lawson."

"I love you too, Luke Harding."

EPILOGUE

An autumn leaf spiraled down from an aspen tree, twisting in the breeze before landing on Sophie's open Bible. She smiled at the perfect red-gold heart shape nestled against Proverbs 18:22—"He who finds a wife finds what is good and receives favor from the Lord." Her fingers traced the delicate veins of the leaf as the late cool September air carried the scent of cinnamon and apple cider from the reception preparations across the yard.

"There you are," Virginia called, climbing the slight rise to the grove of trees where Sophie had retreated for a few moments alone.

Sophie closed her Bible, carefully preserving the leaf between its pages. "I needed a little quiet time. It's getting rather... busy down there."

"That's one word for it," Virginia chuckled, settling beside Sophie on the wooden bench Luke had built specifically for her on this spot. "Lily's directing the flower arrangements like a five-star general, Abigail's inspecting the tent setup with her tape measure, and Ray is hovering over the catering staff like they might abscond with the prime rib."

"And Pastor Sam?"

"Rehearsing his sermon for the third time, as if he hasn't officiated dozens of weddings in the past." Virginia's eyes crinkled with affection. "He says yours and Luke's is special. He wants to get it just right."

Sophie's heart swelled. Four months ago, she'd arrived at Ironwood Creek Ranch a stranger, wounded by betrayal and desperate for a fresh start. Now, on her wedding day, she was surrounded by a community that had become family in every way that mattered.

"I never imagined it would be like this," Sophie confessed, gesturing toward the transformation below.

The ranch had been converted into a wedding venue straight from a fairytale. A white tent billowed gently in the autumn breeze next to the barn, its sides rolled up to showcase the mountain panorama beyond. Wooden chairs arranged in neat rows faced an arch woven with autumn flowers and trailing greenery. String lights crisscrossed overhead, ready to twinkle as daylight faded. The trees surrounding the property had begun their seasonal transformation, painting the landscape in fiery hues of amber, crimson, and gold.

"Second thoughts?" Virginia asked.

"Not a single one," Sophie replied without hesitation. "Just... overwhelmed. In the best possible way."

Virginia patted her hand. "That's exactly how a bride should feel." She glanced at her watch. "Speaking of which, your groom will be back from his mysterious errand soon, and you, my dear, need to start getting ready."

Sophie nodded, taking one last look at the grove of trees—the place where, just six weeks ago, Luke had dropped to one knee with a vintage ring that had belonged to his grandmother.

"Okay," she said, rising from the bench. "Let's do this."

***

"Stop fidgeting," Ray instructed, straightening Luke's bolo tie for the third time. "You look fine."

"Fine?" Luke repeated, adjusting his western-cut jacket. "A man aims for higher than 'fine' on his wedding day, Ray."

The bunkhouse had been transformed into an impromptu groom's quarters, with the ranch hands functioning as both groomsmen and comic relief. Gus paced nervously by the window, his tie askew, despite multiple attempts to fix it. Ed and Dan played cards at the kitchen table, while Eric meticulously polished everyone's boots to a military shine.

"Handsome as a movie star," Gus offered helpfully. "Dashing. Debonair."

"Have you been reading romance novels?" Dan called from the table, not looking up from his cards.

"He's been reading the thesaurus," Ed countered, laying down a card with a triumphant slap. "Read and weep, partner."

Luke checked his watch again, a pulse of anticipation quickening his heartbeat. In less than an hour, Sophie would be his wife. The thought still stunned him—how quickly and completely she had become essential to his life, how perfectly she fit into the spaces he hadn't even realized were empty.

"You got the rings?" he asked Ray.

Ray patted his pocket. "Safe and sound, just like the last four times you asked."

"And the surprise? Everything's ready?"

"All set up exactly as you wanted," Ray confirmed. "Though I still think you're crazy for planning this particular exit strategy."

Luke grinned. "Sophie will love it."

A knock at the door interrupted their conversation. Pastor Sam entered, his presence immediately calming the room.

"Just checking in on the groom," he said, clasping Luke's hand warmly. "How are you holding up?"

"Good. I'm ready," Luke replied simply. "More than ready."

Pastor Sam nodded, his eyes reflecting an understanding that went beyond the surface meaning. He'd witnessed Luke's journey—from a grief-stricken survivor to a man embracing life and love again.

"I was just reviewing my notes," Pastor Sam said, "and I realized something. You and Sophie—your story is one of the most beautiful examples I've seen of God's perfect timing. Not your timing, not my timing, but His."

Luke nodded, throat suddenly tight with emotion. "I spent so long questioning His plan, especially after Jake died. I couldn't understand why things happened the way they did. But now..."

"Now you see the bigger picture unfolding," Pastor Sam finished gently.

"Parts of it, anyway," Luke agreed. "Sophie couldn't have walked into my life a day earlier or later. It had to be exactly when it happened—when I was ready to let go of the ranch but not quite able to, when she needed a fresh start but also guidance. Everything aligned so perfectly that I can't call it coincidence."

"Divine orchestration," Pastor Sam said with a smile. "Now, that's a phrase worth including in my sermon." He checked his watch. "Speaking of which, it's almost time. Shall we?"

Luke nodded, taking a deep breath. The ranch hands gathered around him, their usual joking manner replaced by genuine emotion.

"Proud of you, boss," Ray said, clapping him on the shoulder. "Carter would be, too."

***

"Hold still," Lily instructed, securing another pearl-tipped pin into Sophie's upswept hair. "One more... there! Perfect!"

Sophie gazed at her reflection in the antique full-length mirror that Virginia had brought over specifically for the occasion. The woman staring back at her seemed both familiar and transformed—her blue eyes bright with happiness, her cheeks flushed with anticipation, her blonde hair elegantly arranged with small white flowers tucked among the curls.

Her wedding dress captured everything she'd wanted—simple elegance with touches of vintage charm. The ivory satin skirt fell in clean lines from a fitted bodice, with a delicate lace overlay extending to three-quarter sleeves. The neckline was modest but flattering, and the back featured tiny covered buttons trailing down to her waist.

"You look absolutely breathtaking," Abigail declared, her typically brusque manner softened by genuine emotion.

"Like something from a fairy tale," Lily agreed, dabbing at her eyes with a lace handkerchief. "Our Sophie, a bride!"

Virginia approached with a small velvet box. "Something borrowed," she said, opening it to reveal a pair of pearl earrings. "These were my mama's. She wore them on her wedding day."

"Virginia," Sophie breathed, touching the lustrous pearls reverently. "They're beautiful. I'd be honored."

As Virginia helped her with the earrings, Katie Morrison appeared in the doorway, her children beside her.

"Sorry we're late," she apologized, ushering Emma and Michael into the room. "Someone insisted on picking flowers for the bride." She nodded toward Emma, who clutched a small bouquet of wildflowers.

"For your hair!" Emma announced, holding up her collection proudly. "Uncle Luke says you love wildflowers best."

Sophie crouched carefully, mindful of her dress, to accept the gift. "They're perfect, Emma. Thank you."

Lily immediately set to work incorporating a few of the blooms into Sophie's hair, while Michael stood awkwardly by the door, clearly uncomfortable in his suit and tie.

"You look so handsome, Michael," Sophie said with a warm smile.

The boy's serious expression relaxed slightly. "Mom made me wear the tie."

"Luke's wearing one too," Sophie confided.

A hint of a smile touched his lips. "Are you nervous? Mom says people get nervous before weddings."

Sophie considered the question honestly. "Not nervous exactly. More like... my heart knows this is exactly right, but it's so big, so important, that I can hardly believe it's happening."

Michael nodded solemnly, as if her answer made perfect sense to him. "Dad would've liked you," he blurted. "Uncle Luke says so."

The simple statement, delivered with a child's directness, touched Sophie deeply. "That means a lot to me, Michael. Thank you."

A knock at the door signaled it was time. Ray entered, his face softening as he took in Sophie's appearance.

"Well now," he said, his voice gruff with emotion, "aren't you a sight?"

"Everything ready?" Sophie asked, standing as Virginia handed her the bridal bouquet—a cascading arrangement of autumn blooms in rich burgundy, cream, and gold, accented with sprigs of wheat and tied with a simple satin ribbon.

Ray nodded. "Just waiting on the bride."

When Sophie had planned her wedding, one detail had given her pause—the traditional father walking the bride down the aisle. For a brief moment, she'd considered walking alone as a symbol of her independence. But then Luke had suggested Ray, and it had felt perfectly right.

"Would you do me the honer, Ray?" she asked, offering her arm.

Ray cleared his throat, blinking rapidly. "The honor's all mine, Doc. All mine."

***

The autumn breeze carried the strains of violin music as guests settled into their seats. Luke stood beneath the flower-adorned arch, Pastor Sam beside him, watching as the ranch hands—his groomsmen—took their places.

Though small by some standards, the gathering represented the heart of Riverbend Valley. Shop owners, ranchers, church members, and neighbors filled the rows of chairs. Dr. Patterson sat near the front, beaming with pride. Sheriff Wilson and his deputies occupied a row toward the back, their presence a reminder of the community's protective embrace. Even Phil Needham from the boot shop had closed early, his wife beside him in her Sunday best.

Luke's gaze drifted toward the mountains in the distance, their peaks tinged with the first dusting of snow. He then looked toward heaven and knew Uncle Carter and Jake were watching, perhaps sharing knowing glances about the man who had finally found his way forward without letting go of what mattered from the past.

The music shifted, signaling the approach of the bridal party. Katie walked first, elegant in a deep burgundy dress that complemented the autumn setting, followed by Emma, who took her flower girl duties with solemn importance, scattering maple leaves and rose petals with careful precision.

The guests rose as the traditional wedding march began. Luke's breath caught in his throat as Sophie appeared on Ray's arm.

She was radiant—not just with the conventional beauty of a bride, but with something deeper, a joy that seemed to illuminate her from within. Their eyes locked across the distance, and for a moment, everything else faded away—the guests, the music, the spectacular setting. There was only Sophie, walking toward him, her smile reflecting everything he felt in his heart.

Each step brought her closer to Luke, closer to the future they would build together. As Ray placed her hand in Luke's, the older man's eyes glistened with unshed tears.

"Take care of each other," Ray said softly, before stepping back to take his place.

Pastor Sam's voice rang clear in the autumn air: "Dearly beloved, we are gathered here today in the sight of God and this company, to join together this man and this woman in holy matrimony."

The ceremony unfolded with meaningful simplicity—readings chosen to reflect their journey, vows they had written themselves, the exchange of rings that symbolized their unending commitment. When Luke slipped the wedding band onto Sophie's finger, joining it with the vintage engagement ring, his hands were steady despite the emotion threatening to overwhelm him.

"I, Luke, take you, Sophie, to be my wife," he said, his voice clear and certain. "To share the joy of the skies and the steadfastness of the earth. To stand beside you in storm and in stillness. To honor your independence while offering my strength. To build with you a home filled with faith, purpose, and love. This is my solemn vow."

Sophie's eyes shimmered with tears as she responded: "I, Sophie, take you, Luke, to be my husband. To embrace your calling while pursuing my own. To comfort in times of grief and celebrate in moments of joy. To create with you a legacy of compassion and service. To love you completely, today and all the days to follow. This is my solemn vow."

As Pastor Sam pronounced them husband and wife, the setting sun broke through the clouds, bathing the area in warm amber light. When Luke kissed his bride, a cheer rose from the gathered community, echoing across the ranch that had brought them together.

***

Laughter, music, and conversation filled the reception tent as evening settled over Ironwood Creek Ranch. Strings of lights twinkled overhead, casting golden light over the celebration. The wedding cake—a three-tiered creation adorned with buttercream frosting and fresh flowers—had been cut and shared, the traditional first dance completed, and now guests mingled freely, enjoying the food and festivities.

Sophie, cheeks flushed from dancing, made her way to a quiet corner where Luke stood in conversation with Rex Webster.

"There she is," Rex said warmly as she approached. "Congratulations, Mrs. Harding. You've done what many thought impossible—grounded our favorite pilot."

"Only in the ways that matter," Sophie replied with a smile, slipping her arm through Luke's. "I'd never ask him to give up flying."

"Good woman," Rex approved, raising his glass of sparkling cider in salute. "Speaking of which, my Marlene is signaling that it's time we old folks head home. Thank you both for a beautiful celebration."

As Rex departed, Luke drew Sophie closer, brushing a soft kiss against her temple. "Having fun, Mrs. Harding?"

"The best," she confirmed, leaning into his embrace. "Though I still can't believe Lily managed to wrangle everyone into line dancing, including Sheriff Wilson."

"The night is full of surprises," Luke agreed, a mysterious glint in his eyes. "Speaking of which..."

Ray approached with a mischievous expression on his face. "Pardon the interruption, but I believe it's time for your... departure."

Sophie glanced between the two men, noting their poorly concealed excitement. "Our departure? But we're not leaving until tomorrow morning. The honeymoon flight—"

"Plans change," Luke said enigmatically, taking her hand. "Trust me?"

"Always," she replied without hesitation.

Luke led her toward the center of the tent, where Ray was already gathering the guests' attention with the traditional announcement that the bride and groom would soon be departing. Confused but intrigued, Sophie allowed herself to be guided through the crowd, accepting last hugs and well-wishes.

"Luke, what's going on?" she whispered as they reached the tent entrance.

"Follow me," he said gently, leading her in the direction of the north pasture.

The guests trailed behind them, their curiosity matching Sophie's own. As they crested the small rise beyond the barn, Sophie gasped.

There, in the open pasture, sat Luke's Cessna 182, "Sky Dancer," illuminated by portable lights. A red carpet stretched to the aircraft's steps, and the plane itself had been decorated with flowing ribbons and a hand-painted "Just Married" sign on the tail.

"Luke?"

"Our chariot awaits, Mrs. Harding," he replied, his eyes dancing with pleasure. "I thought, what better way to begin our life together than soaring above the place that brought us together, under a sky full of stars?"

"But..."

"Ray and the guys took care of everything. The honeymoon destination remains the same—that little coastal inn in Maine—but I thought we'd start the journey tonight, under the stars, while we fly to Missoula, where I reserved a honeymoon cabin for the night."

Sophie's heart swelled with love for this man who continually found ways to blend romance with the unique elements of their life. "You're amazing, you know that."

The wedding guests formed an impromptu honor guard along the red carpet, cheering as Luke and Sophie made their last farewells. Lily dabbed at her tears, Abigail beamed with uncharacteristic sentimentality, and Virginia offered a final blessing as they passed.

At the plane, Ray waited to help Sophie board, mindful of her wedding dress.

"Take care of our ranch while we're gone," Sophie said, impulsively hugging the foreman.

"Count on it, Doc," Ray replied gruffly. "It'll be waiting for you both when you return."

Luke completed his preflight checks, then climbed into the pilot's seat beside Sophie. As the door closed, sealing them into their own private world, he turned to her.

"Ready for our next adventure?"

Sophie looked at her husband—this brave, thoughtful man who had opened his heart to her despite past wounds. Who had shown her what true partnership meant, and who had given her not just a home but a community and a future filled with purpose.

"With you? Always," she said.

The engine hummed to life, its vibration familiar and reassuring. Outside, their friends, and neighbors waved farewell, their faces illuminated by the plane's lights. Luke guided the Cessna expertly down the makeshift runway, and with a smooth acceleration, they were airborne.

Sophie watched through the window as Ironwood Creek Ranch grew smaller below them—the tent with its twinkling lights, the barn where they'd first met over a foaling mare, and where they'd just exchanged their vows. All of it part of the foundation of their life together.

As they climbed higher, breaking through a thin layer of clouds, the vast Montana sky opened above them—a canopy of stars stretching to infinity. The moon cast silver light across the landscape below, highlighting the contours of mountains and valleys that had become home.

"Look," Luke said, pointing toward the east where the first hint of aurora borealis shimmered on the horizon—curtains of green and purple light dancing across the northern sky, a rare and magical display.

"It's beautiful," Sophie said, reaching for his hand.

"Nature's wedding gift," Luke suggested. "Or maybe just a reminder that some things are worth waiting for, worth fighting for."

Sophie squeezed his fingers, overwhelmed by the symbolism of their position—suspended between earth and sky, between past and future, held aloft by both science and faith.

"I love you, Luke Harding, with everything in me," she said, the simple words carrying the weight of all they'd overcome to reach this moment.

"I loved you yesterday. I love you today, and I'll love you tomorrow, Sophie Harding," he replied, his voice steady and sure.

Below them, Ironwood Creek Ranch receded into the distance. Not an ending but a beginning—the place where two wounded hearts had found healing, where a community had become family, where two houses would be transformed into homes. And above them, the infinite sky stretched out like possibility itself, a reminder that their journey together was just beginning.

As the Cessna banked gently westward, carrying them toward their honeymoon destination for the night, Sophie leaned her head against Luke's shoulder. In that perfect moment—surrounded by stars, wrapped in love, and filled with gratitude—she knew with absolute certainty that she had found exactly where she belonged.

Not just a place, but a person. Not just a ranch, but a purpose. Not just a house, but a home.

And in that knowledge was the greatest peace of all.

Leave A Review

If you enjoyed this book, please consider leaving an honest review
on Amazon

Visit Our Website:

www.tarabaisden.com

Visit Our Amazon Author Page HERE

Find Us On Social Media:

Facebook

Facebook Author Page

Instagram

About The Author

Tara Baisden is a Contemporary Christian Inspirational Romance author who proudly calls the beautiful state of West Virginia her home. Nestled on a sprawling mountainous property, she is surrounded by the peace and serenity of nature. Her days are happily spent in the quiet of country life, writing heartwarming stories of love, faith, and second chances. Tara also enjoys quilting, working in her garden, tending to her beloved pets, and soaking in the beauty of her surroundings.

With deep roots in West Virginia, family is everything to Tara. One of her favorite pastimes is gathering on the front porch with loved ones, sharing stories, laughter, and enjoying the simple, meaningful moments that life offers. When she's not crafting her novels, Tara can often be found exploring the rich history of her home state, visiting local historical sites, and, of course, stopping by every bookstore she passes! Her passion for reading and discovery always fuels her next adventure.

Tara is the author of the Laurel Ridges series of novels, as well as the Riverbend Valley series of novels, of which have been beloved by fans of inspirational romance. Her novels reflect her love for faith, family, and the timeless beauty of the world we live in.

Known for her sweet and clean romances, she creates characters that feel like family and settings that make readers want to visit again and again.

You can find out more about Tara and her latest releases at www.tarabaisden.com or follow her on social media for updates and behind-the-scenes glimpses of her writing process. Stay connected—you won't want to miss the heartfelt stories of love and family she has in store!

Also by Tara Baisden

<u>Riverbend Valley Series</u>

#1 A Cowboy's Second Chance

#2 Wanderlust & Wild Horses

#3 Heartstrings on the Horizon

#4 Runaway in Riverbend Valley

#5 Mended Hearts

#6 Healing Hearts

<u>Laurel Ridge Series</u>

#1. Season of Hope

#2. Finding Grace

#3. His Perfect Plan

#4. Love Redeemed

#5 Snowbound Blessings

#6 Sheltered Hearts

#7 Restoring Faith

#8 Love Rekindled

#9 Where She Belongs

www.ingramcontent.com/pod-product-compliance
Lightning Source LLC
Chambersburg PA
CBHW010606310726
48969CB00010B/2591